CROP DUSTER

A NOVEL OF WORLD WAR TWO

•JDB•Communications,•LLC•

JOHN D. BEATTY

JDB Communications, LLC
West Allis, Wisconsin

CROP DUSTER

A NOVEL OF WORLD WAR TWO

JOHN D. BEATTY

Also from John D. Beatty

Sergeant's Business and Other Stories
The Liberty Bell Files: J Edgar's Demons
The Past Not Taken: Three Novellas
This Redhead: The Dialogues

The Stella's Game Trilogy

Stella's Game: A Story of Friendship
Tideline: Friendship Abides
The Safe Tree: Friendship Triumphs

For Evelyne

My Love,
My Life,
My Muse of Fire

Not Long Ago

Dover AFB

Long is the way, and hard,
That out of hell leads up to light

John Milton

T he weather was cool and misty when the C-130 gently broke through the light overcast and landed on the rain-slicked runway. With a slight squeal of brakes and a roar of turbofans, the plane rolled to the end of the runway in an otherwise unremarkable routine landing.

This aircraft finished a flight that began a lifetime before, in a freezing maelstrom thousands of feet above the earth.

Several men quietly waited by the Military Mortuary hangar opening, watching as the plane taxied towards them. A man in a worn tweed coat asked the one in the latest Armani, "Where'd they find him?" Despite their apparent differences, their tone was of old friends in private conversation.

"The Germans were building a bridge over a river about where we crossed it and a couple of bones and his tags turned up," the Armani replied. "DNA in the bones types to his daughter. That satisfied the DoD and my sources."

As the plane's ramp descended, it revealed an Air Force Lieutenant General standing in front of the plane's only cargo: a single, flag-draped casket. An Army and Air Force honor guard entered the plane to carry the casket out. "PreSENT...hARMS," a sergeant loudly whispered, and, as one, a squad of armed guards alongside the ramp snapped up their rifles in silent salute.

At the edge of the hangar, a small man in a long leather coat slowly brought his feet together and snapped his right arm into a closed-palm salute.

As the honor guard carried their burden out of the airplane, five who waited stood at the foot of the ramp. The honor guard transferred their burden to a cart brought to the ramp's edge.

The pallbearers pushed the cart slowly, carefully, as if they were afraid to harm the occupant. Though the journey from the ramp to the hanger was short, for these once-young men it had been thousands of miles and decades. They included a prominent writer, an engineer, a powerful New England congressman, the Lieutenant General, an arithmetic teacher, and an industrial tycoon. A gust of wind ruffled the uniforms, the loose-fitting suits and coats, the hat brims of the civilians and the wrinkled skin of the civilians, the fine hairs and the dipped colors of the military.

The pall-bearers felt the wind not at all.

"Or...*DER hARMS*," the sergeant whispered, and the rifle squad snapped their rifles back to their sides.

Once inside the hangar, the Lieutenant General placed a jagged, slightly curved, green-painted piece of aluminum adorned with a large script letter "D" atop the coffin.

Spring 1925
McCook Field, Ohio

It is easy to be brave behind a castle wall

Welsh proverb

It was drawing dusk when the Studebaker ground to a halt in the gravel road in front of the row of officer's quarters. The uniform 2-by-4 and clapboard houses on both sides, held together by paint and plaster, were as unique as duffle bags and served the same purpose — to hold the soldier's worldly goods. The car stopped in front of the house with "LT. L. MILLER" stenciled on the mailbox. A lieutenant and his diminutive wife got out of the car and went up the gravel walk to the front door. It was a familiar walk, but with some sadness, the little lieutenant realized it would be the last. A tall woman answered the knock on the door, wearing the slightly harried and worried expression of an Army wife who just got marching orders again. "Hi, Jimmy, Joe," she said, letting them in. "Larry's in the back with Johnny. I'll go get him."

"That's OK, Babs," Lieutenant Jimmy Doolittle said. "I need to talk to him alone for a bit. Chew the fat with Joe for a while." Doolittle passed through the house in only a dozen steps, finding Miller and his little son just outside the kitchen door. Miller looked up.

"Hi, Jimmy," he said blankly. "I guess you heard." Miller, a big man with gray, flashing eyes most of the time, watched Doolittle dully, rubbing and wiggling his big, raw hands absently.

"Hi, Larry; how's the ace, Johnny?" Doolittle, a small and impish man, sparkled when he spoke, his wiry frame bursting with potential energy.

"Oh, I'm OK I guess, sir," 5-year-old Johnny answered, his face drawn and solemn. "Dad says we have to move again."

"Well, he may be right, unless I can talk some sense into him," Doolittle replied. "Go find that sister of yours and see if your Aunt Joe can't scrape up a couple nickels for some ice cream down at the PX." Johnny trudged off in search of Sally, two years older than he. The two men sat on the stoop, silent, watching the dusk change the shadows from gray to purple. "It only means you can't fly in the Army, Larry," Doolittle began. "It doesn't mean you have to resign."

"I can't raise two kids without flight pay on a Lieutenant's paycheck, and I will not get promoted in an army that cuts officers every year. Besides, it's more than that, Jimmy," Miller sighed. "I can see better than anyone else at McCook can, and I've got a civilian optometrist that says so. Eaker took me off flying status because...well, you know." The shadows were darkening from dusty purple to deep blue. A light breeze ruffled the sparse grass, kept sparse by Miller's active children.

"Larry, Ira didn't have any choice," Doolittle drawled in that peculiar, made up patois he affected with friends. "He takes orders from Hap Arnold, and Hap has his priorities, and they're for the good of the service. We just can't afford to make waves right now."

"Jimmy, you were born making waves," Miller growled. "I just make the wrong kind; expensive waves."

"Unpopular waves," Doolittle agreed. "But I didn't think they'd go this far."

"What I can't understand," Miller said bitterly, "is why everyone thinks an Italian artillery officer knows so goddamn much about aerial bombardment."

"Douhet? He flew for the Italians during the war."

"Yeah, but only for a year or so at the end," Miller spat back. "Why does everyone think that bombing from the air is so much more effective and terrifying than any other form of warfare?"

"Mitchell and Arnold both think Douhet's on the right track."

"Billy Mitchell could fart in a burlap bag and Hap Arnold would call it divine truth," Miller sniffed. "Aerial bombardment won't change ground warfare. How could it?"

"You know better than I do what the trenches in France were like," Doolittle said pointedly, "living like moles for years at a time, trading a thousand men for a yard of gain. *You* were there; I wasn't. We have to avoid repeating that." Both Miller and Doolittle were passionate defenders of both their country and of their point of view. They argued long into the evening, but both knew there was no point in further discussion. Miller, a *Lafayette Escadrille* flyer, felt that the entire foundation of US Army aviation was based on unfounded theories and suppositions with no evidence that, by his reckoning, was a pleasant-sounding but cartoonish way of not thinking about the blood of war. Doolittle, an aviation theoretician who knew more about the mechanics of flying than the uses of airplanes, could only argue based on the doctrine as he understood it, *not* from first-hand as Miller could. The theoreticians, including Ira Eaker and Henry H. "Hap" Arnold, spent a great deal of time and political capital on selling daytime horizontal precision bombing. Others, like Claire Chennault, were arguing about fighter defenses and dive-bombing. A few, Miller among them, were arguing for a "big tent" of integrated air operations that included all types. There was blood on the wall of all these discussions, but no one brought much evidence or experience to the table to prove their points except for the British "air policing" experiments in the Middle East, and those results were mixed.

"Well," Doolittle said at length, surrendering without malice in a fight where he had no stake, "what are you going to do?"

"Take Babs and the kids up to the farm, I guess. My brother can't work it since he fell into a machine a few years back. Guess I'll make a go of farming for a while. Got that old Jenny to fly. Maybe I'll fly some mail contracts."

It was well after dark when Jimmy and Joe left, but little Johnny Miller lay awake in his bed, remembering what two men argued about in his backyard—the future of war.

Spring 1925

Marburg, Germany

*It means that we shall lose our heads along with the rest
And stop weighing right and wrong*

Woodrow Wilson

How short this ritual is, Lothar Thielmann thought, watching the children bravely fighting back their tears. Eduard and Helga, his parents, lay side-by-side as they had been in life; Elisabeth, his wife, lay a short distance away, separated now only by earth. The minister finished the service, nodding to the gravediggers to lower the coffin into the ground.

Die Grippe—the horrible influenza epidemic—had ravaged central Germany just after the war and had killed Thielmann's father. His wife perished bearing young Otto in 1920, and now his mother had died of a heart ailment. With food still so costly and money worthless, life in Germany would not get much better soon. That left Thielmann only with his father's small butcher shop and his dilapidated farm to eke out a living for his children.

Walking slowly away, Anna, his oldest at fourteen, consoled her youngest brother, five-year-old Otto, still so small. His son Ulrich and his same-age uncle Georg-Hans, Lothar's ten-year-old brother, marched stoically behind them. Lothar, who had been an intelligence officer during the war, followed his children, deep in thought. The *Stahlhelm*, the only German veteran organization that Lothar paid any attention to, had paid for the simple funeral. He only had money for a few more weeks—if prices did not go up again—and nothing on hand to either sell or slaughter. There were a dozen waterfowl, a pair of goats and a cow at the farm, yielding a bare sustenance for his family. "I wait in line for a day for a kilo of bread, and I have four mouths to feed now. What am I to do?" he asked himself.

"We must rise," someone shouted across the square. "Russia has showed us the way! Even now Soviets are forming all across Europe, committees of workers who will seize the means of production from the thieving capitalists who steal your labor, who own your homes, who foreclose your mortgages..."

"We must fight," another voice shouted from another corner. "We must hunt out the November criminals, the Jews, and the Bolsheviks. It is they who betray you, who steals the food from your very mouths, who pollutes our blood with the ideas of Slavs and Jews. We must fight to cleanse our land of the subhumans, free ourselves from the bondage of Versailles, and proclaim our heritage as the protector of Europe from the hordes of Asia, just as the Teutonic Knights held back the Turk and the Mongol. We must proclaim our right to free Germany of the filthy Jew, the crucifiers of Our Lord..."

I wish they would make more sense and less noise, Thielmann thought. They confuse the children so.

"I am so sorry for your loss, Thielmann," old *Herr* Baumer was standing in Thielmann's shop doorway, hat in hand, as he trudged from the graveyard. "I wondered if you couldn't help me."

"How may I be of help, M*ein Herr*?" Baumer had been an engineer at the electrical plant in Giessen to the south and was now a well-off pensioner. Thielmann's shop was below Baumer's small apartment, on the corner of *Marienerbadstrasse* and the *Birkeplaz*, just north of the main Lahn River canal.

"I've inherited a small herd of swine from my brother, who recently died. I know nothing of swine, but you have a farm, do you not?"

"I know nothing of swine either, *Mein Herr*, other than their slaughtering. I don't know how I can be of help." The two men had known each other for decades, but the *Glaswand*, the eternal barrier of social etiquette between Germans, had yet to be penetrated between them.

"Well," Baumer explained, "my brother had a son who is also a swineherd, and who is looking for a place to stay. When my nephew is broke and sober, as he is now, he is a good man and a good swineherd," he chuckled, "but when he has money, he is a drunken wastrel. I was hoping you would let him tend the herd at your farm. I would split the profits with you evenly, and of course, the costs." Baumer squared his shoulders quickly, like a private caught slouching by a corporal. "I will be responsible for my nephew's upkeep, of course, until there is a profit."

"How big is the herd?" Thielmann asked, thinking quickly. Perhaps he could build a swine yard by blocking off part of his yard. They should only need a small mud pit...perhaps in that small hollow by the barn...they don't wallow except in summer, and then only by day. That much he knew.

"Not especially large, I don't think," Baumer muttered after some thought. "At least I don't think so: twenty sows, half in row; four boars; perhaps thirty piglets."

Gott im Himmel, Thielmann thought: most butchers don't see so many pigs in a quarter these days. At thirty pfennigs—no, a Mark— to the kilo the piglets alone are enough to provide for another year. Tended well, perhaps forever, even at half profit. And more on the way! By fall the sows should have thrown their litters, and I can enlarge the pen, and I should be able to afford to freshen Maria. "We would have to slaughter some piglets to buy feed," Thielmann said guardedly, hiding his excitement and relief as a good businessman should. "I have a neighbor with pigs, just lost his boar. We could sell stud services...or a boar."

"Yes, of course," Baumer answered. "I don't know about such things, so I leave it to you and Adelmar, my nephew. The herd could be in Marburg next week. There is also a season's feed, I'm told."

A season's feed is a season's profit and saves the piglets. Thielmann suddenly had a reason to hope for the future, but held a nagging doubt in his mind. In a time of hard money and even harder food, Baumer could set himself up for life...outside of Germany perhaps, but life nonetheless...on the profits of just selling out. "Tell me why, Baumer," he asked earnestly. "You could sell the entire herd for a handsome sum... perhaps a thousand *Geldmarcks*." The old Empire's gold currency was the only stable money in Germany just then, but was so rare that they only saw them in business transactions and large estates: a thousand *Geldmarcks* was worth perhaps a large house, or twenty years' living expenses. "Why do you come to me with this...business proposition? Should not your nephew inherit, anyway?"

Baumer looked pained after Lothar's question, his wizened face briefly shrunken. But as the children came into view from the *Marienbadplatz*, he brightened. "My brother made it clear that Adelmar cannot inherit. Your wife was so kind to me after my Lorelei died during the war, and we had no children. We took such private delight in your children. I just thought that I could help them out and we all could profit. Neighbors should help neighbors, should they not?"

"They should indeed, *Herr* Baumer. They should indeed."

In an alley next to the shop, a young man with balled fists watched the Thielmann children coming up the street. He was particularly interested in young Anna, whose fair hair and deep dimples reminded him so much of his late mother as she lay in her coffin.

Otto thought Baumer looked like a thin Father Christmas.

Summer 1935

Northern Wisconsin

Spirit, that made these heroes dare.
To die, and leave their children free,
Bid Time and Nature gently spare
The shaft we raise to them and thee

Ralph Waldo Emerson

Т he sun was just rising on the horizon, red from the storms of the night before. The trees spread out beneath him like an undulating carpet of green, riven by firebreaks and the odd road here and there. The trees meant lumber, paper, jobs, houses, books, newspapers. In northern Wisconsin, the trees were big money. The paper and lumber companies that owned the millions of acres of standing pulpwood treated those trees like gold — living, green gold by the acre.

Oh, this is number three and my hand is on her knee;
Roll me over, lay me down and do it again.
Bop, bop...
Roll me over in the clover;
Roll me over, lay me down and do it again.
Bop. bop...
Roll me over in the clover;
Roll me over, lay me down and do it again.

John Miller finished his song/timer and shut off the sprayer valve, starting his long bank north again. The spray was a new insecticide that Miller couldn't pronounce let alone remember; the target was the trees, and the enemy was tent caterpillars; the song took ten seconds to sing; one pass. This was his first full summer spraying the trees for his father, having spent weekends in the winter carrying cargo and mail.

The flying service was in profit, finally, with three sprayers and a Ford Tri-motor for cargo. Supplementing the flying business, Larry Miller and his son overhauled and rebuilt airplanes, including those for Mitch Canby's fledgling Air Peshtigo, the first scheduled airline in that part of the state. Young Johnny, fifteen and recently licensed to fly without passengers, had dreams of flying for Canby in another couple of years. Especially if...nope, Johnny thought, cracking the valve again. Even though Sally was sweet on him and him on her, Canby just got engaged to Doris Whittaker, puzzling everyone, unless Doris was in trouble. But no one spoke of such things except in hushed tones.

Oh, this is number four and I'm knocking on her door;
Roll me over, lay me down and do it again.
Bop, bop...
Roll me over in the clover;
Roll me over, lay me down and do it again.
Bop, bop...
Roll me over in the clover;
Roll me over, lay me down and do it again.

Valve off and bank south again. It would have been deathly monotonous if Miller didn't love flying so much. The wind, the sun, the vibration of the engine, the exhilaration of lift and turn, and it was monotonous. As he turned south, he thought he saw something as he swung around...a speckled cloud, incongruous and pulsing. *NO! They can't be here yet!*

Fish-tailing the Jenny and boosting the throttle for power, Miller headed for the cloud, easing the stick back for height. Gotta make sure... don't panic for no reason...think, then act...act with knowledge first, then passion. As he approached the oddity to the southwest, he tried to reason the dimensions...five miles wide, probably ten thousand feet high when they're moving, maybe more...three counties deep. Yes, they were grasshoppers...locusts...the modern version of the Black Death.

They'd been hearing about them for a month, starting somewhere in Kansas and Missouri. Funny winds and the Dust Bowl seemed to drive this swarm northeast through Iowa, where they devastated the corn, Minnesota, where most of the oats went, and now Wisconsin, and the trees. To crops they were devastating, ruining a season's harvest. To the trees they would be disastrous, ruining two generations of green gold, a century of growing.

There was no doubt, and there was no time to wait. Johnny could hear their clicking and buzzing over the engine. He banked away for a furious run to the base camp an hour away, where he could recharge his tanks with insecticide. But the swarm was about two days from the trees; one pass through them may have meant nearly nothing, hardly stopping them. Not that it would matter, since he'd have to fly through them. He couldn't fly high enough to go over and the winds aloft would have scattered the spray too much. Far below in the swarm's path was mostly state and federal land, technically owned by no one, with untended old-growth and second-growth, marshes, and swamps. It wouldn't slow the swarm more than a few hours.

But the flocks might.

Just to the south was the booming metropolis of Ladysmith on the Flambeau River. Ladysmith was a high spot in the marshes, attracting tourists in the spring and hunters in the fall. At this time of year, the flocks of ducks and geese were at or very near Ladysmith on their way north, fattening on the cattails. The night's storms would have grounded them this late, Miller hoped. One low-level pass at the North Marsh and the Western Reservoir and I'll get a half-million waterfowl aloft. Once aloft, the flocks will head for the food, the easy prey, the 'hoppers and the cornfields under them. Then maybe the ruckus will attract the martins, and, with luck and enough noise over Flambeau Ridge, what we really need...I hope.

Scribbling a hasty note and stuffing it into a steel pipe with a streamer attached, Miller made full throttle for Ladysmith. He dropped the pipe on the main drag through the town, hoping someone picked up the note (someone usually did) and called his dad for reinforcements, then told the authorities about the approaching swarm. He then turned north, down on the deck over the marsh, the prop wash serrating the placid waters below. As hoped, the ducks and geese took to wing in a flurry of feathers, quickly forming into their majestic mob-like formations of imperfect vees and ells, flying noisily in circles, then heading for the 'hoppers.

Miller's second pass, over the Western Reservoir (behind the Western Dam, a flood control project), got more feathered flocks into the air. A below-treetop pass over the honeycomb caves was less rewarding, but it got some of the ominous black bats to come out. They'll smell or hear the 'hoppers, Miller thought, and will come out after them, eating two or three times their weight every night. A glance at the instrument panel: no gas. Great; just hope I've got enough cash...

13

***

Johnny nursed a cup of coffee at the table while his father talked to the paper company on the telephone. "OK...Thank you, sir. Good bye, sir, and thank you again." Three days of struggling against the swarm of locusts had worn him out, flying spray supplies for the bigger ships that could do damage to the swarm, moving people out of sprayed areas, waking up the flocks in the morning and "herding" bats at night. But he had saved many fields of crops and most of the forests of trees, with food, jobs and generations of lumber preserved. "Well, Stan Oldman at Wherry Paper and old Ben Follet at Regent Paper and Pulp all think you're God's gift to aviation, son," Larry Miller boomed, beaming. "And while I wouldn't go that far, I think your initiative in using the ducks instead of flying into that swarm showed real potential. Yessir, real potential. We've got the spraying contracts all locked up, and Oldman wants to talk about executive transport."

"What was that about the governor, Dad?" Sally wondered, pouring more coffee. Sally had grown from a precocious tomboy to a sweet-faced beauty, more so at a diminutive five-one. She'd taken over the household duties after her mother passed away in the last round of polio in '27, but diligently finished school and was pursuing a nursing degree.

"Oh, yeah: the governor wants to meet you, talk about a commission in the State Guard. I didn't have the heart to tell him you were only fifteen."

"Yeah, but I can pass for twenty." At six foot one and a hundred and ninety pounds, he sure could.

"Your decision, but I wouldn't do it. You'd be the only real flyer in the 'Guard, and they wouldn't know what to do with you. I say it's best to stay clear of them, for now. But Oldman wants to give you a scholarship, four years paid-up..." What in hell for, Johnny Miller wondered. I just did what had to be done. What's so special about that?

Summer 1935

Marburg, Germany

With 2,000 years of examples behind us,
We have no excuse when fighting, for not fighting well

T. E. Lawrence

Marburg was a small, pastoral town, surrounded by hilly, rocky farms that grew an abundance of milk cows and sturdy horses, fresh-scrubbed children and stolid adults. The town had grown from a small market town with a crossroads to a big modern market city with a railway station, a university, and the tomb of Erich Ludendorff without taking on too much in the way of heavy industry or too much support for the Nazis in bigger cities like Munich and Berlin.

Old Baumer was harmless. He lived alone above the Thielmann butcher shop, told old folk tales to the village children, and harmed no one. But he was a proud German who had marched to Paris in 1870, and was decorated by the Kaiser himself. He spent many an evening alone in the Gasthaus, eating his simple meals and drinking his three beers, attending church on Sunday mornings and visiting his wife's grave Sunday afternoons, spending his last years in peace, bothering no one.

Baumer avoided political and ideological discussions, lately becoming all too commonplace. But one evening at the Boar's Head Tavern, from his seat at his usual table, he heard arguments he could not ignore. "The French too weak and decadent," he muttered what he just heard. "The French weak and decadent," he had muttered when he heard it. "The French may be many things, young man," he chided Alois Zimmer, "but weak is not one of them. Ten Frenchmen held my entire company up for half a day at Metz, not because they were weak. And the defense of Paris in 1914 kept us from getting there, not because they were decadent. We didn't get there because the French fought like tigers. Do not underestimate your enemies, my young friend. That may be your undoing."

Ordinarily, such an exchange would have gone unnoticed. But Zimmer was a beefy young lay-about who had never been known to hold a steady job until the Party hired him to be a leader of the Hitler Youth. For reasons of pride, this kind of rebuke from an old man was not to be taken lightly.

Zimmer was not only arrogant, he was angry. How dare this old man question the *Führer*? How dare this *Jew* defy me in front of witnesses?

Marburg's Nazis may have been few, but they were just as vicious as those anywhere. When the old man tottered home that very night on his usual, never-varied route, three boys in brown uniforms followed him, swaggering arrogantly on the rough cobbles. Ahead, three more appeared, similarly attired and similarly threatening. "*Juden*," one of them called to the old man, who ignored them. "*JUDEN*," went the call again, and just as before, ignored. Three of the boys, each a head and a half taller than Baumer, stood in his path, blocking the sidewalk. "Excuse me," the old man muttered, stopping, "but I would like to get home. Let me pass, please." The six laughed without mirth.

"He would like to get home," the barely literate Zimmer mocked jovially, his eyes full of fury in the dim streetlight. "Well, old Jew," he said, "that is simple. All you have to do is say, 'The French are weak and decadent and I am a Jew.' That's all. Say, 'the French are weak and decadent and I am a Jew.' Say it."

The old man raised his steady gaze up to Zimmer, his face defiant, voice steady. "But neither would be true," he said.

"Oh, but they are true, old man. They are true because the *Führer* and I say they are true."

"How could the *Führer* know anything at all about me?" the old man protested mildly. "And besides, you yourself have seen me in the church on Sundays. All of you have. I am not a Jew!"

"*You are a Jew*," the leader yelled, slapping the frail figure across the face in fury. Though it reeled slightly, the proud old frame would not stagger. "I say you are a Jew!"

With that, one boy threw a punch into the old man's kidneys, and suddenly there was a flurry of fists and feet as the old man crumpled to the cobbles, crying piteously, "No! No! I am not a Jew! No! Help me, please!" Others had been on the street, avoiding the attack with their eyes, some even crossing the street to avoid seeing it. A pair of policemen lolled just a few blocks away, their backs turned to the altercation.

Just rounding the corner across the street, two figures came upon the scene, one they had heard of many times before. Otto Thielmann was walking home from the boxing ring, where he had been training for a match the next week. Though small for his age, he had developed powerful shoulders and lightning speed. With him was his good friend Gunther Rickmann, a large boy of muscular build. Though it had happened in Marburg before, this outrage, this beating of the helpless, had never happened in Otto's sight, or in Rickmann's. It would not go unanswered.

Crossing the street at a dead run, both shouted at the small mob, still flailing the old man whose cries were becoming steadily weaker. Two of the bullies turned to meet them, fists balled, poised to spring like street brawlers. But their new opponents were not street brawlers; Thielmann had won six successive boxing matches by knockout in as many months as Rickmann had trained him to do. Before the first bully had a chance to warn off these interlopers, he met Rickmann's hammer-like left hook on the side of his head, while another other took three successive, blurred jabs in the stomach from Thielmann's right. Both collapsed in the street.

Suddenly, the remaining four realized that someone was interfering. "Get away," Zimmer boldly shouted, the old man's blood dripping off his fists and shoes. "Or you can enjoy similar treatment." Zimmer was part triumphant, part terrified, with fear rising in his face. But this was not the physical fear that one fighter shows another; it was the fear that animals show when suddenly they are no longer the hunters, but the hunted.

"He is just an old man," Thielmann said evenly, "an old man who has done no harm to you."

"But he has, Thielmann," one of the gang said defiantly. "He has defied the *Führer*."

"Shut up, Gretzler," Thielmann spat. "So you have found something to do besides throwing stones at streetlights, eh? Beating up on this old man?" Gretzler sneered, backing away carefully. Zimmer decided that his remaining four goons (the other two were out of action) should teach these two a lesson while making an example of the old man. Drawing his dagger, he slashed at Rickmann clumsily. Rickmann saw the flashing steel in the dim half-light and parried it away easily, grabbing the leader's arm and breaking it against his rising knee with a sharp *crack*. The remaining three flung themselves on the pair, but Thielmann met the first with a well-aimed blow to a solar plexus, shouldering away a second's wild swing, and easily dodging the third's lunge. Zimmer staggered away, yelling for help. The remaining three attacked again. One met Rickmann's devastating uppercut in the jaw and went down, another Thielmann's right jab—a thunderbolt of sinew and bone guided by calculated fury and unerring aim—into his guts, doubling him over for the last time. The last took to his heels just as the policemen decided to take an interest.

***

Thielmann and Rickmann walked to the farm, sharing the old man's weight between them; across the cobbled square, up the winding brick alley, across the rough fields riven with ancient stone fences, around the copse of ancient, mystical oaks. The stone house with the stout timber and slate roof was clean and well-maintained; the huge hearth in the front room blackened by centuries of fires, the worn wooden floor creaking on the foundation timbers.

"He's a remarkably resilient man," Dr. Kelso said finally, pouring a large measure of brandy in the kitchen, "but I don't think he'll survive the night. Who did this?"

"HJ," Otto said bitterly. "Zimmer, Gretzler and their acolytes."

"*Ptui*," Anna spat, "that slug Zimmer! For years he has been chasing me around the square, and then the Nazis come to power and suddenly he's denying he ever knew me, in public at least. The creature, just yesterday..." she stopped, glancing at the doctor. "Nazi vermin!" she finished.

"Yes, but they have made work for many," Otto began, puzzled by his sister, "and we have repudiated that stain of Versailles..."

"To whose advantage," his sister barked. "That old man's?"

***

"They need us in China, Papa," Anna said. "The Japanese are murdering millions over there, and there's famine where there isn't war. Adam is going, and I must go with him." The living room, which had been so warm and cheery, had become cold and foreboding, the clock in the hall ticking away loudly as if to punctuate the silence. The passionate missionary who was once Lothar's daughter spoke with conviction, not asking for permission, but a blessing. "Germany doesn't need us, anyway," she said, eyes cast downward. "Soon they will start slaughtering their enemies wholesale, and I don't want to be a part of it. The Church is all I have left."

It was true, Lothar thought, sad but true. His daughter was a devout Catholic in an increasingly devout Nationalist country, and she was now a trained missionary. Oh, when will all this Nazi madness end? The money is stable, and business is good, but how long can it last with those peacocks in Berlin building an army? And for what? Just last week, he was told to report for a village *Volkssturm* muster. Perhaps, he thought, I can get a situation with my old friend Wilhelm Canaris in the *Abwehr*. "I'm only glad your mother isn't alive to see this," he said at last. "She would be as ardent about them as you are. But, Anna my child, they won't really do anything more about the Jews than they already have."

"Papa," she interrupted, "they will. They mean to kill them, as many of them as they can. And I can't stay to see it."

"All right, then," he said at length, "all right. Go with your Papa's blessing." The girl kissed her father's forehead gently, tears welling in her eyes. "*Auf Wiedersehn*, Papa," she choked, and hurried from the room.

Otto, listening from the kitchen, felt he would never see his sister again.

October 1938

Fischer's Corners, Wisconsin

War hath no fury like a noncombatant

Charles Edward Montague

T he western sky was just getting on to dark as evening descended on the small town of Fischer's Corners. The movie house with its glittering facade of gaiety twinkled invitingly, beckoning the farmers and shopkeepers of the North Central Wisconsin town with the promise of an entertaining escape from their cares and woes. John Miller, eighteen and home from Beloit College for the weekend, strolled arm-in-arm to the theater with his sister Sally, who was home from nursing school. Tonight they would shut out the real world and, like many of their neighbors, visit the fantasy world of Hollywood. Armed with popcorn and Cokes, they went into the darkening theater, finding seats near the aisle just as the house lights dimmed and the curtains drew back.

The newsreels unwound to the narration of Avery Johnson and a stirring Richard Rogers score, with vignettes of the world outside rural Wisconsin. A strip on the World Series dominated their interest; the scenes of Japanese bombing in China were surreal, almost make-believe; the demonstrations of the Lambeth Walk were entrancing; the column of marching Italians in Ethiopia may as well have been a Hollywood back lot for all that it mattered to the audience: swaggering Italians and barefoot Ethiopians sharing the same roads, rifles against spears—talk about surreal. The first anniversary of the Golden Gate was fascinating; the ruin of Guernica by dint of aerial bombing by German "volunteers" was far less important to this audience than the casting of Clark Gable and Vivien Leigh for *Gone with the Wind*. The newsreels gave way to the first short subject, with Larry, Moe and Curly yukking it up over the destruction of a house during an elegant party. John and Sally laughed right along with everyone else, forgetting all about the newsreels.

Then there was another short, a documentary that, in another age, would easily pass for a paid advertisement. It talked about a war in Europe that no one wanted but that everyone knew was coming. And everyone present "knew" that America could—and should—stay out of it. "What do Poland, Czechoslovakia and Austria have in common with America?" the film's authoritative-sounding narrator asked, the screen lit by scenes of contemporary marching columns artfully intermixed with pans of WWI trenches. "Nothing," it asserted to this audience of Central European descendants, most of whom bobbed their heads up and down in agreement.

"Our great first president, George Washington, the father of our country, said to his people: 'Avoid foreign entanglements.' Good advice then; good advice now," the narrator assured his audience. "Two mighty oceans and a Navy that is the envy of the world protect us," it said, showing storm-tossed seas and steel behemoths sprouting mighty guns. "No one can attack our shores without assurance of destruction long before our sons must fight another foreign war for the moneyed interests. The distances are simply too great. We simply have no interest in what Europe or Asia does." To this Depression-era audience, this was a comforting thought.

Next up, the audience was transported from the political to the promising: previews for *Jezebel* and *You Can't Take It with You* hanging in the air of the smoky theater, ending with Benny Goodman's orchestra's *A Flat Foot Floogie with a Floy Floy*, as the last latecomers took their seats. Finally, the feature started—H. G. Wells' *Things to Come*.

The scene opened with three men arguing about a war, a war that hadn't happened yet, a war that no one wanted but that everyone knew would come. Soon. "But war is bad for trade," the merchant said emphatically. "Business will not support a war, I say."

Well's cinematic war comes in 1940, and it lasts, fantastically, incredibly, unbelievably, until 1970 and beyond. It is waged by great crawling fighting machines and acres of artillery, thousands of men, causing the ruin of cities, famine, disease, and destitution for millions of hapless non-combatants.

Then the virtuous policemen in enormous flying machines appear (the film not troubling to say exactly from where except "the

Mediterranean"), dropping bombs on the capitals and headquarters of the evil leaders of the warring factions. Then the people in the cities and the soldiers, defenseless against the aerial onslaught, rise in revolt against those who made the war, concluding a lasting, permanent peace, forswearing all war. "If we don't end war," Raymond Massey's character intones, "war will end us."

In your dreams and the movies, John thought.

October 1938

Nurnberg, Germany

*How horrible, fantastic, incredible it is
That we should be digging trenches and trying on gas-masks here
Because of a quarrel in a far-away country
Between people of whom we know nothing*

Neville Chamberlain

T he night was crisp and clear, and the torchlights gave off an unnatural, almost other-worldly feeling. Otto felt a ripple of excitement as he carried his Youth Flying Corps unit's standard in the victory parade, the one commemorating Germany's victory over Czechoslovakia. This was his first major rally, and the first time he would personally see the *Führer*. On a sub-stage near the dais, Anton Zimmer waited with hundreds of other "honored guests" who were to personally meet their glorious leader.

For three frantic days, the parade had been gathering. Since midday, the spectators, clad in cloth coats and crude woolens against the Bavarian fall chill, crushed together in a few acres of the stadium in a mystical natural bowl built expressly for rallies like this one. The caps and hats, scarves and bare heads of the crowd topped the gleaming eyes filled with the eager expectation of hopeful farmers, tradesmen and factory workers waiting for their Messiah.

Otto was excited too, for he and his entire unit had just signed up for the *Luftwaffe*, and in a matter of days, they would begin their formal training. But this was one of the most important things he'd ever done in his life—to carry the standard in review before the *Führer*. He had many schoolmates and other friends who were signing up for the armed services, but Otto was carrying the standard before the *Führer*.

His participation in Hitler Youth activities was minimal only because he was such a terrific boxer. Still, he was proud of his Germany, how it had come storming back from the evils of Versailles, and now stood proud before the world, defiant in the face of the British and French, a stalwart bastion of the west to stem the tide of the Russian communists. That was about as far as he went with his National Socialism. He didn't subscribe to the racial theories of the Nazis, though he kept his own counsel on such matters. He was much more like his brother Ulrich, at the Naval Academy right then, who held judgment of the Nazis until the fad blew over.

A whistle blew, and the big drums boomed across the crowd. One by one, the marching columns started to march, keeping time with the blaring and pounding music. Soon the columns moved into the stadium, and the parade took the chant up: *"Deutschland Erwache! Deutschland Erwache! Deutschland Erwache!"* At first it was a whisper, but soon it was a shout, a scream, a prayer, an invocation. Deutschland Erwache! From a thousand and a million throats the cry went up, rolling over the crowds, roaring over the music, thundering against the surrounding mountains and hills. *Deutschland Erwache! "Deutschland Erwache,"* Thielmann shouted until he was hoarse. He was holding his banner like thousands of others marching past the reviewing stand, from the army, the navy, the air force, the labor service, the railroads, the fire wardens, the police, the foresters, the frontier police, and every other organization in the New Germany, proud, marching, shouting, *"Deutschland Erwache!"* Germany has indeed awakened, he thought proudly.

The mass of flags and standards marched around the bowl, columns breaking off and reforming like pods of an amoeba, flickering torches providing the only light; the masses of humanity packing the stadium shouting, screaming; flags and standards flapping and swaying with the movement, bearers marching in perfect synchronization with the sound of their pounding boots reverberating in time with the throbbing drums and blaring horns over the crowds; Party functionaries on the reviewing stand in a cornucopia of uniforms, arms outstretched, saluting the banners and flags as they marched by; newsreel cameras panning and pulling, wire recorders running, flashbulbs popping, radio commentators pressing their headphones to their ears and shouting over the din. And when their marching circuit was done, the black and gray, brown and blue mass stopped again precisely where it had begun, as though it had never moved.

Then, as if shut off by a switch, the stadium was silent, and a single light shown on a stage, where a small man in a brown Party uniform stood, his hands folded before him. Quietly, almost timidly at first, the small man spoke. He spoke of Germany and of Germans, of pride, and of cowardice, of other nations, and of strength. With rising confidence, he spoke of a holy task, of a work only barely begun, of an enemy within Germany, within all of humanity, which must be expunged. He talked about a Red menace, and the decadence of Europe, and the weakness of America. Many of the words rang true for Thielmann, but not all of them. Why the Jews? And what was this about a "stab in the back" in 1918? The Navy mutinied because they had no bread, and the Army was starving, pushed by the much stronger and better supplied Allies. Germany just wore out, he thought, and the Kaiser gave up. That was what Papa said.

But the small man in the brown suit went on, a fervent rage building within him, and his effect on the massed crowd of angry, proud people in the stadium was palpable, hypnotic, addicting. "Then, when we have the Jew where we want him, we will crush the very life from him, even while he pleads for mercy!" This brought a cry from the crowd, an exaltation of assent. "And I shall not rest until this task is done, and Germany stands alone at the pinnacle of humanity, as the true leaders of the Aryan race, as the purifiers of the world! *Deutschland Erwache! Deutschland! Deutschland uber alles!*" With this, the crowd went into frenzy, right arms thrusting at the stage in salute, every throat crying, "*Deutschland Erwache! Deutschland uber alles! Sieg Heil! Sieg Heil!*" The sound echoed over the mountains, across the land, and across the continent. Otto was transfixed, hypnotized by the rhythmic chant and pounding music, weary from the cry, proud of Germany, but ashamed of the hideous lies that carried it forward, to a future that very few at that rally could begin to understand.

Later that same evening, Zimmer was still numb from his visit with the *Führer* (he walked by within three meters of me, Zimmer thought, and looked in my direction! Did he see me?). To celebrate, he and his newfound friends took over a small, out of the way inn where the beer was flowing from Party kegs and the women were willing—or at least they were said to be. As excited as he was, the young girl he managed to get onto a table was not as compliant as he had imagined she should have been—or wanted. After training her to obey with a few judicious blows, she finally did what he wanted. Regrettably, however, the cow died. Odd, Zimmer thought, how aroused I became again when they carried her out.

***

"Today, my young whelps," Lieutenant Colonel Heinrich Kaltz said while spreading his arms wide, "you shall learn the basics of air tactics and strategy." Those words marked Thielmann's entry into the stunning universe of air combat, far advanced from the basic flying and aerobatics he'd already been taught. His teachers were, mostly, veterans from the last war, but some, called "Spaniards," had more recent experience in the *Legion Kondor*.

"This," Kaltz said, pointing to a drawing on the wall, "is what we call the 'line of idiots.' It is a simple formation, easily executed, and makes those that use it easy prey for the wise ones who do not." The instructor moved the simple felt figures of airplanes on the wall behind him. "As you can see, they line *your* targets up in columns as they attack *their* targets from the stern. Your task is merely to get your four-machine swarm behind the last one and shoot him full of holes. You can take turns on the lead, if you wish. If you are quick and the enemy is slow, you will destroy them all." The plan was simple, the logic elegant, and the effect devastating.

Kaltz was a big man, and at 48 he was elderly for a fighter pilot, but he had flown on von Richthofen's wing just before the Red Baron died. "He was too tired," Kaltz had told them, "he'd been at it too long. He didn't know when to quit. There is a certain point beyond which no man should still be flying. I stopped combat flying twenty years ago. I'll not fly combat again." Kaltz was called "the Hawk" in *Luftwaffe* circles for his tendency to swoop down on unsuspecting students from above them, a strategy he embraced in the original Flying Circus. "Always get a height advantage on your opponent, even if only a few meters," he would say, "for who has height and the speed that goes with it, wins."

"There is nothing a horizontal bomber can do that cannot be more accurately done by the dive bomber," another instructor told them later. "It is implicitly logical that the dive bomber, placing bombs and gunfire where they will do the most good for the soldiers in the field, is the most effective use of air power on land."

"The heavy bomber attacking defended cities," another instructor assured them, "is much too risky for the value returned. Antiaircraft artillery and fighter interception make the heavy bombers much too vulnerable for practical use in so-called 'strategic precision bombing' against targets that can defend themselves. The Americans and British, however, believe there to be some value to it, but we know that this is a false belief. Therefore, heavy bombers are given little attention by the *Luftwaffe*, self-protecting heavy bombers no thought whatsoever, and the preposterous notion that 'the bomber will always get through' that the Englishman Baldwin came up with is given no credence at all. Besides, what happens strategically is irrelevant. Once we defeat the enemy's army on the ground, they will always sue for peace."

Throughout his early instruction in air tactics and strategy, Thielmann was slightly uneasy at some things his instructors taught. Use of flying machines as a weapon was still fairly new, he thought. Who can say what may work and what may not with new aircraft being developed all the time? Ideas originating from experimenting based on engagements nearly devoid of opposition such as Ethiopia and Spain were not yet proven, but the leaders of the *Luftwaffe* embraced them as if they were facts. Perhaps, Thielmann thought uncomfortably, it was easier to embrace dubious theories as enlightened truth in a land where people were considered not quite human because of their religion. "What about Nanking," Thielmann once asked. "The Japanese burned it practically to the ground in air attacks."

"Unopposed, they could have used paper kites to destroy Nanking," had been the answer.

"But they *were* opposed. Our own intelligence said that the Chinese have a quite large Air Force, some flown by Russians and even Americans," he had replied.

"The Chinese are subhuman scum, incapable of anything in the air other than the simplest of tasks. No, the Chinese Air Force is not even worthy of the name. The war in Asia has little to do with us in Europe, where we know how to build real flying machines and fight air wars. Spend less of your time on nonsense taking place elsewhere, Thielmann, and spend more on what we teach you here."

So he learned about the low-level bombing used by the JU-88s, the dive bombing used by the Stukas, the raking of ground targets by the HS-123s and Messerschmitts, hunting for enemy bombers and fighters in the sky.

Always get the height advantage...watch for your leader...hold your formations loose...don't get too tied up in tactics outmoded before you use them, level bombing is a waste of time... dive bombing will inherit the kingdom...air warfare is for fighters and dive bombers by day and the odd level bomber by night, "mostly to keep the populous awake," his teachers said, "night bombing has no tactical or strategic value. The *Luftwaffe* will infrequently have use for it."

September 1939

Detroit, Michigan

If there be one principle
More deeply rooted than any other
In the mind of every American,
It is that we should have nothing to do with conquest

Thomas Jefferson

The radio sputtered the announcement of Chamberlain's last ultimatum to Germany. "War with Germany again," John Miller muttered. He was in Detroit with a load of machine parts for the Ford Rouge plant.

"And we should stay clear of it," the counterman said. "We want nothing to do with another foreign war."

"We may not have much of a choice," Miller responded quietly. "They may attack us first."

"Then we should negotiate a quick peace," the counterman said. "Lindbergh says the German Air Force can't be beat, and anyone who thinks different is nuts."

"Slim Lindbergh's a horse's ass," Miller retorted, having remembered his dad expound on the subject of the Lone Eagle's pronouncements about the *Luftwaffe*. "He's a hopelessly vain peacock who's easily flattered. Hell, he's just an airmail pilot and reservist who was the fifty-second guy to fly across the Atlantic. Just so happens he was alone at the time."

"What war?" someone else said. "Says right here that Mister Ford says that there *ain't* no war over there. It's just a concoction of the moneyed interests."

"*Huh,*" Miller sputtered, taking the proffered paper. He read the editorial with incredulity.

"What about what the radio just said?" Miller replied.

"If you know what's good for you, young fella, you'll wise up and pay attention to Mister Ford, and you'll have more respect for true patriots like Colonel Lindbergh. *They* know what's what. I ain't too sure about there isn't a war over there in, where, Poland? That Chamberlain fellow, he don't lie too much, I don't think, and besides, who would make up a war?"

"I heard the Poles invaded Germany," another wag began, "invaded them before the Germans hit 'em back. From what I know of them Polacks down in the steel mill, well, they ain't too bright, so I figure maybe the Polish would be dumb enough to pick on somebody a lot bigger than them."

September 1939

Kutno, Poland

For any madness of their kings,
It is the Greeks who take the beating

Horace

Expertly, Lieutenant Thielmann turned his ME-109E after a Polish P-23 *Kara* bomber, which was struggling desperately to outmaneuver or outrun the German attackers. Its escorts of gull-winged Potez fighters were all gone, and this bomber was trying desperately to finish its mission to bomb the German bridgehead over the Warta River. After a stream of Thielmann's cannon shells struck the engine and wing root, it exploded in midair. "*Horrido*," Thielmann called on the radio, proclaiming another victory.

Gazing about for more targets, Thielmann heard his group commander, Major Ernst Belzer, give the recall signal for all his flocks to come home. Finding his leader, Lieutenant Philip Kutz, Thielmann slid into position behind his left wing and headed west again to their forward airfield outside Poznan.

Thielmann pushed the sadness away, earnestly hoping that there would be no more such holes in him.

After supper that evening, a mongrel dog that had wandered onto the base several days before was the butt of the flyers' jokes. They fed him scraps from the table, watching his antics as he jumped and dove and spun in the air after the airborne morsels. He had a shaggy short coat of brown and black, with a white chest and gray feet. His muzzle was strong and pudgy, eyes of chocolate brown that entranced. He stood about knee-high and weighed less than twenty kilos.

"Why would they attack Germany, these Poles, and what war are they fighting, anyway?" one wag asked aloud, "certainly not this one. Why, they don't know how to fly those obsolete crates of theirs any better than my grandmother!" This was met with great merriment by most.

"For not knowing how to fly," Belzer said gravely as the laughter died down, "they have killed more than a hundred *Luftwaffe* pilots since they invaded us, and two from this *Geschwader* alone. Think about that, my son." The wag fell quiet. Thielmann had heard about the Polish "invasion," but the more he thought about it, the less sense it made. Still, it *seemed* plausible, but...

"What about Spain?" someone asked Linz. "How good were the Spanish pilots?"

"It wasn't the Spanish we worried about so much as the Russians and Americans," Linz said. "The Spanish had heart, good stout heart, even if they were flying castoff French and British junk. But we avoided the Russian and American volunteer squadrons, whatever they flew, in our HE 100s. Our Messerschmitts could handle them all right, usually..." he said, trailing off.

"I fear the Russians and Americans," Belzer said softly. "I fear them because they do not fear us. All of Europe is afraid of the *Luftwaffe* in the air, but not them." Linz nodded assent. The room was quiet for the rest of the night. As Thielmann walked to his billet, he told his orderly to find the dog, bathe him, and bed him down comfortably. "What will you call him?" the younger man asked.

"Gunther," Thielmann said, retiring into the darkness.

***

The SS Lieutenant looked vaguely familiar, with a slightly slack-jawed expression and dull, lifeless eyes. He was dressed in the immaculate black, red, and gray uniform preferred by the Reich Security Service. As Thielmann approached, the Lieutenant lanced his arm into a *Hitlergruss*. "Heil Hitler," he said. Thielmann returned the salute by limply touching his cap with his right hand.

"My congratulations on your successes in the Polish campaign, Lieutenant Thielmann," the officer said silkily, with a familiar ring to his voice. Where have I heard him before...?

"Thank you, Lieutenant. I have been as fortunate as my opponents have been unlucky." Thielmann regarded the vaguely familiar figure with the annoyed interest of the warrior for the bureaucrat. Golden pheasants, Thielmann thought derisively, strutting pretty birds, with about as much brains.

His countenance was familiar, but not altogether known. There was something very wrong with his jaw, Thielmann thought. What was it...?

"I've come on a somewhat delicate personal matter, Lieutenant, about your sister." The SD man purred in the way of a cat for a mouse.

"Anna," Thielmann said, slightly apprehensive. China was a very dangerous place for a missionary, and the family feared for her. "What of Anna?"

"Not her, actually, but her husband. Do you know his family?"

"I've met his parents, his brother and his aunt, but that is all. Why?"

"We have information, Lieutenant, that he may have obtained his medical degree under false pretenses."

"How?" Thielmann said, somewhat confused and growing annoyed. The Lieutenant's face was becoming more familiar and more disgusting.

"Well, it seems that, let me see," he said, consulting a paper. "Yes. It would seem that he got his degree in 1932? May 1932?"

"Yes, that sounds right. What does that have to do with me, or with Anna, for that matter? That was before they met."

"Well, apparently, his maternal grandmother is an unfit person to have a German physician for a grandson. Did you know that?"

"Unfit? How unfit? She has been dead for many years, yes? She lived in Vienna, yes?"

"She expired in, let's see...1921, yes, and she lived in Austria. Nevertheless, she is unfit. Jewish." *Juden*. The word stuck to Thielmann's brain like a nettle — annoying, a little painful, especially the way the Lieutenant said it. *Juden*, pronounced with the same contempt as for the Black Death or the influenza, as if to excise the fiend by exposing it. The tone was typical for Nazis, but in this context, it was nearly nauseating.

"How is it that the dead are fit to be anything but dead, Lieutenant?" Thielmann was becoming more than vaguely annoyed, suddenly realizing that this Lieutenant was none other than Alois Zimmer, the HJ thug who beat up old man Baumer. "What does a dead woman's religion have to do with a degree conferred years after they buried her?"

"The Decrees clearly state that German universities cannot award degrees to persons of Jewish blood and *Herr* Adam Kelso, your brother-in-law, was conferred a medical degree from the *Universitat Koln...*"

"Yes, but years earlier. You are making such an accusation about a degree conferred before the law was passed?"

"There is no limitation on the law, Lieutenant. Kelso was required to report his ancestry, and failed to note his Jewish origins when the law required it. He has violated the law. I only enforce the law, Lieutenant," Zimmer purred at last, as if to close the subject for good. There were vague hints of triumph, German officious innocence, and Nazi arrogance all at once.

"Really, Zimmer," Thielmann replied, "you only enforce the law? Anna and her husband Adam Kelso are in China. How will you enforce Nazi law there, eh? You enforce the law? Beating up an old man whose worst crime was calling you an idiot? What part of the law was that, Zimmer?"

"Do not get *too* comfortable, Lieutenant Thielmann," Zimmer snapped, drawing up to his full height nearly half a head taller than Thielmann. "Baumer, that old *Juden*, was an enemy of the Party. He..."

"Was as much a *Juden* as you are, you horse's ass. Do you think I *wouldn't* remember, Zimmer?"

"I don't care if you remember or not, Thielmann." Zimmer clicked his heels together officiously. "I am here to tell you that our agents in China will find Adam Kelso and bring him to justice. Any warnings or assistance you or your family provide him will make you enemies of the state. And that sister of yours," Zimmer sneered contemptuously, "she, too, will be punished as the law requires. *Both* of them..."

"Are far beyond your feeble reach, Zimmer. You cannot bluff that, obviously." Thielmann was weary of this game and determined to end it as decisively as he could. "Tell me, Zimmer, how is your arm?" Zimmer glared at him violently, malevolently, triumph gone to reveal sudden, unreasoning, animal hatred. Thielmann stared back with contempt, turned, and walked away.

Thielmann tried not to think of Zimmer for some time without success. He believed a pink rhinoceros would have been easier to forget.

May 1941

Labrador, Canada

Friendship is love without his wings

Lord Byron

T he pilot of the big tri-motor set his manifest and flight plan nonchalantly on the customs counter. The bored official glanced at the name "Adam Adams," the certainly contrived route it said he took across eastern Canada, the manifest listing "farm machine parts," and thinking idly that the forgers were obviously running low on imagination. "Adams" retrieved his stamped forgery and walked away, directing the unloading of his ship.

John Miller was in St. Johns delivering another load of "farm machine parts" that looked suspiciously like aviation instruments, forbidden to be delivered to "aggressing powers" by the Neutrality Act. The night before, he'd flown to an abandoned iron mine in northern Michigan, changed the ID numbers of his ship for those of an empty Canadian tri-motor waiting there while picking up the fake papers, and sprinted over the border just after dark. All this, he groused in his head, because Congress can't quite get it through their thick skulls that this is *all* our fight, not just Europe's. Silly-ass Neutrality Act.

After unloading the double-bound crates (more than one had burst open during handling, causing embarrassing moments in Canada and arrests in the 'States), Miller went into the terminal again for some coffee and to see about fuel and a cargo for the return trip. While Miller was negotiating with the proprietor of an air freight forwarding company he'd done business with in the past, someone burst into the terminal lobby, breathless from a long run.

"Any pilots with planes," he shouted. "Any pilots with planes; may I have your attention, please? We've just received word that U-boats have struck an outward bound convoy fifty miles out. A ship that was not, I repeat, not, with the convoy, has been torpedoed—an American ship. The ship is foundering and believed to be under surface attack. I need pilots to go out and find the ship. Please, does anyone here want to help?"

"You gotta ask," Miller said snidely. "Hell, I'll even buy my own gas. Give me a bearing." In a half hour, Miller was scanning across the flat, featureless ocean, looking for telltale signs of a ship in distress. Next to him was a slightly overweight RN observer, scanning the same blue-gray sea with binoculars. The bearing had put the stricken ship roughly fifty miles east- northeast of St. John's, some two miles behind the convoy she wasn't, repeat, wasn't with. Five other Americans with false papers were flying search patterns, including a Beech Staggerwing Miller had flown when the paper company's regular pilot was too soused to fly. All had an observer, but the three multi-engines also carried inflatable rafts and a volunteer foolish enough to jump into the dark cold water if conditions warranted.

After three numbing hours, Miller finally saw what he took for an oil slick gleaming in the reflected sunlight, and, as he followed the slick east, saw a tangle of wreckage, rafts and boats mired in oil, bobbing on the sea. Miller banked around the waving, cheering survivors, cold and soaked with oil. He dropped to fifty feet when the "jumper" opened the door and pushed the rubber rafts out as they inflated. The rafts contained blankets, fresh water, rudimentary first aid supplies, and pemmican cans. A hasty message tied to a life preserver assured them of rescue in a few hours. Miller wondered how long they could last in the open water with night coming on. A radio call back to St. Johns of the survivor's position returned disturbing news—this wreck couldn't have been the American ship since the American was still afloat, or so the radio said. Miller resumed the search until dark.

Next day dawned overcast and cold, but Miller and the other searchers out of St. Johns went out anyway, with diminishing hopes of finding their countrymen since the ship had sunk in the night. The convoy was long gone, and rescue ships out of Labrador and Argentia had failed to find anything. Attacking neutrals, Miller thought wearily, German U-boats are attacking neutrals. Why are we still holding out? What will it take for us to get into this war that everyone knows we will get into "soon," that Henry Ford had first said didn't even exist?

A fire on the horizon brought Miller to another dying ship. The freighter's crew was scrambling into the boats and rafts, fuel oil blazing, and a German submarine stood off to one side, waiting—a black jackal on a lead-gray sea, deck gun manned and ready for the *coup de grâce*. Miller, engulfed by rage he couldn't control, muttered "*Damn neutrality*," and suddenly dove on the sub, which, having spotted him by then, was busy trying to dive. With spray from the blowing ballast tanks splashing on the tri-motor's windshield, Miller smashed the U-boat's periscope with his right wheel, causing his unarmed tri-motor to jerk heavily from the impact as he barely recovered inches off the angry pewter sea.

"If my country won't by *God, I will*," he shouted as he circled the wreckage with the enraged U-boat's machine guns chattering away at him. "Throw the rafts off," he yelled at the jumper in the back, "I gotta get outta here!"

***

By the time he'd got back to St. Johns, it was nearly noon, but news of his attack on the German U-boat had preceded him. A seagoing tug with another tow had arrived on the scene an hour later and picked up the survivors with their fantastic story of a tri-motor that had sunk a sub by ramming. "Adam Adams" landed his tri-motor on the macadam with little difficulty and a great deal of sparks, the evidence of the attack unavoidable. "Well," a slightly haggard RN commander told him, "I'm not sure you would have sunk it, but it's definitely back to Germany for him, with his periscope torn off. That's one less Hun U-boat for about two months. I appreciate it Mr....uhn, Adams, is it?"

"Yeah," Miller responded. "But not near as much as those guys in the drink did. Did we ever find the crew of that American ship that got hit yesterday?"

"No, I'm afraid not."

The next day, an envelope arrived at St. Johns stuffed with money—Canadian, American, Dutch, and Norwegian. A note in it said: "For your trouble and to fix your wheel."

May 1941

Maleme, Crete

Next to a battle lost, the greatest misery is a battle won

Lord Wellington

T hielmann landed his plane on the Maleme airfield, his engine smoking badly from British flak hits. He had shot down another Hurricane that day—a South African by its markings—and had lost another Katchmarek; wingman. In two years of war, Thielmann had earned the nickname der einsame Jäger, the Lone Hunter, because he always seemed to outlive his wingmen—he'd had ten by Crete—while scoring ever more victories. He had lost three wingmen in three weeks fighting the RAF in Greece, and had two machines so badly shot up he had to nurse, cajole and coax them back to base. During the Channel battle in the fall of 1940, he had reached thirty victories. They awarded him his Knight's Cross on the day that Goering called the Luftwaffe a "pack of cowards" for not defeating the RAF. His nickname followed not long after.

From the air, Crete looked to Thielmann like it was made by someone who used too much stone and not enough dirt—a twisted maze of jagged, craggy rocks and hills, cracks and patches of trees, punctuated by huge expanses of rocky plains that didn't know what level *meant*. The merciless Mediterranean sun beat down on the dry, featureless hummocks of dead, dry soil that was most of Crete. The scrubby trees and stony pastures were still strewn with discarded parachutes and other detritus of war. The airfield was dotted with the wreckage of destroyed airplanes—British, Italian, and German. In knots around the field, tired Germans guarded tired Englishmen, Indians, New Zealanders, and Greeks captured in the battle.

The dead were only now being recovered from the terrible struggle for the island. The German dead were lined up in orderly rows, covered with parachutes, tarpaulins, shelter quarters, or whatever was at hand. The Allied dead were being lined up on the field opposite. It struck Thielmann that the only differences between the rows of the dead was the side of the field they were on, their uniforms, and those doing the gathering. The intelligence men were searching the Allied dead for anything useful; the German dead were being searched for ammunition and equipment. Even the dead were being put to good use in the new Germany, he thought, struck by a slight irony for which he was too weary to contemplate.

After directing a pair of oil-covered blackbirds to repair his machine, Thielmann trudged across the field towards the hangars, some still smoldering from fires caused in the battle. Outside the shed, acting as a makeshift terminal (the real terminal had been destroyed) Thielmann bundled a piece of cheese and flat Greek bread into a crude sandwich, washing it down with warm water. He passed some conversation with a tired Captain acting as airfield commander. "We will make aviation fuel available on an as-required basis," Thielmann was told, "but first the wounded have to be evacuated."

The wounded were even then arriving on trucks and carts, walking and limping, as two JU-52s were warming up. The *Tante Jus* were tired, ragged, and holed in several places. The injured passengers—requiring medical attention not possible on that barren desert of an island— were being carried one by one into the planes. One engine emitted dangerous, oily smoke. "Aren't there other crates available?" Thielmann asked, alarmed that wounded men were being subjected to such dangerous transport.

"No," the embattled Captain replied, "they shot up nearly all our old Aunties up in the attack. These two have been flying nonstop for nearly a week."

My God, Thielmann thought. There were over five hundred transports when the attack began, and now these two are all that is left? Just today I shot down a man who came from half a world away to this Godforsaken, evil place to fight me. What sort of victories are we winning? And against whom are we winning them?

December 1941

Milwaukee, Wisconsin

I have told you once and I tell you again;
Your boys will not be sent into any foreign wars

Franklin D. Roosevelt

The anteroom of the recruiting station smelled of old linoleum, shoe polish, and sweaty men in damp clothes. They bleached the woodwork white in just a few days of street mud and rock salt that thousands of earnest young patriots and had tracked in. The dim brass-and-glass chandeliers turned the overcrowded anteroom into something that greatly resembled a cattle pen. John Miller waited with the rest, listening idly to snippets of conversation around him:

"...I heard the whole of the Green Bay Packers signed up for the Marines ...Yeah, just yesterday I seen this funny lookin' guy eyeballin' the Allis-Chalmers plant, and I think he was a spy...Naw, them Japs are invading the Panama Canal right now....I tell ya it's the Nazis what bombed Pearl Harbor...Yeah, and them Mexicans are gonna be on the Jap's side...Naw, them Japs're too nearsighted, couldn't see to fly airplanes...Well, I'm gonna deliver a big bomb right down old Tojo's throat, just let me at 'em...I tell ya, I got it from a guy whose brother's in the Navy...Yeah, we got a fleet right now goin' right over there to Tokyo gonna blast the place to smithereens...We know that the Nazis have set up radio stations in this country, and they're gonna be here any minute...Why, I heard that...I got the straight poop from...Now listen to me...And just where in the hell is Hawaii, anyway..."

The din of men in idle conversation and deep rage, ringing telephones, a tinny radio blaring in the background, and the seemingly mindless whirl of the army recruiting office that was wholly unprepared for the rush of new recruits that now confronted it, was almost unbearable for the grizzled veteran sergeant at the intake desk. "Aw right you guys... SHADDAP!" he shouted. "They'll be plenty of Japs and Nazis for you to tango with by the time you get there. Somebody *shut off that damn radio!*" The noise subsided, abating slowly, as if to wait for the unwary before it struck again. "OK, you, what's your name?"

"Miller, John Miller," he said, adding, "listen; who do I talk to about the air corps? A guy last night said..."

Only barely hiding his disgust and frustration, the sergeant growled, "Sure, he said we need fighter pilots. Yeah, we do, but I don't decide that. Ya see this here," he said, holding up the form with Miller's name on it. "This here form is you, as far as I'm concerned. What happens after you leave that spot right there, I really don't *give* a good goddamn. You are the three thousandth warm body I've handled in the past three days, and I'll tell you like I told them, you'll get your chance to say what you want to do for the Army, but—" he broke off and stood up suddenly, "HEY! SHUT THE HELL UP YOU EIGHTBALLS! GODDAMMIT I LOST MY EARS IN THE LAST WAR, AND YOU MEATHEADS WANT TO DRIVE ME OUTTA MY SKULL! FOR THE LAST TIME, SHADDAP, GODDAMNIT!" The room stilled again, waiting. "Awright, Miller, take this form down the hall behind me here and have a seat on the bench. Somebody'll be along to take you for your physical. Next man, step up. HEY C'MON, MEATHEAD..."

Miller left the crowded anteroom and went down the hall lined with young men standing, sitting, talking, and waiting. When the time came, he stripped as instructed and was poked, peered at and prodded by a team of doctors and orderlies, only a few in uniform—in what might charitably be called a cursory physical exam—ensuring only that their subjects could leave the room under their own power. Throughout the ordeal, the young men's casual humorous boasts did little to break the tension of an otherwise dull, frightening experience.

For most of the ordeal, Miller found himself behind a man who looked much too old to be doing this. He was a wiry little guy who looked like someone who'd worked too hard in his lifetime to be risking his neck in the Army. The man was...well, older than the rest, but it was hard to say just how old. "Hey, Dad, what're you doin' here? You should be home in bed."

"Name's Milliken, not 'dad,' and what I'm doin' here is the same thing you assholes are doin'. Now mind your own damn business or I'll tap-dance on your gizzard," he finished with a snarl. After what seemed like hours, the production-line physical ordeal was over, and the men herded single-file into yet another hallway.

As the young patriots waited, they were treated to the continuous sounds of military records in the making: the urgent preparation of paperwork by a handful of harried Army clerks whose calm, well-ordered peacetime routine had been suddenly, unceremoniously, disrupted just days before. The sounds of scuffling, shuffling, clattering, file drawers and cursing wafting into the corridor were barely muffled by thin walls and open transoms. A telephone was *always* ringing somewhere, and someone was *always* shouting for *another* form that had suddenly been depleted. The steam radiators in the chair-lined hall seemed almost superfluous in the damp, dim hallway, overheated by the feverish activity of a handful of men who were suddenly expected to perform the work of hundreds.

A major in an immaculate uniform strode slowly down the corridor, scanning the faces of the young men looking up at him. The officer's uniform had rows of ribbons, some British. Atop the ribbons were a shiny set of pilot's wings. He stopped at Miller, searching for that unmistakable quality of hand, mind and body that made for a good pilot. "OK, next hero," yet another harried corporal shouted. "OK, sit down and gimmie your stuff," the corporal groggily intoned. Miller sat in the proffered seat. The corporal glanced at the forms Miller handed him and said, as if he really didn't care (and by then he really didn't), "All right, Miller, can you do anything special? You fly planes maybe, or jump over buildings in a single bound?" As if he had waited for this moment all his life, Miller carefully placed his pilot's license and his pilot's log on the desk in front of the corporal. The stunned corporal regarded the documents like they were French postcards.

"Well, sonny-boy," speaking with the condescending tone career NCOs can only use on new men, "I've seen some excellent forgeries in my time, but if these ain't real, I'm a monkey's uncle. If you're lyin' they'll know in a few days, ya know, and they'll make you wish you'd never been born. Federal offense, ya know, falsifying enlistment."

"I'm not lying," Miller said, a little indignant. "I can fly."

"Hey, Major Scott," the corporal shouted, "got one here for ya, I think."

The major came quickly, grabbing up the log books and lifting them into the light as if they were holy writ. "How many hours does this add up to?" Scott asked, scanning through the log at the long columns of closely scribbled entries.

"Well, sir," Miller said confidently, hopefully, "I've been flying crop dusters and air freight for six years now and the logs show about two thousand hours single engine, nearly two hundred fifty multi-engine, and ninety hours instrument, and instructor ratings in single, multi and..."

"What were you flying?" the major interrupted, shooting a quick glance at the earnest young man.

"JN-4s, mostly," Miller answered quickly, eager to please as a puppy learning tricks. "I've ten hours in Beech Staggerwings, and all my multi-engine time is in Ford Tri-motors. My dad has a flying service up in..."

"You give any thought to the Air Corps, son?" the officer asked.

"Uh, yessir, I thought I'd..."

"Shove him through, Corporal," Scott said, cutting him off. "When you're done with all the paperwork, bring everything up to my office up on the fourth floor. The sign says 'Officer Recruiting,' among other things. Let me make a few calls on the license and logbook, OK? I'll give them back when you come up."

"Well, I'll be damned," Scott muttered a few minutes later, looking at the signatures in the logbook. "Larry Miller's boy is joining the Air Corps. Sure as hell hope he makes better friends than his old man did."

***

The hotel room was small, intended for only one sleeper, but three young men were now sharing it: Miller, a young Lutheran minister named John Fallon, and Rusty Earnhardt, construction engineer. All three had taken the oath to their country just hours before, and were now "in it for the duration" as the going phrase suggested. The three were just returning from dinner (at government expense, of course), and would wait in this room for the word that their orders had arrived. No one had any notion how long that would be.

They started talking about themselves as the time and boredom wore on. Miller talked about his flying, Fallon about his wife and child on the way. And Ernhardt about building bridges and dams. "How'd you come to fly, John?" Ernhardt, a decidedly pleasant but flinty man of thirty, was by far the oldest of the three. He had been an officer in the Civilian Conservation Corps, and had been building highways in rural Wisconsin just a week before.

"My dad flew in the last war," Miller answered. "He learned to fly from Jimmy Doolittle himself. He brought the bug home and gave it to me as early as I can remember. Taught me how, and I've been doing it ever since. Why'd you build bridges?"

Earnhardt grinned. "I got the bug from my dad, too. It got so he couldn't do anything else. Gave me the bug, and I've been at it since I was fifteen." A sideways glance at Fallon, and the red-headed builder remarked, "How is it that priests 'get the bug?'"

Fallon grinned, "pretty much the same way, only Our Father is a little more persuasive." At this, the three laughed heartily, breaking up the slightly nervous tension of the unknown, the unforeseen. Out in the hall, other young officers-to-be were joking louder. Earnhardt went out into the hallway, leaving the door ajar. For Miller, it had been a long and grueling day of traveling, standing, sitting, filling out forms, answering the same questions a dozen times. For Fallon too, it had been wearing, but not quite so wearing as to shut off his thoughts completely. "You know," he said quietly, gazing out the door, sucking on his ever-present pipe, "patriotism is an astonishing thing. It's a lot like religion, actually. It starts with fervor and proselytization, then it changes, either to disillusion or to deeper faith. I wonder how many of us that signed up today will still feel the same way when it's all over."

Miller stared at him, then blurted, "what's in this for you, pastor? You won't get drafted; you got a wife and kid on the way. Why're you here?"

Fallon blinked his sloe eyes as if just awakening, then turned to Miller. "You," he said simply, and turned back to the door.

We serve because our neighbors are serving, Miller thought, and because this war is something bigger than ourselves.

December 1941

Smolensk, Russia

I saw a man this morning,
Who did not wish to die;
I ask, and cannot answer
If otherwise wish I

Patrick Shaw Stewart

Thielmann flew west into the setting sun, glad that the daily ordeal was over for him. But for the ground troops outside Moscow, the long Russian night was only just beginning—freezing in the bitter cold of the worst winter on record—with precious little winter gear at hand...and none forthcoming. For a week the half-wild Siberians and Uzbeks, battle-tough Red Guards, brutal horse-borne Cossacks, and hordes of T-34 tanks that German Intelligence in their wisdom had missed, thundered across the frozen steppe in a series of counterattacks that had sent the German Army reeling in retreat. And Hitler said "No retreat. Not even an inch."

He had never seen the Ivans in such numbers in the sky, with British Hurricanes and their own MiGs and those half-wooden flying tanks called Sturmoviks. Every day the *Luftwaffe* went out to wrestle with these Russians, strafing the roads, bombing bridges, artillery emplacements, tanks, anything that helped the enemy. Although they nearly always won individual fights, by the end of each day the Russians were still advancing, the Germans still retreating, the *Luftwaffe's* efforts apparently wasted against an ever-growing, ever more skillful Ivan that no longer flew the line of idiots that allowed many German pilots to gain huge victory counts.

The swarm found the airfield and put down on the icy strips, braking carefully to avoid skidding off into the trees or into parked planes. They taxied to their hardstands surrounded by sandbags as night was enfolding them. The pilots stomped their feet as they entered the shack. Shaking off the omnipresent Russian mud from flying boots. Gunther jumped happily around, to Thielmann's quiet delight. Thielmann waved noncommittally to the strangers that peopled his unit. Linz had been killed over Moscow by Russian flak a month before, and they had moved Kutz up to Group two months before. When he had the energy to think, he missed them.

Since the invasion of Russia began, Thielmann's squadron had been filling with strangers. He barely knew his fellow pilots; most of them were half-trained children, more boys than real flyers. Even so, little holes appeared in his soul when they were killed in the twisting hell overhead, little holes he did not want, but got anyway. His was the last sortie to return. That day he bagged another *Rata*—an obsolete Russian fighter—and a Hurricane. But if the British are managing to send the Ivans planes, he wondered, how can we stop them? Methodically, he peeled off his flying coat, his silk scarf, his muffler, and oversweater. The orderly took each in their turn, carefully folding them over his arm. "So, Bohr," the pilot muttered, "how did we do today?"

"*Sehr Gut*, Captain," the orderly said with some conviction. "Lieutenant Pangre brought down three MiGs today, raising his total to forty. Soon he may even catch up to you." Thielmann grinned slyly at the orderly, an old pensioner of no value any longer other than as someone's servant.

"You think so, eh Bohr? Perhaps you are right and I can go home. Perhaps..."

Thielmann was interrupted by a breathless corporal bursting in, shouting, "It's happened! It's happened! The *Führer* predicted it, and it has come to pass!"

"What's happened, Gerd? What?" Thielmann wondered what was so wonderful that the *Führer* had predicted. What of the hordes of Russian *untermenchen* gnawing like a white saw on a German tree, and in a hundred degrees of frost! Why didn't the *Führer* predict *that*?

"The Americans! We're at war with the Americans!" Thielmann sat heavily on a chair behind him. So, *that* has happened. Now the *Amis* will come, and we won't be able to stop them. Between the Americans and the Russians, Germany and all of Europe will be crushed. Someone muttered, "Nothing but syphilitic Jew gangsters, nothing to worry ourselves about..."

"Who make much of the ammunition the Ivans are shooting at us," Thielmann muttered. "A land of factories we cannot even attack."

"Dangerous talk, Thielmann," someone from a dark corner said. "Treasonous talk..."

"And what can they do to punish me, you rat? Send me to Russia? Piss off with your treasonous talk!" Thielmann didn't believe in much any longer, but he believed in the sheer, huge, wearing numbers of the Russians. Thielmann thought of his brother Ulrich somewhere in the Baltic. Will the Navy sortie now with big ships and stop the Americans from helping these English and Russians? Can you stop them? Can anyone?

Germany is doomed, Thielmann thought darkly, but I dare not say it to anyone.

January 1942

Seattle, Washington

For now sits expectation in the air
And hides a sword from hilts unto the point

William Shakespeare

The shrill scream of the plant whistle reached every corner of the Boeing plant. Clarence John "Jack" Farr stood up from the engine he was mounting on the Flying Fortress, wiping his greasy hands on his coveralls. Another day, another five engines mounted, he thought. Wearily, he sidled to the catwalk on the wing's leading edge, gratefully clambering down to the plant floor. A reserve Captain, too frail to do much for this war, was hurrying towards him. The captain was ostensibly the commanding officer of the factory-training unit Farr had been assigned to two days after Pearl Harbor. If he hadn't just been getting out of a leg cast, he'd have gone to the Philippines with his Flying Fort, and he wouldn't have to suffer this martinet. Ah shit, he thought. "Sergeant Farr," the captain called, breaking into a run. "Sergeant, I have good news for you," the captain wheezed, waving a sheaf of papers.

Farr stopped in mid-stride, thinking that the only good news was his transfer to the Philippines with his ship. But, no, not likely anybody is going into the Philippines since the Japs just walked into Manila. "What good news. Sir." Farr disliked the captain intensely, since he was essentially an administrator commanding highly skilled aircraft mechanics. Come to think of it, Farr thought, I never had much use for many officers.

"I got orders for you... flight engineer in a new B-17 squadron...

forming in Kansas... you're to report to Sheppard Field in a week for Flight Engineer School..." Farr ignored the rest of the captain's words; he'd heard enough. He snatched the orders from the captain's hands and headed for the nearest exit at a dead run.

January 1942

Pavlo, Germany

In the distance, the battle thunders grimly on,
Day and night, groaning and grumbling non-stop,
And to the dying men patiently waiting for their graves,
It sounds for all the world like the words of God

Wilhelm Klem

The telegram was short, simple, and cold. Wilhelm Steger, Reservist, was to report to the mobilization station for an assignment. He handed the telegram to his wife—his sturdy, long-suffering Anna, with whom he had shared his life for half a century. Once again, he was about to go off to war.

Soon his daughters all knew that their Papa was to go. So many men had already gone: his oldest daughter Berta's husband was in Greece, her sister Wilhelmina's husband was in Sicily, her sister Katarina's fiancée was in Russia, and their cousin Georg was on a cruiser in the Baltic. Many were dead or hurt: Stephanie's friend Frederic had been killed in Poland; neighbor Udo lost a leg and an eye in Africa. And now they were calling for the old men.

Steger was not as old as all that, and he was still a skilled carpenter—as skilled as he had been in the last war when he was with the old Air Force. He knew something of engines, he knew airframes, and he knew the men who flew them. He paid a visit to an old friend in nearby Erfurt. There he learned that the call-up notices had been sent prematurely, but that aircraft mechanics—especially the old-style craftsmen like Steger—were in short supply, and if he wanted to stay out of the infantry, he might want to think about it.

"They will come down to me some day, perhaps soon," he told Anna. "It will perhaps keep me out of the infantry."

"But, the farm," Anna protested. "I can't keep it going without... you." She knew other farms were being worked by wives whose husbands were away. With three daughters still at home and whoever she could hire, it would be difficult just to keep it going. But Steger's cabinet-making paid for the extra horses that the farm needed to make up for the lack of petrol. There simply wasn't enough money to keep going without it. "No aircraft mechanic is going to make what you do."

"We will *have* to make it do, Mama," Steger sighed, staring into a gloomy corner of the kitchen. "Mechanics make more than those poor infantrymen."

"Perhaps," she said finally, resigning herself to the idea. "And it's probably safer."

January 1942

Kelly Field, Texas

The outcome of a battle depends not upon numbers,
But upon the united hearts of those who fight

Kusunoki Masashige

I t was cold and dusty at the train station, and the bus ride to Kelly Field wasn't a whole lot better, just draftier. Miller, in his freshly modified officer's uniform with Lieutenant's bars still coated with enamel, took in the flat Texas landscape with as much detachment as he could muster. The orderly room was a linoleum-and-fresh-paint structure like most of the military buildings he'd seen so far, with a swinging door on creaking hinges that let him in. "Lieutenant Miller reporting," he said to the First Sergeant, who took his orders without comment. The NCO read the name and his eyes got wider. "Just a minute, sir," he said, and picked up the interphone. "Lieutenant Miller's here, sir...yessir, I *will*, sir." He motioned Miller through the only other door.

"Lieutenant Miller, sir, reporting under orders," he reported with a salute to the major seated behind the desk.

"Where the *hell* have you been, Miller?" the major growled. "We were expecting you a month ago." Stevens Patton, a prewar lieutenant, was one of the busiest administrators in the Air Corps. It was his job to turn civilian pilots into military ones.

"Fort Knox, sir," Miller answered, "OCS."

"Who sent you to OCS?"

"Uhn, recruiting station...sir?"

"Oh shit, not again," Patton answered. "There's an arrest order out for you: I don't know how you got in the gate." With Miller's puzzled expression, the major continued, "Right...*not* your problem. I'll deal with *that* later. Let's see your orders." He perused them for a moment or two. "You got the orders sending you to Knox?" Miller handed over the only thing he had with his name and "Fort Knox OCS," on it: a pay stub.

"OK," Patton sighed at length. "We'll get this straightened out, eventually. You're the third new pilot this has happened to. Just remember this, for further information that you'll never need: if you can already fly, the Army Air Corps has its own commissioning means, and we're it. You leave here and you're commissioned. But...Christ on a crutch...you're already commissioned. Nuts, what a cock-up! Billings!" Patton shouted. "Billings, get in here with your pad!" Patton looked back to Miller. "OK, I'll tell you what," he said, rising from his desk. "We'll get you checked as far as we can without releasing you...can't hardly take your commission back...and we'll see what goes from there. Find a bunk, get some flying gear from Stores, and be at the 1400 briefing: four this afternoon, in case you haven't figured it out yet."

"I believe the Major means either 1600 or..."

"Yes, of *course*, ya...*two* this afternoon; now get outta here. Billings! Get your ass in here!"

Three weeks of purgatory I didn't need, Miller thought. And I missed Christmas because of it.

***

Miller's first flight that afternoon was in a Stearman primary trainer. His first solo was an hour later, followed by a rubber stamp in his new log book. Aerobatics testing was harder, just because he'd never done it much, though he passed. Formation flying with twelve other flyers two days later was a real experience. After a week at Kelley, Miller and five other pilots transferred to Myers Field in Florida, where they were introduced to their Seversky P-35s. The P-35 was—or at least had been—a front-line fighter and was far more responsive and less forgiving than Miller was used to, and was the first closed-cockpit single-engine monoplane he'd ever flown.

There were classes, briefings, question-and-answer sessions, more briefings, more classes, more flying. Miller was exempt from most of the OCS-level drudgery. But the basic flying that he knew like the back of his hand differed from what the Army taught.

Finally, they preached the official doctrine of strategic aviation—that his father railed against—in no uncertain terms. "Dive bombing is suitable against ships and the like, and low-level bombing of tactical targets invites destruction from ground fire. However, we *know*, from experiments and trials that the heavy bomber," a lieutenant colonel severely intoned, "protected by numerous guns and close protection by fighters, will always arrive over its target, regardless of where that target might be, hit the target with an average of 70% hits, and return safely." They met this declaration with some silence, and some quiet whistling among the murmuring. "With the certainty of daily bombardment, it won't take long for the people to rise up against the harshest of tyrants and compel them to sue for peace. The fighters need only protect the bombers on their missions and the war will be over in a matter of months."

"Excuse me, sir, but did that work on *England?*" was a question that was not allowed.

January 1942

Mosalsk, Russia

Whites like ants, too many to kill

Red Cloud

T hielmann listened to the winter wind howling across the steppe in the predawn gloom, flapping the flames in the barrels that warmed the airplane engines. The crystalline snow that it carried stuck to every surface, turned to ice, and stung like nettles on the skin.

Through the hoar-frost coated window of his hut, he watched the tiny, indispensable, horse-drawn *panje* wagon as it creaked and bumped along the iron-hard frozen ground, stopping at each plane with fuel for the fire barrels. The native horse was quite immune to the intense cold, unlike the men, who cursed it with every breath, every clumsy movement, and every moment of their frigid and miserable lives.

In the cluster of tents, huts, trailers and temporary structures that passed for barracks and ready rooms at this forward airfield, the pilots and ground crews were stirring from their restless sleep, buried in blankets, clothes, straw, or whatever else they could find to keep warm. The first men up stoked the fires in the stoves and hearths, blowing life into the glowing embers of the night before. Soon the generators were running at full speed again (no one dared turning them off in this cold), and the bare electric bulbs added their brilliant glare to the dim glow of the gasoline lanterns and the heating fires. Once again, Thielmann's unit was showing signs of life.

They had moved forward from Smolensk a few days before to help the beleaguered ground forces hold against the waves of Russians pouring out from behind the Ugra River. As the men wakened and washed, dressed and stretched, they could hear the dull booming of heavy artillery and occasional crackling of small arms from the battlefront. The night before, they had listened as the Night Witches, the Russian bombers flown by women, attacked a nearby unit. Thielmann had thought that the partisan's communications network must be breaking down, or *his* unit would have been a target, as well.

At the south edge of the Smolensk-Moscow highway, the group's presence at Mosalsk may not have been very significant in itself. But to the Russian pilots flying the *Sturmoviks*, what Stalin called "bread and air," they were much too close. Thielmann knew it was only a matter of time before they had to pull out and roll back again, or had to defend the field itself.

The day before, Thielmann had flown four sorties against the bridges at Kaluga and Polotnyany, spraying the packed roads with cannon, dropping small bombs. He had seen the Stukas throw their big bombs at the bridges in the morning, only to return in the afternoon to see the spans repaired. So far, there had been little contact with the Red Air Force.

The group had been in action continuously for sixty-one days. Of their original thirty aircraft, they now could boast fifteen. The forward field at Mosalsk had twelve operational machines, for which the flyers had congratulated the blackbirds profusely. No longer was there much talk about the new Germany or discussions of ideology or the superiority of German arms. For these men, there was only the day-to-day grind of fighting the Russians, the weather, the supply system, and fighting more Russians. Spare parts were at a premium, and the group had not seen a replacement airplane since October; their last replacement pilot had arrived in November, and the Ivans killed him in his first week at the front.

Thielmann rubbed the sleep from his face, across the stubble of his beard. His dark hair had become unruly, his face a disaster of skin rashes, flea bites, and chilblains. He felt slightly dirty all the time, and he always had a feeling of exhaustion and impending doom. Now, at this makeshift field, he was denied even the simplest of comforts available at Smolensk. And he missed Gunther.

His current wingman stretched across the tiny aisle. Bruno Stumpp was a big blonde Bavarian—a woodcutter before they drafted him—with broad shoulders and a round face. He had been Thielmann's wingman for three months, which was remarkable; it was the longest he'd had a wingman since the fighting over France. Sharing a loaf of hard bread and some slightly rancid cheese, the pair ate silently, washing their breakfast down with the burned grain beverage that passed for coffee. "We tend our machines from horse-drawn carts, Thielmann," Stumpp groused, watching out the window. "How's that for irony?"

"Too tired, Stumpp," Thielmann sighed. "Irony is for the warm and the well-rested." There was little other conversation in the cluster of connected structures, as if talk would take too much energy from the already weary men.

Their commander, Major Gustav Goerlig, rapped his knuckles on a board for attention. Goerlig was a well-liked Saxon with a pained expression, but Thielmann thought him to be somewhat timid. Goerlig regarded the Nazis as beasts to be feared, rather than as vermin to be despised or fools to be ignored as most of his men did. "This morning, gentlemen, we are to escort a flight of HE-111s to the Ugra River Bridge at Yukhnov, where they are supposed to bomb it to bits. Takeoff is at nine o'clock. All available aircraft will be used. That is the only scheduled mission."

Thielmann and Stumpp shared glances, thinking blank, cold thoughts. Bombers flew high, and the higher one flew, the colder it got. Parachuting from an aircraft at three hundred meters is much safer in this weather than parachuting from a thousand.   They finished their breakfast without discussion. Outside, the blackbirds were starting the engines, and the armorers were out with their hammers, breaking the guns loose from the ice that froze their mechanisms solid. Horse-drawn fuel wagons drew up to each fighter, topping off the fuel tanks. They had refueled them the night before as a defense against condensation, but evaporation in the extreme cold sometimes took several liters of fuel, especially in high winds. The sound of this activity was barely discernible over the wind, even from a few meters away.

As the appointed hour grew near, the pilots donned their flying suits and all the warm clothing they could put under their parachute harnesses. As they heard the engines kick over, they started the long, cold journey across the frozen field to their planes. Miraculously, all twelve planes could fly. Takeoff at the appointed hour was routine, launching six at a time across a frozen waste of withered grain covered in snow and ice. The escorts met the fifteen Henkel twin-engine bombers in the appointed place and headed in the appropriate direction. Then a very inappropriate incident occurred: equals attacked them.

Screaming at them in attack out of the barely risen winter sun, a Russian Guards Fighter regiment of thirty Yak-3s attacked both the precious bombers and their weary escorts at once. In their first charge, they damaged three bombers and two fighters, with one bomber heading for the ground. The German fighters sprang at their antagonists warily, knowing that they were not only outnumbered but also, at this height, possibly outclassed. Thielmann and his wingman turned after the Russians, picking out a pair in the rear for an attack. The Yaks, rather than staying in their sights, looped away with a snap-roll that Thielmann's weary mind could barely follow. Twisting sharply after their quarry, Thielmann tried again, and was again confounded. Thielmann watched a Yak blast a bomber into bits with a single pass as two more German bombers headed for the earth, and two German fighters joined them.

Soon, the Germans were attacking the Yaks with renewed vigor and skill. Thielmann finally downed one and lined up another before metal and glass blasted forward through the Messerschmitt's cockpit and a gust of frozen air hit Thielmann's neck and back. As he maneuvered violently away from his attacker, Thielmann looked around him to see another swarm of Yaks and of *Würgers*, Focke-Wulf FW-190s, spinning and swarming in the adjacent sky. Tired, he hesitated on the scene for a moment too long, and was rewarded by more cannon damage. My God, he thought, they *have* improved their flying.

Smoke trailed behind him. His instrument panel was wrecked, and as he started a tight turn, his plane would not respond. A quick glance to his rear revealed that his tail surfaces were nearly gone, and the Ivan had punched his fuselage full of holes. Got to land or get out, he thought, but where is my wingman? Not here...Russian territory. Banking to the west, Thielmann pointed his nose for friendly troops. In a few short minutes, he knew he could go no further. He lowered his landing gear and set down on a frozen road, not knowing which side of the line he was on. To the east and north, the air battle raged on. He glanced at it bitterly as he clambered out of the cockpit. Checking the damage, he saw the radiator was punctured, the oil lines were shot away, and the tail frame was hopelessly weakened. Sadly, he lit a piece of paper from his pocket, tossed it onto a trail of his fuel on the road, and ran west. In a matter of seconds, he heard an explosion...and then everything went dark.

Three hours later Thielmann awoke on a hospital train, six pieces of metal buried in his back and both legs broken. He thought bitterly that his flying career was over.

Perhaps my flying days are over, Thielmann thought.

May 1942

Rucker Field, Kansas

Without a people's army, the people have nothing

Mao Zedong

Miller came in the orderly room as ordered, and was conducted to the presence of Major Boris V. Throck, commander of the newly formed 190th Heavy Bombardment Squadron. Miller saluted in the prescribed manner, Throck returning the salute in the distracted fashion of all technicians annoyed with the practice. "Have a seat, Miller," he said, shuffling through some papers on his desk. His black hair was clipped tight to his skull, and his crystalline blue eyes belied his eastern European origins. He looked like a craggy cliff with the battered face and frame of a prizefighter, but had a surprisingly gentle manner, a compact body, huge arms, and a deep, gravelly voice with a vague accent Miller couldn't quite place: not Scandinavian or central European, but kind of both. "Are you any relation to Larry Miller, a good flyer—outspoken if I remember right—who resigned from the Army in '25?" Throck asked, not looking up.

"Why, yessir," Miller answered, slightly surprised. "He's my dad."

"Hm," Throck muttered. Even the slightest sound from him seemed like rumbles of distant thunder. "I understand your mother passed."

"Yessir, in '27. Polio."

"Sorry; I didn't know her, but I knew your dad."

"Yes sir. The Major has the advantage of me; I don't recall you."

"I don't believe we ever met," Throck said, finally looking directly at Miller. "OK, the reasons you're in here. First, your records from Kelley and Meyers say you can't fly aerobatics worth a tinker's damn, though well enough not to get killed. Is there any truth to that?"

"I'm afraid so, sir. I just never got to learn it much."

"Well, with a Fortress you won't have to worry a whole helluva lot about aerobatics. But I got this annoying note here says you're to be arrested as AWOL. You know anything about that?"

"Well, yessir, I think so. The recruiting station sent me to OCS at Knox and I've been a month behind ever since. I suppose they haven't straightened it out yet."

"Yeah, you're right, *they* haven't." The peculiar emphasis on *they* was more than a little disquieting. "The FBI was just here wondering where you were. I gotta deal with them assholes on top of everything else I gotta do. On top of that," Throck continued, the muscles on his neck bulging, "there's another small matter of a broken German submarine. You know *anything* at all about *that*, 'Mister Adams?'"

Oh, shit, Miller thought, now what am I gonna get into? "Well, sir, I..."

"'Well, sir, I' *what?*" Throck spat, his voice rising with every syllable. "You committed a hostile act against a power engaged in a conflict in which the United States was not involved! That makes you an embarrassment to the United States and puts you firmly on the top of my *official* shit list. You know what that means?"

"Ah," Miller gulped, "I think so, sir..."

"No, you don't. You don't have any *Goddamn* idea. What you *want* to say is that the couple thousand Americans who enlisted in the armed forces of other states at war with Germany and Japan also risk their citizenship, despite the crying need for combat experience in the American armed forces. As they rejoin the ranks of the United States military now that hostilities have commenced, we can take advantage of their deep well of experience. Do I make myself *clear?*" By this time, Throck was practically screaming, but suddenly his voice dropped to practically a whisper. "What it *really* means is I've got you, but there ain't a lot I can *do* with you because I can't get you a security clearance until they straighten this mess out." He added hastily, "So, a Ford Trimotor with one wheel gone. How'd you land her?"

The transition startled Miller, but blurted out; "low power on both outboard engines, don't set the bad one down until the tail's down, followed by lots of sparks and a sudden jerk. You can't taxi it worth a damn afterward, though."

Throck made a face somewhere between a grimace and a grin. "That sounds reasonable; plausible even. Whatever possessed you to charge a submarine with an unarmed aircraft? Never mind; listen, if you had to, how would you land a B-17 with one wheel?" Miller glanced over Throck's shoulder at some hand-drawn certificate or other, announcing some casual, made-up honor for 'Boris the Bold,' and another for 'the Mad Russian.' Miller continued his gaze up the wall to stare briefly at the ceiling.

"Well, sir," Miller began, "the Fort's a bigger plane, a lot heavier. But, I suppose something similar, but the Fortress isn't as...nimble...on the ground as the Trimotor." Miller tried to think of something smart without going for the book answer, which Throck probably knew by heart. "Trouble isn't the weight, though; I think it's the sheer size. Momentum is greater; the sudden stop would tear the airplane apart..."

"Hm," Throck responded, not particularly impressed. "Think about it. All this bullshit makes you a headache. Are you getting the picture?"

"I think so, sir," Miller sighed. "Does that mean I'm grounded?"

"Fortunately, no, but you're not deployable. That means you can't be sent overseas any time soon, and I need good pilots to get 'Forts over the water starting in two months. Except for the fact that you can't tell a split-s from a shit brick, you're one of the best pilots I'm likely to get for some time. Do we understand each other?"

"Uhn, yes, sir."

"Good. Now, on to other things: I need a squadron check pilot. The check pilot certifies other pilots as fit to fly in type and weather, makes sure the pilot's logbooks are up to date, all that kind of horseshit. It's a pain in the ass, but the regulations require it. Your personal logbooks and licensing papers say you're instructor rated. You game?"

"Uhn, all right, sir. Just show me the regulations."

"See Clay Cole, the adjutant. As for the other things, I'll figure the mess out; with a hundred Americans just repatriated out of the RCAF last week, the State Department will probably drop the whole thing soon enough. Staff call tonight 1800, and you're staff now. We've got a flight this afternoon if the weather holds. You got any questions? I thought not. Now get outta here. I'm busy. My door's always open, but I ain't always behind it."

Miller stood and saluted his way out of Throck's office. In the orderly room outside, the clerks failed miserably at pretending they hadn't overheard a thing.

Captain Clay Cole was a rounded, genial-looking officer, perhaps a bit overweight, wearing old and tarnished wings and a glass eye. As adjutant and both ground and acting air exec (until Captain Ernie King arrived, expected any day) he was somewhat harried, but took the time to gently explain the role of check pilot to Miller: it was half the air exec's job.

"Let's see." Cole muttered when he was done explaining the regulations, "you've been a first lieutenant since...end of March...and we need captains...you're eligible...maybe I'll take it up with the Major."

"What makes me eligible?" Rank had not been important to him since he'd only been in the Army just shy of six months.

"You're in the Army Air Force, you can fly, you haven't had any actual charges sworn out on you, and you have a pulse: never mind about that AWOL thing; that's just an administrative punishment that I'll tear up as soon as I send it out to the AG. Squadron's authorized four flight captains and two ground. So far we have one flight and one ground. Need to look into that..."

***

Jack Farr held his hand across his brow to block the stunning glare of the mid-morning Kansas sun as he looked out over the ocean of airplanes parked on the apron. He had just arrived from gunnery school at Randolph Field and was eager to get started on his new ship. The tail number was scribbled on a piece of scrap paper in his pocket, but he'd already memorized it: xxx5251, fresh out of the Boeing factory.

As he walked towards the line of Fortresses sitting quietly in the sun, he felt the light breeze off the prairie, smelled the new-cut grass and fresh paint of a brand-new base, and the unmistakable scent of airplanes. He relished the overheated smell of paint and electrical instruments and hydraulic fluid mixed with the exhaust from aviation-fuel engines. He had lived and breathed Fortresses for six years. Making flying machines work was about the only thing he had in life. Still in his Class A's, Farr found his new ship in an hour, but was slightly distressed to see someone already working on one of his engines. "Hey Mac," he yelled up to the stranger, partly hidden inside the engine cowling.

"Hey yourself," a muffled voice called back. Farr looked around to see an old pickup truck with a toolbox in the back, parked under the ship's nose.

"What're you doing in my airplane" he called up, getting a bit hot.

"YOUR airplane!" the voice called back. "*Who* called it YOUR airplane?"

"The Army," Farr shouted back, getting annoyed at the invasion of his territory.

"Well, they told me the same thing," said the voice, which now had a face over the cowling, "when they made me the airplane commander. Miller's my name. Who're you?"

Airplane commander? A goddamn wet-behind-the-ears pilot working on my ship? Hell no, this ain't gonna work. "Jack Farr," the flight engineer called back, still angry, but now unsure what to do about it. He'd been in the Army long enough to know that NCOs did *not* question the actions of officers, regardless of how stupid they were—either the actions *or* the officers—until he had something to question *with*. "Hey, listen, uh, sir. Is there anything I can do for you?"

"Yeah, there is," the voice called back, now back under the cowling. "Your papers say you were a mechanic on B-17s. Grab a 3/8 inch open end and get up here. This coupling doesn't want to seat right. Tools're in the back of the truck." My papers, Farr wondered. What in the hell does this guy think he is? I only just blew into base. Puzzled, Farr rummaged briefly through the toolbox in the back of the truck, found two appropriate wrenches and clambered up the ladder. "Better strip your jacket off," the voice said. "This damn thing may break loose." Farr took off his jacket and carefully stepped up to the engine.

Miller had his hands around a hydraulic feed line, jockeying a bulkhead coupling into position on the engine mount, socket in one hand. Another coupling rested in a pile of oily rags next to him. He had his jacket off and his sleeves rolled up, but he was still fairly covered with oil.

"Damn thing was leaking, so I replaced it, but the line was too short in the first place," he said, gesturing to the heavy brass coupling. "Line stress must've done it in. Now, if you can grab the flats with your wrench, I may be able to get part of the clamp on the longer end of the line. That should do until we can replace the whole damn thing." More than a little impressed, Farr did as he was asked, and the pilot started the clamping bolt around the line, tightening it only part-way with his socket wrench. "There," Miller said with finality, "that won't put too much more strain on it. See if you can get about six feet of hydraulic line out of those supply types, can ya? I don't like these damn couplings...too much heat and pressure. I'd prefer a monolithic line, just one piece from the tank all the way back up."

"Uh, yeah, I mean, yessir," Farr muttered. "But, um, they're easier to build like this. I was...How'd you find the leak," Farr wondered, looking at the angled jaw and honest face of his hulking big pilot.

"Oh," Miller said distantly. "I saw it from the ground. Wet panel on the engine cowling always makes me nervous. You weren't around yet, and the crew chief hasn't reported yet, either."

"Oh," Farr said, not sure what else to say. "Sir, how'd you see my papers when I just now got to the base?"

"Well," Miller said with a boyish grin, "when they gave me this ship, they gave me a list of available flight engineers, and you were among them. I wanted somebody with at least as much mechanic experience as I've got because I didn't want to have to do it all myself. They said I could have you."

Farr was a bit overwhelmed that he, personally, had been hand-picked for this ship. "Just how much experience do you have, sir?" Miller gave him an encapsulated version of his father's business and his flying experience. No wet behind this guy's ears, Farr thought. This guy might be all right...even for an officer.

"Oh, one more thing," Miller said as they climbed down. "I just heard that your last airplane arrived in Australia about a month ago. All hands are safe and sound. More than we can say about the poor airplane, though. Hanger queen, I hear."

"Why thank you, sir," Farr said, suddenly jubilant, "I think a lot of those guys. And she was a good ship." As they wiped their hands clean, they talked about the airplane. Miller had been waiting for three days for his crew to arrive and was tiring of it. "Did any of the other crew arrive yet?" Farr asked.

"Bombardier a couple days back; name's Kearns. He's a flight school washout, just like the rest of them. Good man, though. Got a pool of gunners; I'll let you pick them out. I wasn't expecting you for another week."

"Well, I had two week's delay en route authorized, but I didn't have anywhere to go, so I just came here."

"No family?"

"No sir. Got an uncle's a rancher in Montana somewhere, but I haven't seen him in twenty years."

"Hey, do us both a favor," Miller said with a grin. "If nobody's around, just call me John. All this 'sir' business makes think my dad's around somewhere."

"OK, uh, John."

"You ever fly a 'Fort?" Miller asked.

"Just the right seat," Farr answered, somewhat taken aback. Enlisted pilots? Not in my lifetime.

"OK. First chance we get, I'll let you land this one; you need to get the feel of it because it may come in handy one day. I want everybody forward of the bomb bay to do it at least once. Squadron commander's name's Throck..."

"Boris the Bastard Throck? No shit? Aw, Christ, I'm doomed."

Miller hadn't heard that one yet....and why 'doomed?' "Um, yeah, but I only heard about the 'Mad Russian' and some 'Boris the Bold' moniker. Why? Is he bad news or something? I only met him a few days ago."

Farr wondered briefly if he'd overstepped. "Last I heard, he was flying for the Finns and got shot down somewhere in the middle of... aw, it don't matter; probably bullshit, anyway. I hear he flew fighters against the Reds in Poland, then China, Spain, Ethiopia, even South America. Where there's shooting going on, there's Throck flying whatever he can get off the ground, or so the story goes. I hear tell he's just as good a flyer as Jimmy Doolittle. Dangerous, though, from what I understand. 'Only death will stop me,' he told some guy who told him not to fly some suicide mission in...hell, I dunno where. Guess it wasn't so suicidal after all. Still," Farr went on, thinking he'd talked himself into a hole, "I'm not sure I'd want to be commanded by someone who's braver than everyone else."

"Huh," Miller grunted, not sure what to think. It was clear that Farr had been in the Air Corps for a very long time, or he had a vivid imagination, or both. Throck was a disciplinarian, certainly, and he had a short temper, but didn't seem tyrannical...yet. He had different ideas about billeting the crews, about flying practice and the like. Miller was so new at all of this, he had no way to tell if it was wrong—or right. That would have to come later.

"Uh, John," Farr interrupted, "I really ought to sign in, I guess." Noticing that Miller's collar held Captain's bars and his jacket Lieutenant's, he felt emboldened to ask: "Um, sir? Shall I refer to you as a lieutenant or a captain?"

"Ah, captain, since yesterday morning. I haven't had time to change everything over yet, and the PX doesn't *have* any more," Miller sputtered, glad for a change of subject. "You get settled in, find your billet, and we'll see about getting some gunners. We're supposed to have a co-pilot this afternoon..."

***

The afternoon was slightly gray, but the same balmy breeze wafted across the prairie. The takeoff of the four Fortresses was routine, with Farr watching his pilot carefully over his shoulder. They flew around for a few hours in formation, practicing the tedious throttling up and back, jockeying around, maintaining a position relative to three other moving aircraft trying to do the same thing. As exercises in futility went, this was pretty close to the ultimate, Miller thought darkly.

"Throck to Group," the squadron commander called over the radio, "let's try this again tomorrow. Get the feel of your ships for a while and let's talk about it tonight. Throck out."

Miller and the other pilots banked off for some maneuvering room, relieved not to have to fight a seemingly losing battle before becoming completely familiar with their planes. As Miller flew north over the endless nascent fields of wheat, corn, rye, alfalfa, and soybeans that covered the landscape, he was reminded of his other profession. With a few gentle banks, some altitude changes, and other routine maneuvers, Miller put his new ship through quite a workout over the budding crops.

Dour-faced Elias Kearns of Massapitic, Georgia, Bombardier, certified competent to act as temporary co-pilot on Miller's ship (they washed him out of flight school for a recurring middle-ear problem), flew in the right seat. The promised co-pilot had not yet reported. Ernie Block, on left waist, was a rusty-haired ranch hand from Elko, Nevada, who did fairly well in gunnery school. Beanpole-thin Chuck Payne on the right waist didn't do as well, but was a boat-builder in his native New Hampshire, and Farr thought that might come in handy someday.

Throughout the flight, Farr moved through the ship, looking over the controls, the airframe, the connecting hoses, wiring, instruments, and a plethora of other details, noting every setting and indication as he went through.

The two enlisted men in the waists were getting used to their new ship, as well. They had trained on Digbys—DB-18s—which differed greatly from this ship. They watched the countryside float by, and under Farr's direction learned what they should watch for during flight, maneuver, climb, descent, and anything else the pilot should find it necessary to do.

After about three hours of acceptable flying weather, the sky darkened to the west. Not liking the look of it, but not tired of flying

—as if that was even *possible*—Miller decided to take his ship home. Following the bombardier's compass track (which he did well, Miller thought), he set his heading for the field. On the way in, he set up the C1 autopilot, engaged it, and sat back to watch it work. A most extraordinary thing, he had decided when he first tried it. Flying in an airplane while it flies itself. Then suddenly, the airplane started to bank to the right, all on its own. Miller disengaged the autopilot, righted the airplane, and checked the instruments. "Flight engineer to pilot. What was that?"

"Unknown; autopilot seemed to want to turn right. Trying it again." Suddenly the airplane did a diving bank to the right, jerking the yoke out of Miller's hands. Recovering the controls, Miller again slapped the C1 off...but it didn't turn off.

"Pilot to flight engineer; aircraft is *not* under control. *Find* a way to disengage autopilot, and NOW!" Miller pulled the yoke with all his strength while throttling back the engines. Miller heard a *crash* behind him and suddenly the yoke responded. With almost all power gone, the bomber continued to fall until Miller managed to regain control, leveling off at nearly tree-top level and skimming over the spring corn just like a crop duster. "Pilot to crew: clear your drawers. We're under control."

"Uh, Waist to pilot: What happened?"

"Flight engineer to waist: we won't know until we get on the ground. Looked like an electrical problem to me." Miller looked over to his bombardier, who seemed unfazed by the experience. "You all right, Kearns," he shouted over the din of the engines. He bobbed his head up and down.

"Copilot to pilot: four engines on-stream, sufficient power and fuel to reach home field. We should be in sight of the field in about twenty-five minutes. I have informed the field of emergency." "I'm OK," he shouted off the intercom. "You did real good, sir."

The rest of the flight was uneventful.

Dutifully, Miller filed a report on the "incident."

May 1942

Cologne, Germany

For a single general's reputation
Is made out of ten thousand corpses

Ts'au Sung

S itting on a stone bench outside the bunker, Thielmann smoked the last bit of his cigarette, watching the gathering darkness in the east over the city, idly scratching Gunther's ears. Pangre rescued Gunther from Smolensk after the Russians overran the Mosalsk pocket the day after Thielmann was shot down, delivering the little dog on his way to the Channel front. Thielmann had just heard that Pangre was shot down over the North Sea. I shall miss him, Thielmann thought quietly, even if he was an insufferable ass. Even insufferable asses can be good flyers, and someone should miss them.

It was an overcast evening, damp and cold in the spring air. The city of 800,000, settling down for another night, winked and blinked in the distance. They will come tonight, he thought. The clouds should clear tonight about midnight, and unless they are fools, they will come tonight—and the Tommies are no fools.

It had been two weeks since they removed the casts from his legs, but still the stiffness remained. The metal shards in his back from his exploded airplane were long gone, but the memory haunted him still. Thielmann had volunteered to work at the *Himmelbett* station not because he knew anything about night intercepts (he didn't), but because life at the convalescent hospital was endlessly boring. Even if he couldn't fly just yet (that would be another few months, he was told), he could at least feel as if he were doing something.

And the something he was doing was spending hours on the telephone, vectoring the night fighters in on the British bombers as they approached Germany. They usually came in groups of up to two hundred in long, isolated lines. The long-range *Freya* radar would find the incoming streams, pass the information to the more-accurate, shorter range *Würzburg* sets, which would pass the information to the searchlights while Thielmann relayed the course, position and speed to the night fighter fields and the orbiting *Himmelbett* radar-spotting controllers...then the game would begin. Only it wasn't really a game. Until now, the British had been ineffective in their bombing of German cities and factories. Once in a while they got lucky and hit something important, but usually they were not a lot of trouble. But the Tommies horribly burned Rostock, and the Germans hoped they remained ignorant of the damage they could really do if they tried.

Much to his private delight, Thielmann's old instructor, Kaltz, was assigned to the same sector station. It felt awkward at first, but gradually Thielmann got accustomed to the idea that someone he had known in his halcyon days before the war was still alive. Over the months, he had become nearly numb to the bitter agonies he still felt when he heard of—or witnessed—someone he knew being killed.

Thielmann stubbed out his cigarette and stiffly descended the steps into the bunker, Gunther loping lazily behind. Inside, the orderlies and duty clerks were preparing for the evening, laying out pencils, forms, paper, checking telephones and radios. The senior officer, a jocular Colonel named Gatt, was just coming into the operations room. "*Guten abend*, Captain Thielmann," Gatt said, as light-hearted as ever.

"*Guten abend*, Colonel," Thielmann responded. Thielmann liked the older man, even though he was a Flak officer and not a flyer. He had an unusually cool head in tense situations and had excellent instincts about the incoming plots. He was usually right. "Nasty night tonight, but supposed to clear," Thielmann reported.

"Yes, but not until late," Kaltz interrupted. "Still, they can take off in the wet and hit in the bright."

"Yes. The British will come tonight. Perfect for them," Gatt finished. With that, the three officers began their early duties, signed the required forms, briefed their enlisted men and the junior officers in the duties they already knew, and settled down for the evening. After Gatt retired for the first shift around eight in the evening, Thielmann and Kaltz settled down to a luxury: real coffee, one cup for the night. "So, *Herr* Kaltz, what brings you down into the trenches, eh?"

"Oh, several things," Kaltz smiled ruefully. "I got into a disagreement with the *OKL* staff, and my friends thought I should go out to the field units, get the feel of the real *Luftwaffe*."

"You must have very highly placed friends."

"I shot an SE-5 off Herr Goering's tail in 1918, and an American SPAD off Milch's in the same year. The *Luftwaffe* may be very young, but it has a long memory."

"So, what have you been finding out?"

"I've been finding out that we need to do something different from what we have been doing. I have concluded that in our current structure, the best we can hope to do is hold our current status. But as our enemies grow stronger, we will inevitably grow weaker because of pilot attrition. We have no time to replace the experienced pilots we keep losing. We need to develop a core of teachers and real tacticians that can develop new techniques, especially as the Americans arrive."

"An operational test unit?"

"Yes, one that isn't broken up every three months, made up of aces that are not tied to a single doctrine."

"A testing unit of aces," Thielmann said distantly. "What an honor it would be to be a teacher in such a unit." Kaltz watched his young friend carefully.

***

At about eleven, reports of low-level air attacks on the forward fighter fields in Holland and France started filtering in. Sometimes such attacks were political,   more for British propaganda than anything else, for they infrequently did any damage. But this time there was a disturbing pattern: even though no damage had been done to radars or aircraft, the fighter strips had been badly cratered. Thielmann noted his suspicions in the duty log book and sat back to contemplate. *If I'm right, it's right in line with Cologne.* Thielmann walked up to the situation map as the plotters marked the strikes. "Have we any aerial reconnaissance tonight," he asked Pluskut, a sad-looking Prussian *Stabswebel* with a wooden leg who handled non-fighter coordination.

"*Nein, Mein Herr,*" he said. "Conditions are not favorable over England for reconnaissance tonight." Thielmann grunted assent, turning back to the situation map. XII *Fliegerkorps* headquarters at Zeist, which controlled all the night fighters, had been hit, too. Coincidence, or...

Around midnight, all three officers agreed they should alert Cologne. Twin-engine bombers had penetrated the Kammhuber Line of patrolling night interceptors and appeared to be headed towards Cologne. Kaltz cranked the special line for the *Gaulieter* of Cologne. "This is Kaltz. The British may be coming. Yes, Cologne is the probable target."

As the city locked down to receive yet another raid, the warning sirens wailed their mournful, urgent tune at 12:13 AM. Half an hour later, the flak batteries in and around the city opened fire on the first British pathfinders, flying too low for radar detection. The fire brigades began fighting the fires started by the pathfinder's incendiaries. The great city itself was dark, and as the final warning sirens were fading in the distance, Cologne prepared to receive its 105th raid of the war.

"Captain," one of the radar operators called, "I think I'm having some difficulty here." Thielmann went to the operator's control set for the long- range *Freya* and peered over the operator's shoulder. In the green haze of the sweeping display, he could see far too many contacts coming from too many directions.

"Have you checked the set?" Thielmann asked, who even with his little experience could tell that there was something very wrong with the display.

"Yes, I have. It doesn't make sense."

"Keep watching," Thielmann said, rushing to the telephone. "Kordt, raise the technical section and get someone down here to look at our oscillator." Some minutes later, the three officers were watching the oscillator with amazement. "And you say there is nothing wrong with the apparatus," Gatt asked the operator and the technician, who had just finished his checks. Assured in the most stringent terms that there was absolutely nothing wrong, they watched in growing horror as three massive patterns of blips and bumps made their way across the tiny display.

"*Here,*" Gatt whispered. "They are coming *here...hundreds* of them... more than *ever* before...perhaps a *thousand...now.*"

"Baumer," Thielmann called out, echoing dully in the barren room, "Call the fighter fields at Venlo, Deelen and Twente. Tell them we may be under heavy attack. It looks worse than Rostock. TELL THEM!!" he shouted, hoping the hellish recollection of the rare British success would jolt them into attention.

The telephones jangled and buzzed in the clammy concrete room. Junior officers and men were posting the results. Intercepts, sightings, soundings, all confirmed what they had already suspected—a huge concentration of bombers was headed their way...now.

There was no time to think, reflect, or philosophize while the sounds of thousands of laden engines droned overhead and the dull explosions of bombs reverberated into the bunker. An occasional off-target bomb shook dust from the concrete roof. Gatt contacted the flak units in Cologne, Thielmann called every night interceptor in the area, and when he exhausted those, he called the day fighters. Kaltz coordinated the civil defense teams in Ehrenfeld, Lindenthal, Zollstock, Nippe, Deutz, and the Old Town itself. For an hour, the telephones rang and chattered as men (and the occasional woman) hustled about the cavernous bunker. Thielmann expected the activity to slacken at any moment...

An hour and a half after the attack had begun, night fighter pilots returning to their fields to rearm and refuel were convinced that British bombers were still approaching Cologne. Already over five hundred had been estimated over the city, and the oscillator still showed streams of blips headed their way. A guard stumbled drunkenly into the bunker, pale and wan. Thielmann and Kaltz bolted outside.

Mouths agape at the glowing spectacle to their east, they could feel the heat of the monstrous fire engulfing Cologne some three kilometers distant. The roaring blaze, the howling draft feeding the maelstrom, the explosions and incendiary blooming of bombs still tumbling out of the bomb bays of British bombers was clearly audible. The searchlights and flak no longer probed the darkness overhead. One by one, the reporting centers stopped sending. The sight reminded Thielmann—dimly—of a torchlight parade in Nuremburg. Is this what that parade had come to?

And still the bombers came...

***

It was nearly noon the next day when Thielmann and Kaltz drove into Cologne to find the *Gauleiter*. The smoke and dust permeated everything, the devastation and the sheer horror of that one night unavoidable. Hollow shells of what had once been buildings, twisted wrecks of vehicles, tram rails bent in the heat, cobblestones shattered, water flowing in gutters from ruptured mains, power lines sparking in gutted houses. And the people—hollow-eyed and weary, dirty and thirsty—queued up by the few dispensary trucks for the Red

Cross workers to give them their pitiful cupful of water. Thielmann and Kaltz looked around them in silence as they rode through the blackened horror that had once been a magnificent city.

Driving down a twisted alleyway half-filled with rubble that had been a wide boulevard, they came to the buttressed walls of a cathedral, where Kaltz told the driver to stop. An old priest sat on the steps outside, holding his head. "The ceiling collapsed," the priest babbled, "and everyone inside was crushed or burned and I have been left behind why have I been left behind why has God chosen me why not some other more worthy soul why me oh merciful Jesus why me..." Kaltz gazed up at the magnificent stone edifice, a hollow shell, with tears welling in his eyes as the priest babbled on.

"Why," Kaltz finally managed, then went back into the car. "My wife and I were married there," he wept as they drove off. "My oldest son was christened and baptized there. And now, this: why, Thielmann? Why?"

The English are responding in kind to our bombing of their cities, Thielmann thought. Watching the old priest, he could not separate his feelings from the shattered landscape and incinerated rubble.

August 1942

Rucker Field, Kansas

The only thing harder than getting
A new idea into the military mind
Is to get an old one out

Basil Liddell Hart

T he three months of working-up training had moved along as well as could be expected. Miller's crew came together from several varied backgrounds, but tried to work together despite the gnawing assurance that, one day, they would be on the other side of one ocean or another, fighting to stay alive.

Mitch Berg from Stowe, Vermont, was assigned as Miller's copilot. Phil Egan, the tail gunner from Nashua, New Hampshire, was pulled out of the gunner pool the same day. At five foot four, Ray Otto from Long Island was the natural choice for belly gun position, assigned just a few days before Oscar Feynman from Bad Axe, Michigan came in from the radio school at Scott Field, Illinois. Bob Smith from Wheeling West Virginia, the navigator, was the last to be assigned.

But the flying crew wasn't all Miller had to work with. Just after Farr arrived at Rucker, a lanky Alabamian with the unlikely name of Casmir Philukuzki ("Just call me 'Casey,' suh," he drawled when he met Miller) was assigned to Miller's ship as the crew chief. "Now just how in the hell," Farr wanted to know, "does a southerner like you get the name of Casmir?"

"Wall, hell, Jack," Casey drawled, "that was easy. I was born in Crackau, Poland in nineteen and eleven. When the Krauts threw us out in '17, my pappy brought us ovah heah to where my great-uncle

Stanislaus had a thrivin' business in Mobile, and the rest is history. Just nevah saw fit to change the name, is all."

Casey's assistant crew chief was a small boy from Iowa named Willie Williams, straight out of the school at Keesler Field, Mississippi, whereas Casey had been in the Army Air Corps since 1927. Though big for his age, Williams *had* to have lied to get in. Because he had an aptitude for all things mechanical, the Air Corps looked the other way. Farr, Casey and Williams kept Miller's ship flying longer and better than damn near every other ship in the 190th.

They were joined by three other squadrons—the 191st, 192nd, and, with inscrutable Army logic, the 610th—to form the 299th Bombardment Group (Heavy) by the end of July. But by August, the Group still didn't have a real commander, and the situation was becoming dire. Because Throck had a decade's seniority on the most senior officer present, he was promoted to full colonel (after being a lieutenant colonel for about a week) and was made acting Group commander, at least until they got to wherever it was they were going. From what source Throck's first commission originated, no one quite knew, and no one was sure how many "leave-of-absences" he'd taken from the Air Corps. As for their final destination, the betting pool, run by a New England rich-kid bombardier named Jackson, had England three to two.

As the crews learned their trades, the ships sprouted names. The pilot usually selected the names, but some skippers gave the crews a chance to put their two cents in. Naming an airplane in 1942 was a ritual as individual as the crews that flew them. Many were symbolic of the war itself: *Hitler's Headache, Tokio or Bust,* and *Hun Hunter.* They named some after home towns: *Detroit Demolition, Spirit of Lexington,* and *Pride of Jersey.* Some after women: *Maryanne, Daisy Mae, Karen.* And there were, of course, other themes; *Midnight Lace, Shady Sadie.* The ship belonging to the 190th's squadron commander, Major Ernie King, was *The Throne Room.* They promoted King from captain on the same day they promoted Throck to colonel. Throck's ship was *The Mad Russian.*

Farr convened a crew meeting after a three-hour cross-country navigation practice mission to determine a name for Miller's airplane. A clandestine meeting among the eight NCOs an hour before the real meeting—the one with the officers—had already decided what that name was to be. When nominations were asked for, there was only one. "*Crop Duster,*" Farr declared. No one had any other suggestions.

They passed the hat and an artistic radio mechanic was paid a double sawbuck to paint the name in big, bright orange and yellow script letters on the green aluminum nose, joined by a *busty* lass in a *short* skirt carrying a dust rag. Miller never said what he felt about the name, and nobody ever asked.

***

Another typical dog day in the middle of America, the blistering sun beating down on the crops and on everything else. In the rarefied air of gunnery practice, the day was proving to be another hectic waste. *That damn sleeve is the hardest thing for most of them to hit,* Miller wrote in his journal. *Less than 20% came even close.* He decided he had to have a little talk with his gunners, but first he had to get it through his flight engineer/senior NCO's head that this target practice was the most important thing they were doing right now.

On one particularly balmy evening in a borrowed classroom, Miller and Farr got into a heavy discussion about the self-protecting bomber. It wasn't that Farr lacked appreciation for what Miller wanted to say; it was just that his commander's approach was so new to him it wasn't making much sense. In gunnery school, he'd been taught on slow-moving sleeves and the occasional fast mover across the front. But his pilot was presenting an original picture of what he expected the enemy to do.

Drawing diagrams on a chalkboard to simplify the problem, Miller broke it down as well as he could understand it. "Look," Miller said, "the Japs and Krauts aren't stupid. It'll take them about a week to figure out that the most vulnerable points on a Fortress are on the long axes—dead ahead and from the rear. Of the two, dead ahead is probably the best choice. He's only got the top guns to worry about, and your field of vision is pretty restricted. So if he comes in just below the flight deck, nobody's gonna be able to shoot at him."

"But, John, from head-on, he's gonna have to get a real lucky shot into the flight deck or the engines to do any good. From the rear he's got lots of wing surface to try for, not to mention the engines. And when he does that, he's a sitting duck."

"Not even close, Jack," Miller said ruefully. "Improbable things happen all the time. We're at less than 20 percent hits right now, and that's on a towed sleeve that's not maneuvering, and *not* shooting back. If they use the slow attack from the rear much, he'll get cut to pieces—

85

the rest of the formation will shoot at him too. Look," he said, drawing numbers on the board, "the Fortress cruises at about 170, and the Messerschmitt hits about 350 at top speed full boost unless he wants to risk blowing his engine by flying faster. But he won't fly that fast if he wants to hit something, so let's say he's at about three hundred. Closing speed from the rear is then about 130, and flying through our formation gunners he's not even going to get close, normally. So what's our clever bad guy do? He hits us from head-on, where he can fly at a safe 300 or below and close at a rate approaching the speed of sound at 25,000 feet, and we can't even get a *bead* on him."

Farr stared hard at the board for a moment, running it over in his mind. If this guy's right, Farr the military aviation engineering pioneer thought, everything we said about the self-protecting bomber is so much bullshit. If this guy's right, we'll be lucky to survive more than a few attacks. Holy Christ. But, the NCO in him thought, he is in command, even if he's a raving lunatic. "OK," he said thoughtfully, "I'll try to sell it, but I don't..."

"You've gotta do better than that," Miller snapped unexpectedly. "You've GOT to convince them that their gunnery's crucial. Damnit, Farr!" Farr started at Miller's unexpected vehemence, "it may be my ship, but they're sure as HELL your gunners. You've GOT to get it through to them , or we're all dead ducks."

Farr the NCO was in charge again. "Yessir, I'll get it through. But perhaps if the Captain would like to..."

"Oh, can the military shit, Jack," Miller said. "This is important. What do you want me to do?"

"Explain it to them the way you explained it to me." Miller bobbed his head in agreement, too weary to respond otherwise.

***

The next night, the entire crew was in the same classroom, but in a peculiar seating arrangement. Egan faced the back wall; a row closer to the front, Block and Payne sat with their backs to each other, facing the left/right walls. Closer to the front, Otto faced the back in his belly gun position, as did Feynman, a row ahead of him in his radio gun position. Farr's top turret position sat two rows ahead. Miller and Berg sat next to each other just ahead of Farr. Smith sat sideways, looking out to the right side of the room in the navigator's seat, and Kearns sat in front of the room in the bombardier's seat.

"OK, now," Miller said, "Let's think about this for a while. Notice that from head-on, only Farr can really shoot at someone. Now, how long do you think it'll take the enemy to figure that out?"

"Oh, maybe a week; two tops," Berg remarked casually.

"OK. So, let's admit that the first B-17 missions will have been at least a month before we get into the European theater, providing we get orders tomorrow. And we've been flying B-17s against the Japs since before the fires were out at Hickam Field."

"OK," Feynman said slowly. "So..."

"So both the Krauts and the Japs already know where our weakest point is, and we haven't even got *into* it yet." Miller paused to let this sink in, because they still looked puzzled. "They are already devising ways to take advantage of that weakness. They are working out tactics to attack us from head-on, from twelve o'clock high. I'm mortally certain of it."

"You mean like playing chicken," Smith drawled.

"Yeah, just like that," Miller responded. "Only this guy's shooting at us, and Farr can't go below, what five degrees above horizontal?"

"Not and still hit anything," Farr replied.

"Makes me mighty nervous," Kearns quipped, "out here in front of God and everybody and nothing to shoot back with..." Nervous laughter punctuated the remark.

"Yeah, well, maybe it should. But think about it. You waist gunners, you can't swing any more than, what, maybe close to the wingtips?"

"Yeah, a little short, really," Block answered. "Given the recoil of the Ma Deuces, even then, we're taking a chance."

"So the waist guns are..." Payne began.

"A waste of weight," Farr continued. "The belly gun's our only other defense. How high can your guns get, Otto?"

"No more'n maybe fifteen degrees below level. Above that, the guns'll fire, but I can't see the sights right."

"There, ya see? Now, how long do you think it'll take for the Krauts and Japs to figure that one out?"

"What're you trying to say, sir?" Egan asked, still facing the back wall.

"That if you get a shot at something coming across, it may be the last one you get. They ain't gonna hang out there like target sleeves. They'll be coming at us head-on at a speed equal to theirs *plus* ours— near *500 knots*...and *maybe* from the tail. You guys have got to improve those gunnery scores or the bombardier's gonna catch it. And if that happens, the Government ain't gonna be too happy losing one of their expensive bombardiers."

"Neither's the bombardier," Kearns muttered.

Outside the classroom, Throck listened intently , thinking this kid was truly a chip off the old block, another genius perfect for this business. His dad, Throck's old friend, punched holes in this "self-defending bomber" pipe dream and got bounced for his efforts. Now that the Brits half-proved him right, their only hope for survival was formation flying. If that failed, there'd be a string of coffins all the way back here with American flags on them.

There was only one way to sell the idea of the long-range, heavy bomber to Congress in a tight budget period—by not considering the fact that the enemy would adopt their tactics to meet the threat. Building a force of projection based on wishful and short-sighted thinking is not the best way to go to war.

But in 1941, this was what the United States had.

August 1942
Salzburg, Austria

It is as a soldier you make love,
And as a lover, you make war

Marie de Saint-Exupery

The late summer weather in the Alps was most salubrious for German pilots recovering from serious injuries. It seemed like years since Russia and Thielmann's last combat assignment. The scars on his back from the metal shards that had been his plane were still there and bothered him when the weather changed. His legs were still stiff, his nerves were still raw, and his stomach troubled him from the rotten food in Russia, but he was recovering.

Since June, Thielmann had spent most of his mornings teaching basic fighter tactics and maneuvering to frightened, swaggering boys barely out of school. Other mornings, it was basic flying, trying desperately to fight off what Goering himself called the Plague: the rash of flying accidents, with terribly inexperienced pilots in worn-out airplanes colliding with each other in bad weather, and getting lost when flying blind, and lacking the skills to nurse crippled machines to earth. To increase their confidence, Thielmann organized a boxing club, encouraging his young charges to learn timing and, above all, anticipating what their opponents might do.

But some of the news from the battlefront was encouraging. The Army was plunging deep into southern Russia, fighting for the Caucasian oil that Germany desperately needed; the U-boats were sinking American ships right on their doorsteps, by all accounts; and Rommel had pushed the British almost into the Nile. But still the British fought back, bombing Europe practically every other night, somewhere.

Western France and the Low Countries had become a graveyard for *Luftwaffe* pilots recovering from the horrors of the eastern front, with the British bombers by night and the fighters by day.

Now the Americans had joined in, bringing with them four-motors even more fearful than the British: the Flying Fortresses—*Festungen* to the Germans—and their larger brothers, the Liberators. They also brought twin-engine Marauder bombers and twin-boomed fighters named Lightnings that had fearsome firepower; there were rumors that more powerful machines called Thunderbolts were on the way. Some of his fellow instructors had fought British versions of the Festungen, and those encounters did not end well. The intelligence people were relating fantastic stories about these rugged machines in the Pacific, how they seemed to absorb damage beyond all reason, beyond all imagination; even, incredibly, to survive ramming by fighters. The Americans had built flying machines that feared nothing.

On one particularly glorious afternoon, Thielmann was determined to put all of that out of his mind. Instead, he was going to fly a sailplane in the mountains, so he *might* forget about British and Americans and Russia and green pilots...for a while. He squeezed himself into the small, confining cockpit, lowered the canopy into place, tried the controls to his satisfaction, and signaled the winch operator that he was ready. Slowly at first, the sailplane bounced heavily on its single wheel; then, with gathering speed, the tail lightened, the nose lowered, the wind buffeted the canopy, and the launch ramp sloped upwards beneath him, spiriting the fragile, long-winged glider into the air. At once, Thielmann left behind him all his pain and cares and woes, soaring encased in a fabric cocoon, buffeting in the wind, dancing on the drafts and breezes, swooping among the clouds and mountain passes, bright sun dazzling in the western sky. For a few hours, nothing else existed but Thielmann and the sky.

Swishing across a ridge, he felt the tug of gravity, yet he was far away from the field: a downdraft had captured him. As he lost forward speed, he circled for an updraft while looking for a big enough clearing to land in, if necessary. It only took a few minutes to realize that the weather had changed the thermals, and soon he would *have* to land. Searching around the ground below, he found a large meadow on a hillside and pointed for it. Flaring over a gust of air rising enough to brake him, but not let him climb, he set the glider down gently in the soft grass, coming to an almost imperceptible stop. He opened the canopy and climbed out. Strange, he thought, I never saw this meadow before. How many times must I have flown over it? Lighting a cigarette, he sat carefully on the nose of his glider, basking in the warm sun and silence of wind rustling the pines, the rich smell of fresh mountain air and greenery. For a rare moment, he was at peace on earth.

It was several minutes before he knew he was not alone in the meadow. Gazing around him, he saw a young woman in bare feet with a simple *Dirndl* and snowy-white blouse scrutinizing the back of his glider. She looked as if she were born to these mountains, with burnished blonde hair gathered in simple plaits, fair, blonde skin browned by the sun, and the simple expression of innocence of the country folk. Seeing him stare at her, she said, "Hello."

"Hello," Thielmann replied, surprised at the sound of his own voice. He could not think of much else that made any sense.

"Did you want to land in my meadow?" she asked, sauntering toward him.

"Well," Thielmann stammered, "it was either the meadow or the trees, and the meadow made for a softer landing."

"That's good," she replied, then asked, "how long do you wish to stay?"

"Stay," Thielmann asked, "Stay? Why, I don't know. I haven't thought about it."

"Well, then," she said, "you can stay for as long as you like. Do you fly a lot?"

Stay for as long as I like? Here, with her? But she said something else. Do I fly? Do I? "Some," he heard himself say, feeling awestruck—almost smitten—by her simple beauty, and struggling for speech and rational thought. What is it I do other than sit in this quiet mountain meadow staring at an angel? What have I ever done before? What else ever mattered?

"Flying must be terribly exciting," she said, stretching her slim, bronzed neck up to look at the passing clouds. "I wish I could fly, too." What, Thielmann thought, an angel that does not fly? She looked back at him with astonishingly beautiful china-blue eyes. "What's your name?"

Name? Yes, I have a name. What was it? "Otto," he managed, still staring at the smiling, angelic face.

"Otto," she repeated, "Otto. That's a good name for a flyer. I am Elsa. Elsa Portz. Did you come from the airfield at Salzburg?"

He almost melted at the sound of her voice saying his name. Airfield? Salzburg? Yes, Thielmann thought, stirring from his reverie. "Yes. I'm teaching other pilots down there."

"Oh, that means you're a very skilled flyer," Elsa burbled child-like. "How was it you came to land here instead of there?"

A child of the mountains drew here me; by an angel who does not fly, he thought. "Lost my breeze," he said simply. Gathering more of his senses, he stood up from the glider's nose. "Would you mind, *Fraulein*, if I enquired about a telephone? The field will miss me soon...."

"Oh, there's a telephone in the cabin," she said. "Come." And with that, she turned and walked away. Still partly entranced, Thielmann followed her. They walked along in silence for a time, through the lush green grass of the meadow and into the tall evergreens and their cool, fragrant shade. "It's 'Frau' by the way," Elsa said once they entered the shadows, "but my husband died in a U-boat somewhere."

Those words pulled Thielmann violently back into the present, into the pain and horror of the war. But spells, like laws, are made to be broken. "I'm sorry," he said humbly.

"Oh, it was years ago," Elsa said. "Since I've been up here, I've forgotten all about it. And Uncle Peter helps me enormously."

"Do you and your uncle live up here always?"

"Oh, no; I came here with Uncle. We live in Hamburg, but Uncle got into an...altercation with the authorities. So the family thought I should bring him up here." The rest of the trek down the mountain and up the next was largely in silence, Thielmann trying to imagine what sort of altercation her uncle *could* have gotten into with the Nazis and survived. He also pondered how he might scheme to stay in those beautiful mountains forever *without* abandoning his comrades still fighting.

***

The cabin was typical of Alpine hunting lodges, with stone-and-log walls and a timbered roof sodded against the weather. Inside, the furniture was simple and sturdy, the hearth enormous, the cool dark enormously inviting. It was getting dark by the time they reached the place. Even if he contacted the airfield, Thielmann doubted they could find him that night. Still, he called the field using an obviously disused instrument, discussed his "predicament" briefly, and hung up. "Well," he said with all the seriousness he could muster, "it looks as if I'm stuck here until at least morning, unless you have an automobile."

"Well, we do," Elsa said, "but the mountain roads aren't safe at night. You can stay here. We have plenty of room." As she spoke, a man entered the cabin through a back door. Standing nearly two meters tall with a stunning shock of steel-gray hair, he smiled at Elsa, then approached Thielmann, hand outstretched in welcome. "We have a visitor, Elsa? Hello, I'm Lutzow- Verein."

As Thielmann shook hands with him, he struggled to remember that name, where he had heard it before. As Thielmann listened distantly to Elsa's explanation of how he came to be there, he recalled reading about the exploits of a plucky colonel in Africa during the last war, of how he led the British in a merry chase for years, tying down thousands of men with just a handful of Europeans and Africans. Good God, Thielmann thought, I'm in the presence of an angel and a legend. "*Herr General*," Thielmann began, remembering the rank as being appropriate. "I'm honored..."

"Ach," the old man sniffed, "please forget the rank, young man. Up here, there is no time for such formalities. I will call you 'Otto' and you may call me 'Peter'. Will that be all right?"

"Yes," Thielmann said, only slightly uncomfortable with the familiarity and the rare privilege of being able to use the familiar *du* with someone—a living legend no less—that he'd only just met. But still, he was prepared to go to nearly any lengths to be anywhere near Elsa for just a little longer.

Their supper of venison and mountain onions was better than any meal Thielmann ever remembered. Elsa changed from her traditional dress to a warm sweater and stout trousers as the sun went down over the mountains. The hearth was lit, warming the lodge and filling it with the odor of burning pine. With brandy snifters filled with warm liqueur, the three sat in the enormous chairs around the fire. "So Otto," the old man declared, "Tell me about yourself, about the *Luftwaffe*, and of your role in it."

Quietly, with as much detachment as he could manage, Thielmann told them about his life, his family. He talked about flying, his eyes dancing with excitement. But then he finished with "...and then I joined the *Luftwaffe*, and the war began."

"Ah, yes; the war; I had heard of it," the old man said. Not a word was spoken for several minutes as they stared into the fire. "I have lost two sons in this war. Perhaps if I had taken up that Bohemian corporal's offer of an ambassadorship, it may not have..."

"Uncle," Elsa chided. "Don't let's....."

"Elsa, dear, you are much like your Aunt Martha was," Lutzow-Verein grunted. "Neither of you ever let a man say what he means. Your father, that scoundrel, he makes sure no one ever says anything that..."

"Uncle," Elsa snapped. "Our guest doesn't..."

"Our guest needs to know the truth. Your father, my brother-in-law, is a Party thug; a policeman who uses the law and his position to silence everyone who doesn't believe as he does, or doesn't say the things he says." Elsa looked away, frightened and angry. She wept.

This exchange confused Thielmann. This was genuine dissent, not the mild disagreement of weary Germans or a family spat. As a member of the *Wehrmacht*, he was not a Party member, but they expected him to support Germany and its leadership, see the war as a necessary response to Germany's enemies, or face certain punishment.

"This war," he said out loud, surprising even himself, "is an evil, vile, hurtful thing. I just wish I knew how it happened, why it began in the first place."

Lutzow-Verein considered Thielmann for a long moment, then threw another log on the fire and sat on a three-legged stool next to it. "The Party led us to believe that someone else was to blame for our problems," Lutzow- Verein said simply. "Versailles happened because well-meaning men believed that someone had to be brought to book for the murder of their 'Gilded Age,' and so it had smashed many thrones to kindling. We had the supposed stain of Versailles, which we repudiated long before the war began."

He rubbed his hands together, eyes shining in the firelight. "The last war was very simple for me. I was in Africa; we got a telegram; and we were at war. This war was more subtle. Austria and Czechoslovakia baffled me. 'Sudeten Germans' I wondered, what sense does that make? Hohenzollern Germany and Hapsburg Austria had not been one since the Crusades. Poland? We began a war with England and France because of a tiny strip of land between the Prussias? Rubbish. If Versailles was a grievous mistake compounded by misunderstanding, then this entire war is a compound tragedy. I believe a conference of men who never saw a single trench in the last war would have rectified Versailles in a few hours, and this whole mess would have been avoidable. I venture to say, Otto, that even you believed Versailles was punishment, eh?"

"Yes," Thielmann said, hollow voiced in reflection. It is all a mistake. It was a gruesome, ghastly, monstrous mistake that needn't have happened. Why is it so clear now? Why not before? "What of the Bolsheviks? Certainly they would have tried to spread their evil savagery if Germany..."

"If Germany *what*, Otto? Had not invaded Norway and France or tried to humble England? I remember a popular saying from the last war; 'God punish England.' Punish England for what? Germany was marching before England because Russia did. We were England's friend before we invaded Belgium in 1914, and we only did that because the General Staff could not re-imagine their plans against Russia without invading France. No, my friend, if we want, we can find many excuses, but none of them would make any sense. The Bolsheviks I do not worry about. Their brutality and the weaknesses of their system are plain. They survive on hatred as much as the Nazis do, and when no one can remember who to hate, when their enemies are too strong to be battered down by their mighty hammer on its rotten handle, their system will fall, just as the Nazis will fall."

At great length, the old soldier stood up and stretched. "Oh, I talk too much and say too little. I'm for bed. You children enjoy the fire. In the morning, we'll get your flying machine out of the meadow. Good night."

The fire was warm, crickets chirped in the forest, and a light breeze rustled the fragrant branches. Thielmann felt reassured by the old general's talk, his views on Germany and the Nazis. After the general left, Elsa filled brandy snifters, brought sweet cakes from the kitchen, and sat beside him on the sofa. They shared stories about their families and childhoods, and the occasional shoulder bump in laughter.

Yes, a good night, Thielmann thought, a very good night indeed. We have this moment, and laughter, and guarded kisses. That is enough, for now.

November 1942

Reykjavik, Iceland

The graveyards are full of indispensable men

Charles de Gaulle

J ust after six in the evening, *Crop Duster* lifted off the steel-plank runway just as a snow squall hit. Miller was flying, Farr sat in the right seat, a transit radio operator was in the back, the bomb bay was full of fuel, the waist full of electrical parts, and a transit navigator sat in the nose.

His small crew had been joined by a passenger—a WREN courier who'd been stuck in Iceland when her Lancaster transport broke down. She and a companion were carrying some hush-hush messages for the North African invasion that had begun that very morning. The traffic was especially vital; the crew was told, and had to get across immediately, leaving behind the other B-17 and the nine Lightnings that arrived with him just twelve hours earlier.

The flight plan called for an eight-hour flight, but they had fuel for twelve if need be. He would fly east first, turning slightly east-southeast for the Faroe Islands, then make for the Orkneys southeast, then due south for Scotland. A weather front north of the Shetlands might have required diversion from that route. The violent turbulence of the storm he'd launched into vibrated and rumbled the plane's skin loud enough to interrupt the familiar, comforting drone of his engines. Outside, an occasional boom of thunder and flash of incoherent lightning punctuated the turbulence. "Not bad," Miller muttered. "I've flown worse. But not for eight hours at a crack."

The radio room was constantly in touch with England and with Iceland, and reports as to the dimensions and conditions of the bigger storm were passed up every now and again. After a couple of hours, it seemed to calm down some, and Miller could relax a bit. Turning on the autopilot gingerly, he called the navigator. "Pilot to navigator, can you get some coffee up here? Sure appreciate it."

"Navigator to pilot: roger, wait one." A few moments later, the plane was unexpectedly buffeted by turbulence. Miller regained control, and it died down again. A few minutes later, one of his passengers was on the flight deck carrying two steaming cups...and wearing the better part of another.

"I'd meant for the navigator to bring that," Miller shouted over the droning engines.

The young woman seemed unfazed. "Not at all, Captain, not at all," she yelled. "He seemed terribly busy, and as I have nothing essential to do, I just thought I might run this errand. No trouble at all." She was the younger of the two, with enchanting green eyes and light skin. For all of that, she seemed a bit too polished, too refined to be a courier in the WRENs. Then again, Miller had never met an Englishwoman before. Still, young women were young women, no matter what country they were from, but this one just seemed a bit out of place to be doing this.

"Have a seat," Farr shouted, sidling out of the copilot's station. "I've gotta see a man about, uh, gotta check the batteries." She sat gracefully—almost too poised and too graceful—in the hard seat, seemingly unaffected by the whole business.

Miller scanned the instruments continually, sometimes glimpsing her out of the corner of his eye. She made a great show of interest in the plane. Finally she asked, "How long have you been flying, Captain?" She sounded genuinely interested.

"Since I was fourteen; nearly eight years now."

"Is that common for young Americans?"

"It is when your dad runs a flying service and he needs to make ends meet by moving more cargo. I started crop dusting, actually. Better money in it, more real profit."

"Crop dusting? What is that?"

"Well, you put some chemicals in a tank, say a pesticide or an herbicide, put the tank in an airplane, fly the airplane over an infested field, and spray the chemicals on the field. Nothin' to it."

"That is fascinating," she said. "I'm not sure if that's done in Europe."

"I'm not either," Miller answered, suddenly convinced that he had heard her voice before, that the profile looked somehow familiar. "We were some of the first to try it. That's why it's so lucrative. And it works really well under the right conditions. Dad got the idea from a paper company; that's who started it. Treating a million acres of paper trees four times a year for tent moths can be expensive any other way."

"Who taught you to fly?"

"My dad. He's still flying. Probably be flying when they bury him."

"Has the war affected him much?"

"It's affected everybody, miss." Miller said, staring at her.

"Please call me Alexandra—Alex, if you wish, John."

Alexandra, Miller's mind raced. *Princess* Alexandra was a name he remembered from a newsreel...and a picture of a young woman stepping out of a boat. "Yes, uh, am I supposed to call you 'your highness' or something?"

"John, you are not a royal subject, and I am not a royal princess," Alexandra yelled, slightly amused. "I have a handful of titles that, if properly framed, might cover a small wall. My full name, if you *must* know, is Margaret Alexandra Victoria Charlwood-Essene Mountbatten, Serene Princess of Montefalcon, and Grand Duchess Mountbatten. I'm what you might call a kissing cousin to the House of Windsor. Please call me either 'Alexandra' or 'Alex.' Now, about your father..."

Miller stared at her for a long moment. She seemed stern in her amusement and determined to have her way. She was only a teenager, Miller thought, when her small country was overrun by the Germans. "Miss, I don't know that I..."

"John, *please*! I shall call you John, now that we're such good pals." She'd become gently insistent, affecting a slight smile with an odd curl to her lip...not exactly a pout, and not quite a snarl. She wasn't as much asking as she was informing, with a hint of pleading. "You and I are only three months apart, and I have *so* few friends my age. It would honor me to count *you* among them."

"How...would..." Miller sputtered, before he remembered the RAF men hanging around his airplane when they boarded...and his personnel and pay records were inside. Well, what was he supposed to do now? And how could he say no to those eyes? Resigned, he replied, "Dad joined the Civil Air Patrol—actually they drafted our trimotor—just to keep getting enough gas to fly, but now he has a priority- type job as an aircraft mechanic. He's got the contract to fix all the CAP aircraft that come into his area. That's lots of ships, he says."

Alex gave up her seat when Farr returned and gave Miller's shoulder a friendly pat as she left the flight deck to join the navigator in the nose. Miller went back into the routine.

The storm tracked south of the Faeroes right into the path of *Crop Duster*, requiring the unwanted diversion. The rocking, pounding turbulence came back, and then got worse. Concerned about icing on the fuselage and control surfaces, Miller engaged the deicer boots to snap off whatever had accumulated on the wings' leading edges. He dimly hoped the turbulence itself would help prevent a heavy build-up.

Droning across the sky, the navigator started complaining that the radio beacon seemed to be out of whack because the signal just wasn't making sense. Too far north, he thought. "Think it might be a Kraut?" Miller asked.

"Could be," he answered, "or it could be atmospheric bounce. I've heard guys talk about the possibility, but nobody's proved it yet. There's a stronger signal on an alternate wavelength that *seems* right. I'll do some plots on that."

A few minutes later, he called back. "I think the screwy signal has to be Krauts. It'd track us into the Arctic Ocean. It must be a Kraut ship, or maybe a spoofing station in Norway trying to screw us up." Miller acknowledged the call, scratching a hasty entry in his logbook. That's why they give us navigators for the ferry: Smitty wouldn't know the difference.

Eight hours into the flight and still north of the Shetlands, the radioman called up to the cockpit. "England wants an ETA, sir."

Tell England they can go to blue blazes, he thought darkly. What in the hell is so important...ah, oh yeah, her. "Pilot to navigator, you got an ETA?" At that instant, a sudden burst of light enveloped *Crop Duster*, shooting blue lines through the airframe accompanied by a loud BOOM!, and the droning of the engines was suddenly, briefly, interrupted. Lightning, Miller mentally gasped. We've been hit by lightning!

"Pilot to crew," Miller called, hoping the intercom was still working. "Everybody call in." Frantically checking the instruments and relieved that the ship seemed none the worse for wear.

"Radio to pilot: command transmitter's shot. Both radio compasses seem to be knocked out."

"Navigator to pilot; my receiver's dead. Magnetic compass works, but there's more error."

"Flight Engineer to pilot; four engines turning; vacuum pumps appear to be OK so the instruments *should* work."

"Passenger to pilot: what was *that*?"

"Just a little lightning strike, um, Alex," Miller answered, trying to remain as calm as he could. "Nothing to worry about; happens all the time." Not when I've gotta navigate on instruments, he thought darkly. If I lose my horizon...he didn't want to think about it. If I were over land, I'd set it down right now, but.... "Pilot to radio; get on the liaison transmitter. If you can raise anybody at all, tell them we're still flying. Navigator; I'm going down on the deck: can't trust the instruments right now. If I maintain a steady course of 180 magnetic from our last known position, we should hit Scotland before too long."

"But the drift..."

"If *you've* got a *better* idea, I'm all ears...No, I thought not. OK, everybody strap in; this is gonna be one helluva ride." Miller pointed Crop Duster's nose towards the angry, battered sea. At a thousand feet, with wind and rain buffeting the ship, he leveled and trimmed on a due-south heading that he hoped would find land in an hour or less. He had fuel for another three hours, but he was tiring of fighting the controls in the cold damp of the cockpit. Farr helped him steady the ship as it bounced and bucked, varying in altitude by as much as two hundred feet. The radio room was silent.

Lumbering, bouncing over the wave-tossed, pewter-colored angry sea, Miller tried to concentrate on the job at hand and not think about his aching shoulders and legs, having flown *Crop Duster* for nearly nine hours, fighting the weather for two of those...and still no sight of land. The radio room had raised an Irish station that was relaying information to England. Slow and clumsy, but it worked.

With an hour of fuel left, the rain and snow rising vertically on the windscreen, Farr pointed excitedly out his window. Squinting through the dense wet, they could see a storm-lashed coast off to the west, not where it was supposed to be. Banking sharply, Miller pointed *Crop Duster* towards the landfall, hoping he could find a piece of level ground soon.

In minutes, they were over land Alex declared was "somewhere around Kinnaird Head. Aberdeen will be to the south." Miller hoped she was right. If accurate, he was only about a hundred and fifty miles off course.

And right she was. An RAF fighter strip became the surprise host of a strange B- 17 landing without radio. Finally coming to a halt in a light rain, the crew and passengers clambered out of their flying prison, peeling off flying suits as a staff car drove up.

Two men emerged from the back seat of the car, one very British in ascot and high collar, the other a rather disheveled-looking American. Snapping open an umbrella, the ascot darted to Alex, while the American gamboled up to the flight crew. Miller thought it curious that he could make the distinction on sight, but not as curious as having a reception committee where he wasn't expected. "Captain Miller," the strange American began testily, "half of goddamn England is looking for you. You're three hours late, and you're dangerously close to creating a diplomatic incident that could have catastrophic consequences to the alliance. Now suppose you tell me..."

"Looking for ME? What the hell for?" He had already put enough of the picture together to know exactly what this bureaucrat was babbling about, but he wasn't about to give him the satisfaction. He figured if Alex and her companion were incognito in Iceland, there was a reason. "All I've got aboard is spare parts and some message traffic that..."

"Message traffic!" The man was apoplectic. "Message traffic?!?! Why, you lop-eared, nickel-plated idiot, I'll have your ass in Alaska on the next slow-boat! Don't you know who...?"

"SIR," a stern voice called out, causing all present to whip around to the source. "This very skilled pilot has just completed a most arduous flight and is quite exhausted. You are chastising him without due cause. I'll not have it, do you hear? I *shall not have* it!" Open-mouthed, the American gaped at the young woman, now standing in front of him, her legs apart, flying trousers open and jacket removed revealing a coffee-stained sweater, with rain and wind whipping through her hair, hands on hips, her face a statement of angry defiance.

The ascot, eyes rolling, held the umbrella over her head while getting soaked himself. "Your highness, please," the ascot said, "the gentleman is from the American State Department, and..."

"Oh, please *do* be QUIET, Sir Reginald," she snapped. "I don't care *who* he is. I'll not tolerate this injustice." The ascot, thoroughly mortified at this sudden rebuke, fell silent. "Now, sir," once again directing her anger at the American diplomat, "you will apologize to the captain, and to his crew. If you had only ASKED why he was late, you would realize that he was deceived by a German submarine, struck by lightning, and lost use of his primary radio. No other pilot in the WORLD could have accomplished such a flight. And you have the AUDACITY to criticize him? In*deed*, sir! In*deed*!!" All during this exchange, Miller's crew stood dumbfounded, while he himself grinned slightly, as if getting a mild joke.

Sheepishly, the now-thoroughly chastised diplomat muttered a few words and bowed away, never even sneaking a glance behind him, slinking back into the car. "Your Highness," the ascot said, "we shall have to go..."

"Sir Reginald, please," she replied, "I wish to thank these brave men."

One by one, Alexandra, Princess of Montefalcon, took Miller's crew warmly by the hand, thanking each. She lingered briefly with Miller, and then suddenly pecked him softly on the cheek, saying, "Thank you, John," as she stepped back.

Miller thought the ascot would die. "Anytime, Alex," he grinned.

***

The engineers and contractors were still working on the facility when Miller and *Crop Duster* arrived at the 299th's new home later that day. Surrounding USAAF Station Number 221 was farm country, raising sheep and cattle, wheat and rye, kids and hard times, a picture book eastern English county with ancient masonry and wood buildings, houses with thatched roofs, picket fences, victory gardens in every yard, and bicycles everywhere.

Just outside the town of Bartlesby (which was two miles east from the station's perimeter) the local Duke's estate was partly taken over by the Ministry of War for something or other hush-hush. The male population of the village were mostly older, or policemen, or otherwise unfit for service, so the women outnumbered the men three-to-one. Everyone sturdily carried on, seemingly unconcerned that the menfolk were off risking their lives for King and Country.

The Bartlesby station "host command" was the 95th Aviation Engineering Command, a huge and nebulous outfit that had detachments all over England and, as of the morning *Crop Duster* arrived, North Africa. The 95th was commanded by a bandy-legged, barrel-chested brigadier general named Maurice Sanda, who, as the wags had it, surveyed Rome for Romulus and Remus. Their service yard at the western end of the base was a beehive of activity day and night, with damaged vehicles and equipment arriving (but remarkably little ever leaving) round the clock. It was said that there were enough sandbags, steel mat and steel shelters in the depots to rebuild all of Europe.

The 299th was the largest unit on the base, but Bartlesby was also the home of a service squadron of mechanics, technicians, and metal fitters for the 299th, a quartermaster company of supply clerks, a chemical company of hangers-on from the previous conflict, an ordnance maintenance company to handle ammunition and bombs, an MP company to watch the gates and perimeter, an antiaircraft battery to protect the field, a detachment of meteorologists to guess at the weather, four gas defense specialists who wondered what they were doing there, paymasters to hand out money and ration coupons, motor mechanics to keep the five hundred plus vehicles and generators running, radio mechanics for the electronic gear, and signalmen so they could talk to everybody. There was also a hundred-bed base hospital, a small PX and canteen, four mess halls, two officer's and three enlisted men's clubs, a USO/Red Cross club/office, and a sewing shop/cleaners/cobbler's shop.

For once, someone had given at least fifteen minutes serious thought about where this station would be, and what purpose it would serve. Because it was right next to a railway siding, Bartlesby was also a depot for other Eighth Air Force stations in the area: the 105th Bomb Group with B-26 Marauders in Nichols 10 miles north, the 110th Bomb Group of B-17s and the 210th Fighter Group with P-38 Lightnings co-located 12 miles southeast at Vincent St. Niles. Because the Bartlesby station was a depot, they reserved a corner for the 872nd Quartermaster Transportation Company (Truck). As with most truck companies at that time, they referred the 151 men and 4 officers assigned to the 872nd as "colored troops."

But the Americans were not alone in that part of England. In Boorston, six miles east, was billeted a squadron of radar-equipped RAF Beaufighters. At Trentonshire Down, just two miles south, the Belgians kept a squadron of Spitfires. At Veech's Hall, six miles west, a depot company dignified with the title of 3rd Polish Parachute Brigade provided replacements and administrative support to the 1st Polish Parachute Brigade, then in North Africa with British Eighth Army.

Fifteen miles due east at Richard's Cove, a dozen French torpedo boats of the 9th Squadron, 4th Motor Flotilla were based, running people and cargo to the Resistance, as well as lifeguard duties for the RAF and USAAF, and inshore patrols. And Bartlesby itself was the home of the Bartlesby Battery of the Royal Artillery, which, the day Miller arrived in Bartlesby, hit the beach at Algiers with their 25-pounders.

The field itself included two 6000-foot-long parallel concrete strips, reinforced with steel matting and stretched by two thousand feet of packed gravel on both ends; with a third 5000-foot steel mat diagonally joining them, surrounded by taxiways and revetted hardstands for fifty aircraft. The hangars and service shops for aircraft and equipment maintenance were all "tempos;" corrugated steel pole barns of a variety of makes, shapes and sizes, as were the living areas for the four thousand men and sixty-odd women (mostly nurses, but there were also sixteen Red Cross girls and eight USO volunteers) on the station.

They made the headquarters structure on the northern end of the field of concrete block; the control tower and the signal shed had started life as water towers. Clay bunkers housed ammunition and bombs, similar in construction to the air-raid shelters. Cylindrical steel fuel storage tanks dominated one end of the field. They made other buildings of concrete, steel mat and sandbags. Stick-built storage sheds, sod and stone barns taken over from local farmers were used for paint storage. Tents housed a few unlucky flyers whose billets they had not yet completed, as well as parts of airplanes being worked on that couldn't be squeezed into the hangars. No one could imagine that any planning or thought had gone into the layout and construction of the Bartlesby station.

It was from this site that forty-eight heavy bombers were to carry the war to Germany in the face of one of the most powerful, battle-hardened air forces in the world.

Miller thought we're going to a lot of trouble for the mere two or three months everyone's convinced it will take to get the Krauts to see reason.

***

The Red Cross club at Bartlesby was carpeted and paneled with plywood for more insulation. The idea was that if the inside was warm, it would feel a little more like home. There were pictures on the walls of landscapes and small towns, the map of the 'States where everybody stuck a pin in their hometown, posters exhorting the troops to buy bonds, keep their mouths shut and watch out for gonorrhea...and a dartboard. The club also sported a piano, assorted second-hand tables, chairs and couches, a phonograph/radio, two Ping-pong tables, and a brick fireplace built into a corner. It was a pretty homey place if you came down to it. In the corner opposite the fireplace was the plywood counter where the Red Cross girls handed out reading materials, puzzles, games, coffee, doughnuts, soft drinks, and idle conversation to long successions of GIs with nothing but time on their hands and thoughts of home.

Miller looked around the room for Amy Bartlett, a small girl with a big smile from Rhode Island that he'd chatted with the night before. Doing duty behind the counter was Alice McPhee, a double-chinned brunette from Oklahoma with a pleasant demeanor. She was in an animated conversation with a gaga radio tech who stared at her ample chest a lot, and a new face Miller hadn't seen before. She was a rather stunning raven-haired girl with hair clipped short to her head and a statuesque pose even under the shapeless British Red Cross uniform. "Hello," Miller said, "I was looking for Amy."

The brown-eyed stranger smiled at him winningly. "I'm sorry, Captain, but it's her night off. Perhaps I can help you?"

"Uhn, well, no. Just thought..."

"Oh, you must be John," the girl purred. "Amy chattered about you in the flat. I'm Grace Henley." They shook hands politely; Grace's grip was stronger than expected. "I can ring the flat for you if you wish."

"Flat?"

"Well, barracks, I suppose."

"No, no thanks. It's nothing urgent. I didn't know we had any English doughnut dollies."

"Doughnut dollies...oh my, how you Yanks have names for things. Yes, well, a few of us offered to help on some posts. Would you care for coffee, John?"

"Sure."

"Sugar, milk or awful?"

"Awful, I guess. Not much for coffee in England?"

"Not many of us acquired the habit here, but our tea is often much the same. So, what do you think of Perfidious Albion?"

"What?"

"England."

"Oh. I haven't seen much of it yet. Just some fighter field up north and here, and I haven't even been outside the station."

"Yes. We've been thinking of a tour group for you."

"That'd be swell if we find the time. Say, how'd you get this job?"

"Well, I did a stint in the A.R.P."

"What's that?"

"It stands for Air Raid Precautions. I was one of those dreary people who went about getting everyone into the shelters, shouting about lights from the street. Quite a dull job most of the time."

"Unless you did it maybe in London during the Blitz..."

"Oh, but I did; wearing all the same. You have no idea how much water a fire hose can put out until one's aimed at you."

"You were in a burning building?"

"Well, no, actually, I was in a shelter *under* the building. Hit by an incendiary and went up like a lamp. The fire wardens were on it in a flash, but still a great gush of water and heat, ash and rubbish all 'round..."

"Maybe I shouldn't have brought it up."

"Oh, it's all right, John. That was years ago. Years and ages, I think sometimes."

"Where's your folks?"

"Folks?"

"Parents."

"Oh, Canada; went there on business in '39 just before the war started and decided to stay. Father's from the last war. It's how he met Mother, actually."

"How was that?"

"He and one of his chums were in a hospital ward in Flanders and the chum's sister was a nurse in the ward. Before anyone knew it, they were married and Dad's chum became my Uncle Edmund."

"Happened just that fast, huh? Yeah, I've known some guys got married a few days after they met some girl. I think they do it just to get in the sack."

"Sack?"

"Bed."

"Oh. Yes, well, perhaps. Still, it is romantic, isn't it? 'We may never meet again, my dear,' and all that sort of thing."

"Yeah, I guess. But women get all sentimental about the most common of things. Like, you know, Princess Alexandra ..."

"Yes, I do; lovely girl and quite spirited. Her country being overrun put quite a brake on that, I should say."

"You know her, personally?"

"Yes; we went to the same school. I was her secretary for a time."

"Secretary? What's a slip of a girl like that need with a secretary?"

"It's something of a blind, really. Lady Hyde-Warner was the official chaperone, but the dear woman was getting on in years. Carolyn and I—we're both expendable of-age daughters of minor nobility and with no immediate prospects (not *then*, anyway)—got the job with the titles of 'secretary' to keep Lord Hyde-Warner quiet in Parliament and to make sure Alex didn't go off the rails somewhere..."

"Expendable...minor nobility?"

"Yes, well, Carolyn is the second daughter of a bankrupt Baron in the Western Marches, and I am the only daughter of a Cornwall Lord who has a married-with-children older brother. Neither of us can inherit a title, so we're expendable."

"Well, I'll be damned. Anyway, she got marooned in Iceland when her Lancaster transport had some breakdown."

"Oh, she was coming back? Whatever for? I thought she was raising money in America. When was this?"

"Couple of weeks ago, but I can't say as I know why she came back. This is pretty common?"

"Not as common as stones, but a couple of times a year. Was Carolyn with her?"

"Uh, yeah; red hair, sense of humor..."

"Yes, and in a lot of trouble now...back in England, and she didn't even ring me. But, you were saying about Alex?"

"Yeah, well, I got elected to ferry her across the water, so we take off and have to avoid this big storm, only we can't avoid it. So we're flying through it and we get hit by lightning..."

"Lightning? Does that happen often?"

"Oh, often enough, but I never got used to it. Fouls up the instruments and radios and gives me the heebie-jeebies..."

"Heebie..."

"Makes my skin crawl, creepy-like. Anyway, we lose voice contact with England but we're still flying. About four hours later we land at some RAF field in Scotland and this State Department big shot's giving me a ration of crap about how I endangered the alliance and all that, and then the princess gets her knickers in a twist..."

"Ration of crap...knickers in a twist...knickers...oh, my, that's *awfully* wonderful...," Grace giggled, "but do go on, please..."

"...about what a great job I did just flying the damn plane. I mean, any one of a hundred guys could've done the same thing..."

"Yes, but you did it there and then," she said, recovering. "Not someone else, you."

"I suppose. Wasn't anything, really."

"It was for her. She's led a fairly protected life, you know. Just being in an airplane over the sea was probably ample excitement."

"If you say so. Say, what do you do when you're not in here serving coffee?"

"As little as possible; this is a twelve-hour shift, you know. No holidays, no days off, save once a fortnight, and then only if you have a relief."

"You wanna take in a movie or something?"

"Take in...movie...oh, you mean go to the cinema? Well, we're not supposed to make engagements with the lads, but for you, I may make an exception. The nearest cinema is in Vincent St. Faith, however."

"OK, maybe we can take one in here on the station. They got some Cagney picture day after tomorrow. It wouldn't be like a date or anything, not with another three thousand guys around and me with the only date."

"I shall be honored, but the rest of us girls off-duty would also be there. Now, John, we really *must* have a chat about that 'knickers in a twist' expression before you use it in polite English company...."

November 1942

Aschaffenburg, Germany

You can't say civilization don't advance, however,
For in every war, they kill you in a new way

Will Rogers

T he weather was not auspicious for new fighter training. The wind was chilly up off the Alps, and clouds formed to the south. It looked like another day of occasional rain. This was a conversion training school. It would familiarize ME-109 pilots like Thielmann with their new FW-190a, but mostly it would train them how to engage their new targets: instead of Russian fighters, they would become bomber hunters against the Americans.

"The *Amis* fat cars—heavy bombers or four-motors—fly in what they call 'combat boxes,' what we call 'herds.' Groups of fighters escort these herds we call 'Indians,' using the close-escort technique that we have discarded. Do not be deceived, however, that the bombers need escorting as their only defense; these crates carry many heavy machine guns—as many as ten each. They use their combat boxes to provide interlocking fields of fire between machines. These herds are very, very dangerous places to be in, and are very dangerous to attack.

"The general idea is to cull the herds, separating the weak from the rest, then finish off these cripples when they are not surrounded by so many of their fellows. Because someone in America got the peculiar notion that no one would attack the bombers from ahead, these machines frequently carry nothing in the nose except a light rifle-caliber machine gun. Therefore, we have learned the most effective attacks are from the front: straight on, head- on. You must fire into the wing roots, into the pilots, into the nose. Infrequently is there any danger there. However, you only have about three seconds in effective range before you must divert to avoid collision."

Riding in the back of the truck with the other new *Würger* pilots later in the day, Thielmann felt confident about his new assignment. The doctors had declared him fit for combat in mid-October, and his nerves had steadied enough to fly high-performance aircraft again. Though he felt he might miss the reliable old ME-109s he'd flown since the beginning of the war (well enough for 64 aerial victories), he was looking forward to flying the powerful, more heavily armed FW-190s.

One by one, the pilots were dropped off at their planes. One by one they trudged to the blunt-nosed, taper-wing fighters, parachutes and flying suits in kit bags slung over their shoulders. For this operational training unit, not much about the routine of manning planes was new. Of the nine pilots, not one had less than thirty victories, and two had over fifty.

Like the others, Thielmann set his kit on the right wing root and walked around his machine. The Focke-Wulf FW-190 was a single-engine fighter with a blunt nose (some models had radial and some had inline engines), ten meter long tapering fuselage and ten-and-a-half meter wingspan. Fully loaded, she could climb at nearly a kilometer a minute and fly at nearly seven hundred kilometers an hour with nitrous-oxide injection. Armed with four 20mm cannons and two 13mm machine guns, Focke-Wulf *Würgers* could fire nearly nine kilos of ammunition in a head-on three-second attack at a closing rate of about two hundred meters per second on an American *Viermot*.

For three weeks, they drummed these tactics into the pilots. First, make contact and parallel the bombers course and speed. Next, execute a wide crossover turn, ending about four kilometers in front of the bombers, flying straight ahead into the formation. Then, press the nitrous oxide switch, full throttle, and as the targets grow larger, palm the firing switch. Then fly over your target to avoid being hit by falling debris and dive quickly down out of the herd, out of the range of the formation's heavy machine guns. Properly executed, the leading bombers were crippled, leaving the herd's protective web of guns so that they could be destroyed individually, leaving the rest of the formation with having to reform their defensive boxes. With luck, they could not do this before the next *Schwarme* of four machines attacked.

Break up the formations...keep the pressure on...keep pounding them...hit the cockpit...cull the herds...don't go for kills inside the herd except head-on...

Finally, the training ended, and they assigned the pilots to a newly forming special unit on the flight route to Berlin at Oschersleben as a group.

***

"Welcome, gentlemen, to Operational Development Group 191, which for the benefit of Allied intelligence, shall be known as JG191, because we don't think they need to know we are an operational test unit," Colonel Kaltz said in the new unit's first briefing. "Other *Luftwaffe* fighter units are made of unique aircraft, but JG191 shall be different. As you flew in, you doubtless noticed the JU-88s and the ME-110 on the other side of the field. They are part of Experimental Battle Group 191, to be known as KG191, as will other *zweimots* or even *Viermots* in time, as we develop our techniques. This double group, gentlemen, has been charged with one mission only: develop tactics that will turn the American bombers away, to make them retreat before they drop their bombs. Failing that, we are to find the best way to destroy them wholesale. For that reason, we are to be known as the Giant Killers. The finest pilots in the *Luftwaffe* will be assigned to the Giant Killers, some briefly, some long- term. Our task is to develop tactics to defeat the American herds."

Thielmann glanced around the room at his fellow senior officers. There was Joachim Pritzler, an amiable Prussian (what a contradiction!) who downed the first English Spitfire over France besides fifty-three other machines. Beside him was Fritz Taube, a Hanoverian test pilot on the FW-190 and co-developer of the head-on attack, with seven *Viermots* and forty other victories so far. And there was Heinrich Bär, the swaggering Swabian with nearly a hundred victories. What a swarm they could form on their own, Thielmann thought. But in this unit, that would be rare. The four Captain aces would each command their own group. As new methods were developed and tactics evolved, 'graduates' transferred out to pass these innovations on to other squadrons, making their task as much development as it was training. For most members of the JG191, the stay would be brief, providing they survived.

***

That afternoon, while inspecting his aircraft, Thielmann noticed a kindly looking, older NCO taking an interest in his *Würger*, who introduced himself as Thielmann's new crew chief, Wilhelm Steger. "So, Steger, what wondrous deeds did you perform to get here? Most of the pilots are aces."

"Oh, nothing extraordinary, Captain," Steger said. "I was a farmer in Thuringia, and in the last war I was an artificer in the old *Luftstreitkräfte*, so they sent me to airplane mechanic's school when I...joined up to avoid...well, the infantry. Who is this?" he said, pointing at Gunther.

"My dog, Gunther; Gunther, this is Steger. He is our friend." The little dog's ears pricked up slightly, nudging Steger's knee. "He likes you."

"It must be the farmer in me, *Mein Herr*. Dogs always seem to get along with me. Are you married, *Mein Herr?*"

"No, I'm not," Thielmann said, "Though I may have found someone..."

"That is good, *Mein Herr*. A fighter pilot's lot is such a lone thing. It is always good to have someone to come home to."

"Well, since Poland, I've had Gunther. You, Steger, surely you have a family." As Steger proudly spoke of his wife, five daughters and beloved farm, Thielmann thought to himself, it is Gunther that has kept me human. For two years, the little dog had followed Thielmann whenever his master was in sight. He gave Thielmann the comfort and reassurance he needed after long hours of violent maneuvering in the freezing, solitary sky, with only other machines and the crackling, tinny voices of the headset to remind him of the human world. Gunther's was his last touch of a living thing before his flights, and the first to greet him upon his return. His coarse fur and wet nose were reminders of a much different time and place; one that Thielmann increasingly longed for, but knew was still a long way off.

***

The Oschersleben base on Germany's North Coastal Plane, just north of the Weser River, was not typical of most of Thielmann's previous stations. This one had real 2000-meter runways, real permanent, purpose-built buildings besides a scattering of traditional trailers and tents, *and* running water. Most of the marshy countryside was inhabited by those who made their living off the river, the sea, or by small farming and logging. The station was modest because JG/KG191 was modest, with a complement of one hundred pilots, three hundred or more technicians, and another hundred staff and other ground personnel, including twenty people working on ejection seat designs and the mechanics of aircraft escape.

Oschersleben's military district had provided two infantry divisions for the German Army by the end of 1942, and there were rumors of another draft to take place early in 1943. They already drafted most of the eligible men, so many of the townsfolk wondered what the draft requirements would be. Most of the people in the Oschersleben area listened to the radio news accounts with a great deal of personal interest, because one of the *Wehrkreis's* divisions was in the Stalingrad area, and the news reports of fighting in the area towards the end of November were, to be charitable, cryptic. It is not clear why JG191 was designated the way it was, but, on the other hand, no one was sure, in late 1942, why the war had lasted as long as it had.

***

Thielmann found the American bombers some thousand meters below, but was wary of the American fighters between them, who hadn't yet spotted JG191 through the cloud bank. Pritzler's group, two hundred meters below and to the left of Thielmann's, was assigned to intercept the Indians so that the other three groups could get through to the bombers, but this band was unprecedentedly large. Thielmann quickly decided (it being his day to be Kaptain for the air battle) to stick to the original plan, hoping Pritzler and his twelve could hold off the Americans long enough for the other three groups to make at least one pass at the bombers. "Altmarck leader to Altmarck four," Thielmann called, "Indians at one five left. Repeat: Indians at one five left."

"Altmarck four to Altmarck leader: Affirmative, I have them. I am engaging. *Pauke!*" Pritzler and his 12 machines dove downwards to the immense American fighter formation between JG191 and the bombers.

While Pritzler engaged the Indians, Thielmann and the other machines would try to separate the herds from each other, to cut down their immense combined firepower. This, they thought, may hit the herds hard enough so that they would turn back.

As Pritzler slid silently under Thielmann's group, Thielmann called to the others of JG191. "Altmarck one to Altmarck attack unit: Boost ahead and turn on me." Thielmann pulled his throttle back while pitching the nose slightly down, surging ahead of the bombers. The others followed him.

As the airspeed grew, Thielmann glanced back to check on the bomber's position, now falling behind. Meanwhile, he glimpsed Pritzler's group just on the edge of the American fighters. As Pritzler dove into the Indians, Thielmann knew, his group switched radio frequencies so as not to confuse the other groups. A *Jäger's* life is complicated enough up here, Thielmann thought bitterly, without having to listen to the troubles of others.

The attack groups wheeled around in a shallow dive following Thielmann's wide bank, the trailing groups now becoming the lead in a crossover turn, forming a thirty-six point wedge intent on driving between the bomber's formations, attacking the leading, low machines in the highest formation to break not only the box formation but the contact between boxes. There were three swarms of four machines in each group's staggered, descending echelon wedge, practiced for many hours and by now instinctive, with Thielmann and the three other machines of his swarm leading ahead and just below, and heading directly for the bombers. Above the bombers and to Thielmann's right, he glimpsed Pritzler's group cartwheeling around the American Lightnings, swirling in dizzying motions. "Altmarck Leader to Altmarck: Noses in. *Pauke!*"

The FWs flashed over the leading box, boring straight into the second- lowest box leader. At just the right moment, Thielmann palmed the gun switch and his guns thundered across the icy space, the lead American Fortress growing in his sights, top turret and cheek guns already sputtering in defiance. As planned, the American evaded downward, right into the sights of his following *Schwarme*. He yanked up the yoke and pressed the boost switch as tracers from sixteen Fortresses crisscrossed the surrounding sky. As he arched over the leader's back, he saw the left inboard engine catching fire. Diving quickly to get out of range of the trailing Fortresses, Thielmann glanced around him. His own swarm followed; smoke trailing from engines on high-boost for too long.

"*Horrido*," Thielmann heard exclaimed, and as he turned around, he saw a Fortress in a dying spin, turning out of control and headed for the ground. One, Thielmann thought, and without culling. This may just be effective.

"Altmarck Leader to Altmarck: Reform and go around," Thielmann called, banking around the back of the Fortress formations as their tail guns fired at him, out of range. Searching for where Pritzler should have been, he saw only Spitfires and Lightnings headed for him. Where is Pritzler, he wondered, knowing that the standard *Luftwaffe* escape maneuver, a split-s into a long dive, was useless against the powerful Lightnings. "Altmarck leader to Altmarck two: Engage the Indians."

"Affirmative," Bär answered, "*Pauke!*" Bär's twelve machines went into a climbing turn to meet the bounce head-on. Thielmann and Taube's remaining twenty-four kept charging around the right of the herd to get in front of the bombers again.

"We are right behind the Indians. Take low," Pritzler called. God, Thielmann thought, in a few moments they could shoot at each other!

"Altmarck leader to Altmarck four: Disengage. Repeat: Disengage. Fall behind me. Altmarck three, swing out right high. Engage the Indians after Altmarck two."

"Affirmative," Taube called back. "Altmarck three, follow me." Taube pulled up hard from behind Thielmann, turning once more to meet the oncoming Lightnings. This escort may have been too large, Thielmann decided, for our small JG to handle. As he struggled to get around the Fortresses again, tracers lanced his path. Indians, Thielmann's mind screamed, they've gotten past all of them.

"Altmarck leader to Altmarck units: report your location. I am under attack to the right."

"Altmarck leader, this is Altmarck two: I am behind the Indians coming down on you."

"Altmarck three to Altmarck leader: I am behind you."

"Altmarck four to Altmarck leader: I am above you moving into attack position on the Indians."

"*Horrido*," Thielmann heard again, this time pivoting around to see a Lightning roll over on its back and the pilot tumble out, as other Indians attacked Thielmann's group.

"Altmarck one," Thielmann called, "break and attack; break and attack." Thielmann threw his machine into his favorite maneuver, a diving snap roll, hoping his wingman had seen him perform it often enough to follow. As he recovered from the roll a Lightning presented its tail to him. Swiftly setting the sight, he palmed the gun switch, corrected his aim, and fired again. The American's left wing sheared off in a minor explosion and the machine tumbled through space. "*Horrido*," Thielmann called.

"Altmarck three four to Altmarck: I am on fire. I am escaping. God grant us..." and then there was silence. Thielmann put the message

117

out of his mind as he swung around for another attack. Most of the Lightnings were now far below the bombers from their diving charge, with a few stragglers still caught in fights with JG191.

"Altmarck, this is Kustrin," Thielmann heard. "We are ahead of you. We will engage the herd." Another group was about to engage the American bombers. Eastern is a ME-109 Group, Thielmann thought. Not much use against the *Festungen*.

"Kustrin, this is Altmarck," Thielmann called back, "Affirmative. Good hunting. We will try again after you pass through if we can." Thielmann watched behind him as he pressed for the head of the bomber herd, his group and several other machines from the other groups falling in behind raggedly. He glanced off to the left to watch the Messerschmitts close with the herd rapidly, their guns sputtering. A leading machine's engine exploded in a cloud just before it had to pull out, and the wreck rammed the unlucky *Festungen* it was attacking head-on. A trailing Messerschmitt swerved expertly to avoid the explosion, firing into another Fortress's flank. It was only moments before the Messerschmitts were through the herd, and three bombers were staggering, one spinning down.

"Kustrin, this is Altmarck: good work. Come around again." Just as he said it, another burst of tracers sprang from behind him. More Indians! Thielmann snapped his machine around, tracers still flying around him. Thielmann threw his machine into a looping dive, desperately looking for others of his JG to help. By then he could see more Focke-Wulf's and Lightnings swerving and dashing through the air, guns thundering over screaming engines, machines exploding, others catching fire; over there, a Lightning rolled out as the pilot fell away; over there a Messerschmitt smoking badly, spiraling downward; and there were two Focke-Wulfs diving on a crippled bomber.

Heavy slugs tore into his tail section. Desperately Thielmann pulled hard up into an Immelmann while boosting to full emergency power, beginning his count: *Ein*...his skillful attacker loops away...*Zwei*... Thielmann pushes the stick over to regain forward control...*Drei*... the Lightning grows large in his sights...*Fier*...Thielmann palms the gun switch and heavy cannon rounds strike home in the Lightning's tail section...*Funf*...Thielmann cuts out the boost and throttles back moments before his engine would explode at full emergency power. The Lightning issues a gout of flame from a severed boom and streams for the ground. *Horrido*! A red light flashed urgently on Thielmann's instrument panel: low fuel. "Altmarck, this is Altmarck leader: Disengage. Repeat: Disengage."

"Affirmative Altmarck leader. Altmarck two; roll out and dive."

"Altmarck three; turn on me."

"Altmarck four; crossover turn out and back. Find the leader and reform."

Ten minutes later, JG191 was winging back downwards, looking for a place to land. They were too far from Oschersleben, but needed fuel soon. There were forty machines in the formation when they landed near Rheims for fuel. They were later credited with three Fortresses, six Spitfires and four Lightnings, and two of their pilots were later recovered unharmed. Four others were wounded, two dead.

JG191 had attacked a herd of eighty Fortresses and an entire fighter wing of over a hundred Lightnings and Spitfires.

With such mathematics, we would all be dead by the end of 1943, Thielmann thought, and the Americans would still have *Festungen* and Lightnings.

December 1942

Lille, France

I begin to regard the death and mangling
Of a couple of thousand men
As a small affair, a kind of morning dash

William T. Sherman

The crew was scared, which was to be expected, considering none of them had ever flown in combat. But only a few of the 299th's ships had even flown a live mission. Idle crew chatter tried to hide the nagging fear—everyone says we're so new they're giving us an easy target...some torpedo plant near Lille...Krauts don't defend French factories, so this should be a cakewalk.

"Engine start," Berg said, watching the red flare from the control tower shoot into the midmorning sky, heavy with mist and thickening cloud deck.

"Let's do it. Stand by to start number one. CLEAR ONE," Miller shouted out the window.

"Start one." Berg held down the engine starter switch at START and pumped the primer. After a few seconds Miller said, "mesh one," and the copilot moved the starter switch to MESH. The left outside engine coughed slowly to life, its huge propeller swinging slowly at first, then with growing speed. The engine coughed, belched fine smoke, and finally started. At the same time, the other Bartlesby B-17s started their engines, breaking the mid- morning stillness of the tranquil English countryside with a great cacophony of noise, first from dozens, then hundreds of engines.

One by one, Miller and Berg brought the engines into life, revving each up to test the magnetos, prop controls, vacuums and pressures, always standing on the brakes just in case *Crop Duster* ran over the chocks. They felt the vibration added by each, listened carefully to the sounds they made, watched their gauges.

"Pilot to bombardier," Miller called, "synchronize left." Kearns watched out the nose window, watching the moving shadow of the intersection of the propellers. "Up, up," he called as Berg jockeyed the throttles until the shadow was still. Smith did the same on the right. Satisfying himself with the checks and the engines, Miller waved to Philukuzki and the wheel chocks pulled away. Brakes released, the bomber lurched forward slightly, the subtle signal to the planes behind him he was ready to go. Shortly, the control tower fired another flare, signaling that takeoff could begin. One by one, the Flying Fortresses lumbered off their hardstands, waddling zig-zag fashion to the end of the runway.

***

The strike went in about noon and was practically undefended by fighters, but the flak was heavy. Someone said that some Liberators were getting hit by the German fighters. The first time he saw flak boiling up at him, Miller thought it looked rather like cotton candy that had got soot in it, and it looked about as deadly. He thought it strange that it was so quiet and appeared so suddenly in the distance, but got louder close up. Spent fragments falling from high bursts clattered against *Crop Duster*'s skin when she flew through it, but seemed no worse than gravel from a loose runway.

A handful of German fighters demonstrated half-heartedly around the 1st Wing on their way to and from the target. They seemed to float around the edges of the group formations, coming in on flank attacks and the occasional stern and once or twice head-on, but in the main they seemed fairly innocuous. Nothing like what they had expected. Still, the 1st Wing lost a Fortress to "unknown causes"—meaning he just didn't come back—and flak and fighters hit nine others. Great introduction to the world of strategic bombing, Miller thought.

As the formations returned to Bartlesby late in the afternoon, RAF fighter squadrons intercepted them over the North Sea. "Fencepost group," Throck called, "account for your neighbors." Once in a while, the Germans snuck an intruder into a formation, usually at dusk, that shot up the airfield. Once, they snuck an FW-200 Condor into a Liberator formation and dropped incendiaries. Someone rumored that the *Luftwaffe* had a squadron of patched-up and salvaged B-17s for doing just that to Fortress groups. No one was interested in finding out if the rumor was true.

The radio men flashed recognition signals at each other with their big signal lights, in codes known only to that privileged class of cabalists that could identify each other after a few flashes or blips. Finding nothing untoward, Feynman reported in, "Radio to pilot: friends only." The RAF sped around the formations, looking for anything that they didn't like, but found little to concern themselves with. A small gaggle of Hurricanes hung a few miles behind, waiting for other intruders. Dusk inbound flights were always somewhat more dangerous than outbound; the crews were tired and not overly observant. Returning fighter groups had learned to count airplanes, waggle wings or flash recognition signals like the bombers did. The penalties for inattention were sometimes dire.

As the group found the runway and vectored in to land, the last of the battle damage became apparent: brakes shot out, landing gear that wouldn't go down, and weakened airframes came out in stark relief. Though there were no catastrophes at the end of the 299th's first strike, there were casualties. One tail wheel had been shredded, causing a fountain of sparks when the ship set down. Another, lacking brakes, skidded out of control at the end of the runway and into one of Sanda's enormous sandbag berms. As Miller set *Crop Duster* down, he took note that at least one of the 40mm flak guns in one of the sandbag towers around the field—manned by Battery A of the 211th AAA Battalion— followed every bomber from approach all the way down the runway. Some speculated that the Germans might try mounting a commando raid out of a captured B-17, and Battery A was taking no chances. Since Bartlesby was a test bed for a lot of techniques and tactics, Battery A's caution was widely seen as something of an experiment in vigilance. At the first sign of trouble, a stream of half-pound high-explosive shells should, it was thought, settle any commando group's hash. After Miller parked in his revetment, the crew dismounted the guns and went off to debriefing.

Debriefing was a denouement for a mission, where flying crews talked about what they saw, how many fighters they thought they shot down, the accuracy and density of the flak, the Fortresses that went missing or had gone down. Theoretically, intelligence personnel did the debriefing, but because of the sheer volume of men needing debriefing, ground officers often conducted them, briefed by intelligence on what to look for and what to ask. It was also where the crews got a belt or two of whiskey at government expense. Ostensibly, this was to take the edge off the trial of air combat and to help ease the dehydration caused by having to breathe oxygen through a mask for long periods.

Usually, the debriefing was in three groups: one for gunners (including the navigator), one for bombardiers, and one for the pilot/copilot. They debriefed crews together, so Miller and Berg went to one debrief, Kearns to another, and the gunners and Feynman to another, all at the same time. Miller didn't have anything unusual to report. The gunners claimed two kills on ME-109s, one on the right waist and top turret, one on the belly and tail. Kearns said he unloaded over the target with unknown effects.

The debriefing over, there was the hard labor of cleaning the guns, and for this, Miller insisted everyone take part. Farr, Egan and Otto had two guns each, but with the bombardier, pilot and co-pilot joining in the party, it was one gun apiece. Miller had an idea that it was good for crew building, but also that familiarity with the guns might come in handy one day. Some guns, they noticed, had ice inside them, and though they didn't jam that mission, there were others that might cause trouble. It was an exhausted Miller that dragged into the late night officer's mess for some coffee and whatever else he had the stomach for. The mess was brightly lit, warm and inviting, with preparations being made for a Christmas party for officers and invited guests. Mess #2, the largest officer's mess, would host the major dignitaries from Bartlesby, while Mess #6, the largest mess on the post, would host minor celebrities and those from other posts.

As Miller selected some dry toast, meat of some sort, and green beans, he took his tray to a table. "Bully beef; that's the ticket," exclaimed whipcord-thin Major Seamus Geoghegan when he saw Miller enter the dining room. Geoghegan was an ebullient artilleryman whose history, like many prewar officers, was a matter of some speculation. His New Mexico National Guard unit was in the Philippines when the Japanese attacked, but it was not clear that he had been with them. It was rumored that Geoghegan was with MacArthur on the PT boat, or escaped Corregidor on a raft, and had the power to stop a locomotive. With a deep southwestern drawl and occasionally affecting an Irish lilt, he commanded the two batteries of the 211th Antiaircraft Artillery at Bartlesby with a mixture of panache, humor, and discipline.

"OK, I'll bite," Miller rejoined, trying to be cheerful through his bone-weariness. "Ticket to what?"

"Now, don't you be pedantic, Pilot Miller," Geoghegan replied. He called all flying officers "pilot," whether or not they *were* pilots. "Your ticket to an eternal and blissful life is what I mean, to be sure."

"Ugh," Miller grunted, "an eternal life like today I'd rather not have, don't you know?" Miller, like most of those who ever spoke to Geoghegan in any casual setting, mimicked his Irish affectation. "And my people got off another boat, too. You're about as Irish as Throck, are you not?"

"Well, 'tis true that I'm Boston born and bred, but my grandfather and his bride landed in Boston from Dublin carrying me father. He fought in the war with the south, too, to be sure." Grinning mischievously, Geoghegan chided. "Have you any idea of your people?"

"In fact, I do," Miller said, thinking about it. "My mother's people were Germans, Scots and Welsh. Mom was a Mackenzie; her mother was a Bulow who married an Infyn. My father's people were English and Irish; McDonnell is in there, as I recall. I think the last of them came to America before the Revolution."

"Aye, that's grand; grand," Geoghegan replied. "You could look up some of your....McDonnell, you say? Of the County Cork McDonnell's?"

"No idea," Miller said. "Are there more than one?"

"Oh, aye, there are McDonnells of Kerry and Galway as well. If your people are of Cork, well, we could be cousins! Ain't that something, to be sure?" Geoghegan slipped from Irish to New Mexican and back again within five words. This could hurt a guy, Miller thought. "Well, I'm off."

"Ah, hey," Miller called, suddenly remembering the ice in the machine guns. "I could use some advice on a professional level."

Geoghegan stopped in his tracks and turned around, a wide grin on his face. "If it's something for a doctor, go on sick call. If not, a priest will hear confession anytime. Anything else and I'm your man." He sat with Miller at a small oilcloth-covered folding table. "Only reason anyone wants to talk to me professionally is about something that goes 'bang,' so tell me your bang troubles. But make it quick, mind; I'm on staff duty tonight." Miller explained about the ice that troubled him as he ate, wolfing down his plate in moments, while Geoghegan listened attentively. "How cold, sixty below you say?"

"That's about right," Miller confirmed. "Any ideas on how to prevent it?"

"Sure, oil, and lots of it." Geoghegan said, all Irish lilt gone. "But your gunners must know that. Let's go speak with the Tycoon."

The "Tycoon" was a slanted reference to the post's POL officer, Major Grant Haan, a mousy New Englander whose favorite possession, it was said, was a photograph of him as a child with John P. Rockefeller, but he wasn't that well connected; the older man in the fuzzy black-and-white snapshot taped on the wall was his grandfather, who spudded a well for John P. but had a falling out later. Haan listened to Miller's explanation, and Geoghegan's expansion of the problem. Having heard them both out, Haan got up from his chair, went across the room distractedly, selected two voluminous tomes from a shelf, and returned to his desk. Flipping through the tabs, he settled on one particularly dense page of tables and notes, pursing his lips from time to time. Suddenly he sat bolt upright, reached for the other volume, did a similar search, heaved a heavy sigh and sat back in his chair.

"The problem isn't the oil but water contaminating it," Haan declared softly. "There's nothing in pure petroleum that can freeze above 80 degrees below zero Fahrenheit. But," he declared, reaching for the volume underneath, "here: 'water contamination of lubricants in extreme conditions is the only component that will form crystalline ice.' In your case," he went on, pulling out the other book, "'qualifiers to lubricant crystalline ice formation must be taken into account in aircraft when the lubricated equipment is subject to direct exposure to slipstream velocity air movement.' There; quite clear, you see."

"Um, sure," Miller added, "the guns are out in the open air all the time. No choice, really. But what do we do about it?

"What have you been using for lubricating the guns?" Geoghegan asked. All traces of brogue vanished. "Bulk machine oil?"

"I guess so," Miller replied. "I know the gunners complain they can't get enough of it."

"We test the water content daily of the fuel and the bulk oil," Haan said, "but water content can be as high as 3% in bulk oil, which may be too high for you. Your gunners use canned oil, Geoghegan." Haan scratched his chin thoughtfully. "Even that might have water content. We'll test cases by lot numbers to see if that's any better. Need a lot of cases at a quart per mission per gun."

"More I'm afraid; twice that." Geoghegan asserted. "A quart before the mission and a quart after, done right. They go up wet, and then get cleaned, and then they're stored. After cleaning, you leave it on, but put more on before you fly."

Haan's eyes widened so much that Miller thought they might fall out. "Good heavens! We've nowhere near that allocation! We'll be out of machine oil before the end of January." Haan, a more than adequate bureaucrat, probably knew just how much was being refined. It struck Miller, at that instant, that the safety of his airplane and his crew—and the entire war effort in the air—could hinge on the peacetime-trivial issue of water content in machine oil.

Thereafter, the AAF tested oil everywhere, and improved its storage methods. The gunners started marking their own oil cans that they tested themselves.

Pearl Harbor was the least of America's unpreparedness problems.

December 1942

Minden, Germany

Peace hath her victories
No less renowned than war

John Milton

Light snow fell in the forest as trucks and cars from Oschersleben arrived at the camp gate. The trucks were carrying two dozen chickens, a dozen geese, forty cartons of cigarettes, and three hams. The cars carried pilots from JG191. At Thielmann's suggestion, they were bringing a little Christmas feast to *Oflag* X, where many of JG191's opponent pilots would spend the rest of the war.

The gate swung open for the little convoy and the cars drove to the commandant's office while guards directed the trucks to the kitchen. The pilots got out of the cars and gazed around them at the camp. The guards in the towers and around the enclosure watched with the impassively bored expression of prison guards everywhere, the tower machine guns pointed high over the knots of inmates. Prisoners watched in small groups outside their plank barracks, unsure of what they were seeing or the rumors that they had heard.

"Welcome, gentlemen," the commandant called from the porch of his office. "I hope you have brought enough for all of them." Colonel Dort was a spindly man with an expansive grin and thin tufts of hair who had been a cavalry officer before they transferred him to the *Luftwaffe* at the beginning of the war. A *Luftwaffe* Major, an austere and bluff officer introduced as Major Greim, joined him.

"We have, I believe," Thielmann answered, "if you only have two hundred prisoners."

"Two hundred and twenty now," Dort answered. "We received more last night."

"Colonel Talbott," Greim called in English. "Would you join us, please?" A stocky American colonel marched up to the commandant's porch. "Colonel Talbott is the senior prisoner," the Major said in German. "Captain Thielmann, Colonel Talbott." Thielmann saluted, which Talbott returned smartly, and the two fliers shook hands, the American noncommittally. "The Captain and his comrades have brought you a Christmas feast, Colonel: chicken, goose, ham..."

"*Und Zigaretten*," Thielmann added. Talbott raised an eyebrow slightly. "*Früliches Weinachten*, Herr Colonel." Talbott turned around to face his men, shouting some orders. In a few moments, the prisoners, clad in a variety of American and Royal Air Force uniforms in various states of repair and cleanliness, had formed into a four-block formation, and a tall captain had joined him near the porch.

"Captain," the captain said in excellent *Hochdeutch*, "I am Captain Maurice, Colonel Talbott's translator. May I enquire as to what the meaning of this is?"

"Just a little Christmas feast for our brave and skillful adversaries, Captain," Greim replied, "nothing more." The two Americans conferred in English for a time.

"The Colonel is uncertain if we can accept it. *Our* authorities may see it as a special favor."

"He's right," Greim interrupted. "Under the Geneva Convention..."

"*Please*, Major," Pritzler said, leading Greim away, "this is a matter for fliers, not jailers."

"Captain," Thielmann said quietly. "Do not look on it as German to American and Englishman. Look on it as from one group of aviators to another. It will probably be the best meal they will have for a long time." The captain and the colonel conferred again.

"Very well, Captain," the captain finally said. "Thank you very much." Colonel Talbott extended his hand to Thielmann again, this time smiling and gripping it firmly. "*Früliches Weinachten*, Captain," Talbott said in not- unacceptable German.

"And from all our men, Captain, to all of yours," Maurice added.

***

As the Germans drove away, the Americans waved and yelled things like "*Merry Christmas,*" and "*up your ass, kraut,*" "*happy new year,*" and "*come back when you have less time*," all of which the Germans took as peculiar seasonal Americanisms. The drive back to Oschersleben that night was boisterous, the men having stopped at a *gasthaus* for supper. Even though Talbott invited their former adversaries to join them in the feast, they politely declined, not wanting to detract from their bounty.

"This was a fine idea, Thielmann," Bär told him. "I wonder what the High Command would think."

"The High Command can think what they like," Thielmann said. "We paid for it, we transported it, and Dort is a friend of my uncle's and will say nothing." The last was a lie, but Thielmann didn't care.

"They are just pilots, you know," Bär said, "and we would want them to treat our men as well as we treat them."

"I think they *can* treat ours better," Thielmann guessed. "They have much more of everything than we, and I've heard that the Americans send their prisoners to America, and the British to Canada. At least there we cannot bomb them as they can bomb their own prisoners. I would think that our men in their camps are much better off."

"You are probably right, Thielmann," Bär agreed, then added distantly, "This war will end someday. I just hope that when we are all in American and Russian pens that someone will remember this Christmas and treat us to a feast." It was only the second time that Thielmann had heard a German say that Germany would lose the war, as he, himself, had felt now for a year. He looked at Bär quizzically, who looked away.

"Happy Christmas, Bär."

"Happy Christmas, Thielmann."

***

Thielmann met Elsa in Hamburg just before New Year's. Their small celebration had been quiet, subdued, with nothing of the gala, festive air so common in Hamburg at that time of year. Very late on their last evening together, they sat quietly in a small bistro by the waterfront, in a dark corner made for such occasions. "Do you think of Gunnar often?" Elsa's husband had been missing since August 1940.

"No," Elsa answered, too quickly. "Yes," she whispered a few moments later, not looking at him.

"Perhaps I shouldn't have asked."

She made a face, as she often did, when she thought of her husband. "No, it's all right. I don't think about him so much as I do about what happened to him."

"What do you mean? Do you wonder if he's dead or alive?"

"No, I'm certain he's dead. They have reported no prisoners from his boat, and it's been two years. No, it's what happened to him...before." She was pensive, guarded, more frightened than sad. She often seemed worn out when she spoke of him. "I hardly knew him, really. We met when he was in Hamburg on leave from the Naval Academy. He was an officer cadet, not quite an officer, but no longer just a sailor. He was funny, made mocking jokes about the Nazis, which infuriated my father. He never drank to excess. Not then..."

"In May 1939, he was commissioned a Lieutenant, and was assigned to a U-boat working up at Kiel. That very day, he asked me to marry him. Uncle and Mother approved, and Father could hardly say no, but they all seemed to fear the marriage. Uncle said something the night before the wedding about 'iron coffins,' but I didn't understand. Father said it was about time we had a Navy man in the family." She made her defiant face, as she often did when she spoke of her father. "As if I cared what that strutting bully thought. I remember Gunnar's first patrol just before the war. We were so happy we hardly noticed that the war had started. All we knew was that we were in love, Germany was strong again, and Gunnar was in the *Kriegsmarine*.

"Then he went out on a second patrol, and he came home smelling of bilge and oil, mold and old sweat. He said he'd bathed before, and it was a week before the smell finally came out of him. He seemed tired, and some of the fire had gone out of him. But when we made love, he was still Gunnar." Her voice drifted off, and she seemed lost in a sea of despair.

"Then came the third patrol, and he came home from the Atlantic smelling worse than before. I had to repeat everything; he seemed angry because of that. He said an attack deafened him three days out of Kiel. The Tommy destroyers dropped their water bombs on him as they circled above them for two days. Is that possible, do you know?"

"No, I can't say. I don't know anything about the U-boats except that I don't like them: too confining. Papa may know, or Ulrich..."

"No, it doesn't matter. We didn't make love after his third patrol. We hardly spoke. He transferred to France, closer to the sea lanes, and said that we may not see each other for some time. He said he didn't want to go to sea again, but that he was being promoted to executive officer because he and the Captain were the only two original officers still with the boat.

"I wanted to hold him, I wanted him to hold me, but he kept staring at nothing with that haunted look, drinking, smoking, and brooding. He left early one morning, and he didn't even wake me, and I never saw him again." She was quiet, near tears. "I've told no one all of that. I don't know if I miss him or not. And now...I don't even know if I loved him."

"I'm sorry, Elsa," Thielmann said, meaning it. "I didn't know..."

"Oh, it's all right. I ought to have talked about it long ago. I sometimes think that my time in the mountains wasn't good. I think I should have stayed in Hamburg and worked with the sailors or something. Make me face the kinds of terror Gunnar lived through...."

"I don't think it would have helped. Even if Gunnar told you, you wouldn't understand. You have to live it. I tried to tell Papa what it was like to fly into an American herd a few weeks ago, but the words failed me. You fly straight at a machine, he shoots at you, you shoot at him, he dives down, you fly over him, and the tracers—the only bullets you can see—fly after you. The air is full of falling and flying debris from the fat cars, from the flak, from other fighters, men escaping dying machines, crates breaking up, shell casings, bombs, bits of people—I got a tooth lodged in my oil cooler once—and all sorts of things I'm never sure of. But you fly through all that, you turn around, some Indians run after you, you evade them, it's cold and noisy. If you have to escape a bad situation with some maneuver that you invent in an instant and that the airplane designer could not possibly imagine, you may pull four positive gravities one moment and two negative gravities the next, your stomach ties in knots, you fart to excess and sometimes liquid comes out, the sun always is in the wrong place, the radio is full of shouting and crackling, the vibration from the guns digs your back into the parachute harness, you wonder what happened to everyone else moments after the first contact, someone is shouting frightening things that make little sense, you charge the herd again and do it all over." He watched out the window, snow gently falling, so peaceful. "I don't think you'd understand the fighting. I don't." They were quiet for some moments.

"Do you think of...." Elsa caught herself before going further.

"The killing? No," Thielmann said with finality, "But I think about the dying; about the wingmen that don't last, and the comrades that simply don't return. But, too, I think about what the bombers are doing, dropping bombs on my friends, my neighbors, and my family. I think about it and I get angry, but one cannot fly angry. One must fly... collected, certain, and calm. But just a few weeks ago, we took some food to some prisoners, pilots and crews just like us. Met their senior officers, briefly...they seemed like fine fellows. I can hate what they do, not them." He was quiet again, sipping at his wine.

"Otto, I'm going to join the Red Cross," Elsa said in the dark stillness. Thielmann, his mind benumbed by drink and weariness, could only remember the ragamuffin Red Cross workers in Cologne handing out cups of water to the survivors of the attack. "They do good work," he said.

"You're not angry?"

"No. Should I be?" Did he have a right to be angry? They hadn't spoken of a future, certainly not as a couple. He'd spent less time with her than he had with most of his wingmen.

"It means a great deal of risk..."

"Being a German in 1943 is a great deal of risk already," he said, reaching for her hand across the table. "You may as well try to get some good out of it."

February 1943

Bartlesby, England

To persevere in one's duty and
Be silent is the best answer to calumny

George Washington

T he bugle blew its annoying, tinny jingle as the wags mockingly recited: "*There's a soldier in the grass, with a bullet up his ass, don't be alarmed, it's only in his arm...*" Assembly: time for the briefing, three and three-quarter hours late.

The cavernous briefing room gradually filled up with pilots, co-pilots, bombardiers and navigators, greeting each other in the easy camaraderie of nervous tension. No one knew what the mission was until the briefing actually started. The group adjutant, a grandfatherly type named Pearlman, entered from the back of the room, heading for the dais. The murmuring and joking was done. This was business. The ground exec, a super-attenuated jerk named Davis, entered just after the adjutant, and shouted "*Atten-SHUN.*" As one man, the officers stood up as Throck walked in.

"Seats, gentlemen," Throck called out, and as one, they sat again. "Today, our target is the Peugeot torpedo works at Brest." He glanced briefly at the wall-sized map that lay behind the drawn curtain. "The fighter cover over French targets has been relatively light of late, but our escort will rendezvous ten minutes before the target IP. However," he emphasized loudly, "the flak over French targets has become increasingly dangerous. Be advised that whole formations of Fortresses can be shattered by these new 'flak fields' that the Germans have been putting together. For that reason," again, inflecting louder, "bombing altitude will be 36,000 feet." A collective groan emanated from the

135

briefing room—that was almost service ceiling for a loaded B-17, and accuracy was impossible. Routine station times, engine start, and all the rest followed. Navigators and bombardiers stayed behind for their navigation and target identification briefings as the rest of the men shuffled out.

Even though it was just a milk run to Brest, one by one the men passed the issue window of the personal equipment room, to pick up their flying suits, boots, helmets, body armor, parachutes, flight rations, oxygen masks, survival kits, aid packets, and Mae Wests , stuffing it all into shapeless kit bags. Some dressed in the locker room next door, but because of the weather (it was still marginal) many anticipated being scrubbed. To minimize the buildup of sweat inside the flight suits, most wouldn't suit up until the station time flare. They put their personal effects into ammo boxes marked with their service numbers, stacking these at the back of the locker room, keeping only their dog tags and their ID cards. Husbands kissed pictures of wives holding newborn children before putting them in. After every strike, they handed the ammo boxes of those that did not return over to the adjutant, so he could decide what to do with its contents. Much would be sent to the next-of-kin, but some (especially embarrassing pictures of girlfriends) would be destroyed.

Officers drew their side arms; radiomen drew their rice paper code sheets sandwiched in celluloid and clamped in metal frames; bombardiers got their target ID photos, aiming points marked with wax crayons; navigators got their three route maps, with flak centers marked with red blotches, and escape routes with white streaks.

In the wide corridor outside the locker room, Father Smith and his three assistants started and finished a Mass about every fifteen minutes (they left out the homily), giving Communion continuously while hearing confessions two at a time on the fly, passing out the same penance to all: a shilling or two bits in the poor box and as many Hail Marys' as the penitent could fit in while over enemy territory. Chaplains Renfrew and Sedelmeyer gave communion to any that wanted it just down the way. Sergeant/Elder Mills recited prayers of deliverance with the 610th's sizable Mormon congregation (many members of the 610th had been in the Utah National Guard), while Lieutenant/Rabbi Greene sang Psalms with the handful of Jews within earshot of the Mormons. Some of the four hundred-odd airmen drawing gear stopped by all four. None were turned away.

As Miller and Berg were leaving the equipment room heading for the flight line train (more a cab stand than a train), their squadron commander, Lieutenant Colonel Ernie King, pulled them aside. "Come with me," King dully intoned. King always seemed to Miller like a morose soul with a voice like Boris Karloff. They followed King behind the building and down a long alley between structures to a vehicle parking lot secluded from most of the rest of the field. As they rounded the corner of one such structure, they beheld a somewhat bizarre assemblage of people: men and women in uniform and out, with two photographers, a movie camera crew, and a brace of generals. Throck was in the middle of all of it, between Princess Alexandra and Grace Henley.

"Captain Miller," an austere and urbane RAF officer in an immaculate uniform smoothly announced, "I believe you have met her Highness Princess Alexandra. This fellow here," he said, nodding at a young man with soft features in an RAF flight uniform, "is her cousin..."

"Nephew," Alexandra corrected, stepping forward with an extended hand. "I'm so pleased to meet you again, Captain." As they politely shook hands, she gave a slight wink that only Miller could see. "Permit me to introduce you to his Royal Highness, Prince Jean of Montefalcon." Miller introduced Berg to Alexandra, who seemed genuinely eager to make their acquaintance. The movie cameras noisily rolled on, and the occasional shutter snapped. With them was Carolyn Smalls, the Princess's ostensible secretary, who glad-handed both Miller and Berg as the cameras followed.

"Captain Miller, his Highness would like to ride along with you on today's mission," the general went on. "It's an important gesture to the occupied people of Montefalcon that they see their royal family is fighting for them, too." Throck tightened his jaw, rolling his eyes slightly, as the other officer spoke.

"Um, yessir," Miller answered in his best military response. Thinking quickly, he began by saying, "the best place for passengers is..."

"His Highness will be your co-pilot, Miller." Throck choked; Miller gaped; Smith coughed. "He has had extensive training in the Fortress I." Miller stared blankly at the general, then at the Prince. It seemed like he was too young to be doing this; he looked even younger than his... aunt? Miller evinced confusion, glancing back and forth between the Prince, the Princess, the unknown general and Throck.

"The...*what*, sir?"

"The Fortress I is the British version of the B-17," Throck answered. "Much the same aircraft, but doesn't carry the waist guns or the radio gun, and there's a few other differences that won't matter. The Montefalcon Air Force has operated three of them since 1941. His Highness has about a hundred hours..."

"Nearly two hundred, General," the Prince said, speaking for the first time while extending his hand to Miller. "I am a Pilot Officer in my Air Force." He grinned as if entertained by a small joke. "Our Air Force has fewer people in it than your unit does, but we had to call it something." Miller laughed as he shook the Prince's hand, which had a surprisingly powerful grip.

Miller had done a little reading on the kingdom of Montefalcon. Snuggled between the corners of France, Luxembourg and Germany, the entire country was no bigger than most American counties, but it had more people in it than Wisconsin. The Germans overran the place in a day in 1940, when both the government and the royal family fled, and its small army fought its way across France while being decimated. Best known for wine and a peculiar aromatic cedar, Montefalcon's royal family and government-in-exile was one of many "guests" of the British, wholly dependent on the largesse of the UK (where the Princess spent much of her time raising funds among the expatriate community) and the US (who was arming two battalions of Montefalcon infantry to be deployed in the Mediterranean, and a squadron of fighters).

Introductions over, the camera crews packed up and moved their gear. A truck was summoned, but Throck insisted—demanded—that Miller, Berg and the Prince make their way to the ship in the usual manner: on the train. Grudgingly, Throck allowed a photographer with a 35mm camera to accompany them on condition that he ask no questions of the pilots about their mission *and* get permission for every shot. The field itself was classified; the MPs could legally shoot loose cameramen.

The three chatted about flying as they trudged. The Prince shouldered his gear bag with a casual precision that seemed odd to Miller, but he didn't give it much thought at the time. Their photographer ran ahead and captured the trio in between the buildings—a casual action shot with full flying kits over their shoulders—in a photo that made the front page of clandestine SOE-delivered papers all over occupied Europe. Berg, who wanted the mission hours as badly as Miller did so he could go home, offered to fly in the jump seat with the radio, where Miller had thought to put the Prince. "Oh, please, lieutenant; please no. I will get in for the cameras, but as soon as we are away, you and I can change." Prince Jean seemed adamant. "I flew last night and I am quite weary. I shouldn't even be out here, but duty calls."

"Last night? You bomb with the RAF?" Berg seemed incredulous that a B-17 could even fly at night.

"No," the boy grinned slightly, as if at another private joke. "You see, General Throck misled you, or rather, we him. Our Fortresses carry no guns at all, and no armor; only cameras. We fly as far as the Polish frontier some nights, even Austria, mapping occupied Europe. I landed, in fact, just before dawn; perhaps four hours ago, at Vincent St. Niles. But this...event...was more important than my rest, you see."

"I thought I'd seen 'Forts flying around here with funny markings...'" Berg said, as if suddenly seeing the light. "Or..."

"No markings at all," Miller said, finishing. "We saw one just a couple days ago, headed east as the sun went down. That was you?"

"Um, no," Prince Jean said, thoughtfully working his oval face into a frown. "Until last night, I was flying out of Kent. I came up here for this...mission. My squadron mates often fly out of East Anglia. We fly out of whatever field we need to get close to our targets."

The trio threw their gear in the back of an idling weapons carrier, hoisted up the cameraman, and bumped and jumped on cranky springs out to *Crop Duster*. During the short journey, Miller and Berg learned young Jean had been flying since he was fourteen, and had logged nearly a thousand hours in the air.

On the flight line, the camera crew, guests and other hangers-on gathered on the hardstand, stunning Miller's men with all the attention. Farr, nonplussed as ever, greeted Princess Alex as he might an old girlfriend during an unexpected meeting while his wife watched. The Princess shook hands with the rest of the crew while Grace narrated briefly (her astonishing memory recalled each crewman's hometown, except for mangling "Bad Axe" into "Bad Apple") as Miller, Berg and Farr pre-flighted *Crop Duster*.

While Throck and King pointed out exactly where the photographers could point their cameras, Miller pulled Grace aside, saying, "she's his... aunt?"

"Complicated, but yes," Grace explained. "His grandfather—King Francis I—married Olivia (Alex's mother) when Alex and Jean were very young, making them technically step-aunt and nephew, though they're less than a year...*yes*, I believe that's right...apart in age. They were practically raised together. Anyway, the heir-apparent, Francis II (the prince from the king's *first* marriage) enjoyed a love match with some minor duchess that no one approved of, but because he was already the heir, they didn't *have* to. No child from Francis I's second marriage can inherit the throne without a *great* to-do, but no one expected the prince *and* his consort *and* their two elder sons to be killed in the first few moments of *this* bloody war. Jean—Francis I's *third* son—is now the declared heir to Francis I's throne because a bunch of escaped ministers and some Montefalcon nobles met in the Commons during the Blitz and *said* it *shall* be *thus*. Olivia is still the Grand Duchess of Montefalcon; she's in London with Alex's two young brothers (and God *knows* what *they* are to be when their little parliament gets around to deciding). King Francis is stuck in Switzerland (he started to escape with Olivia and his family but his car was attacked and he was diverted), technically without a country but with a throne that the Swiss are ambivalent about. The Germans officially erased the kingdom months ago, but all the crowned heads of Europe proclaimed their support for the Mountbatten throne—mostly from London—and there's *thousands* of Montefalcons the world around wanting to fight." She shrugged, making it clear that she knew an American could not *possibly* understand the royal politics of Europe. "Think of Monaco and you may understand."

"Not likely," Miller grunted. "Hey, we've got station time pretty soon. You guys with the cameras and all that need to..."

"Relax, Captain," Throck told him. "Nobody's going anywhere until they get enough pictures to satisfy everyone." Throck joined Miller near the nose of the plane (which had been covered with a tarp to guard Miss Duster's reputation, and the 299th Group's security) while the cameras shot frame after frame of the Prince inspecting the airplane, his Highness getting in the tail door, Prince Jean pulling the engine through with the rest of the crew, and just for good measure, Princess Alex and friends helping to load machine gun ammunition into the plane. Miller vaguely wondered if the lookie-loos knew that Jean knew what he was doing. "Small world, ain't it?" Throck was standing next to Miller and facing away from the airplane, making him barely audible. "You fly his aunt over here, and then he shows up here..."

"You think I had something to do with them coming here, sir? I don't even know..."

140

"No, but *Grace* does." Throck shook his head slightly. "No, it wasn't your *doing* as much as it was your *being*." Grinning broadly, he whispered. "She *asked* for your ship. Yeah; she really did. General Frost, the guy giving the orders on this little dog-and-pony show, said I was to give my full cooperation because she specifically asked for your airplane. I heard about it at three this morning; had to shift the mission profile to Brest, which was why the briefing was late. We were supposed to go to Bremen..."

"While we're being frank, sir," Miller whispered, "the general knows Prince Jean put in a full night last night. Said he doesn't..."

"Yeah, I know. But apparently the timing isn't up to us or to him. God knows *where* it's from. Listen," he said, turning his craggy face to Miller, "it would be a PR disaster if the Prince were to be hurt, or be captured. *Missing* would be better than captured. But whatever you do, he's just one man. The mission comes first. Just don't...." Throck was interrupted by Philukuzki, who muttered something Miller couldn't understand. They are both Polish... Huh, he wondered, what could...?

"Ah, we need to wrap this up," Throck announced. "The weather may change rapidly, so we need to get this mission off. Please, ladies, my car. Cameramen, please load up your truck. General Frost, sir, I must join my crew for the strike." How would Casey know anything about...?

As they strapped in and the last truck left the tarmac, the Prince confided in Miller. "I had asked your general if we could hurry that Punch-and- Judy show so that I could get some sleep: to that effect I bearded your Sergeant Casey to assist me—and a little Polish exercise I haven't had for a bit. I *hope* you don't mind? In fact, I'd rather your lieutenant start..."

"Sorry, sir, but that's a bit late. The catwalk's a dangerous place at the best of times, but before takeoff with a full load it's..."

"Yes, I know. Sorry I mentioned it. Please, while I am under your orders, just call me Pilot Officer."

"'Sir' faster," Miller said back. "But let's get this part of the show started. There's the flare. Stand by to start number one. CLEAR ONE," Miller shouted out the window.

"Starting one," the Prince answered without hesitation, starting the engines flawlessly.

***

The takeoff, the mission, the flying were like a training run. As *Crop Duster* climbed into the group formation, the Prince and Berg swapped places, but swapped back just before the 299th reached the target. The only thing that seemed new to Prince Jean was formation flying, which he thought was terribly dangerous. They saw a few German fighters at long range, calling back to the ground as to altitude and speed, since at that height the German's height finders were inaccurate. The escort—Spitfires this time—showed up and scared the watchers away. A few clouds of flak—dispersed and low—rose to meet them, but they hit no one. The 299th returned to Bartlesby with no casualties, empty bomb bays, and likely no hits on any vital targets. Smith and his fellow bombardiers complained they could barely see the ground, let alone identify the target through the light haze from five miles up. But Throck had ordered the bombs dropped and dropped they were.

Miller and his crew went to debriefing with Pilot Officer Prince (as he called himself), but no one had anything significant to report. They turned the gear in, cleaned the guns (the only part of the day where Prince Jean was clearly out of his depth), and the men dismissed for the day. The cameras and gawkers, Miller took note, were absent. "Care for a repast at the mess hall, your High—" Berg began, expecting him to decline.

"Certainly," the Prince answered before he finished, "I'm ravenous." Surprised, the two Americans led the Prince to Mess #4, also called "Alice's Grotto" for reasons known only to the mess manager, who wasn't talking. It was a small facility that was only sized for perhaps two hundred diners, comprising two smaller Quonset huts end to end and buried in sandbags, but was thought to be the most consistently bland on the post. The menu that day—pork roll, mashed potatoes, creamed corn and apple crumble—was the same at Alice's as it was at every Army mess on that day, worldwide...as it was the last time it was served, and would be the next time. But for men that faced new dangers every day, it was a comfort.

If the fare displeased his Highness, he didn't mention it to Miller or Berg. Instead, he ate the lot in the peculiar (to Americans) manner with the inverted fork common to Europeans. Conversation centered on flying B-17s, hometowns, lightly on family (it mildly surprised Miller to learn that his co-pilot had been married just before Pearl Harbor, but she divorced him when he left for flight school), and lightly on sports. Miller made a feint at being a Milwaukee Brewers fan (which he really wasn't), and Berg announced he was a fan of the Chicago Cubs mostly because his father had been, but he was a bigger fan of skiing. "Don't follow sport much," the Prince said, "but my father was a tremendous devotee of football—what you call soccer, I think."

"I played some in high school, but it wasn't an organized game like our football is," Miller admitted. "It seems to me to be a game that girls can play as well as boys in gym class in very small high schools. I thought polo was the sport of kings."

"Well, yes," the Prince replied, "but not in the house of Mountbatten. Bad luck, you see. Great-great grandpapa was in wine one morning and started a game with some guardsmen. Old fool fell off and got his head in front of a mallet in full swing. Dead, of course, but his noggin scored a point." Miller and Berg chuckled as the Prince deadpanned; "great-great grandmamma banned the game in Montefalcon on the spot, but later married the guardsman." The Americans gripped their ribs, not so much at the joke, but the way he delivered it. Not a muscle in the Prince's face moved.

While they were recovering, the Prince droned on. "Girls play football in America, you say? Before I went to university—Oxford, then Eton, then Sandhurst—my only classmate was my Aunt Alex. Perhaps Alex was born on the wrong continent: she would have loved to play any game like that. We had tutors, you know. Taught me all I need to know to rule Montefalcon, which is decidedly not much except how to negotiate treaties with neighbors that have more policemen than we have people."

"So, where did the reporters go?" Berg asked. "Thought sure they'd want to be here when we landed."

"They certainly did," the Prince interrupted again, "but this is my night off. I get twenty-four hours every fortnight to do what I like, and gentlemen, I like to drink beer in pubs with people who don't want something from me. I want..."

At that moment, Ben Grant, the captain commanding the truck company, stood next to the table. "Mind if I join you, gentlemen? I just got a cup of coffee and would like some new company. Ben Grant, your Highness," he went on, offering his callused hand before he said something distinctly French.

The Prince shook the black captain's hand firmly, answering in French. Though Miller was slightly surprised at Grant's knowledge of who Pilot Officer Prince was, he wasn't shocked. Nearly everyone on the post knew that he was some sort of celebrity because of the photo shoot before the mission, but because they had jobs to do, they saved their gawking for their free time. Grant, Miller guessed, was off duty, but...the French? "I was just congratulating his Highness on his flying service and on his survival," Grant explained. "It gave me a chance to exercise my father's French."

"Indeed, thank you," the Prince answered. "It was excellent, most excellent. From around Paris, was he?"

"Frankly, I'm not sure. My father married my mother after the last war. By the time I went to college, I had learned all the French he could muster. Mother spoke it, too." Grant scanned Miller's and Berg's faces. "You gentlemen care to be my guests at the Bomb Dump?" Though there was no official segregation at the clubs on the post, the Bomb Dump was one of the few that welcomed Grant and his fellow black officers. The others made small provisions, but most only because the regulations required it.

No one had any objections. The evening, for a worn out young pilot, was extraordinarily long. The juke box was playing a mix of American and British music that many of the patrons joined in on. His Highness, it seemed, was a great fan of American Swing. Dancing, however, was not his best subject, though try he did. Lieutenant Jeanie Medina, first shift ward nurse and a part-time stage hoofer, had great fun leading him around like a dog on his hind legs. Miller and Berg tried to keep up with the Prince, but his capacity for liquor was breathtaking.

As the party seemed to wind down, Philip Piesec, the 190th's resident clown, burst into the room with a box of cigars and a double sawbuck. "We did it," he exclaimed. "Lisa's gonna have a baby in August!" Though few knew Piesec well (he was a replacement that had just joined) all were more than happy to take part in the bounty of cigars and drinks.

"Premature, isn't it?" the Prince asked Miller. "Isn't it celebrated after the child is born?"

"Around here, we celebrate a good rain shower," Miller replied. "Any excuse to break the monotony." He pointed to the space above the bar where some paper hearts were hanging. "There's probably one eligible woman for every hundred guys within an hour's drive of here, but we had a Valentine's Day bash, nonetheless. All the gals we could find, all the nurses and doughnut dollies, we pulled into the clubs, and still we wore them out with our sheer numbers and energy." Miller waved his arm around. "Almost none of these guys were out of high school before Hitler came to power, and most of them were likely in grade school; I was. Grant over there, he's probably the oldest here and I think he just turned thirty. Piesec celebrating the conception of a child—hell, just the thought of a new baby—is enough for most of us to pull a cork and dance the night away, even if we're tone deaf. Just being alive is enough for most of us." The Prince seemed to accept this, and bought a round for the house, which caused the house to buy a round for the alliance, which triggered *another* round because it was February, and then there were more.

Miller and Berg poured His Highness into a bunk in the guest hut somewhere around three in the morning.

February 1943

Bremen, Germany

For he who has not folded in his arms
A skeleton, nor fed on graveyard charms
Recks not of furbelow, or paint, or scent
When Horror comes the way that Beauty went

Charles Baudelaire

T here it sat, gleaming wetly in the morning sun, its stubby nose pointed defiantly into the air, elliptical wings swept slightly back as if they were preparing for the tremendous speeds and stresses yet to come. The armament crew was loading the guns when Thielmann approached, Gunther happily bounding along. "Good day today, Captain," Steger said. "I got up before the chickens this morning, and that always means a good day."

"You are a superstitious farmer, Steger," Thielmann said as he ran his hand along the leading edge of a wing. "There is no room for such nonsense in the New Germany. No, say rather that you woke up thinking of the *Führer*, and that means a good day."

Steger smiled slightly at Thielmann's small joke, his cool gray eyes sparkling under a heavy brow, knowing Steger thought the same of the "new Germany" as he did. "*Jawohl, Mein Herr*," he grinned, "I'm so sorry I didn't think of that before. I shall never make that mistake again."

Thielmann walked around his plane, looking for undetected flaws or unrepaired damage. He had no illusions about the airworthiness of his crate. Thielmann's tactics helped him get close enough to make good strikes, preferably in the wing roots or the flight deck. He rubbed his hand across a long patch on the tail section. "Steger, a little more wax here." The crew chief dutifully took the wax out of his box and applied

147

it. Wax helped the airflow across the surfaces and helped cut down drag. Thielmann needed every kilometer of airspeed he could get.

Rocking the plane slightly, Thielmann checked the structure for warping or unwanted bending. Finding none, he climbed up the wing to the cockpit, checking the instruments, the compass, the magneto, the smooth motion of the controls, the action of the throttle, the winding of the inertial starter.

Tentatively, he pushed the trigger on his unarmed guns. Hearing a satisfying click, he released the trigger and gently threw the arming switch. After a similar click, he set the arming switch back off and climbed out. Good for another day, he thought, one more day... "Today, Steger. Today we find out if the new methods work."

"I am certain of success, Captain." It would not be long in coming, Thielmann thought darkly. If it does work, we will kill Americans by the hundreds.

Three hours later, Thielmann and JG191 were vectored towards the American bomber stream; some two hundred machines headed, they thought, for Bremen. The Focke-Wulfs sat at high station, basking in the cold sun; below them beneath the cloud deck, the Messerschmitts that would engage the fighter escorts. Behind them, the stream of Dorniers equipped with heavy rockets. Soon, Thielmann thought; soon.

Bär saw the Indians first, a small group of Lightnings just below them and some twenty kilometers away. As Bär led the attack from his side and Pritzler followed, the Messerschmitts rose to meet more Indians. Thielmann and Taube's swarms held back, for they too carried rockets; smaller than the eight centimeter monsters the Dorniers carried, but still big enough to make maneuvering sluggish.

Thielmann watched the brief battle with the lead escorts with as much detachment as he could muster. Here a Lightning had a wing shear off; there, a Messerschmitt belched smoke and flame, spiraling away; another Lightning cut in half, and another caught fire. But just ahead were the *Viermots*, set into position as planned, just off to one side of the attacking formations. "Siegfried group," a controller called; "execute attack." The first four Dorniers suddenly lurched forward, closing the range on the lead machines of the first herd—*Festungen* this time. At a distance that Thielmann thought was far too great, they launched their rockets, eight in all. As if in a painting, the missiles flamed and smoked across the cold sky into the lead formations, followed a few moments later by eight great clouds of flame and smoke as the lead six bombers crumpled and fell. *"Horrido!"* came from a score of throats as Thielmann and his FWs plunged into the broken herd. Their mutual protection broken, Thielmann himself scored two victories in one pass—one with rockets and another with his guns. His *Katchmarek*, a well-meaning youngster with good instincts named Hanno, flamed another with his rockets. Altogether, Thielmann's swarm downed ten *Viermots* between them: twelve fighters destroyed an entire bombing group. Four more Dorniers blew down another five bombers a few minutes later, and Taube's swarm destroyed all but one of the herd's survivors in a few minutes.

Turn around and go home now, American, Thielmann thought. We can beat you now. Turn back...

But on they came; day after day, and week after week.

***

The small hospital near Warsaw was clean but noisy. For Stalingrad survivors, the real treat was to be away from the chaos of that cauldron. For Senior Sergeant Georg-Hans Thielmann, his reward for winning his Knight's Cross First Class was ten days' "leave" from Stalingrad, treatment for his infected stump where his right arm had been, and some rehabilitation. They flew him out two days after Christmas, but his "leave" was, of course, a fig leaf for his evacuation. With a Knight's Cross, he could never completely leave the Army, he was told, but they may place him on "administrative duties" at home. Time would tell.

The urbane Gestapo man glided through the hospital, looking neither to the left or the right, following an elderly orderly whose starched apron stank of both decaying flesh and bleach. The Gestapo man's pass, signed by the head of the RSHA himself, had confused the hospital administration. "Captain," the hospital director wondered, "this facility is closed to the public, to everyone. How did you even know it was here?" They hid the survivors of the Stalingrad disaster from public view; the public was not even told about any evacuees, let alone whether their loved ones were even still alive.

"Colonel," Anton Zimmer purred, "I need not explain to you how I know what I know. Suffice it to say that I do, and I demand access to *Unteroffizier* Georg-Hans Thielmann. Immediately," he insisted, his small eyes growing wide, "or I may be forced to investigate the National Socialist sensibilities of your inmates and staff. Now, Colonel, inmate Thielmann: where is he?"

The director assigned an orderly to take Zimmer to Thielmann's room that he shared with a blinded SS lieutenant. Zimmer took in the scene from the doorway instantly: two beds, two chairs, and a small table against the wall by the window. The lieutenant was in a chair by the window; Zimmer's prey was reading a newspaper to him. Zimmer dismissed the orderly with a glare; Thielmann noticed Zimmer in the doorway but made no acknowledgement. "*Unteroffizier* Thielmann," Zimmer seethed, "do you not acknowledge superior officers? Stand to attention!" Thielmann, still slightly groggy from morphine given from his last debridement, glance up at him casually. Georg-Hans recognized Zimmer instantly as the village would-be-rake who had once tried to assault a girlfriend who badly scratched the failed Lothario. Georg-Hans broke Zimmer's jaw two years before Rickmann broke his arm.

"Better do it," the lieutenant muttered. "Asshole might have some juice. He needs it to get in here." Thielmann showily and slowly set the paper aside, rose to his feet, clicked his slippered heels and rolled his shoulders back one at a time. Zimmer slowly and noisily strode into the room, making a great ceremony out of ignoring Thielmann. He stopped next to the lieutenant, suddenly shifting his gaze to Thielmann's craggy face while slashing a riding crop down in front of the lieutenant, who jumped up startled and knocked over his chair.

"Stand to attention, you slime! You lacked the courage and spirit of National Socialism to die for the Führer, and you call me filthy names! Swine!" Zimmer shouted, whipping the crop across the terrified officer's face. "I'll have you in a camp before dark! Insubordinate dog," he screamed and whipped again, but this time Thielmann's hand caught the crop before it could swing.

"Enough, Zimmer," Thielmann grunted, pulling the crop away from him with surprising ease. "You have proved that you can beat frightened blind men because they are alive." Thielmann tossed the crop out the door; the small group of staff and patient onlookers scattered back. "Now state your business and get out."

Zimmer stared at Thielmann with unbridled contempt. Years of insults and torments flashed through his mind, each raising a new welt in his soul. "You foolish, foolish turd," Zimmer whispered. "For that I'll..."

"You'll nothing, Captain," an authoritative voice thundered from the doorway. "State your business and get out." Reaching for his pistol, Zimmer turned swiftly towards the door where before him glowered an SS colonel with one eye and a hand missing. Swiftly assessing his situation once again, Zimmer transformed at once.

"I am so sorry, lieutenant; I didn't realize your impediment. Unteroffizier Thielmann, I was merely enquiring as to your health, of course," turning towards the colonel; "we are neighbors, you see."

Turning back, he continued; "I became enraged because of the lack of courtesy. You see, I am a very...orderly man. I demand punctilious courtesy from my men, and I deliver it to all my superiors and, of course, subordinates. I recently saw your nephew Otto, Thielmann; he seemed well, sends his regards. A most remarkable recovery you have made. I wish you good luck in the future. I am so very sorry again, lieutenant. My sincerest apologies." As Zimmer strode nonchalantly out of the room, an orderly who had retrieved his riding crop offered it to him, which Zimmer snatched away without even a flicker of recognition. He nodded perfunctorily to the colonel and glided back to the administration office, where he demanded to see Thielmann's records, and those of the lieutenant and the colonel. He carefully examined each page as he stood at the front counter, and then stuffed the lot under his arm. As he left, he glared at the staff, daring them to demand the records back, making it quite clear that he was bulletproof.

**

"There is not much to go on, *Mein Herr*," the SD colonel offered. "Other than they are all from Marburg, there is really no connection." The colonel sat attentively in the overstuffed chair, his watery whiskey warm in the glass. "I know there should be something, but other than youthful altercations, nothing."

"Huh," the general grunted. "Then why would you, if you were a former HJ leader beat up by another man many years ago, spend so much of your time looking up your..." Suddenly he saw it. "That's it, Colonel. That's the connection." The colonel smiled carefully; glad his chief finally saw what he had known for nearly a decade. He had worked hard to elevate himself in the ranks of the SD, just as the general had struggled to rise in the police. "So," the general said with triumph. "So now we know. And now we must think of what we must do...if it comes to having to do anything. Is there anything in the Thielmann family record that might be...?"

"Dangerous? No, there's nothing in particular to show that. The pilot is a hothead with a soft spot for other flyers (nothing new there) but an ace at destroying bombers; his brother is a weatherman in the *Kriegsmarine*; his father works for military intelligence; the uncle is an unremarkable crippled veteran. There doesn't seem to be anything that could get them in trouble unless one of them slips a tongue and says something stupid; but anyone could do that."

"The list grows, eh, my friend? What was once playful is now treasonous, yes? But our friend Zimmer...what to do about him when—or if—the time comes? But that's enough for tonight. My wife has dinner ready."

March 1943

Hamm, Germany

*Duty is weightier than a mountain, whereas
Death is lighter than a feather*

Emperor Meiji of Japan

The flak was worse than *Crop Duster* had flown in seven previous missions. Still twenty minutes from the primary—an aircraft engine factory—and already the pounding had taken out four ships from the 299th, two from the 190th. Suddenly the world in front of *Crop Duster* exploded in an angry cloud as fragments, like hornets, screamed into her nose. Shattering glass blinded Miller and Berg for a moment as even bigger shards tore through the forward portion of the aircraft.

"Pilot to crew, we're hit in front," Miller called with as much self-control as he could muster. "Report nose to tail."

"Bombardier to pilot: I'm hit *bad* in the leg; can't move." There was silence where the navigator's report should have been.

"Top gun to pilot: I got a fragment in my hip, I think. Not too bad."

"Radio to pilot: Everything's OK here."

"Belly gun to pilot: lost the reflector sight."

"Left waist to pilot: I'm OK."

"Right waist to pilot: OK here."

"Tail gun to pilot: OK here."

"Copilot to pilot: I'm all right. Instruments are pretty bad. Engine controls appear to be functioning. Four turning."

"Pilot to top gun: get forward and give me an assessment." All Miller could see through the shattered windshield was a mass of tangled metal where the ship's nose had been, and he could feel the controls responding sluggishly.

In a few moments, Farr was up on the flight deck. "Smitty's dead. Kearns is dying; big gash in his thigh. Won't make it back, and pitching him out won't help. Bombsight's gone, and so's everything else in the nose."

"OK," Miller said grimly, sadly. "We'll keep up with the formation and I'll jettison when the lead drops. Get Kearns up here so the co-pilot can take care of him." A few moments later, the bombardier was sprawled behind the flight deck, blood gushing out of his leg and many smaller wounds. Miller held on through the flak concentration and pulled his emergency bomb release when the lead ship dropped a few minutes later, calculating an escape route in his head in case he had to leave the formation, hoping to find other cripples on the way back.

Suddenly there was a whoosh behind him and Feynman started yelling "FIRE! FIRE IN THE RADIO ROOM! FIRE!" as the draft roared through the bomb bay and blew open the flight deck's rear hatch, banging Kearns on the head. Miller quickly glanced back and saw there were still bombs hanging in the racks with the doors limply hanging open. Ugly, black, malevolent, volatile incendiary bombs, stuck in frozen shackles. Feynman sprayed the blaze around his command transmitter and the dynamotor with the extinguisher. Flames lanced into the bomb bay along the roof, flashing and melting wire insulation. The frigid blast pushed ahead of the heat like a physical force on Miller's face. Farr feverishly shut down the fuel transfer lines through the bomb bay and the wing root. "No good, skipper," he yelled at Miller. "The bombs will cook off any second. Get 'em outta here!"

Just as he said that, and just as Miller reached for the bail-out bell, Payne surged through the radio compartment and onto the bomb bay catwalk, wrapping a blanket around the remaining bombs just as the bomb shackles opened and released their load...taking Payne with them as they tumbled into space. Roll into a ball, the RAF had told them; it makes you fall faster so you can open your parachute at a lower height, and you'll bounce off other airplanes....

Moments later, the three incendiary clusters blossomed one by one. Farr and Feynman, watching silently through the open bomb bay, waited for the opening of Payne's 'chute. They didn't see it. After a few more harrowing, wrenching moments the fire was out, Farr hauled the bomb bay doors shut, and the hatches were closed up again. Mitch Berg held Ernie Kearns until well after he was dead, while Feynman and Block manned the waists against fighter attacks.

Farr's wound took him off flight status until the end of the month. He had Casey remove Payne's parachute from its stowed position in the waist and got it back into stores quietly. Thereafter, he insisted the crewmen wear their 'chutes at all times. They awarded the 299th a citation. They bombed the Ruhr for the first time.

Chuck Payne, New Hampshire boat builder, was posthumously awarded the Distinguished Flying Cross. Two of *Crop Duster's* crewmen died in a random act of war they could never have seen coming; a third in an act of heroism that saved six others. Miller remembered Smitty's clumsy attempts to land *Crop Duster* back in Kansas, and Kearns's cool aplomb during his first in-flight emergency. It took a while, but Miller got over the feeling that he was responsible for them getting killed. He wondered if Payne had any thoughts at all when he wrapped that blanket around the bombs. He hoped he would never have to wonder about it again.

Crop Duster became a hanger queen. Her nose and midsection were too weak for safety.

***

It was a quiet, miserable-weather day. Miller was at the airplane depot outside London to get a new ship, and Throck was looking into the spare parts backlog. They bumped Throck up to permanent group command with a promotion to his first star in January after the Germans killed the intended commander in North Africa. While Miller inspected new ships out on the hardstands, Throck was inside, arguing with the supply types. The new, untried Fortresses, Liberators, Marauders, Lightnings and the new Thunderbolts gleamed wetly in new paint jobs, unetched by hard use. Many were having the myriad changes that had to go into them before they went to operational units. Many Fortresses had their radio room roofs removed and covered with canvas while they were being worked on.

On another part of the depot, war wearies were being stripped of special equipment before they returned them to their owners. Airplanes, like people, could only take so much punishment. Regardless of how careful a pilot was, or how many times an airplane was repaired, the stresses of combat flight, bearing heavy loads for long periods under strained conditions, flying with many crews and maintained by successions of strangers...it all took its toll. Fighters can only take so many hammerhead climbs, diving rolls, and split-s escapes. Bombers cannot carry heavy ordnance loads in freezing weather for long without showing some signs of strain.

After the special gear was stripped and certain critical parts removed (like the bomb sights or the AFDC gear) the old ladies would go back to their units and be used for training, liaison, assembly ships or, the ultimate fate for most of them, as hangar queens gradually cannibalized for ships still flying, like *Crop Duster* I was now. Still wistfully kicking tires on a new Fortress, Miller heard a familiar voice call, "John Miller!"

Looking around, he saw a familiar figure in an unfamiliar getup. "Canby," he shouted querulously.

"In the flesh," came the reply. "How'd you get here?"

"Well, I'll be damned," Miller shouted happily. "Mitchell Canby; if you ain't a sight for sore eyes." The two men came together in greeting just as Throck was walking into the depot line. "Major," Miller held his friend at arm's length. "How the hell'd you make major?"

"Clean livin' and four thousand hours flight time," Canby replied, throwing off a crisp salute to Throck.

"You two know each other," Throck asked, his shoes wet in the damp grass.

"Why sure, sir," Miller answered. "Mitch Canby owned and operated the first passenger airline in northern Wisconsin. La Crosse, Green Bay and Madison, right?"

"Right," Canby said. "And Duane Greene is flying it all now."

"Greene," Miller said querulously, "with that clapped-out old hangar queen he's got? How in the hell can he..."

"He's flying my old ships," Canby interrupted. "I'm leasing them to him. There's nobody to fly them now."

"Didn't you have a partner?"

"Yeah," Canby said, and suddenly grew solemn. "But he joined the Marines right after I signed up," and he fell quiet.

"What happened?" Miller pressed, instantly realizing he shouldn't be asking.

"Guadalcanal happened," was the quiet reply. "Twelve kills and he got his from a Jap mortar round."

"Sorry. Well," Miller tried to change the subject, "what're you up to now?"

"Stalling the supply system, that's what he's up to," Throck growled.

"He's right," Canby conceded. "I was in Marauder school in Utah and already wearing these oak leaves when the Flight Surgeon decided my game leg was too game to fly combat..."

"The one you broke back in, ah, '37, was it?"

"Yeah; it never set right. Anyways, they tell me I can stay in the Air Force because I know so much about flying and airplanes, but I can't be on flight status. You figure it out. So they sent me here to tell these quartermaster types what real flyers need. I'm supposed to go up to the 105th at Nichols in a few weeks as ground exec..."

"We'll be neighbors, then," Miller offered. "We're up at Bartlesby."

"Yeah, I know," Canby glanced at Throck. "Well, what do you guys need up there? You're the... "

"Replacement Procurement officer this month; next month some other sucker'll be doing it. But I need a replacement ship for one I got pranged a couple of weeks ago."

"OK, I can give you a new ship, but only one. I can't give over much more than that; just one-to-one replacements. We keep losing supplies to U- boats, and the Twelfth down in North Africa is pulling all the priorities, so the Eighth is hurting for everything from paper clips to bombs. Hell, I can't even get ribbons for typewriters..."

"OK, but listen," Miller said. "How about you give us a few of these new ships? We'll hangar some of our worst until we can get the parts."

"No soap," Canby said. "Most of 'em are already spoken for. And you ain't authorized..."

"Sally's here," Miller interrupted.

Canby glared at him. "Doing what?"

"She's a nurse. So happens she just rotated up to Bartlesby last week. Usually she's in London."

Canby looked at Throck, who nodded solemnly. "She just as pretty as she always was?"

"Even prettier. And she's got friends."

"OK," Canby said. "I'll get you three new Fortresses on top of the one replacement ship if you can get me twelve hours on the town with Sally."

"Sure, she'll do it," Miller smiled. "Anything for the war effort."

Throck was silent for a few minutes after they got back to the car. Finally, he broke out laughing. "Miller, you sonofabitch; you peddled your sister's ass for three B-17s! Man, you're the limit!" After a moment or two, he rejoined, "I want to meet this gal worth, let's see...at two

157

hundred and seventy-five thousand apiece...eight hundred thousand bucks!"

"They've been sweet on each other since high school, sort of," Miller tried to explain. "Doris got between them because...well, never mind; besides, I'm not sure. Sally's on rotation up to Bartlesby now: she'll be glad to help out."

***

"For WHAT," Sally screamed when her brother told her about his "plan" at the USO club that afternoon. "You told Mitch Canby I'd spend a night with him in London for WHAT?"

"Three new 'Forts," Miller explained, becoming slightly embarrassed at the commotion, "and keep your voice down."

"John, he's MARRIED," she cried, "and Doris's a friend of mine, sort of. What would I tell her? You know her; what would YOU tell her?"

"I wouldn't have to tell her anything," Miller said. "What she doesn't know won't hurt her. Besides, you know Mitch, he's harmless. He won't do anything..."

"Oh, yeah? He was harmless in the 'States when he could see Doris every day. But she's five thousand miles away now. A lot of married guys are pretty eager when they get over here. How do I know he's still harmless?"

"Well," Grace interjected, "why don't we arrange a chaperone?" Miller, Throck, and Sally looked at her, puzzled. "Well, he didn't say *alone*, did he? And if, as you say, John, he's just an honorable gentleman looking for an honorable night on the town with an honorable lady of his acquaintance, he wouldn't mind some *company*, now would he?"

"Well, I don't know about that..."

"Yes, that's right," Throck said, butting in. "You're absolutely right, Miss Henley. We need those ships and we'll by God get them. Now, what night..."

"Think Friday would be convenient?" Grace enquired sweetly.

"Absolutely," Throck exclaimed, "Captain Miller's available."

"I am? But I've got..." Miller managed.

"Miller, if the President himself sent you on a mission for Friday or Saturday, I'd find a way around it for four new Fortresses. Now, I can provide Miller, a car and a driver, but what shall we set up for a night on the town, Miss Henley?"

"Oh, my, General, not with me: I'm spoken for. But, now..." Turning to the telephone, she picked up the receiver, spoke into it briefly, and hung up. "Line to London," she said. Shortly it rang. "Yes, thank you," Grace answered. "This is Duchess Mayfield calling personally for Her Serene Highness' secretary Lady Carolyn Smalls." Sotto voce to her audience she explained, "Uncle Edmond is a widower so I am allowed the courtesy title for social functions. Works marvelously for...Carolyn? Grace. I needed to ask you when you were up here: did you see my parents in Toronto...I ought to, yes...I saw your father last Tuesday week...yes, but there's a more urgent matter. Is Alex free on Saturday? Can she...no, it's for an evening with two of America's finest pilots and one of the best nurses in the Nurse Corps...happens one of them is Captain Miller...brilliant; can you make arrangements? Be a dear and ring back when you have it sorted. Ta-ta!"

After she rang off, Grace looked pointedly at Throck and Miller. "Special Branch wouldn't allow a Mountbatten to travel that way, General; they will provide transportation. Alexandra's quite taken with you, John. She went on and on about you for days, the poor dear. If I were free, I might be jealous; might do anyway, just for spite." She grinned winningly. "Ah, but the heart wants what it..." and the phone rang. "Yes, I'll hold... Hello, Sir Arthur; Duchess Mayfield...fine, thank you...oh, the Red Room...yes, the war, of course; that will have to do... oh don't be that way, Sir Arthur...yes, of course...yes, at six, then...thank you...very well then...that would be fine, Sir Arthur. Good bye."

Then, off the phone to her increasingly flabbergasted audience; "Sir Arthur is concierge to the Montefalcon royals, and he knows full well that I'm Uncle Edmond's niece, but Uncle and Father sponsored him into their London club, so he knows what side his biscuit has marmalade on." The phone rang again. In a moment, she turned again to Miller and asked, "Would Noel Coward be acceptable for the theatre?" Taking his open-mouthed stare as an answer, she went back to the phone. "Yes, Mr. Pemberton, this is the Duchess Mayfield speaking. A box Friday evening... nine o'clock; thank you ever so much."

"I'll be dipped in shit," Throck muttered. Miller stared at his commander who, for the first time in human memory, had been out-operated.

"Well, it's all pretty pointless," Sally muttered. "I'm not free any night this month. We're so shorthanded..."

"Leave that to me," Throck assured her. "If I gotta bed your supervisor myself, I'll take care of it. Seems I can't do much else for this operation..." She stared at the general, as if disbelieving not only what she heard him say, but what she was about to do.

"I'll call Mitch," Sally sighed. "What I won't do for my brother..."

***

Friday night, the car dropped Miller off at the front of the hotel just as it was getting dark. It would pick him up 48 hours later at the same place. The London metro traffic was finally thinning out as the blackout came into effect, and headlights were scarce in a world of shortages. Miller was presentable in his freshly pressed Class A's, with gold-plated brass (a gift from the crew who had traded three cartons of smokes to Sanda's "elves" for the work) and a full set of ribbons that included a fresh Air Medal that was awarded after he completed his sixth mission just the day before: a milk run to St Nazaire.

Bounding up the hotel steps and through a door held open by an elderly doorman in a tattered overcoat, Miller entered a gilt and plush red velvet world he might otherwise see only in the movies. As directed, he entered the lobby's only working elevator car, manned by a matronly woman who looked as though she came with the equipment, sitting on a stool in the corner. Upon closing the door, she took him to the 12th floor. Stepping off into a tiny unfurnished and undecorated anteroom with two doors, the biggest human being he believed he had ever seen met him. "May I help you sir," the giant severely intoned in a rolling voice like thundery gravel.

"I'm here to meet Princess Alexandra," Miller managed, craning his neck to take in the full khaki-clad length of this enormous person—a sergeant-major, if Miller remembered correctly.

"Who may I say is calling, sir?" This was more a demand for information than a question.

"Captain John Miller of the United States Army Air Force."

"Of course, sir; you are expected." The behemoth turned around, turned a doorknob that seemed to vanish into his hand, and motioned Miller in. Through the door, an older version of Alex brightly greeted Miller; a little taller, with a face a little more angular. "Captain Miller; I am so glad to meet you; I'm Olivia Mountbatten. Alex and Jean speak so highly of you." Leading him into a sedately furnished reception room, she introduced him to two military officers. "This is Group Captain Vauchand of our own Air Force, and this is Captain Groves of the Coldstream Guards." Shaking hands with both men, Miller thought there was something distinctive about the grand duchess' voice, but couldn't quite place it. "Drink, Captain? Alex is running a bit late, of course, but your sister's helping her. She's a real ball of fire, that Sally of yours."

"Something of a spark plug, yes ma'am," Miller agreed, puzzled by the familiar slang from a non-American, "and I'll have beer, if you don't mind."

"I'll get it," the guardsman offered. "Old Milwaukee OK?" Stunned by the thought of a Wisconsin beer in Britain, Miller nodded his assent.

"One for me, too, Captain," the grand duchess called, "we don't have it very often, and I always love the taste of home." Home? The guardsman returned with four open bottles, offering the grand duchess one and passing out the other two. "Here's mud in your eye," the grand duchess said, hoisting the bottle in salute before swigging down a third of it. Grinning at Miller's puzzlement, she explained. "I was born and raised in Hammond, Indiana. My first husband moved us to Montefalcon to build an auto factory for the Mountbatten's business interests before the last war and stayed on to build artillery. The last round of the flu took dear Fred, but I had Alex by then and the royal family was very kind to me. But I always like the taste of home when I can get it. The first we've had since the Fourth of July," she finished before slugging down another gulp.

"Labor Day, ma'am," the guardsman corrected; "if you'll recall, we split that last one." He continued, "My father was in automobiles, so I spent most of my youth in Detroit and Flint. The grand duchess keeps me in her detail because he likes to hear a Midwestern twang once in a while." There was a buzzing sound, very faint but distinct. "That would be Major Canby getting into the elevator." Soon enough, Mitch Canby, resplendent in freshly pressed Class A's, was walking through the same door that Miller passed through. Miller took it upon himself to introduce Canby to the grand duchess and the officers.

"I must see what's keeping the young ladies," the grand duchess muttered, walking off down a long, door-lined hallway. The men shared small talk, comparing Great Lakes weather to that of northern Europe.

"Colder here," the group captain asserted, "especially in those Lightnings they have us transitioning to."

"P-38s, really," Canby queried. "I thought your people were in Warhawks."

"A change in grand strategic plans far over our heads, certainly. We started in those excellent aircraft, but just last week they moved us into the Lightnings; ground support or ground attack, we're told. Well suited for it, I must say. They took out all our machine guns and put in three more twenty millimeter cannons, have us training at attacking barges," he lamented. "But that's a dammed sight better than flying them at higher altitudes. Much too cold, you see. Engines are too far away from the cockpit, and there's too much stuff in the wing roots to pass hot water."

"Well, now," Miller exclaimed, "that makes sense! I wondered why the P-38s always seem so sluggish, bouncing the bandits. They're freezing up there!"

"Indeed," the group captain agreed, "and I should tell you..." he began, but stopped abruptly at the sight of two young beauties floating. Sally wore a red brocade strapless gown; Alex wore an off-the shoulder green satin number that matched her eyes. "John," Canby said after a friendly embrace with his not-especially standoffish date, "after this war's over, remind me to kill you."

"Now, now," Sally purred, "what would you tell Doris?"

He was quiet for a heartbeat, and then jovially rejoined, "I'll still kill him. He cost me four 'Forts and a case of my best trading bourbon."

The grand duchess appeared, grabbing Canby and Miller by the elbows. "If you ladies don't take these handsome gentlemen away, I'll keep them here tonight," she laughed. "Might anyway. Now go," she finished, pushing them all down the hallway. "Captain Groves will escort you down to the car." Led by Groves, who had miraculously changed into a silk suit, the two couples walked to another elevator at the end of the hallway. The operator, a dour corporal whose face was almost the same color as his red stripes, barely looked beyond the door. The doors opened onto a secluded alley where a Bentley waited with the engine running and its driver by the door. While the foursome bundled into the back, Groves sat in front.

"Steven," Alex called through the window, "do please introduce yourself."

"I am Steven Groves, my friends; captain of the Coldstream Guards and Constable of the Special Branch of the Metropolitan Police; I am to be your guide, escort and the head of Her Serene Highness's security detail this evening. If you should happen to spot me outside of this car, I'm failing at my job." The ride in the London blackout was uneventful, with muted headlights on the streets and only the occasional flicker of red light from any buildings.

The head waiter fell all over the princess and her guests, much to the amazement of the Americans. They were seated in a small, secluded corner of the Red Room, an astonishingly quiet place despite the hustle and bustle of every other establishment. "I can't get the time of day outta most English joints," Canby complained. "I oughta do this more often."

"*Noblesse oblige*," Alex explained. "The gentry are always treated thus, even if we have no country." A matronly woman apprehensively approached the table.

"The wine, your Highness," she asked.

"Excuse me," Alex said, taken slightly aback. "You're the wine steward?"

"Stewardess, Highness," she gave a shallow bow, appearing somewhat fearful. She'd been dismissed out of hand by other guests who were genuinely shocked that the Red Room would use a woman as waitstaff.

"Oh," Alex said casually. "Yes; certainly. Yes. What's good, then?"

"We've a fine Bordeaux, Highness. Rothschambeau '21?"

"Excellent," Alex said, and the stewardess retreated. "I understand waitresses aren't unusual in America?"

"True," Canby said. "They're more common than waiters now." A few more minutes of idle chatter and the wine arrived. The stewardess, under the worried, apprehensive eye of the Maitre'd, expertly uncorked the bottle and poured a sip into a fluted glass, setting it and the cork in front of Miller, and waiting.

"Now what?" Miller whispered, leaning slightly toward Alex.

"Sniff the cork, John," Alex suggested, the Maitre'd rolling his eyes, the wine stewardess smiling slightly.

"For what?" Miller was no rube, but he'd never had to deal with wine before, let alone a wine stewardess.

"Oh, never mind," Alex said, seizing the cork and wafting it under her nose. Then, taking the glass, she held it to the light, swirled it around a bit, sipped the wine down, and nodded in approval. The stewardess served the wine without further ceremony.

After a few moments and the onlookers were gone, Alex said, "I have no idea what I just approved of. I've only ever seen others do it;

never did it myself." All four cracked up, much to the consternation of the other guests...and the amused chagrin of the Maitre'd.

***

"So, where's the bill?" Canby asked after the busgirl removed the last sherbet. The busgirl nearly dropped the tray.

"Oh, please, Mitch. Don't ask for a bill," Alex said urgently, slightly embarrassed. "Never ask for the bill. It shall be taken care of."

"I pay my own way, Alex," Canby said evenly.

"I don't doubt it, Mitch. But if there's a Maitre'd and a wine steward, never discuss money in the dining room. And there's nothing to settle; consider it a contribution to the war effort."

"Oh, OK," Canby said after Miller kicked him in the shins.

***

The car was waiting in the queue, hooded headlights barely illuminating the back bumper of the car ahead, other traffic on the street creeping eerily along in the blackout with their dimmed lights cast down to the street. London at night was black as pitch, the streetlights off for the duration, the street signs removed to confuse invaders.

"...So Farr comes up with this rag and plops it down right there next to my coffee," Miller related, "and I look at it and it looks like a big bullet. 'What's this' I say, and he says, 'Kraut forty millimeter round. We pulled it out from between the spar frame and the number two gas tank. If it'd gone off, it would've blown us in half.'"

The audience, including the driver and Grove, listened with rapt attention. "So what was it?" Canby asked. "Just a dud?"

"Not exactly; 'No explosive,' he says, and he fishes out a little piece of paper with some writing on it."

"Don't tell me, let me guess," Sally chimed in. "Kilroy was here." All had a good laugh at that, including Miller.

"No, no. Better than that. It was a note somebody had scribbled in Czech, and said, as near as we figured out: 'It is not much, but it is all I can do.' The eggheads from intelligence said something like it was probably made in a forced labor camp by somebody the Krauts had locked up..."

They finally arrived at the music hall fashionably late (it never started on time). Alex had to explain some nuances of English humor.

164

Noel Coward was in fine fettle, with even a few gags designed for the Americans in the audience (which made up nearly a third).

At intermission, Alex told her story of a week of boating off the French coast at Dunkirk. "So, after traveling for days in motorcars and trucks with no springs, we get to the coast. Carolyn is in tears most of the time. I can no longer feel my bum, and there are great knots of men wandering around, seemingly without direction. Of course, my driver is long gone and we're in borrowed transport.

"So we get down to the beach and there's maybe a hundred boats standing off the shore, but the only sound we hear are the bullhorns of the Navy. 'Form queues' they're saying; 'stay with your units.' So what am I supposed to do?"

"As I recall from the newspaper pictures, there was a pier..." Miller suggested.

"Yes, there was, but miles away from where we were, and Carolyn was getting on my last nerve. But I look out at the boats and there's Grace's Uncle Edmund with his *Marbury Rose*. Providence itself, I think, if only I can get out there. Well, we were hardly dressed to go bathing (we'd been at a dinner party when the air raids started, and hadn't stopped moving since), but I knew there was a way around that. So we nicked some blouses and trousers from some men, who didn't mind watching two young ladies change out of evening gowns with only transparent silky sheaths underneath, and who then somehow cleared a path for us so we could wade out to the yacht. We were chest deep in the icy-cold Channel when we reached the boat, and so delighted when Edmond recognized me."

"Well, I would suppose," Canby muttered, "that he was mighty surprised..."

"He couldn't have been *more* stunned if his hound had kittens. But he pulls us in, and suddenly Carolyn turns around and starts hauling men into the boat. We start pulling off and she jumps onto the roof where there's a Lewis gun strapped to a pedestal, acting like she was Annie Oakley. 'What's all that blubbering?' I ask her. 'What blubbering,' she says. She genuinely could not remember."

"I've heard of that," Sally said. "Hysterical amnesia, the psychiatrists call it."

"You mean it has a name? Heavens, I thought she was...oh, well, I'll have to apologize to the poor dear. Anyway, we can't get back to England anytime soon, and there's work to be done, so we spend the next...what was it, five days...pulling other lads aboard and pitching them up to the destroyers. I never worked so physically hard in my life.

"But at the end, there we are quayside at Ramsgate, and this hulking big Scot says he wants to adopt me. I'm filthy dirty, my hair is in knots, haven't slept in ages, must have looked an awful sight in bloody great sea boots and oilskins and my brassiere is long since gone into the Channel (not that anyone would notice but me and Mother), and this tribe of Celt savages wants to adopt me! Could you credit it?!? Edmund says it's a great honor. All I want to do is get a bath and get to bed, so I agree to it if it would get me out of there any faster.

"And this Scot shouts in that great booming voice of theirs, 'By the Grace of 'is Majesty George' and all that rubbish, 'be it known that Princess Margaret Alexandra' and etcetera, 'and Edmund, Duke of Mayfield' and more rubbish, 'are forever after to be known as kinsmen of the Clans of the Black Watch,' and then some more rubbish. Then they pass around this water bottle with this *awful* French Cognac mixed with some *dregs* of malt whiskey, and they march off with their bloody pipes skirling and *singing* at the top of their lungs. This is midnight, mind you!"

***

At a nightclub after the show, the four danced and drank and told tales to excess. "...So Gable climbs outta his 'Fort with the rest of the guys," Canby related, "and he ambles over to the grass with the rest of 'em for the ritual..."

"What ritual?" Alex asked.

"Post-mission piss," Miller explained.

"...Well, there are all these cameras from Public Relations and brass hats and reporters and Hollywood types standing around waiting to take his picture. Well, Gable paid 'em no mind, so this major from Public Relations comes up to him and says; 'Sergeant Gable, the folks back home would like some pictures.' Well, his group got hit pretty hard that day over Le Havre, and like the rest of the waist gunners he's pretty cold and tired, so Gable just looks at him and says, 'Frankly, Major, I don't give a damn!'"

The combo on the bandstand was a rarity in England: it played American swing like it *should* be played, and not an up-tempo version of the "Pomp and Circumstance." Unfortunately, that didn't give much opportunity for the dancing acceptable in evening gowns, but it led to some marvelous stories.

"So we're all out on deck," Sally related, "and this other ship about a thousand yards away is sinking from a torpedo. The scramble net is over the side (because we're the rescue ship for the column) and I decide the boys in the water needed some help. So I get the gals to shore up a rope and I rig up a boson's seat I remember from Girl Scouts..."

"Girl Guides...?" Alex wondered.

"Girl Scouts in the 'States. But then I remember I don't have any undies on, so we find the smallest sailor out there and get his pants and I pull 'em on and over the side I go into the drink. Well, I grab onto a couple of boys and tow them back, then I spend the next half hour until dawn hanging on the net helping more boys up...."

"And nobody stopped you," Canby asked, incredulous.

"Nope. Then they decide to pull the net up and get underway, so I climb up the net. Well, remember I have a tiny waist and no hips to speak of and this gob we got the pants from had to be about a thirty, so when I get topside, I untie the rope that'd been around my waist...and the pants drop to my ankles..."

"Oh, no," Miller coughed, "And you..."

"...had been hanging on the end of this lifeline, and my robe and nightshirt conveniently bunched up under my armpits. And now here I am in front of God and everybody with no drawers and covered with oil and freezing numb with my pants around my feet and half the Navy is looking at my *boobs* standing at attention and another half staring at my *you-know-what* and *another* half is trying to be noble and pretend I wasn't there. So what was I supposed to do? I just pushed my nightie down with as much dignity as I could muster, went inside, crawled back in my bunk and prayed that I would never see another of those gobs again..."

Not long later, when the ladies excused themselves for a ritual powdering of noses, Miller pressed Canby about why he seemed to hold back, not having more fun. He finally gave in. "I didn't tell you or Sally before, but Doris died in New Guinea."

"What's she doin' there?" Miller slurred. *Died...?*

"Medical Corps; X-ray technician. She didn't *tell* me she was there. Then I got this telegram two weeks ago. Dengue fever, her CO said, she passed right about Valentine's Day. Because married women *can't* enlist, her CO didn't *know* she was married until she..."

"Oh, oh God." Miller replied. "Shit, Mitch, I'm so sorry. You don't expect...but you'd better tell Sally," Miller said, "or I'll have to."

"No, I'll do it," Canby said, taking Sally for a well-timed slow dance after the ladies returned. Miller gave Alex the news. "Oh dear," Alex said. "That does change things a bit, doesn't it?"

"Yeah, you could say that."

When they returned, Sally was silent, strained. "They buried her out there," Canby said.

Buried her, Miller thought, *buried her...*

"She was my friend," Sally said at length.

"Yeah," Canby replied. "Mine too."

"Damn this war," Alex sighed.

"Amen, sister," Canby said heavily, "Amen."

March 1943

Hamm, Germany

Nothing is more exhilarating
Than to be shot at with no result

Winston Churchill

The explosion of the Fortress beneath him blew pieces into Thielmann's machine, shearing off part of the airscrew and tearing through the engine cowling. Hot oil from the engine sprayed back onto Thielmann's cold feet, searing them on the rudder pedals. "Altmarck one leader to Altmarck: I am in trouble. Good luck to you all," he called.

His engine was smoking badly, with flames licking through holes in the cowling's top. He shut off the engine as the unbalanced airscrew kept turning, threatening to rip his machine apart. "Get *out*, Thielmann," he said to himself, attempting to set into a glide path that would take him far clear of the Fortress herd and out of the range of their guns. Ahead of his new course, he saw another Fortress formation under attack by another group. His feet smarting under the strain, he swung his now powerless machine into a diving bank, struggling to keep it from rolling into a spin that, without power, he could not escape.

It was a strange thing, Thielmann thought calmly, to glide silently through an air battle. He could hear, for the first time, the engines of the other German fighters and the Fortresses, the rattling and popping of the guns, and the explosions of dying machines.

His diving bank had brought him ahead of the lower Liberator formation, nearly in the path of an attacking Focke-Wulf, which flashed by within ten meters of his silent, powerless crate, guns blazing at the leading bomber. His damaged machine seemed, for the moment, to be at least glideable. He decided, having never had to parachute before, to try to land his crate dead-stick—without power.

He built up energy in a steep dive, just before his speed went ballistic and his control surfaces ceased to work. As he lost altitude, he leveled his machine off, looking for an appropriate landing place. The ground below was farm country, with new crops in the fields and teams tilling. He wondered vaguely if he should try landing gear, wondering how he might know if they would lock.

"Altmarck two leader to Altmarck one leader: Thielmann, lower your wheels. I'll verify the position."

Bär, Thielmann thought, is somewhere under me. What is he doing here? Still, he was relieved to hear a familiar voice, "Altmarck one to Altmarck two: Down they come," he called, turning the hand crank. "What are you doing here, Bär?"

"I got separated. They are not coming down straight. Try to pull them back."

"Stuck. I'll have to belly land the way I am."

"That field on the next ridge looks soft." Thielmann pointed his machine at the ridge and the dark, freshly plowed soil of the field. "Here I go." There was a hush as Thielmann topped a tree line, still with plenty of energy to reach the field, but then there was a downdraft ahead of the ridge. Thielmann struggled to pull up, his machine's energy bleeding off fast. Just as he thought he had cleared a farmhouse, he felt a bump of his tail wheel bounding off a roof. With hardly any energy or airspeed left, Thielmann fell the remaining ten meters, plowing into the farmer's courtyard, scattering a knot of horses and a flock of chickens in his path, finally coming to a halt in a rather outsized sty. A wave of muddy ooze slapped over the nose of the machine, leaking down into the cockpit. "I am down," he called on the radio. "Give them my position."

"I have you. Help will be on the way. Good luck with the farmer's daughters." Bär swooped overhead, waggled his wings, and was gone.

"Any landing I can walk away from," Thielmann muttered as he opened the canopy, "is likely to be a good one." He unbuckled his seat harness as someone climbed up on his wing.

"Are you all right, sir?" a small boy asked. "You killed Dora."

"I'm fine, boy. Who is Dora?" Thielmann said, climbing out of his machine, a horrified picture in his mind of a German killed by his stubborn insistence on flying his crate to the ground.

170

"Papa's old sow," the boy said.

"Oh," Thielmann said, relieved. "I'm sorry about the sow. No control, you see. These kites don't fly well without engines."

"Is he all right, Johann?" a woman's voice called. Thielmann waved over his head.

"I'm all right. I hit a sow, I'm told."

"Ach, old Dora was just about bacon, anyway. What happened?"

"The *Amis* shot up my engine," he said, slogging through the ooze, the cold muck soothing to his burned feet. "Have you a telephone?" The woman, with a large, matronly figure and a sunny face, scurried up to him.

"No," the woman replied, "but the *Polizei* should be here at any moment. Here," she said, handing him a bottle. "Put some of that in you. Oh my! Just look at your feet." Thielmann looked down to see his feet covered with oil and muck, his flying suit similarly soiled.

"Burned," Thielmann said absently. "I don't know if I should take them off or not. There may be complications."

"Here," the woman said, "sit over here until the *Polizei* arrive." She directed him to a wooden bench under a tree, where he sat and drank. Wine of some kind, he thought, as the stinging pain came back to his feet.

The boy came back again, leading a man, obviously blind. "Hello, *Mein Herr*," the blind man said, "and welcome to our home. I am Leo Herbst. You've met my son Johann and my wife Etta. You are very fortunate, yes?"

"Yes, I am, I suppose," Thielmann admitted, swigging the wine again. "This is the second time I've been shot down."

"Second time," the woman said, incredulous. "Is that really very common?"

"Oh, yes. I have known pilots shot down a score of times."

"My, how exciting," the blind farmer said. "Nothing quite that exciting happens around here. Nothing, but..."

"Leo," the wife chided, "the boy." Thielmann watched them both, puzzled.

After a half hour, the promised *Polizei* had not arrived and Thielmann was wondering how he was about to get back. It would only be a matter of time, he thought, before his own JG191 would start looking for him, providing Bär got back and got the location correct. But it could be the next day before they might arrive. Farmer Herbst tapped with a great, long staff across the barnyard to the bench, where Thielmann's wine was nearly gone and his feet still hurt, though he no longer cared as much. "Could you do me a service, *Mein Herr,* a personal service?"

"All right," Thielmann replied, "If it's something I can do. But my feet..." "Oh, I just need you to look at something for me," the farmer said. "Etta has gone to fetch the authorities for you. If you could come over to the barn, please." Following the farmer painfully the twenty meters across the barnyard, Thielmann wondered what it could possibly be he was to look at. "Etta has forbidden Johann to come into the barn since whatever happened this morning. Please, what is it? She won't tell me."

Lying on the barn's stone floor, and spattered on its walls—all swarming with flies—was what remained of an American *Feldwebel,* his parachute either unopened or missing...it was hard to tell which. He'd made the gaping hole in the barn roof. But for the shattered bones rising from the mass of flesh like defiant tree trunks after a raging forest fire, one would be hard-pressed to say it had been human.

I hope you were dead American, Thielmann thought sadly, long before you got this far. Breaking through the thatched roof would not have killed you, but you would have seen it coming, certainly. "This morning, you say," Thielmann said, barely controlling a rising tide of nausea.

"Yes. Please, what is it?"

"A dead American," Thielmann said dully, "nothing else. I'll send someone around to collect him."

Thielmann thought he would ask Steger and some blackbirds to come and shovel him into a bag, find his identity tags in that pulped mess so we can notify the Red Cross that another American has died over Germany.

And we'll let his comrades at the PW camp bury him, where he's belonged ever since he thought he'd gotten *lucky* again, *just* once more.

Steger later told Thielmann that the *Feldwebel's* name was Charles Payne, and that he was an Episcopalian. He said the service at the PW camp was simple but beautiful.

April 1943

Bartlesby, England

You've time to get hungry, while you're waiting
For someone's death to get a living

Moliere

Miller got a new flight deck crew: big Norm Thomas from California as bombardier, and tall, older (26) Harry Royce from Montana as navigator. The pair was a highly trained team of the new Lead Crew dogma just then getting currency in the Eighth Air Force. The Lead Crew notion was that the lead aircraft in the formation would identify the target, home in on it, and the whole formation would release the bombs when they did. *Crop Duster* wasn't fortunate enough to be a Lead Ship, yet. They designated *Crop Duster* an Alternate Lead Ship, to slide into position when the leader was no longer leading. But Jackson and Reynolds, the other lead crew in the 190th, stayed with Ernie King, the 190th's commander, in *The Throne Room*, and Thomas and Royce went to *Crop Duster.*

Ernie Block was a good enough gunner to be tagged as an instructor at Bassingbourne. In his place, *Crop Duster* received Collins Digman, a sandy-haired farm boy from Notre Dame, Illinois. To replace Payne, she got Fiorello Calisto, a swarthy kid with a quick temper from Queens. The 299th group was split one day not long after the two waist gunners reported, with the 192nd and the 610th Squadrons going to St. Nazaire, by then dubbed "Flak City," to hit the docks and sub pens, and 190th and 191st to hit the locomotive shops at Antwerp.

Crop Duster launched just before dawn and got back from Antwerp by noon, easily completing the strike in full fighter cover. Waiting for the rest of the group, the returned flight crews played baseball with the ground crews, or read and reread mail (or pretended to) in silence, waiting. No one wanted anything to do with airplanes just then. Not yet. Not now. A fast-moving spring squall just after the other half of the 299th launched had left everything slightly damp and chilled. The men in green and brown waited on the ground, watching the sky to the east, straining their ears for the droning of the Fortresses. Even with the air of spring, they could think of little else than their friends coming back. At about three, the control tower said they'd hit the primary and were headed back. Fighters had attacked heavily before the target, and were hitting again. No word on losses.

The sun was low in the west when the first of them was heard from: one had to ditch in the Channel, eight survivors pulled out of the drink. Another went into a RAF Coastal Command field short on gas: ten survivors, six wounded. Then they started coming around the field, their engines straining as they swept over into the pattern for the downward leg, ground crews straining to read the names, flight crews looking for familiar friends....

Mary Dear...Berlin or Bust...Five Aces...Midnight Lace screamed in, brakes gone, trailing parachutes to stop her...*Hell on Wings...Kansas Cyclone...Rosalie* tripped a flare for her wounded, and the ambulances chased after...*Cobb's Crib...Wrath of the Lamb...Detroit Demolition* in with a flare, flaps dangling from her wings, fuel trailing...*Screamin' Meemee...Hitler's Headache... Spirit of Jersey* bumped in, two engines out and a huge hole in her right wing. Twenty-three of twenty-six operational ships were accounted for in the 299th. *It Beats Relief* was seen to go down burning; *Cowboy Carnival* and *LuAnne* dropped out of formation and headed back alone. By nightfall, the two stragglers reported from alternate fields.

Mitch Berg got the word that night that he was getting his own ship in another group. *Crop Duster* had a little party for him that night, hoisting a few beers to their copilot's new assignment and his continued good fortune.

***

Some people, Miller thought two days later, just shouldn't be expected to do everything like others can. Atwell was just a kid, really, a year younger than Miller, but a boy nonetheless. The beads of sweat boiling on his forehead just weren't consistent with the kind of flak they were getting, which could have been much worse. His hands shook badly; although it was cold—about twenty below—it just wasn't that cold. His voice shook; his reactions were quick but too deliberate, not instinctive. He jumped too much in the close flak bursts. He'll get used to it, Miller told himself. We all did.

Miller set the autopilot on time, releasing the controls so Thomas could line up the target and count off the scale, watching the lead ship for the release. It was point-flak, not box barrage, which meant the gunners were having some trouble shooting through their own smoke screen.

It was still enough to destroy both Atwell's nerves and two Fortresses.

April 1943

Oscbersleben, Germany

And gentlemen in England now a-bed
Shall think themselves accursed they were not here;
And hold their manhood cheap whiles any speaks
That fought with us upon Saint Crispin's Day

William Shakespeare

There was a chill in the air from the sea, freezing the rainwater on the prop tips. Thielmann and other senior officers were philosophically discussing the nature of the American daylight formations, and whether their methods were working. "How many angels dance on the head of a pin, Taube," Kaltz said. "The crux of the whole matter lies not in whether or not they turn back, but in how many of them come in each attack. If we can keep bleeding them, we will be successful."

"Do you really think so, Kaltz? If so, then we were successful in the Channel battle and the Tommies should have surrendered three years ago."

"No, no, Taube," Thielmann said. "That's not it at all. The point is, or is getting to be, how badly we can maul them each time they go out. If we can convince them that their daylight tactics cannot succeed, we may get them to switch over to night attacks, when at least we can get twelve hours of rest..."

"I cannot agree, Thielmann," Bär said. "We must convince them that their bombing efforts, both day and night, are ineffectual. That they are sacrificing too much for too little return. Only by stopping the bombing campaign altogether can we preserve the *Luftwaffe* for the battle against the Ivans..."

"I have to agree with Bär," Pritzler joined in. "We are the only arm that the people can see. If we cannot demonstrate outright power, the morale at home will suffer, and as any fool knows, it was morale that killed us in the last war." The room hushed, with all staring at him. Oh yes, they knew it. They hadn't said it out loud for over a decade, but they knew it. "We can only do that by clearing the skies of the *Amis* and the Tommies," he finished.

"Can we really expect to do that, Bär," Taube said, incredulously. "Have we even come *close* to stopping *one* attack?"

"I don't think it's a weakness of tactics," Kaltz said. "I don't think it's a weakness of ours at all. I just think that it's the strength of the allies. They have so much, and can throw it away at will. What was it Rommel said about the Americans in the desert? First to run..."

"... And first to rally," Thielmann finished. "I heard that a few months ago, but I wasn't prepared to believe it..."

"Moltke the Elder knew it," Pritzler the scholar said. "He was an observer in their civil war. He said he watched Americans charge a stone wall for over three hours in winter cold without a living man coming nearer than a hundred meters, and still they did not stop until nightfall. Pure tenacity..."

***

It was a week after that conversation that JG191 first encountered the Thunderbolts. The Americans had been sending Lightnings and Spitfires on their escort missions until March, when a few of the tubby fighters were encountered over Rotterdam by an ME-109 group; the encounter did not go well.

But that April morning, while searching for the stream of *Viermots* near Hanover, JG191 met with a swarm of P-47s they'd only ever seen before in pictures. In moments, Thielmann and his comrades were scattered by the American's diving charge. "All Altmarck units climb to three-five and head west; engaged Altmarcks dive to escape."

This was manifestly bad advice; there were no aircraft then flying that could dive faster than a P-47, but Thielmann and his comrades could not have known that. In the wild melee that followed, two Altmarck swarms (one of Thielmann's; one of Taube's) dove into a split-s; Thielmann's swarm was destroyed, and he considered himself fortunate to be alive. Taube's swarm lost two machines to extensive damage, and the pilots had to bail out. Bär shot down a Thunderbolt, but he credited it to pure luck.

That evening, the pilots were quiet, reflecting on the day's events. "We simply could not get around them this time. What a surprise those crates are!" Pritzler, for once, was at a loss for what to say.

"Are they that maneuverable?" Kaltz had to put something into an official report that didn't look like an excuse, since Goering had made another "*Luftwaffe* cowards" speech the day before.

"No, but..." Thielmann began.

"They are fast, powerful, and very rugged. I put at least ten cannon rounds into one and I saw no effect." Taube tossed down another tumbler of liquor. "*Mine Gott,*" he muttered, "What we shouldn't give for a group of those. They almost seem..."

"Russian," Thielmann finished. "Rugged, fast, and powerful; superb aircraft. How the Americans came up with them, I have to wonder."

"It's..." An orderly entering the room interrupted Kaltz. "*Yes*, Ringe," he said, irritated.

"There is a uniformed *Gestapo* captain here for Captain Thielmann."

The others looked at Thielmann quizzically. Why would the *Gestapo* want me? Thielmann wondered; probably just something routine. When they appeared in uniform, it was almost always some routine matter: in their well-fitted suits, one had cause to worry. "We shall come back to this," he said as he left.

"What is it now, Zimmer?" Thielmann sighed, plainly annoyed, not returning the obligatory salute. He noted Zimmer had been promoted to Captain.

"I congratulate you on your continued good fortune, Captain Thielmann," Zimmer smiled falsely, no honor in his voice or in him. "I wish you continued success against the enemies of the *Reich.*"

"You didn't come here to hand out laurels, Zimmer. What is it?"

"Oh, a minor matter, really. I have a probably false report about you and *Luftlag X* last Christmas. I just wanted to clear the matter up."

"What about *Luftlag X*? It is a prison camp. We visited it last December and left behind some food. What of it?"

"Yes. Apparently, the food was distributed to—and this is the minor point—the enemies of the *Reich.*"

"So? Talk to the camp administration. We were not present when the food was handed out. Why come to me?"

"Well, incredible as it may seem, the camp cook has reported that you directed it to be given to the enemies of the *Reich*. There cannot be any truth to that, can there?"

"What if there was," Thielmann replied, growing increasingly weary and even more annoyed.

"Well, that would be most unfortunate. That would give aid and comfort to the enemy. That would make things very difficult for you, and for your family."

"Zimmer," Thielmann whispered, barely controlling his rage, "say you are not threatening me or my family. Say you are not."

"I do not threaten anyone, Captain Thielmann. I only report on what I know. This may be a matter for higher authorities, but I..."

"Zimmer," Thielmann said hoarsely, his eyes bulging with fury, "you are threatening my uncle, a decorated hero of Stalingrad who lost his arm in one of the final successes in that hero's graveyard? You are threatening my brother, who lost his toes fighting the communists? You are threatening my father, a personal friend of Admiral Canaris? Zimmer, say you are not?"

"Well, I...no. I charge *you*, Thielmann, and that old man in charge of this highly suspect unit. I..."

"Kaltz? You threaten Kaltz? Kaltz, who saved *Reichsmarshall* Goering's life in the last war? And me? Zimmer, on any given day I fly in the face of a thousand heavy machine guns at least once; as often as six times. And you threaten me, a decorated flyer with over seventy aerial victories? *What* do you threaten me with, Zimmer? *What?*"

"I don't threaten, Captain, I merely report..."

"I know you are not serious, Zimmer, so I dismiss you. Goodbye, Zimmer." Thielmann walked away, leaving Zimmer dumbfounded and incensed by the utter dismissal of the power projected by his uniform and insignia that worked so well with nearly everyone else.

"By the way, Zimmer," Thielmann called behind him, "how is your arm?"

May 1943

Bartlesby, England

I propose to fight it out on this line if it takes all summer

Ulysses S. Grant

T he small officer's club was dimly lit and reeked of stale whiskey, sweat and cigarettes, quiet even though it was full. The patrons were holding a wake for eighty of their fellows that went down that day. Clay Cole came in with a young new second lieutenant, gazing around the room. Against a far wall was a piano no one was playing. Over the bar were photographs of Hollywood actresses no one was ogling. Not even Betty Grable, Veronica Lake, or Barbara Stanwyck elicited so much as a glance. Scattered around the room, tables of officers were silently knocking down very large drinks. At the bar, nine officers were holding a muted conference.

"Look, if the gyros go in backwards, and they can, the C1 will think a 45 degree down attitude is straight and level. If it gets a downdraft and the autopilot's on, the pilot may just be too damn tired to disengage the damn thing, and the ship will go down screaming."

"But there's been no indication that that could happen before. Nobody's ever reported anything..." Marty Ballache, a pilot with as many missions as Miller, was trying to catch what Miller was pitching.

"I did, in Kansas," Miller said emphatically. "Some moron installed a new main gyro backwards, and my flight engineer had to kick out the main electrical panel before we got under control again."

"Did Boeing ever hear about it?" Piesec seemed dimly interested, not clowning this afternoon.

"*Hell* if *I* know. I wrote it up, but it's probably still in the file box I dropped it into."

"Well, I'm not ready to blame the autopilot," Ernie King finally added. "And I signed off on your report. I know it got to the manufacturer, but that's about all. Seems to me like, well, maybe it's a sort of...I dunno... release." The other pilots stared at their squadron commander, slightly offended that anyone could bring up the subject so soon.

"You mean suicide," Miller said, as the other pilots gazed at him incredulously. Atwell had been his copilot...

"Well, yeah..." The offender started, and then trailed off. The other officers studiously returned their gazes to their glasses or to nothing at all.

"That could be it," one of them said, after a long pause. "A pilot just so damn tired he noses in just to get some peace and quiet; a copilot who wants the same. Seems to make sense..."

"...And Atwell knew I didn't want to," Miller whispered after an even longer pause. "So when we get back from a run over Kiel, he goes behind the paint shed and blows his brains out." He said it with such detachment, it seemed inconceivable that it had happened only hours before. Some of them, Miller included, were fugitives from the law of averages—the one that said that five missions were average and six miraculous. The war for them had become a game of craps played with human lives instead of money or ration stamps. Sometimes the players just didn't want to do it anymore.

By then, Miller had two nicknames. The one used to his face by officers was "Iron John Miller," supposedly because he brought back airplanes that no one else thought was possible. He once landed a two-engine B-17 with two feet of each horizontal stabilizer and most of the rudder shot off. Instructor pilots in other groups often consulted him to advise on how to land cripples. He tried to take it all in stride, and as a matter of pride: he could do something no one else seemed to be able to do.

The other nickname that the enlisted men used, the one that Farr had started more than one fight over, was "Killer Miller," because he had a nasty reputation for bringing back a lot of dead crewmen. By the time he had fourteen missions, he had gone through nearly two complete crews, except for Farr. What that cruel epithet failed to acknowledge was that Miller brought more crewmen back alive than dead.

Cole sidled up to Miller at the bar, fresh lieutenant in tow. "Captain Miller, can we have a word? Colonel King; here's Lieutenant Witt all signed in. You met him yesterday." Miller threw back the remnants of his drink and pulled away from the discussion, following Cole, King and the new officer to a miraculously empty table. After sharing introductions, King went to the bar for fresh drinks and Cole left. After a moment, Miller stared at the new lieutenant.

"So, you're number three." Jerry Witt's china-blue eyes, fair complexion and unruly blonde hair made him look the part of a member of the Master Race.

"Yessir," Witt replied eagerly. There was a long pause before Miller said anything more.

"Where'd you get your training?"

"Kelley, Scott, Selma."

Another pause, "Where're you from?"

"Chicago."

This went on for another five minutes or so, with an eternity between questions. It was just general stuff, mostly—any family, how long in England, etc.—but throughout, Witt felt like Miller's glances weren't so much at him as *through* him, like he was seeing someone behind him. Witt's attempts at idle chit-chat were met with monosyllabic responses.

"Well, I hafta tell ya," Miller said at length, "'cause you'll likely hear it from somebody else soon enough. My last copilot blew his brains out about four hours ago. So forgive me if I don't get too excited or too friendly. I'm just too tired." Right about then, King returned with the drinks.

Miller excused himself to the latrine. Witt and King were alone. "Is it just me, sir, or is he really a cold fish?" the junior officer asked.

King weighed his answer carefully before responding. "He's a fugitive from the law of averages, and he knows it. You are his third copilot. Like I told you in my office, one other is dead, so is most of his original crew. Learn this quick: it's easier to lose strangers on your ship than it is to lose friends. For that reason, Miller doesn't *want* to know you. All he wants is to work with you and get back home again." King regarded his glass of whiskey as if it were a particular species of bug. "In a time of peace, we hope all our friends outlive us. In time of war, we don't." Someone started playing the piano...badly. King looked calmly at the young man, measuring his words and his tone with care. "John Miller is probably one of the best pilots in the Army Air Force. He's got more time in the air than most instructors have in the chow line, and he's pushing his luck. He just finished his fourteenth strike, a bad one over

Kiel. We lost eight ships today, eighty guys, and had twenty damaged. He's done fourteen strikes—more than the average crew—hell, more than the average airman does."

King pointed up to the bar, where the eight officers were continuing their discussion. "See them guys up there? They started the war together: them, Miller, and fifty-odd other pilots, when the 299th was declared operational last December and started receiving missions. Those guys up there and Miller are all that's left."

Witt listened in stunned silence, gazing around him at the men, a few much older than he, drinking, smoking, murmuring. He suddenly realized he had joined a very exclusive club, with the only membership requirement being that you had to risk your life and defeat all the odds. "All of them know," King continued, "that whenever they get together like this, the odds are that there will be at least one less of them than there was the time before, and sometimes it's worse, and it'll be worse yet. You might call them lucky. But call them cursed right now and call them lucky when the war's over. They came over here expecting to be going home in three months, tops. That's what we'd been teaching since the 'twenties. One strike per German city and that's all she wrote. Well, they've been here for six months now, and the only guys they know of going home are in coffins. And we've hit some German cities a half-dozen times already." King stared into space, his voice hollow. "I guess we got *that* wrong."

Miller returned to the table as King finished talking. "I wanna give Feynman a medal; a Silver Star," he said, looking at King. "He shot down two Messerschmitts and fixed the tail control cables on the ship today."

"OK," King said. "Write up the request, get it to Clay Cole and I'll get a citation cut." The two men went on about different subjects for a time, and then they entered the discussion of formations. Both had much the same opinion by then, but didn't come to voice them too often.

"A self-protecting bomber's so much bullshit," Miller said with uncomfortable conviction, "and I'm not too sure anymore about 'precision daylight bombing', either." Witt suddenly became very frightened, thinking, what they told us for all these months can't be wrong, can it...?

"In its purest theoretical form, yeah, I agree," King rejoined, "but what we do in the meantime soaks up German resources in ways that're hard to do otherwise. We've just about won in North Africa, we've taken back a few islands in the Pacific, and the Russians are grinding them up, and they're losing about a thousand people an hour doing it. We're doing a valuable service here."

Miller absorbed this quietly, but a rage within him was building. "But what we do doesn't hurt them," Miller suddenly blurted. "For six months I've been dropping bombs on targets I rarely see. Did we have anything to do with North Africa, or Russia or the Pacific? For us, this damn war's just some abstract terror we live through once a week. It's a kind of game we keep playing that we don't know all the rules. Hell, we don't even know we can win. I'm tired, sir. I'm tired and I don't think I can see a point in all this."

Almost immediately, a deep hush fell over the club, and Miller looked slightly embarrassed, as well he should have—he'd just blurted an over-loud shared sentiment of futility common to the bomber crews. Other officers were staring at him, wishing they hadn't heard it, wishing they'd had the courage to say it, but glad they didn't.

King sipped his drink, setting it down carefully. He turned to look at the young pilot calmly, much as a grandfather might an errant child. "OK, you're tired and you can't see what you're doing here," he said in an even voice. "We're all tired. But you know, so are the Germans. I got a briefing the other day on our last strike into Hanover, when we hit that airplane factory. The plant was back in production in about a week, but they had to dismantle three repair shops to do it. They can only keep up with battle damage for so long until they're just spread too thin. Every mission we shoot down fighters they have to replace somehow. Every now and then, the pilot doesn't get out, and they have to replace him. Just remember, we've—that's all the Allies—got a lot more people that we can put into bombers to knock down those fighters. So yeah, we're all pretty tired. But think of this: when you finish twenty-five missions you'll be able to go home, to go back 'Stateside to train other B-17 pilots. When a German bomber pilot makes 25 missions, he gets to stay right where he is and do *another* 25. I think we'll wear them out a lot faster than they'll wear us out."

Miller studied King's smooth face, trying to absorb what he had been told, to accept the nuances of the theory, as if looking for a map, a way out. "Does that make sense to you? Sir," Miller asked, after a long pause.

King stared hard at his glass and then squeezed his eyes shut. "Some," he said finally, immense pain in his voice, "but it's not a matter of making *sense*...it is what it is...it's our reality...we deal with it by focusing on our jobs." King rubbed his forehead vigorously, as if wiping away a tremendous burden.

"Look," he said, his normally even voice becoming loud and somewhat more Karloff-like, "all you guys are my responsibility. I have to send up the casualty feeder reports not only on your crew, but on everybody else's, and I have to report on every ship that doesn't come back, whether anyone saw them go down. I have to write all those letters, see that their gear is bagged up, all that shit. If YOU can't see the point, that's your problem. But I have NO CHOICE in the matter, OK? I NEED to know there's an end purpose—and an end—to ALL this." He wasn't angry at Miller, and there was no rancor in his voice. He was only saying, "that's *my* reason. You figure out your own."

"Yessir," Miller said, and continued smoking, staring off into space. The other officers turned away, slightly embarrassed, as if they had been staring at something unpleasant for too long. Witt felt as if he'd intruded into a private feud and had little concept of what was really being said. He studied his glass, then his new pilot for a time. My God, he thought, will I be like that six months from now? He preferred not to think about it, opting instead for the relative numbness that drink could provide. He hastened to the bar and ordered three more drinks. When he returned to the table, neither King nor Miller had stirred.

After what seemed an eternity, Miller whispered, "Oh, Christ, enough o' this," and stood up, looking around the room. "Where is he... *there* he is," and made a bee-line to another table where he hauled another officer named Brubeck to his feet by his collar and commanded, "Come with me." He marched him to the piano, pushed the piano-player off the bench, plopped Brubeck down in his place and growled, through clenched teeth, "Roll out the Barrel."

Softly, Brubeck played the familiar tune. Miller slammed his fist on the keyboard and shouted, "BANG IT OUT, GODDAMNIT!" The playing got louder as Miller turned around to the astonished officers present. "NOW SING YOU IGNORANT BASTARDS! SING!"

Roll out the barrel;
We'll have a barrel of fun...

Stomping around the room and yelling furiously, "Sing, you meatheads, or I'll beat the bejesus out of all of ya!" Miller shouted as a man possessed, punching the air with his fists like a crazed maestro.

Roll out the barrel;

We've got the blues on the run...

Now John Miller stood about six feet two and weighed in at about 220, and when he said someone should do something, especially at the top of his lungs, it usually got done.

Zing! Boom! Tararrol!

Sing out a song of good cheer!

Gradually, but with growing volume and fervor, the officers sang the familiar tune as Miller browbeat the recalcitrant into line. Even Smith and Lincoln, two officers from the truck platoon jammed into their "colored officers only" corner, had joined in. "Sing, or I'll beat your damn brains in. SING I SAID!"

Now's the time to roll out the barrel;

For the gang's all here!

"AGAIN," Miller shouted, and Brubeck started from the top. No one was about to call these "festivities" to a halt. Chorus after chorus belted out in the tiny, smelly, dimly lit room, and all the while, Miller urged them on, accompanied by Brubeck's masterful playing. After the fourth repetition or so, Miller sat down again, and the room was much as it should have been all night: men laughing, drinking, swearing, lying about their exploits and conquests, talking about their homes, another time, another place.

May 1943

Marburg, Germany

I am short a cheekbone and an ear,
But I am able to whip all hell yet

John M. Corse

T he war had not yet been cruel to Marburg: harsh, perhaps, but not nearly as cruel as it had been to, say, London or Cologne. But Marburg was a small town in comparison, with little to attract the attention of most of the outside world. Once in a while, Allied bombers would confuse the confluence of the Niesse and the Lahn Rivers outside the town for something else and drop some bombs and slaughter a few cows, but little else.

The Thielmanns were having a reunion, of sorts, gathering at Lothar's empty butcher shop on the town square, itself almost devoid of foot traffic. Lothar arrived first, riding a freight train from Wilhelmshaven where he'd been working for the Abwehr. The farm, now worked by a neighbor, was much the same, but dustier than he recalled. Then again, he hadn't been there for some months. His butcher shop too was dusty, the shelves long empty, the massive block clean, freshly scraped, and unused. His brother Georg-Hans arrived in a borrowed staff car from a rehabilitation hospital in Bavaria, resplendent in his infantry *Unteroffizier* uniform, empty right sleeve pinned up neatly, Knight's Cross with oak leaves gleaming on his tunic pocket. He was gaunt, a mere shadow of the man he once was.

Ulrich hitched a ride from an Army caravan from a naval hospital at Kiel and arrived at the shop, clopping his way across the square balanced by two canes. Learning to walk again without toes was a long process, but he was getting the hang of it. Otto flew in a *Storch* borrowed from the headquarters for the occasion, the last to arrive; his small body with the huge boxer's shoulders seemed too tiny for his uniform, his Knight's Cross a little more weathered than his uncle's. There was little expressed joviality between them. German formality, even in family gatherings, still held them in its grip. And the memory of the death of friends—and even acquaintances—strained their relations with everyone, even family.

"What do we hear of Anna?" Ulrich asked his father.

"China is an evil place," Lothar sighed. "I get a note once in a while in the diplomatic pouch. It is full of starvation, disease, pestilence, petty cruelty, neglect, and constant warfare, and in the Japanese-occupied zones it is worse, she says. But she and Adam are well. How are they treating you?"

"Well enough, I suppose. The *Kriegsmarine* says I may not fly for another three months at least. In two weeks I'm to report to a coastal station in France as a weatherman. If I can't fly at least I can try to predict when the English are coming. How long were you out of the cockpit, Otto?"

"Let me see; I was shot down in December, out of bed in May, flying trainers by July, so seven months. What do they tell you, Uncle?"

"I'm to be posted to an infantry training barracks at Baumholder. I'm in a special ward of Stalingrad survivors for now, and all we do is brood all the time. It depresses even me. If it were not for this Knight's Cross I'm wearing, I wouldn't have even been able to come here. I see you got one too, Otto."

"Yes, I did, but only for being a better shot and being slipperier than the rest."

"How many victories do you have now?" Lothar asked.

"Seventy-five confirmed, thirteen unconfirmed."

"My God! That's a tremendous number," Georg-Hans exclaimed.

"Illusory, Georgi; merely night and fog. Some are for victories of landed machines; some are for idiots in a cockpit. Mine are nothing like your accomplishments."

"What accomplishments? You know how I got this medal? I robbed a bakery, that's all. I robbed a bakery less than a hundred meters from a position we'd been in for a week, and it cost a hundred Germans to get that bakery. A hundred Germans that had been eating rat meat for a month killed a thousand Ivans that fight all day on a fistful of grain and a swallow of vodka. No accomplishment, Otto."

"Is that how you lost your arm?" Ulrich asked.

"I got drunk. That bakery had casks of vodka, so when we got there, we all had a swig or two. That Russian fire in a bottle got us pop-eyed in moments. I fell into a hole and a piece of iron bar went through my arm. Well, in my company, I had men who had been shot three times and were still on their feet. So I pulled it out and ignored it. It got infected, and they had to take it off. But as a reward for threatening an adjutant with a grenade to attack that bakery, they gave me the oak leaves for the Knight's Cross I got in France, and they gave me ten day's leave out of Stalingrad. How did you lose your toes, Uli?"

"That was nothing so dramatic. I was watching weather developments off the Estonian coast and my machine got jumped by some MiGs. I went into the water and was frozen by the time they got to me. They took my toes to save my feet."

"Watching weather developments? What on earth do you mean?" Lothar asked, genuinely interested because the weather always interested farmers and butchers who *relied* on farms.

"Some eggheads have guessed that the weather can be predicted more accurately if we can see it on radar; actually measure the size of weather fronts. Perhaps they are right, but our radar just isn't good enough."

"Surely," Otto interrupted, "there has to be a good enough apparatus to see something as dense as a thundercloud."

"Yes, but thunderclouds are far denser than the more common rain stuff," Ulrich said with some disgust. "We've tried other equipment, but even fog is transparent to our instruments; except we can't see through it well enough to identify other planes."

"I'm sure someone is working on that," Otto declared. "In fact, I know they are."

"Perhaps; MiGs jumped me. What shot you down? "

"It was Yaks for me. Bastards learned to fly overnight as far as I was concerned. Thirty of them jumped fifteen Messerschmitts out of the sun. Got most of the bombers we were escorting, too. It's all a tremendous waste, as far as I could tell."

"Why a waste?" Lothar asked, concerned that Otto had gone too far.

"Because for all the good we did in our late-fall drive on Moscow, we could have spent that time, fuel, not to mention those lives, fortifying what we'd gained by September. The *spadenpaulis* didn't even have winter clothes."

"No, we didn't." Georg-Hans agreed. "We had the Ivans to keep us warm that winter. Between General Winter, Marshal Mud and Mother Russia, we never stood a chance. Once they attacked, we just started moving backwards. I was in the Crimea that winter, but I think that whole godforsaken country turns into an icebox in November and an oven in June."

There was a silence, suddenly, in the small butcher shop. Otto and Lothar each chose that moment for a furtive glance out the shop window, and then at each other...still no pedestrians...good, that's good. No one looked at the others, no one spoke, no one moved. "What are we doing?" Georg-Hans whispered.

"We are watching Germany die," Lothar said, "Murdered in her sleep."

"We're not asleep, Papa," Otto said. "We're trying to save her..."

"We *have* to be rid of the Nazis. As long as they are about, they will kill Germany. It is inevitable."

"The Nazis aren't killing Germany, Papa," Ulrich said, "but they are not saving them, either."

"They're looting France," Otto said flatly, "and as much of what else they've conquered as they think they can get away with."

"We did most of the conquering on their orders, Otto," Georg-Hans chided. "Nazis don't conquer a lot. Good at giving orders..."

"But we've had some successes," Ulrich said. "Africa..."

"Lost," Lothar said. "It is only a matter of hours now." Ulrich stared at him, stunned. Reverses, yes, but to lose a continent...

"Yes," Otto added, "that makes sense. The radio has been talking about the 'brave defenders of Tunis' the same way they talked about Stalingrad just before...oh, sorry, Georg-Hans."

"Think nothing of it, Otto."

"I think they've broken our codes," Lothar said softly, knowing that just mentioning the idea was grounds for execution.

"Enigma," Ulrich said. "How?"

"It is mathematically possible. The entire system is based on a pre-war commercial machine, so it cannot be that difficult to duplicate. And we think they may have a naval machine..."

"Then we must change it," Otto said. He knew of the strange typewriter-like device, but had never had to use one and knew nothing of it other than it took weeks of training to operate correctly.

"Cannot be done," Lothar said evenly. "There are over thirty thousand of them in use. If they have cracked the basic pattern of the nine-rotor naval machine, the rest are vulnerable. It would take years in peacetime to change the codes and retrain the operators. It would take forever in wartime."

"And we were making lip rouge until last Christmas," Ulrich said. Silence again.

"I saw Zimmer a few months ago," Otto said.

"You, too? What did that turd want from you?" Georg-Hans wondered.

"That pest from the *Spiesenstrasse*?" Lothar wondered. "The little creature chased Anna around for a while and did odd jobs until the Nazis came?"

"Him; yes, I remember that little coward now," Ulrich said. "Tried to steal from the tomato garden once and I boxed his ears. Didn't the *SA* throw him out?"

"Perhaps," Otto replied, "but he was the *HJ* leader here and the *SS* took him in. He's a *Gestapo* captain now..."

Lothar said, "He came to see me in '39 about Adam's grandmother. I threw him out."

"You, too, Papa? Ha! That's good," Otto rejoined. "I reminded him that Rickmann broke his arm."

"When did he do that?" Ulrich asked.

"Let's see. Late '35, I think, you were at the *Marineakademie*. He and his henchmen beat up old *Herr* Baumer, so Gunther Rickmann and I put a stop to it; too late, regrettably."

"The old man who lived above the shop? I wondered what happened to him," Ulrich said. "He was such a kindly old soul. Told us scary stories on summer nights down by the river, remember, Georgi?"

"Oh, yes; frightened us to death. How is Rickmann, anyway?"

"Dead; Poland." Silence again.

"What's happened to the Jews?" Otto was genuinely interested, but asked timidly.

"Resettled...I think..." Lothar began.

"No," Georg-Hans said flatly, savagely. "If they are not in their homes or out of Europe, they are dead or in the Russian forests. I know where thousands of them are buried, in a big pit outside Kiev, a place called Babi Yar. I know. I delivered them there. I therefore wish never to discuss the matter ever again on pain of remaining drunk for the remainder of my natural life." They looked at him—nephews, brother— as if he had just sprouted an additional head.

"Concentration camps?" Ulrich asked of no one in particular. There had been persistent rumors of such abominations before the war began; almost a fairy story of a place called Dachau, rumors that defied common sense.

"Probably," Georg-Hans answered. "I don't know. I don't want to know. I know too much already."

"My God," Lothar whispered, "what have we done?"

"I don't *know*, brother," Georg-Hans answered, "and if it were not for the Ivans, I'd say surrender to the Tommies and the *Amis* today and hand them the Nazis on a plate."

"I'm not sure that would satisfy them, Georgi," Ulrich said. "Not after the last war..."

"I wouldn't worry about another Versailles, not with Stalin over there. No, we must prevail, Uli, or they shall partition us between the communists and the west, and Germany shall never have peace again."

"I have some...peace," Otto said. "A young woman I met last year. Elsa Portz is her name." His father, brother and uncle all stared at him eagerly, glad for something else to talk about. "She's a widow; her husband was in the U-boats and has been missing since 1940. Her maiden name is Greitz...."

"Greitz," Lothar asked. "I know of an Adam Greitz, lieutenant general of police and commandant of the northern police district. Can there be a connection?" Otto stared at his father for a long moment. "*Herr General* Greitz handles security on the North Sea and Baltic coasts. He often speaks of his son-in-law, who he claims perished, while sinking an American battleship. False, of course, but there it is."

"He's her father, and she hates him. Does he speak of Elsa?"

"No," Lothar said. "He never mentions her."

"That would explain a great deal," Otto said. "She won't even mention his name without bitterness." They chatted long into the night, sharing wine, cheese, and bread.

They wondered to themselves if they would ever see each other again.

***

Otto and Elsa were together on holiday for a precious four days in a small village in the hills west of Marburg. They spoke of much, but they said nothing at all; deciding things would take too long. They swam in a small lake in the evenings, made love in the mornings;

walked the hills and ate cheese and drank wine in the afternoons. On their last afternoon together, Elsa became sad while they gazed up through the trees at an azure sky. "What will we do, Otto? You flying and fighting, me waiting for bombs to make others homeless. What is happening to Germany, to us?"

"Is there an 'us,' then," Otto murmured. "We haven't spoken of it since Christmas. What does 'us' mean to you?"

"You and me, Otto; Germany is finished, I think. Uncle will be shot, probably. My parents; Mother has hitched her cart to a rising Nazi star and I cannot help her. What of..."

"Of us, *Liebchen*, we can only hope that we all survive..."

"Then stop flying," Elsa said, suddenly adamant. "Go to that Florida place and stop flying." He could do it, he knew; others had gone to the Bavarian resort the *Luftwaffe* had turned into a rest camp for flyers that everyone called Florida. Many went and came back refreshed; Taube had, so had Pritzler. But others went and never came back, taking themselves off flying status altogether. Yes, he could go...but would he ever go back to flying afterwards? Because he didn't know, he didn't know if he should go. He loved to fly, but the hunting was getting... stale, and at the scale that the Giant Killers had reached, viciously frightening...and sad.

"I could," he answered, suddenly as serious as he could make himself while lying naked in a wood next to the one person in the world that he genuinely cared about, staring at the sky. "But can we abandon our friends to their fates?" He rolled over in the pine needles, looking at her angelic face. "Can you abandon your Red Cross work? The city will be bombed again, perhaps soon. What will you do if you just run away and they devastate the place, like Cologne or Rostock? Besides," hearing a faint airplane engine in the distance, "where would you go?"

She cried, great quaking sobs making her whole body shake. "I can't...give...you...a...future..."

"No, *Liebchen*, I cannot expect more." He held her face in his hands and smiled. "There will always be an 'us,' as long as we remember 'now.'" And they made love as the contrails swirled overhead and the spent cartridge casings fell gently into the trees.

My love for Elsa knows no boundaries, Thielmann thought, breathless in the shadows. I want so very much to be with her forever, so I can forget the killing at which I have become so adept.

June 1943

Bartlesby, England

When things are going badly in battle,
The best tonic is to take one's mind off one's own troubles
By considering what a rotten time one's opponent is having

Archibald Wavell

The dense fog was enveloping most of England that morning, and Bartlesby's share was well-nigh impenetrable. The field, normally a noisy hub of activity, was eerily silent, as if wrapped in chilly, soggy cotton wool. Since there was no flying, there was ground training, and ground training varied a great deal. The 610th stayed in their billets performing aircraft identification drills, or at least that's what the training schedule said. The 192nd was hanging around their Fortresses pretending to practice aircraft evacuation. They said the 191st was training in emergency repairs, and the 190th was down for maintenance, which meant that Miller and his crew had even less to do than on normal non-flying days.

But since there was a fog, and since Bartlesby was one of the ten lucky bases that had a FIDO system, Miller's additional duty as assistant FIDO officer was suddenly important. Lacking anything else to do, Witt followed him around.

FIDO stood for "Fog, Intense, Dispersal Of," a Rube-Goldberg seeming device that actually worked despite the occasional guffaw the unknowing uttered when first told about it. It comprised several troughs filled with gas and lit by brave and fleet of foot souls. Oversized fans blew the heated air over the longer runways, raising the surface temperature and dispersing the fog. As Witt wandered behind Miller in astonishment, Miller checked the fuel lines, burners, and lubricant levels on the overlarge fan oilers.

"These fans get real hot," Miller explained, "so we put these big oilers on the drives and sheaves." Miller started briefly as the air-raid siren yelped and then was quiet. "Guess the engineers gotta test that stuff, too," he said sheepishly, slightly embarrassed at his reaction. Then his ears picked up a distinct sound in the dense, wet air. "Maybe it wasn't a test," he muttered, pivoting towards the end of the runway. Others near the strip had heard the same distinct sound, and were straining for the source. The air-raid siren yelped again and then turned to a mighty wail.

"AIR RAID! THIS IS NO SHIT! AIR RAID," the loudspeaker thundered, "ALL PERSONNEL TO YOUR STATIONS! AIR RAID!"

In the white, gloomy silence, the men started running around, seemingly aimlessly. The ground guns (20mm cannons mounted on trucks) and the 40mm antiaircraft guns on the sandbag gun towers began to slew about looking for targets. Most of the Bartlesby base's men were hustling off to the sandbag and corrugated iron air-raid shelters.

Few had actually got to the shelters before the attacker appeared at the end of the field. A JU-88 with the left engine out and the right sputtering broke through the thin "fog tunnel" roof and lined up on the left runway, and as soon as Miller could see it the gun towers began hammering away, but stopped almost as soon as they started as Geoghegan shouted a 'check fire.' Miller watched in amazement as the German medium bomber, badly damaged in several places in the left wing and cockpit area, struggled to stay level. "Weather ship," Miller said, "must've been hit over the Channel. See that weird antenna on the roof?" he pointed out to Witt. "Radar; usually unarmed, but the RAF shoots 'em down, anyway."

Watching the struggling cripple trying to land, Miller felt transformed, as if it was no longer important that he was an enemy, and under slightly different circumstances, they would try to kill each other. At that moment, it was simply one pilot was watching a fellow pilot trying to land in a dangerous situation. "Hold it steady," he murmured, watching. "Nose up...wings level ... not too much power... you've got all the runway you need...hold it steady... that's it ...hold steady..."

The German descended quickly, bouncing badly at mid-runway, but somehow maintaining control. "He may not have much throttle control," Witt offered.

"Mm," Miller responded. "Probably not much aileron or flap control, either. Come on," he said, trotting after a small truck that had started out to the strip. Suddenly there were hundreds of men making for the runway, led by a dozen vehicles. The JU finally came to a halt three-fourths of the way down the runway, and the trucks and jeeps were following behind.

Bartlesby was privileged to have assigned to it the 335th Engineer Company (Aviation) (Firefighting/Rescue), part of Sanda's immense engineering command. The men of the 335th were pioneers in the highly specialized tasks required to save crewmen in airplane crashes. First on the scene was hulking Chief Warrant Officer Mike French, former Public Safety director for Nome, Alaska, in his fire truck. After playing water on the fuel leaking on the wing tanks, they sprayed carbon dioxide on the engine fire. Next to arrive was Casey Philukuzki and a dozen mechanics on a deuce- and-a-half. They were the only armed party to arrive for some minutes, with Philukuzki himself brandishing a fifty-caliber that he had dismounted from one of the air defense positions.

Next on the scene was Chief Warrant Officer Steve Latham— former Forestry Department fire chief in Utah—and his rescue crew with their five-ton truck. With little ceremony or hesitation, Latham's crew ran their ladder up the side of the ship, smashed in the remains of the cockpit glass, and started hauling out the crew. Their training, like the rest of the station's emergency crew, precluded any thought about nationalities. Their job was to get in and get the crew out. Nothing else really mattered at that moment, not even if they were dead or alive. The ambulance squealed up just as they handed the German pilot down. Doc Tippie, a third-year medical student from Illinois who became a physician's assistant when he enlisted after Pearl Harbor, roughly hauled him away from the scene.

The rescue crew was pulling out the second crewman when Throck shouted, "HOLD IT!" and everyone turned to look.

"More foam," Chief French bellowed. "I'm outta foam!"

"Wait a minute," Throck shouted again, "this is a German!" Activity, except for Chief French and his fire crew, seemed to stop. Miller glanced at the wounded pilot being attended by Tippie, at rescuers poised in mid-stride, then at the stricken ship, and finally back at Throck.

"No nationalities in the lifeboats, sir," Miller said, and everything went on as before.

"Well," Throck sputtered in frustration, "at least disarm him, Doc." Tippie distractedly removed the pilot's pistol from its holster and tossed it to an aide man.

"You'll be all right," Tippie said in passable German. The pilot had a gash across his forehead, some superficial burns on his hip and a fragment in his arm. The second German, lying in a litter, was much worse. His back was badly burned, and he had parts of his seat imbedded in it.

A large audience was gathering around the JU as an MP gun jeep with Greene aboard roared up and a dozen armed MPs surrounded Tippie and his patients. "Give 'em some air," Tippie growled at them, "they're not going anywhere." By then, the JU had been on the ground for all of five minutes.

The fire was out, and the aircraft was safe for the rubberneckers like Miller and Witt to move in to have a look.

The German pilot started yelling something at the rescue crew, who were just then climbing off the airplane. "He says there's somebody else in the ship," Witt offered. Throck moved toward the German, a seemingly too-young, frail man with blondish hair and too-old blue eyes. Throck questioned the pilot in fluent Polish-accent German, Witt in his native tongue that he learned at the knee of his Saxon parents.

"Back of the flight deck," Throck shouted, "where the bomb bay should be." The rescue crew used one of their air-powered cutters to slash through a jammed bulkhead door, and then there was quiet again. Latham poked his head out of the hole.

"Doc," he shouted, "this one don't look good." Tippie hustled up the ladder and down into the dark compartment, emerging in moments.

"Rogers," he yelled at his aide man. "Get Doctor Hamman. Quick." Then he said to Throck and all those who would hear, "Not good at all. Got a piece of the aircraft frame stuck in the back of his neck between the third and fourth cervical vertebra and coming out under his chin. We can't move him without shutting off his lights for good. Don't quite know what to do." Then he walked to the German pilot, who was waiting anxiously for some news.

He chatted with the pilot briefly, with Throck and Witt providing translations: Tippie's college German was woefully insufficient. The litter patient was only barely conscious, murmuring faintly. The pilot seemed as distressed as any of the thousand airmen standing around the JU might have been when told the same thing about one of their crew members.

"What can you do?" Throck asked. "We gotta get this thing off the runway."

"Not much without killing him," Tippie replied. "If the dura of the spinal cord has been breached, there may not be much hope at all, and it's just a matter of time. If it hasn't, and I can't know without more tests, we may get him out if we remove the splinter with him, but I don't know. He's at a funny angle, back jammed into a rear corner. Difficult to get to. Too much movement could cut his jugular, carotid, valgus nerve, do all kinds of damage, finish what's already started."

Satisfied, Throck rattled some instructions to his adjutant, the owlish Colonel Baker Hughes, essentially closing down the field. He'd catch some hell, but right then he was looking at someone who may have been going down for the last time, and he was throwing the life preserver.

The MPs started to haul the German pilot off, but Miller stopped them. "He can stay here." An MP Sergeant gazed at Miller, and then looked to Greene. Greene shrugged, and they dropped the matter. The ambulance did, however, take the second German off to the base hospital.

The doctor arrived shortly after and confirmed Tippie's diagnosis. After a brief discussion, the two went back to Throck. "Not much that I can add," the doctor said. "He needs a neurologist, a few hours, and a miracle. I'm a pediatrician by practice. The nearest neurologist would be in London. Even if we can get one here, we can't hardly get at the patient. Trouble is, he's not dying. In his present state, we can keep him alive indefinitely. Move him and he might go, though." So this is what it had come to, Miller thought bitterly. We have invented so many ways of killing each other that we could save people only to have the medical profession just let them go. There has to be another way...

"What if we cut the ship apart?" Miller shouted. The crowd turned to look at him, at first with surprise, then with some eagerness. Throck talked to the pilot.

"Let the pilot have a look," Throck replied. After a few moments, he came back out of the plane.

"We'll have to brace at the midsection and aft of the bomb bay," Witt translated. "But he's seen his maintenance guys do it with an overhead crane. He thinks he can remember how."

Throck and Sanda conferred briefly, each pointing to the airplane, waving arms in the air, and gesturing to various parts of the field. They had known each other for about six months, and their relationship was mostly harmonious: Throck took care of the flying part, and Sanda the ground part. But this had to do with airplanes and the airfield, a gray area.

"OK." Throck said, taking charge of his unit again. "Philukuzki, get a couple of beam hoists out here. Rich, I want your best metal fitters out here. C'mon, *hustle, chop-chop, get the lead out!*"

At the same instant, Sanda began shouting at his people. "Bliss, we need thirty thousand feet of sandbags, a thousand yards of perforated mat, and six ten-inch steel I-beams out here *right now,* and I mean *yesterday!* De Witt, find me enough portable compressors to power five pneumatic jacks. Billings, see how many light sets you can string around. C'mon elves, move out, we ain't got all day..."

***

By mid-afternoon the JU was in pieces—forward portion, wings, with the bomb bay and tail kept at precisely the same angle as they had been at landing by a mountain of sandbags and a jumble of I-beams, steel matting and jack stands. Tippie and Hamman were in the bomb bay watching the patient, who was full of morphine and breathing deeply. The German pilot was directing the removal of the remaining sheet metal from the center section, and the Technical Intelligence guys up from High Wycombe were inspecting the cockpit and the instruments as they came out of the ship. The RAF eggheads had showed up at about noon and were mildly protesting the butchering of a perfectly suitable aircraft to save a German, but they just didn't understand. The man in the plane wasn't a German just then: he was a fellow flyer in trouble.

In the center of this dismantlement was John Miller, a self-appointed liaison between the engineers and ground specialists and the aviators and their mechanics. Miller found the water drain when Haan needed to know how to de fuel the wing tanks. When Geoghegan needed help dismounting the JU's only machine gun, it was Miller that got an adequate translation from the pilot how the pintle worked. When Sanda's engineers showed up with the first I-beams, it was Miller who devised a pair of quick A-frames from steel mats. He was just a semester short of a mechanical engineering degree, so he knew a little about machinery: that, and spending much of his childhood overhauling airplanes in a pole barn had given him more than enough experience for this little job.

It just so happened that the chief neurologist of the whole Army Air Force was in England, Dr. A. N. McCartle. He had arrived just as the nose section was pulled away. In his world of academic medicine, nothing ever happened that fast or expediently, and he seemed stunned as the airplane was being pulled apart. He made a cursory inspection of the patient, conferred with the other two medical men present, thought about it for a minute, studied the results of a spinal tap performed a few hours before, and then clapped his hands together. "OK, we've done everything right. Now, get the rest of the sheet metal away from him. He hasn't lost that much blood, but with all that morphine and his general condition, I want to pack his blood in case we cut the carotid when we separate him from that frame. What's his type?"

"That's the bad part," Tippie said. "He's AB Negative. Nobody on the station's AB Neg."

"Not true," a voice said, and the three turned to the voice. Sergeant George Owen, a Mississippi River boatman from the truck company, stared at them, arms across his chest. Owen was, like all the men in his company, black. "I'm AB Neg."

The three medical men glanced at each other, silently exchanging the same arguments that had been fiercely exchanged in the medical community for a generation. "The blood supply is segregated," Hamman said feebly.

"For no damn good reason," another voice boomed. "And you gentlemen know that as well as I do. And I should know it's segregated because I'm in charge of the colored part."

The source was a barrel-chested Negro officer with a caduceus. "Cooper's my name," he said. "Up here for a medical check on the coloreds because Jim Crow says the white doctor here can't. Now," he went on, his stentorian voice rolling over the field, "you've gone through all this trouble to save this guy and all you need is a pint or two of blood. The sergeant here wants to give it. Hell, I'll even take it *for* you."

"Dr. Dean Cooper, I presume," Hamman replied. "Doctor of Medicine from Howard University in 1932, residency at All Saints in Memphis. You've reorganized the American parasitology and hematology departments in Britain, started on the British, and you're moving to hematology and even virology. I've read some of your work; brilliant." With that, he extended his hand. "Tell us, doctor, if you'll have a look at the patient and no one objects...Anybody here object?" he shouted at the crowd.

The asking was obligatory in the political atmosphere of the time, but seemed odd at the moment. "Yeah, I object," someone in the back of the crowd shouted. "I ain't gonna sit still for no..."

"*Cossack*," Philukuzki snarled, socking the protester in the jaw and knocking him to the ground. Throck stared at the lanky crew chief, still shivering at the word *Cossack*. "What else was I to do, Boris Vissaryonovitch?" Philukuzki asked in an odd mix of Alabama-accented Polish-Russian.

Childhood visions of horse-borne murder flashed in their minds, no less terrifying than any other night riders. "They murder us because we are Poles, Casmir Pietrovitch, and because they are *Cossacks*," Throck answered in a similar, mixed dialect. "He got what he deserved." Though no one else on the field understood a word they said, they knew what they meant.

"I would be delighted, doctor," Cooper replied. A brief glance was all he needed. "Ice, gentlemen; pack his spine and his head in ice to reduce any swelling. I believe a pint and a half of blood should do, providing the donor can stand it."

McCartle slapped himself on the head in a comic gesture. "Ice; of course; damn, where's my head today?" He looked at Cooper with a little disdain mixed with dubious respect. "And just *how* would you propose we..."

"Life vests, doctor," Cooper replied without hesitation or malice. "Tear them open, fill them with ice, and sew 'em back together with..."

"Riggers," Sanda shouted; "we need ten rubber tubes for five pounds of ice each, and wool socks for insulation. While we're at it, get the portable ice machine out here. *Hustle*, elves, *hustle!*" Then to McCartle and Cooper, Sanda yelled; "That do it?" McCartle, too stunned by the lightning-fast responses to make sense, nodded.

"You'll have the blood in fifteen minutes, doctor," Cooper said, grabbing Owen by the elbow.

***

A week later, Miller and Witt visited the hospital outside Manchester where wounded PWs stayed. They had brought cigarettes (always useful in a PW camp, the MPs had said, even if one doesn't smoke), and clean socks. The pilot was recovering, but his copilot had died of pneumonia. After introductions and informal chatter, Witt told him. "Oh; that's sad. I didn't know him that well. I know the weather observer better."

"He's *Kriegsmarine*, isn't he?"

"Yes, but we'd flown together on the Baltic. How is he?"

"He'll be stiff in the neck, maybe, they say. How did you find the field?"

"I saw a thin patch in the fog after we were hit. I was so busy trying to get away from the Indians that I lost track of my position. I dived into what I thought was a cloud bank and saw it. Uli—the weather observer—was badly hurt, and so was Wolf, the copilot. I couldn't get my bearings because all my instruments were smashed. But I had to get down to get them some help." They exchanged pleasantries for a time. The Americans said they would bury the copilot, as was their custom, and that the Red Cross would inform the next-of-kin.

"The weather observer's pay book," Witt asked, showing the pilot the small gray booklet borrowed from the MPs. "Lost his tags somewhere in the scuffle. This is his right name?"

"Yes. Thielmann," the pilot said, "Ulrich Thielmann."

June 1943

Oschersleben, Germany

Distant drum, sweet music

Turkish proverb

The old *Gasthaus* had, in its time, played host to six generations of German soldiers. Its blackened roof timbers had silently listened to long tales of places like Torgau, Waterloo, Königgratz, Metz, Tientsin, the Marne, and Tannenberg. For this one evening, they would stand mute witness to the regaling tales of a *Luftwaffe* fighter unit, toasting one of its most celebrated members who had just beaten von Richthofen's score. For the occasion, all the pilots and ground staff had, of course, been invited. As a matter of courtesy, they also invited the *Fliegerkorps* commander and other senior officers, all of whom respectfully declined in deference to the fact that such occasions were not for them, but for the men. Off in a tiny corner, a young man was pounding away a popular tune at a badly tuned piano, while a plain but earnest young woman sang along, nearly in the same key but not quite; nearly in time, but not exactly. Regardless of her musical talents, the young men in the serge blue uniforms were getting riotously drunk and increasingly infatuated with the well-endowed and gallant torch singer.

Thielmann sat quietly in the corner with Kaltz and his wingman of the moment, Felix Reicher, sipping his beer and schnapps, enjoying the relative calm. He felt oddly at peace, with a quiet detachment he could not quite explain. He had felt that way only occasionally and with great effort since he met Elsa in her mountain meadow when he had the time to think of her. Recently, he had not a lot of time, but wedged in a few moments each day, usually when he was playing with Gunther.

The torch singer sat on the old upright piano after being unceremoniously deposited there by several aircraft mechanics who were hanging on her every movement. With her split skirt exposing just a bit of naked thigh, her audience was even more enthralled. She dutifully sang out to her audience yet another slightly out-of-tune piece while the piano player diligently played more or less along.

"Amazing, isn't it," Kaltz said, watching his men and their evening's entertainment. "Just a few hours ago we were pulling Polenz out of his cockpit, and no one had any notion of being entertained. A few hours before that, you were fighting off Thunderbolts over Holland. And now here we all sit while that poor *Mädchen* tries very hard to entertain us, probably trying much harder than is necessary. I wonder, though, why her accompanist isn't in uniform."

"Can't you tell," Thielmann said with a grin, "he's completely deaf." Kaltz and Reicher chuckled. "I wonder if we don't have someone here who can play a little better."

"Well, I'm not *certain*, but I *think* Taube has some musical training," Thielmann said, looking around. "Taube," he shouted over the din when he spotted him, "can't you relieve the piano player for a while?"

"*Natürlich*," he shouted back, "but who will tell the poor boy that he cannot play?"

"I can," Pritzler said, standing up. The two aces, who between them had more than two hundred victories, weaved their way through the crowd to the piano, surrounded as it was with young drunken *Luftwaffe* men watching the slit skirt rise higher and higher. "Piano player," Pritzler loudly declared, setting both hands on the young man's shoulders, "You have done the *Reich* a great service this evening, but now I relieve you. Go now and rest, my young Siegfried. The *Luftwaffe* thanks you." The anemic musician was not one to miss a broad hint when he heard it, and besides, they had paid him in advance. He rose from the stool and went to the bar, still populated by a handful of regular customers. "Now, for your musical enjoyment this evening," Pritzler shouted to the audience, "our own Captain Heinz Taube, late of the Oschersleben Philharmonic Orchestra and Hunting Society, will accompany the talented *Fraulein...* er, what is your name?"

"Gloria Spanek," the singer offered demurely.

"*...Fraulein* Gloria Spanek," Pritzler finished with a flourish worthy of the greatest showman. Taube first played a range, tentatively at first, then with greater fervor, while the torch singer watched in amazement.

After a brief discussion, the two played *Edelweiss*. The room grew silent as the magical, mystical notes filled the smoke-enshrouded space. The torch singer had found the correct key, and her beautiful voice rang like a clear bell. Quietly the men sang the familiar tune, thinking of home, of wives, and parents, of friends and mountains, farms and forests, of anywhere but there....

Suddenly, Taube pounded the keyboard in frustration. "Useless, I'm afraid," he said with finality. "Quite useless."

"What, Taube? What's useless," Pritzler said. "The song was lovely."

"The piano: shot all to hell." There was a slight murmur in the crowd.

"I know of another piano," someone said. "Just down the street."

"Well, then," Pritzler declared, "we must go and borrow it." Kaltz mildly tried to stop his men, but knew that they were much too drunk to listen to reason. The mob bolted out of the *Gasthaus*, led by the Sergeant who knew of the other piano, which was quickly found in yet another *gasthaus*. "We are borrowing this instrument in the name of good music," Pritzler told the frantic innkeeper as they pushed it out his door. "We will return it when we are done."

Hoisting the instrument over curbstones, pushing it past slightly astonished lookers-on, the men managed to get it into the Gasthaus they started from in only a few minutes. Taube took one look at it, traced the gleaming letters STEINWAY with an appreciative finger, dropped his cigarette into his beer, and sat ceremoniously on a stool. First, the range, the same range, but with a much improved sound. Then, without hesitation or music, the *Luftwaffe* ace began Rachmaninoff's *Prelude in E Flat Minor*. The haunting notes chilled the spines of all who heard it in the overheated space. Even the torch singer watched in amazement as Taube played the beautiful music. Eyes languorously closed, feeling only the sounds and the keys, Taube hypnotically poured the music into his audience, washing like a rising tide over their sensibilities. Then gently, ever so lightly, he closed, with the notes still ringing in the blackened rafters. "Much better," he declared, "much better. Now, *Fraulein*, where were we?" The torch singer once again parked on the piano lid, and began again.

***

Somewhere near one in the morning, Kaltz rapped his glass on the heavy table for attention. "Gentlemen," he called out, "I have for our honored guest," bowing slightly to Thielmann, "a number of congratulatory messages that I should share with you. First, of course, from *Reichsmarshall* Göring: Congratulations on your eighty-first victory, and *etcetera*. Next, from *Generalmajor* Galland: Congratulations and *etcetera*. There is also a message from General Wolfram Richthofen: 'my uncle's score was brilliant, but your achievement' and so on and so on. Then, last but not least: 'Live long and fly well, my brother. Priller.'"

At hearing the name, the crowd grew silent, questioning. "Ach," Kaltz exclaimed, "Pips!"

"Oh, yes," Pritzler said, "Commander of JG26, no? Quite the flyer." Quite the flyer indeed, commanding the fighter group with the highest victory total in the *Luftwaffe*.

The music resumed, the congratulations were passed much later, but Thielmann kept only the last. The piano, somehow, never quite made it back to its owners.

June 1943

Wangerooge Is., Germany

We few, we happy few, we band of brothers

William Shakespeare

As missions went, this one hadn't been all that bad. Not exactly a milk run—over the North Sea island and a convoy cuing up in its lee—but not nearly as bad as Germany. *Crop Duster* came in with all crew members alive and only Digman slightly wounded by shrapnel. The rest of the group was coming in more or less intact, with two cripples using other fields and no losses; all in all, not that bad a strike. Miller set *Crop Duster* down on the runway in the usual manner, tripping out a flare for his wounded man. He brought her around to the hardstand and shut down the engines. A truck drove up as the crew debarked, and the gunners laid their dismounted guns in the truck bed as Philukuzki trotted up. "How'd she handle, Cap'n," the chief drawled.

"Pretty all right," Miller answered, pointing to the left outboard engine. "Look at that number one again, will ya? Every once in a while she'll lose oil pressure, but it comes back up in a few minutes."

Philukuzki studied the offending power plant from the ground, as if trying to divine its problem by osmosis. Farr stood next to him, reciting the list of symptoms the engine exhibited. "No particular overheating we could notice. I just wonder if a piece of sludge in the sump isn't trying to circulate every once in a while." The lanky crew chief nodded blandly, trying to work out a solution in his head that would solve the problem without having to dismantle the engine.

"We only got one spare left on the station," he muttered to Farr. "Can't afford to strip this one for an intermittent problem, 'cuz we got three other ships with dead engines. No, sir, can't strip this one. Gotta think of somethin'..." Farr left Philukuzki to mull over the problem as the rest of the crew was hauling Digman out of the ship and onto a litter. He'd caught a flak fragment in his right thigh ...it'd bled a bit, but wasn't serious. The jeep hauling the litter carried the rest of the enlisted men to debriefing while the officers rode the gun truck. The last of the squadron was landing as the crews were getting to debriefing.

The debriefing over, the crews stowed their gear and were preparing to clean the guns. As they moved out, Throck announced to the debriefing room; "we stand down for a week for maintenance and training. Make the best of it." Mild cheering and some loud conversation greeted this unexpected boon. Standing down meant no missions, at least in theory. There would be plenty of flying, but no missions. Thomas, carrying a telegram, came up to Miller, who was slinging his kit bag onto his back. The bombardier looked a little more than happy.

"Sir," the heavy-set Californian began, "Request permission for two days leave." Thomas was technically correct in asking his pilot for such permission, although all Miller did was approve of it. They got the actual paperwork and permissions through the squadron.

"Sure," Miller said. "What's up?"

"It's my dad," Thomas said excitedly. "He landed in Liverpool a week ago and he wants to see me." Thomas's father was a senior merchant marine officer, and the only family Thomas had. "You want to come along?"

"Well, I don't know..." Miller started, not wanting to intrude.

"Oh, no, don't worry about that. Besides, he's here, in Bartlesby. Says he's got sick of wharf rats and seamen, so he came here. It took two days for the Red Cross to find me. Got the telegram here," Thomas finished, holding up the paper. "I want to bring the whole crew, if I can. Take you all out for a drink or two. C'mon."

"All right, I'll get it cleared. Just one night, though. Can't have too much fraternization, you know." As they parted, Miller thought that that could be a problem if someone wanted to really make one, what with officers and enlisted men socializing together, especially with an officer who theoretically outranked the lot of them.

The permission—to take an entire crew off station at one time—was obtained by declaring it to be a special occasion to "improve relations with our brave merchant sailors" (nobody bought it, but it looked good on paper). Adequately attired in their finest Class A uniforms showing only some locker wear and green tarnish on their brass, the crew loaded into a truck borrowed for the purpose and set off for the town soon before dark.

The most popular pub in town for the Americans was called the Blind Dragon. Legend had it that the local Duke's ancestor had once defeated a rival by blinding him. Since the Duke's family coat-of-arms had a dragon's head, some wag had named the establishment in honor of the event, and had since been blessed with the Duke's patronage. Since the inn had been around for the better part of three centuries, the legend was easy enough to believe.

Once inside, they guided Miller and his men to an immense table near the back. Other public houses had had dust-ups between the "allies" billeted in the area, but the innkeeper, a spritely little Victoria Cross winner from the Boxer Rebellion, turned none of his comrades-in-arms away; he just kept them apart from each other. He wasn't anti-American, just careful, like all innkeepers who wanted to prevent embarrassing incidents.

Before they were seated, a big man in a spotless but worn blue uniform with four wide gold stripes on the cuffs greeted them. Captain William Tecumseh Sherman Thomas was a bear of a man who embraced his son unashamedly, laughing all the while with all the gusto of his life. He shook hands with Miller and all his crew, bellowing out greetings for each. "Lieutenant, how are ya...Sergeant Farr, you look like you've been here a while... Come on, all you guys, let's get started."

The barmaid delivered beer in huge glass mugs as they sat around the table, and all took the first sips gingerly. Captain Thomas made a face at the bitter, swearing, "Damn, I never will get used to English beer." Most of the crew chuckled in relief, glad that they didn't have to be embarrassed by saying what they thought. "It grows on me every night, though," he continued, which was met with more laughter.

"So, where are all you guys from?" the Captain bellowed, looking at Miller to start. One by one, the crew read off the list of their homes; northern Wisconsin...Chicago...Montana...southern Illinois...Iowa ...Florida...Queens...Arizona...the Army.

The conversation shifted only slightly, with generalizations about home, baseball, England, relatives, friends, and women. As they ate dinner with not a little fervor ("Anything better than Army chow" Digman quipped), conversation had not come close to touching on the war. Then someone, no one remembered who, asked, "so how long're you ashore, Captain?" As if by signal, all was still in the dimly lit alcove, as all sounds of food and drink and camaraderie seemed to suddenly stop.

The Captain stared into space for a moment, and then said quietly, "I really don't know. Lost my last ship, so now I just hitch along with convoys when they need me."

Thomas was aghast. "You lost your ship, Dad? When? How? I mean..." The big man just smiled at his son, shrugging almost imperceptibly and watching the boy with tired eyes.

"Yes, I lost her. Oh, I know, not supposed to talk about it, but, well, I'm just, oh..." he trailed off, blankly looking at the ceiling. Suddenly the whole crew was embarrassed, knowing that some unwritten rule of wartime conversation between warriors had been breached, and the magical flood of fear and pain and exhaustion that were ebbing away in the dim corner with good food and beer was suddenly backing up, and they would have to live with it again. Just as suddenly, the big merchant Captain banged his ham-like fist on the table and called out: "publican; more beer, and keep it coming." A schoolgirl had replaced the old man, fresh out of the garden and carrying a tray of mugs, easily weighing as much as she. The crew absently cleared the tray without so much as a thought to the bearer, who left crestfallen. Bloody Yanks, she thought, overfed, overpaid and over here....

The sailor leaned forward, tilting his head in that universal gesture of the yarn-spinner, beckoning his audience closer to hear a tale of danger and daring, of heroism and heroes, the kind of story told just once in a lifetime, never heard again or repeated, always remembered in a deep cellar of the mind, taken out and admired for its horrible beauty when the occasion warrants it...

And what a story it was! One of flashing torpedoes, listing ships, seas filled with junk and bodies, brilliant feats of engineering and seamanship, hurling bombs, popping flak, diving bombers, dying men, burning oil, exploding ships, shattered bulkheads, and a brave ship beached because she couldn't anchor and live, delivering three months of aviation gas to the flyers on The Rock called Malta, the Allied bastion in the central Mediterranean, so the Germans and Italians had to run an Allied gauntlet to Rommel's troops in North Africa. At the end, he was wistful, reflective, and the crowd was silent. "Great story, Cap'n," Farr said irreverently, "is *any* of it *true?*"

Thomas let out a great roaring laugh and the crew joined in. "Every *word*, my lad, every blessed *word* of it!"

June 1943

Verville, France

Know therefore that the sword is a cursed thing
Which a wise man uses only if he must

Li Po

Thielmann's encounter with the Lightnings had ended badly, although he had got one. Expertly, he jockeyed his crippled fighter to the ground, lining up on a road as an emergency runway. At the end, heavy shells from their 12.7mm guns and the 20mm (although Thielmann wondered if one of them hadn't had something larger) had damaged his engine, forcing him to land. As power diminished, he lowered the landing gear and set his plane down on the road. Clambering out of the cockpit, he inspected the engine. As he thought, several fuel lines were torn away, and the fuel pump had been destroyed. Now all he had to do was wait for help.

He watched his fellows still engaged in the sky above as he paused for a quiet smoke next to his plane. As he watched, he saw a parachute blossom directly overhead, observing its descent with growing interest. American, he thought, walking to the next field where the 'chute was landing. The pilot landed heavily, with a cry of pain on impact. Curious, Thielmann walked deliberately to the crumpled heap, brandishing his pistol. The parachute had caught a breeze and was dragging its occupant across the field. Thielmann ran easily in front of it, deflating the silk. He walked the shroud lines down to the pilot, who was struggling to get free of the cumbersome device. "*Stop*," Thielmann shouted. "*Ich hilfe.*"

Hit in both legs, the American valiantly tried to get up. Releasing him from his parachute harness, Thielmann forced him to stay down. The American was a Captain with reddish hair and a face full of

215

freckles, which now was little better than a mask of pain. Thielmann relieved him of the pistol from its shoulder holster and sat down beside him. Staring at each other, both wondered what would happen next. For you, the war is over, Thielmann thought. For me, it will still go on. I wonder which of us is more fortunate.

To break the stalemate, Thielmann offered his colleague a cigarette. The American declined, reaching into a shirt pocket for one of his own. He hesitated briefly, then offered Thielmann one. The German accepted, lighting his prisoner's cigarette and inhaling gratefully of the Virginia tobacco now so rare in Germany.

After a few minutes, an Army truck drove across the field, followed by a gang of farmers coming up from a nearby field. "Do you have an aide man?" Thielmann called out. Summoned to their calling, a white-helmeted aide man and two litter bearers piled out of the truck and began working on the American almost immediately. A young Lieutenant got out of the cab and came up to Thielmann as the soldiers piled out of the truck to form a ring around the American. The farmers, armed mostly with pitchforks and shovels, angrily demanded the American be turned over to them.

"Your victory, sir," the lieutenant asked.

"I do not know," Thielmann answered, "but I doubt it. I want him turned over to the *Luftwaffe*, Lieutenant, not the Army or those savages in the SS."

"Of course, sir ..."

"I expect to visit him in the hospital in a few days, and it would be far better for you if I found him well," Thielmann added as officiously as he could manage, writing the pilot's name and service number from his tags.

"Yes, sir ..."

"Now, what is your name and unit for my report?" The Lieutenant, his ill-fitting tunic and lack of awards marking him as a reservist recently called up, handed Thielmann his pay book.

"Now, I'll be turning in his watch and other personal effects to the *Abwehr* for evaluation to relieve you of the responsibility."

"Of course, sir; thank you, sir ..."

"They listed my brother missing over the *Kanal* last month, Lieutenant. I want this man treated as if he were my brother. Do you understand, Lieutenant?"

"I understand completely, sir; most completely. Is there anything else, sir?"

Yes, there is, Thielmann thought darkly. Find my brother, stick both our ranks up your ass, and "end the war," you poor little shit.

July 1943

Bartlesby, England

It is incorrect to hold a theory of equality in all things,
But there must be equality of existence
In accepting the dangers and hardships of war

Mao Zedong

It had started out as not that bad a strike, but the run to Vegesack turned into a nightmare on the way back. Calisto had his head blown off by the same flak burst that cut Digman in half, and probably the same burst that cut Feynman's air supply. By the time Thomas got back there Feynman was frozen solid, skin black and taut, eyes staring blankly at nothing, frozen open.

Miller brought *Crop Duster* and the rest of his crew home safely and set her down at Bartlesby routinely. He waddled to her spot on the hardstand and parked her, just as he always had. The medics hauled the dead out before the officers had crawled out of the nose. As usual, Miller was the last out. He felt a little strange, weak. Can't concentrate, he thought. Nothing's clear. Get out and go to debriefing, he thought. Then he shook, vaguely at first, then getting worse. Oh God, he thought, I'm not that cold but I can't stop shaking...can't let the men see me like this bad for morale can't stop gotta stop gotta stop oh Christ I gotta stop this...

Witt saw him first, fortunately for later events. He pulled his pilot under the nose of the ship, away from the knot of crewmen waiting to go to debriefing. The shivering got worse. Miller's face was white as death, with sweat pouring off in sheets. "Oh my God, skipper," he murmured, "hold on skipper hold on," then, "FARR," he yelled over his shoulder. Old soldier Farr could tell this call for help meant come quick, and did just that. With a quick glance, he knew what had to be done.

"Hold his shoulders," he told his copilot. In a blur, Farr's fist sunk deep into his pilot's lower abdomen, forcing him into a ball on his knees. "Hold on skipper," he whispered, "just hold on hold on...I'll get the medic," he told Witt.

"MEDIC," he yelled across the field. "MEDIC! MEDIC OVER HERE!" An ambulance made a U-turn across the grassy field, heading for *Crop Duster*. By now, the crew was getting curious about what was happening to their aircraft commander, in the nature of all enlisted men. "Get to debriefing," Farr told them. "Skipper's got that bug that's going around."

But the bombardier and navigator were made of sterner stuff than that, and were not about to take instructions from a mere master sergeant. "It's OK, Harry, Norm," Witt told them. "Just that bug that's been going around."

"What bug?" Thomas enquired, still approaching.

"THAT bug," Witt shot back. "Now go to debriefing!"

Oh, Royce thought, *that* bug. The bug that makes you shake and sweat, the one the flight surgeon pulls you out of the lineup for, the one some guys never quite get over. *That* bug. "Come on, Norm," he said to Thomas. "Nothing we can do here."

Still on the ground doubled over and shivering, Miller's mind raced at astonishing speed, but he only managed to make little whimpering sounds. Gotta stop can't stop gotta stop can't stop can't let the men see me like this bad for morale oh God my guts hurt I hurt all over oh Christ I just shit my pants oh God I gotta stop this ...

Witt held Miller close to the ground, keeping his head down out of the light. Hold on, skipper, just hold on it'll be OK we'll take care of it hold on skipper hold on don't give up now too much gone too much left hold on skipper hold on..

Farr was waving his arms frantically over his head, waving off the other pilots and crews. "Just that damn bug, that's all. Go on to debriefing. Go on." All the while he was thinking, keep cool skipper, just keep cool I'll take care of the ship and I can handle these kids called officers and all these other nincompoops that say there's no such thing as combat fatigue your ass there ain't...

"Jerry I shit my pants," Miller finally squeaked, "I shit my pants where's the men get me outta here oh Christ I gotta stop..."

"Hold on, skipper, hold on," Witt whispered in Miller's ear. The ambulance finally pulled up and Doc Tippie tumbled out of the back. Instantly assessing the situation, he gruffly ordered Witt "get me a wrist," as he pulled a syringe out of a pocket. The copilot pulled out one of Miller's arms from under him and pulled a sleeve up. Tippie stabbed Miller's wrist and shot some morphine into it. "When did it start?" he asked.

"Just before Farr started yelling," answered Witt, feeling Miller's shaking ease.

"Good. Where's the crew?"

"Gone to debriefing," Farr said, standing next to them but still watching out for bystanders.

"Good. Good job. Let's get him into the ambulance," Tippie said, picking Miller up by the shoulders.

"You want the litter, Chief?" the driver yelled.

"Good God no; that's the last thing I want. Just walk him into the ambulance. You guys," Tippie said to Farr and Witt, "you can go on to debriefing. I'll take it from here."

"Over my dead body," Farr growled, helping his pilot into the truck.

"Good," Tippie said. "Good job."

Miller only vaguely heard the last exchange. Oh Christ oh I'm tired so tired so tired....

***

It was nearly dark when Miller woke up. Witt was sitting in one of only two chairs in his room, reading a year-old magazine. Miller's head was fuzzy and his tongue thick, like he was waking up from a rather pleasant drunk but without the headache. "Ugh," he moaned.

Witt set the magazine down and waited. For hours he had waited, watching Miller sleep heavily, then lightly, then heavily again. Doc Hamman called it exhaustion, since he was rational before they put him under. Nothing to worry about.

"Hey John," he called.

Miller picked his head up off the pillow, but was too tired to do more, then set it back down again. "Hey Jerry." There was a long pause. "Guess I lost it, huh?"

"Lost what?"

"My nerves."

"Doc don't think so. Says you're just wore out, that's all."

"Oh," Miller said, and went back to sleep.

"What do you make of it, Lieutenant?" King asked the veteran of five missions, while rising from the shadows of an unlit corner.

"I think he's just tired, sir," Witt offered.

"Well, I think he is, too. We need to get him off the station for a while. Farr tells me his ship needs an overhaul, anyway. We're sending him out to Bermuda."

"Witt's not my...original name; it's von Gleichwitz. My grandfather changed it when..."

"Your family landed on Ellis Island, I know. You had to say as much for your security clearance. What of it?"

"Well, nothing sir, but...I was born in Germany. I have family there. I speak the language. I..."

"Wanted to go to the Pacific, I know. You want to quit?"

"Nosir; I'm just wondering if I'm going to end up like him."

King looked up at Witt; a hardened veteran at 21 who, with five missions over Europe, had already beaten the odds. "If you think about it too long, you might. Go tell the adjutant to cut the orders for him for Bermuda. And call his sister. Go on." Witt left, closing the door softly behind him. King, after a few more moments, went after him.

Throck, sitting in another corner, stared at Miller for a few moments, lighting a fresh cigarette. "You wanted to know what this was for, son," he whispered to the dark. "Well, I can tell you what it's not for. I flew a job into Paraguay back in '34, during a little bullshit war over a piece of desert called the Gran Chaco. It has some of the richest deposits of bat guano in the Western Hemisphere, and the killing over that bat shit got so bad that polygamy became legal.

"What this war is not for, son," he said softly to Miller's sleeping form and the enclosing darkness of the room, "is bat shit. It's for something better than that. I hope to God it is, anyway."

***

The train was packed, with some units moving to England from North Africa. Miller stood at an open window, watching the omnipresent green of the English countryside slowly slide by. Inside, the train was a sea of people, some sitting, some standing—soldiers, sailors, airmen (and women), and the occasional civilian—joking, jostling, smoking and swearing. Witt had called Sally to tell her where he was going, but that she wasn't allowed there. "Routine rest rotation," he said. He wasn't sure she believed him.

The trip south took nearly all day, bumping along the ill-maintained roadbed, apparently stopping at every cluster of buildings on the way. People got off and on, tickets were sold, and conductors punched and squeezed through the cars between every stop. The news hawkers were shouting about the landings in Sicily. In one compartment, the crap game changed players, but kept on playing.

In one corner, a sergeant with an arm in a sling and a Ranger diamond on his shoulder impassively watched the countryside, his chest bemedaled and gleaming. His hollow-eyed face was impassive, betraying no emotion, as though cut from solid granite, with the thousand-yard stare of men who had seen too much, cared too much, felt too much. Everyone else in the car ignored him. Miller offered him a cigarette. He stared at Miller as if he'd come out of a dream, accepted it with a nod, and went to the next car.

Wartime English towns and cities were busy places, if dingy. Traffic comprised a few automobiles, a huge number of trucks, and oceans of bicycles and pedestrians, with the odd bus or tram car thrown in. Windows were taped in front of heavy blackout curtains, government buildings and those taken over by the government were sandbagged, street vendors hawked their wares, newsboys shouted their headlines, and people seemed to go about their business oblivious to the occasional pile of rubble or ruin that dotted the towns—silent reminders of the Blitz.

Miller got off at the little hamlet of Gylmyn that overlooked the western Atlantic coast of Wales, with rolling hills climbing to the sky on all three sides. The "rest camp" had been a tuberculosis sanitarium converted by the Americans. The town thrived on fishing; boats were continually being loaded for the fishing grounds or unloaded after a catch, leaving the town smelling like three-day-old haddock at least two days in five. The Royal Navy had a small boat training center nearby, and every once in a while, a destroyer or frigate damaged on a convoy would stop into the little harbor for repairs. Gylmyn boasted three pubs, a small hotel, and five machine shops, besides the small port facilities and the usual collection of small shops. Being out of range of German aircraft, with too small a harbor for a naval base and too small a population to support an air base, the war had barely affected the village.

The place had got the moniker "Bermuda" because, of all the rest camps that the USAAF ran, this one was the most prized and the most restrictive. Doctors had to send the inmates there, and doctors had to release them. The alternative, as the entire Air Force knew, was permanent and involuntary removal from flying status. Everyone knew it was a hospital, but it was also a rest camp. The "guests" were only required to eat lunch (served from 11 to 2), meet with a counselor every day, and keep out of trouble with the locals. The fifty-odd "guests" were paired in generously sized rooms, each with a window overlooking the sea. It was the one facility in Britain where the staff outnumbered the inmates.

The camp was middling size (some 600 acres), but the main administration building, prominently centered on the grounds, looked as if they had plucked it straight out of a fairy tale, complete with two turrets, sixteen chimneys, and two wings. The land featured sprawling white buildings with wide sidewalks, broad porches of the sanitarium, and dotted with gazebos.

Miller was out on the bluffs looking at the sea and listening to the birds the first morning. Being there—watching the sea—felt good, better than nearly anything since he came to England. There were a dozen-odd other flyers there, but they did not converse: they barely acknowledged each other. Miller was there, like most of his fellow inmates, until about noon, when an orderly came around with a truck to take them to lunch.

Miller's first appointment with a counselor was at two that afternoon. He found Major Edmond Dent at the Doctor's Lounge in the main administration building. Dent was a slight man given to girth, with a kindly manner and a pair of protruding ears that made him somewhat clownish. "Play gin," was the first thing he said to Miller.

"Some," Miller replied. "I'm better at poker."

"Me, too, but two-handed poker is dull." They sat at a long table on a veranda facing the road. The deal had changed three times before either said anything, and Miller noticed Dent wasn't keeping score.

"In my head," replied Dent. "You're up fifteen points."

"How's that? You've only taken one hand."

Dent was unperturbed. "Eh, it was big hand. I've only had one pair higher than fives." Miller fell silent again, shuffling cards absently, not caring about the outcome for another four hands. Dent pushed the deck at him once again. Miller ignored it, staring at Dent passively. "Not interested anymore?" Dent sounded like he was trying to be as amicable as he could be.

"Why? What kind of counseling is this, anyway?"

Dent shrugged. "Maybe the kind you need; the kind where someone listens who has absolutely nothing to do with you or what you do. You want to talk, talk. If you're tired of playing cards, that's OK. Our session is about over." Dent looked out to the road, where the hard-pounded gravel and flint darkened in the building's shadow, "Mess hall's open till nine. Good tonight: roast beef."

"Any idea how sick I am of roast beef? That's all we get in this country."

"True, but it's that or mutton." Dent tried something of a grin. "Ever had mutton for a month straight, or maybe a year?" Miller admitted he had not. "OK, let's meet again tomorrow. Same time, same place. Go do something physical, baseball or badminton maybe, or bowls. Odd game, that. Still light out on the west lawn, and there's always a game of some sort on. Then at 9 tonight there are four different discussion groups around the place: join one, *any* one. We'll get together again tomorrow."

Miller squinted at him, suspicious. "What the hell kind of therapy is this? Don't you want to...I dunno...talk about my mother or something?"

Dent rolled his eyes, plainly disgusted. "Oh, how I *hate* the Freudians; screwed up everything for the rest of us." He pointed at Miller sternly, like a schoolmaster lecturing some miscreant. "Look, you want to talk about your mother, fine. You can talk about your father, your girlfriend, your best lay, your worst enemy, your hemorrhoids if you want to, anything. All you have to do to get out of this place in the next two weeks is meet with me every day at two, sit in a discussion group every night at nine, eat lunch and tell the United States Army Air Forces the answer to one question, and one question only: what in the hell do you think you're doing here in England? And your answer had better be damn convincing." He toned it down a notch. "My job, God help me, is to get you to figure that one out. Now go and do something physical and join a group discussion tonight or I'll send your ass stateside tomorrow."

Startled, Miller sputtered, "But you..."

"I, *what?*" Dent snapped again. "My responsibility is to the Air Forces, *not* you. Now get going." Dent had taken on the persona of the severe schoolmaster, and it made Miller feel like he was back in class being scolded. It was hard to say exactly what he felt: a mixture of rage, confusion and fear, but not the physical kind of rage. More the internal kind that comes of unfocused, unresolvable frustration. He had been fearful on and off for weeks, but not of being killed, but of disappointing his unit, his crew; like a team captain who'd lost his drive, didn't know how it happened, and didn't know how to get it back.

As instructed, he passed through the building's wide halls to the east lawn. He joined a four-man baseball game in the third inning. Miller had never been a particular fan of the game, but he had played some in high school: his game was flying. The score was 55-61 in the fifth inning with four outs to the inning and two pitches for each at-bat. Since fielding was, to be kind, slow, standup homers were pretty common. Miller's team's pitcher was a red-headed major; the other two players were captains. Their opponents comprised two lieutenant colonels, a major and a brigadier general. Miller relieved a colonel in the infield who said he'd played seventeen innings straight, and he needed to sit down. He fielded as well as he could without a mitt, got nine home runs (easy under the circumstances) flied out three times, and got tagged out three times (hit twice in the back and once in the shoulder). Miller's team won 104-98 after seventeen innings.

He went to the mess hall with his teammates and choked down some potatoes, cabbage and coffee, passing on the beef. The major was a B-24 pilot who had been in England since the fall of 1942; one captain flew B-17; the other flew Mosquitoes in a photo-recon squadron. All had more than half their required missions before rotation. After dinner, they passed some time looking for another group for their nightly discussion. None of his newfound friends had been at the sanitarium for more than one night. They found their former baseball opponents and another half-dozen guys near the front of the main building.

There were quick introductions ("acknowledge rank here but don't pull it" they were admonished), where Miller found out that senior officers surrounded him: he was one of only five captains (and no lieutenants) among the inmates. "We all know why we're here," a colonel with a deep Georgia drawl began. "Some part of us isn't working anymore."

"Yeah," a youngish major replied. "But which part?"

"That's what we're here to find out. Say, has anyone heard about the Yankees lately? First place again, I hear...anyone know anything about Cleveland...how about Detroit?" Much of the talk centered on baseball for about an hour, and then it swung to movies, then English food, then football, then a few jokes about English beer, then women, then there were some deep thoughts about the landings in Sicily. "Wonder if they're planning on driving into Germany through southern France...I wouldn't think so; too far away to supply well...how long are the Italians going to hold out...what are we doing here in England if all the action's in the Mediterranean?"

The conversation stopped, suddenly, as though someone had thrown a switch. Before that moment, no one had said a word about flying.. "We're closer to Germany here than anywhere else we're flying from," a long and lean lieutenant colonel said with a New England clip. "Bombing Germany makes them pull back from..."

"Where?" Miller surprised himself by asking. "We drop bombs, lose a few airplanes and crewmen and go home. They rebuild, we do it again. How long do we have to do this?" No one had an answer, and the group broke up about midnight.

The second morning found Miller at the bluffs again, soaking in the sun and the salt breeze. He had no thought of war, no thought of anything, no fear, and no pain. He just stared out at the ocean, watching the clouds roll off the water, the birds dancing and swaying as they followed the fishing smacks, coming in and grabbing up the scraps they threw off. "Ever get tired of it?" someone down the bluffs asked.

"Of what?"

"Flying." The stranger down the bluffs was Miller's pitcher from the baseball game.

"I remember when I was a kid," he said at length, "and I'd lie out on the front lawn after Dad cut the grass, watching the clouds and the birds, and I'd think about flying. It's about the only thing I've ever thought about, ever since I can remember. And I've been looking up at the clouds and thinking about how many bandits were behind them, how high we'd have to climb to get over it, whether the target was overcast when we got there. But I don't think about flying. I think about bombing, fighting and dying. Killing...not really."

"Did you lose your dream?"

"No. I know where it was. It got killed."

"What killed it?"

"The war, Pearl Harbor, me, or the krauts: it doesn't matter."

"Maybe you can have another dream. Make a new one."

"Maybe, but I want to know what they killed the last one for. There has to be some reason. Maybe freedom and democracy don't mean much when you're born to it. It can't mean as much to us as it might mean to some Czech in a forced labor camp, or an Englishman whose whole family got blitzed."

"Maybe not, but maybe we're fighting for them, too."

"Maybe so; but would they fight for us?" Miller flashed briefly on the note Farr found in a 40mm shell. *It is not much, but it is all I can do.* Christ, he thought, they already are.

That afternoon, after a light lunch of egg salad and apples, Miller found Dent in the lounge. They went back to the eastern porch, with Dent carrying a checkerboard. They played the first game in silence.

"Two weeks," Miller finally said. "Good rest."

"It's diagnostic." Dent replied, not taking his eyes off the board.

"Diagnostic? What kind of a..."

"I'm not," Dent said. "I have—had—a nice little gynecology practice in Connecticut; I only studied and practiced enough psychiatry to graduate. The Air Forces put me in this job because...well, because they didn't need that many gynecologists, but they needed people to evaluate other people for what they were worth. Like you, I do what I'm told."

"So, what happens in two weeks?"

"You either go back to your unit or back to the States, depending on what I think. To start with, based on your record and my talks with your unit, I think you're the best damn bomb-truck driver in England and we can't afford to lose you. That's the long and the short of it." Dent said it as matter-of-factly as if he were reporting the weather.

"Then..." Miller blurted, confused.

"Then it would be unfortunate if we had to send you back, but it would be unavoidable. You see," Dent went on, triple-jumping to end a game, "there's no shortage of pilots, but there's a shortage of leaders."

"Leaders?" Miller had been hearing broad hints about major's leaves for Killer Miller and his *Crew Duster.* "You mean..."

"I mean that the Air Forces have spent a great deal of money and have a great deal of faith in all of you here in Bermuda, or you wouldn't *be* here in Bermuda. Think about it: every inmate here is a senior officer—or can be soon enough—with at least two thousand hours in the air. Lieutenants that wear out in England we just rotate home, but you guys we can't spare. You're here because..."

"I cracked up?"

"No, you didn't," Dent replied sharply. "'Cracked up' is a poor term. Here, it's called 'combat flight exhaustion' because it has a unique combination of symptoms. For instance, when was the last time your feet felt warm?"

Miller considered the question. "I can't remember."

"As expected," Dent said with a note of assurance. "Your feet, if we took a temperature, may be warmer than mine, and I haven't flown in twenty years. Other psychiatric practitioners, especially in the Pacific, call it 'long- term flight stress reaction' or even 'flak-happy.' Whatever anyone calls it, it seems to strike, especially among flyers, almost exclusively bomber pilots. That's why we find Captain Barres's experience—he's a recon pilot—so interesting, but I frankly think it's just because there are more bomber pilots than recon pilots, that's all."

"Exhaustion?" Miller thought about this for a moment. "It is pretty wearing work."

"Especially in the cold." Dent and Miller had stopped moving, staring at each other. "You get cold?"

"So cold it takes everything I've got to stay warm," Miller said at length. "The suits and heaters help some, but my feet still get cold. And it's noisy. Engines droning on and on for hours, static in the headset, top turret firing a foot over your head with concussion that makes your eyes bug out, and when it ain't static or a beacon on the radio, somebody's hollering about something bad headed your way...

"And it stinks. Stinks of sweat and your last meal. Oxygen mask doesn't always come real clean. Sometimes you throw up, or lose control of your bowels in your suit," he said, shifting his weight uncomfortably. "The stink doesn't come out very fast. Sometimes the ship smells like blood, especially if somebody got hit bad at low altitude and it doesn't freeze before it soaks into some plywood deck. And gasoline and hydraulic fluid, and the stale insides of the oxygen tanks, and ...fear," he whispered, "always smells like fear. And death."

"Why do you do it?" Dent asked. He started to look and sound more like a kindly uncle than a schoolmaster.

"Sure as *hell* ain't for God and country," Miller responded. "It ain't for that. You do it because it's gotta be done and you can do it. God is someone—something—you pray to at twenty thousand feet with an engine out, half your crew hit and three hundred miles from base and the flak's still rising, and the bandits are still coming in, and you're running out of ammunition. Home is a place where letters come from, and where letters get sent to. Country is a set for a movie, nothing more."

"Everything else is abstract," Miller sighed. "The only thing that's real out there is your ship, your crew, your unit, and those bastards trying to kill you. Nothing else makes sense. Nothing else exists. Not women, not family, not friends who aren't up there with you. We have more in common with Kraut pilots than we do with anyone else."

"So I've heard," Dent said officiously. "You guys all think you're in one big fraternity. Can't you imagine that thinking that way could be dangerous?"

"What? No," Miller replied curtly. "There's a common bond: maybe the same conditions. It's like this: there was a JU88 did an emergency landing in the fog at our field a few months back. The pilot's crew was all hit. One was dying, and the pilot knew it. But that pilot knew that if he landed anywhere but Russia, his crew would be taken care of. We've had ships in the group surrender, just land when they knew they couldn't make it back, especially with wounded aboard. We've bailed out crewmen that wouldn't last, though I haven't. Most of the time, we hear back that our guys are in this hospital or that camp, or that they got buried in that graveyard; once in a while with pictures. We do the same for them, though I don't know about the pictures. But when we gotta fight, we fight. When we don't, we'd really rather not." Finally Miller murmured, "Ya do it 'cause it's gotta get done. We gotta bomb, they've gotta defend. Flying's like climbing mountains, you do it because it's there, and 'cause everyone else around you does it. Patriotism's just so many words when you're holding somebody's femoral artery together to keep him from bleeding to death."

"Something you talk about just to sound brave," Dent sighed, lighting a cigarette, "but you never believe a syllable of it when you're up there. Not a syllable..." he finished, his voice trailing off.

Miller stared at Dent, surprised. How did he know? "When I joined up," Miller said after a time, "the night before, we were all great patriots, bragging about what we'd do once we got to war. The next night I spent with another guy, like me, inducted officer. I was a pilot; he was a chaplain, a helluva nice guy. Said he'd finished seminary the previous June and was just settling into a new church, had a wife and a baby on the way. I asked him what his stake in this was, and he just looked at me and said 'you.' Never forgot that."

"Lots of guys cope by drinking and swearing and smoking and whoring, but everybody does it different," Dent said at some length, as the shadows played on the gravel again. "You cope because you have to, because you can, and not everybody can..." his voice fading.

"You know, the flight surgeons are the first line of defense against what I call preoccupation disorder. Sometimes you have bad dreams. You shake for no reason sometimes. Sometimes the flight surgeons take you off the duty list because you don't laugh at dumb jokes. Sometimes they take you off because you laugh too hard at dumb jokes." Miller thought about the Ranger sergeant on the train, wondered if his thousand-yard stare had shortened yet. "I think your biggest challenge, John," Dent said, sounding far away, "is that you only have flying. You should think about another hobby."

"Another....what? Flying is my *hobby*? It's..."

"For most people, a means to an end, but for you, it's been the reason for your existence for, as you said, as long as you remember," Dent added carefully, straitening up in his chair. "But it's turned on you, hasn't it? It's the same for most of the guys here. You need some kind of distraction. You could take up maybe painting, or baseball, woodcarving, or darts, race cars; something to distract you from what they expect you to do every day. Now," Dent leaned forward, his elbows on his knees and his chin in his hands. "Why are you in England?"

Miller thought of the 40mm shell again. "It's not much, but's it's all I can do."

If flying is a just preoccupation, Miller wondered, what have I got left?

That afternoon, Miller's team lost 109-90.

July 1943

Rotterdam, Holland

Nothing can make injustice just but mercy

Robert Frost

The American four-motors drove relentlessly on despite the savage attacks by four fighter groups, including the destroyers from Kaltz' "Giant Killers." Taube, the battle captain for the day, rallied the attackers for another push five kilometers off the left wing of the bomber stream. "All Altmarck units: gather at point Gustav: repeat point Gustav." Taube sounded tired, weary even. The night before, he'd been depressed that Kaltz group, specially designed for one kind of mission, and was failing despite its high kill ratio: no attack yet had turned back an American bomber stream.

Again, the JU88s fired their rockets at the leaders, and again they fell as the rockets blasted them apart. As the leaders fell out and the herd broke up, the fighters pounced on the cripples and vulnerable bombers suddenly without flank protection, but the bomber stream went plowing on and ever on like castles in the air. One bomber caught fire after Thielmann poured cannon rounds into the wing root. The pilot held the machine level as the crew piled out one by one, several through the bomb bay. One parachute opened just as the owner dropped out, catching in the open doors. There he was, towed behind the inferno; battering in the slipstream, trapped forever in its wake like a fly in ancient amber, no air, freezing, and it appeared as if there wasn't anything anyone could do about it.

As if in slow motion, Bär's machine slid up behind the blazing bomber. For what seemed to be an eternity, it hung in the air behind the roaring blaze and its doomed passenger. Then Bär fired into the dark, struggling, doomed bundle, and it dropped into space just before the bomber nosed downward. Thielmann called out as he swooped around again. "Good shooting, Bär."

"I could not leave him..." Thielmann heard, and the war went on as before.

***

As Thielmann and his group (with no casualties that day) returned to their home field, the four aces tested the flying skills of their charges. Though the flyers in JG191 were more experienced than most, few of them had more than two hundred hours in the air. "Altmarck one: take up high station on a base course of nine zero degrees," Taube called. "Altmarck three; left station on base course 80 degrees. Altmarck four: trail station on base course 100 degrees. Altmarck two: low station on base course 70 degrees. All Altmarck units are to fly on the given course for twenty minutes and rejoin on a base course of nine zero degrees in forty minutes over the Estuary. Good luck."

As the squadron broke up, each leader would only listen as the next senior pilot gave the orders for the formation: in fact, Thielmann dropped out of the lead and fell back behind his squadron to observe their formation discipline. All in all, he was pleased. Though the base course was into a headwind, his young pilots (and they averaged just two years younger than he) kept together fairly well.

"Altmarck three three to leader," one of his men called out, "Enemy formation below, heading 270. Cripples, I believe." Thielmann had to strain to see the two airplanes far below. One was making a turn to the north, the other continuing on. "Altmarck three one: join me. Altmarck three squadron; continue with the problem." Joined by his wingman, Thielmann banked and winged over into a long dive.

Both of the enemy machines—Liberators—were heavily damaged, but neither one had lost an engine. At a very low height, Thielmann thought he should leave them to the coastal flak guns, but something caused him to approach cautiously. The tail gun on one was completely blown off, and the upper turret was nothing more than a few shards of glass and metal. Large gaping holes were where the waist guns should have been. They had shot away part of one tail, and the flaps and ailerons waved uselessly in the wind. Curious, Thielmann pulled into a shadow position just off his right wing. The co-pilot's side was red with frozen blood, and the roof appeared to have been shot off completely. How is this thing still in the air? Thielmann wondered. Slowly Thielmann edged his machine into a wingover, looking down on the stranded bomber. To his surprise, there appeared to be no one in the cockpit. Abandoned and still flying, Thielmann wondered. "Altmarck three one, blow it down while I check the other."

Thielmann had to race to catch the other cripple, racing towards the coast and the relative safety of the Allied-dominated sea. But still there was the coastal flak to contend with, and Thielmann thought again he should allow them to destroy this last Liberator. As he caught up to the enemy machine, he saw a burst of machine gun fire towards him; still alive on this one, eh?

Thielmann began a belly approach and just before he palmed the trigger, something fell out of the bomb bay, and another, and another. Thielmann quickly overshot the Liberator, and then swooped around for another pass, climbing slightly to get an angle on a fuel tank. Far below, three parachutes blossomed, and the Liberator continued on. Curious, Thielmann quickly looked at the cockpit, which was another shattered ruin, but there was still a live pilot flying the machine. Thielmann saw the landing gear slowly coming down. Knowing that there was a *Luftwaffe* field only a few miles from the coast, Thielmann fired a burst ahead of the pilot to get his attention. Gesturing at the enemy flyer, Thielmann waved and pointed. The American bobbed his head up and down as the landing gear continued to fall. The descent of the Liberator was steady, controlled, and Thielmann followed the machine all the way down to the field, a night fighter station, landing just after.

Thielmann rushed his harnesses off as the enlisted men helped him out. An officious-looking lieutenant approached him from across the field. "Captain," the lieutenant wheezed, "are you claiming the capture?" Thielmann hadn't really thought about it. "You know that a capture, even of a four-engine Liberator, is only worth a point, but," he hesitated, looking at the large red *R* on Thielmann's tail, "I see you have many points already. Lieutenant Dolmen, Captain, at your service."

"Thank you, Lieutenant," Thielmann said, striding towards the Liberator. "I did not shoot this machine down; I only found it. My wingman should be along soon, and...there he is." Another Focke-Wulf lit on the end of the runway. Armed Luftwaffe men were emerging from the wounded Liberator, shaking their heads. "What is it? How many are inside?"

"None, sir," a corporal reported. "At least none are alive: there are three dead on board, and the pilot gave up the ghost as I was trying to get him up. Sorry, sir."

"Yes," Thielmann said, staring at the Liberator. Large holes in the wings had leaked away much of the fuel, and large pools of blood had gathered in the fuselage. All the bombs had been dropped, but one was still in the rack, and still armed. The ordnance men were stroking their chins, trying to imagine how to get the two-hundred-fifty kilo monster out without blowing up.

He held his machine in the air, Thielmann thought, knowing he was dying, and his crew got out as they could. German pilots have done similar things over England. I wonder then if the English are as accommodating as we are when surrendering to the inevitable. Perhaps they think of us as being as human as we think of them.

July 1943
Hamburg, Germany

In time of war, the devil makes more room in hell

German proverb

Miller stretched stiffly in a swivel chair, yawning widely. It was midnight, and he had the Staff Duty again. His hair hurt from not washing it, his stomach was tight from too much coffee, his throat rough from too many cigarettes. David Roy from Chicago, his new radio man and runner for the night, dozed fitfully in the corner. Miller thought he'd go out and have a look-see around, get the cobwebs out for another six hours before he got relieved. Walking around outside the squadron office in the damp, humid chill of an English summer night, he thought he glimpsed a glow off to the east. At first, he dismissed it as an illusion of a too-tired mind. He rattled some doorknobs, looked under some ships on the flight line, passed a few minutes with Jack Allis, staff duty for the 191st, and generally just ambled around for the exercise.

Just before he went back inside the office, he looked out to the east again. Winking, he thought, flickering like a fire. Can't be dawn, that's not for another four hours at least. Gotta be a fire, just no telling how far away. Well, the cobwebs were gone, but now he was vexed by a problem with no apparent solution, so he went back to see Allis. "What do you make of it?" he asked Allis as they both stood on the runway, watching the eastern horizon.

"Fire on the coast, maybe?" They called the constable in Bartlesby. No, no fires reported; certainly nothing that big. Coastal Command knew nothing, had heard nothing. The French boat basin had no answers, but they were seeing the same glow. By then there were other

237

officers and NCOs with the duty for their units, mechanics off the flight line, MPs, and hospital orderlies out on the runway under a blanket of stars, staring and pointing at the glow in the eastern distance. Someone thought to contact Fighter Command to see if they had seen anything. The response was tight and uncooperative, just like on any other occasion. Bomber Command's answer wasn't as polite. Security, they said.

By then, both Throck and King had been roused from their beds by the ruckus, and looked into the matter with at least as much success as anyone else had had. Some enterprising souls broke out a map and compass, shooting bearings and extrapolating positions, calling Nichols and Vincent St. Niles to see if they saw the same thing in the same place. The meteorologists stroked their chins and gazed at the dim light, then started calling weather reporting stations and other stargazers.

Finally, Fred Trent, the lead navigator in the 610th who flew with the RAF before Pearl Harbor, called one of his friends in Bomber Command. When he came out on the tarmac to join everyone else (by then it was nearly a hundred guys), even in the half-light of the dark they could see the pallor in his face as he stared out in the distance, not focusing or seeing. Shortly, Miller called for quiet as they heard as the laboring engines of a large aircraft echoing across the countryside.

"Lancaster," Trent said absently. "They hit Hamburg again tonight; nine hundred bombers. That's Hamburg out there."

"Hamburg," Miller exclaimed. "Hamburg's near four hundred miles out!"

"Three ninety," Reynolds said, staring at the glow in the distance, "and right on the bearing."

"But how big would the fire have to be..."

"Bigger than any fire anybody ever saw..." As the word spread to the watchers on the runway, a stunned hush fell over them, and one by one, they drifted off. "I heard the Brits call it Operation Gomorrah," someone said to no one in particular.

Miller watched the dancing glow on the eastern horizon until the rising of the sun obscured it.

***

On the Saturday night before, Bomber Command had sent seven hundred bombers to the ancient city at the mouth of the Elbe. Millions of sheets of tinfoil for the first time jammed the German radar as they dropped over a million pounds of firebombs.

On Sunday, the Eighth Air Force sent a hundred planes, dropping nearly two hundred tons of bombs on the firefighters and sleepless survivors. British Mosquitos hit the city again on Sunday night.

The Eighth dropped another hundred and fifty tons of bombs on Monday.

On Monday night, another seven hundred Bomber Command machines attacked again.

On Tuesday morning, the *Luftwaffe* High Command wrote the city off as not worth saving.

Tuesday night it rained in England, and the fire reached the main Hamburg gas works.

Wednesday night England was enshrouded by fog, and they lost power in most of Hamburg.

On Thursday morning Thielmann, desperate for news of Elsa and her uncle, flew to Bergdorf on a "liaison and inspection" mission fabricated by Kaltz. As he drove towards the city, clouds of gas and ash wafted across the sky, rising from what had once been Hamburg, sometimes called the Armpit of Europe.

Crowds of refugees in pitiful states met his borrowed truck. Rich and poor shared the crowded roads, military traffic mixed with civilian and civil. A squad of firemen from Dresden slogged their way into the city, followed by another from Berlin. As he entered the city. weary Polizei made cursory inspections of his orders before waving him on. Firefighters from all over Northern Europe still battled smoldering buildings and flaming gas mains, running patched hoses and bucket strings from the few surviving water mains and from ships and boats out in the Elbe. The fire had coated everything and everyone with a fine patina of blue-gray dust. High explosive bombs, Thielmann thought, only they make that dust.

Thielmann found Elsa's apartment gutted, but no news of her. After enquiring at the police office in Wandsbeck, he finally found her working in a nearby cellar wearing a soiled Red Cross apron and some obviously borrowed clothes, passing out clean water to those few who chose (or were required) to remain. "Uncle is in Austria," she said wearily, "but I have to stay here. As you said before, Otto, *someone* has to stay." Looking around him at the crowd of wan faces coated with sweat and grime and exhausted beyond all description, he decided that perhaps he, too, should stay for a while. Five raids in three days were enough, he decided. The British will not come back again.

Thielmann reported (as was required) to the *Flakartillerie* commander, a one-armed Colonel with red-rimmed eyes and a grimy face named Brazen. He found the officer inspecting several of his men wounded the night before when a building next to a flak tower collapsed. "Why in the name of God would you want to stay here, Captain? This isn't a city anymore; it's a charnel house. Even the *Luftwaffe* has written us off."

"I know that, Colonel, but I have a friend here and, well, I'm here now and you need help." Brazen gazed at him impassively, wearily.

"Well," he said at length, "a genuine selfless hero, eh? I didn't think I would live so long as to see another one in my life," he said with a slight chuckle and a tiny grin. "So, what shall I do with you, eh? Do you have the *Kriegsakademie* and your Knight's Cross?"

"No, Colonel," Thielmann replied regretfully. "I have been flying a great deal, but I did some fighter control work in early '42 at Cologne..."

"Cologne?" Brazen exclaimed. "Then you know Odo Gatt!"

"Why, yes, I do."

"Ach, why didn't you say so? Why, he invented these needles," Brazen exclaimed, pointing to the round concrete edifice behind him. "Come with me. I'll show you the place."

Together they walked to the flak tower, a concrete and steel cylinder with a flared base and a blockish structure on top rising ominously above the ocean of rubble and burned-out shells of buildings that had once been southeastern Hamburg. Standing fifteen stories high and forty meters in diameter, the tower designed for two 15 centimeter antiaircraft guns, three smaller caliber guns, a crew of fifty, and 5,000 refugees from the neighborhood. It had its own water system, power, telephone, radio, and a hospital in the subbasement. The roof and footings were conical, the sides at the base nearly five meters thick.

"The theory is simple," Brazen explained. "At Cologne, they caught most of the flak batteries in fires that didn't rise above perhaps twenty meters, so we build these towers three hundred meters tall. If a bomb should hit them, they slide down the roof, you see, and the base is solid. We think it can withstand the blast of a five hundred kilo bomb at the base without damage to the structure."

"Impressive," Thielmann said earnestly. "How many people can you accommodate inside?"

"Well, we're well beyond designed capacity now. Why?"

"As I said, I have a friend here..."

"A friend, yes, but family?"

"Well, a very good friend..."

"Make her your family," Brazen said absently, "and bring her here; now."

"Why?" Thielmann asked, suddenly very frightened. Brazen stared at him with the urgent, desperate expression of a condemned man who suddenly glimpsed his gallows.

"Now," he repeated, in exactly the same tone as Gatt had many months before...*Here! They are coming here!*

***

Thielmann found Elsa still in the cellar and bluntly said. "Come on. We're getting married."

She didn't have much time to think, even less time to feel as they raced to find a magistrate—anyone who could do the deed quickly.

"A girl generally likes to be asked these things; to think about them for a while; to savor them," she had said over and again, but Thielmann pretended not to hear. They are coming again tonight, his mind screamed; again, tonight. Along the way, Elsa picked a rose from a disheveled garden and clutched it throughout the "ceremony." They answered the requisite questions: Otto Wilhelm Thielmann, born Marburg, 1920; Elsa Frieda Greitz steyer von Lutzow-Verein Portz, born Hamburg 1919, widow of Gunnar Portz, declared killed in the *Kriegsmarine*. Thielmann had given her his *Luftwaffe* ring. Twenty minutes and ten Marks later, they were married in a *gasthaus* next to the burned-out City Hall.

***

The meter-thick wooden core steel doors swung noisily on heat-distorted dry hinges as they entered the tower. Inside the dark, dusty, hot , spiraling staircases wound up the curved sides, each crowded with people, most sleeping or merely lying down, all dirty, many burned or otherwise hurt. Men, women, children packed together hip to shoulder, cheek-by-jowl, thirsty, hungry, frightened, weary, waiting for the nightmare to be over, for someone to tell them it was all a mistake. "There are nearly ten thousand in here, nearly as I know," Brazen told them. "We ran out of food for them this morning. Find me ten thousand rations, can you? I realize it isn't much of a wedding night, but..."

"I can try," Thielmann whispered, "I can try." He turned to Elsa, bravely gazing around her at the sea of human misery, still in shock from suddenly becoming a wife again. "I have to go out for a little while," he told her, holding her face in his hands, gazing once more into those angelic blue eyes he'd fallen in love with in a mountain meadow less than a year before. "I'll be back in an hour." Stooping down to Gunther, he scratched the little dog's ears. "Take care of Elsa, Gunther. I'll be back soon."

He had found four hundred kilos of Army bread and a truckload of beef at a railroad siding at Glinde in the south about 8 that evening. He persuaded an overweight Lieutenant to part with them by trading a case of wine he had found in a ruined hotel. He led the trucks to the flak tower and then went off in search of more food at the miraculously only slightly damaged Elbe docks.

It was nearly three hours later—about 11 o'clock that well-lit night—before he pointed his truck back towards the flak tower. Behind him in the western gloom, he saw the stabbing of searchlights and the dim popping of antiaircraft guns. The pathfinders, he thought. The first *Tannenbaumen* of string flares lit the shattered Hamburg landscape with their eerie, yellow glow about fifteen minutes later, as Thielmann was still maneuvering through the rubble. Weary firefighters and police merely looked up at the flares, too tired to even think about another night of fires and bombs. The water mains were all broken or bombed-out, so there was little most of them could do.

A few more moments of frantic driving brought him to a blocked street just as a string of firebombs landed behind him, raising a sheet of fire. Still three kilometers from the flak tower, Thielmann abandoned his truck and started climbing up the heap of rubble blocking the street. Behind him, the heat rose, and all around the dust wafted into his face.

He ran.

The burned-out shells of buildings and occasional hulls of trees cast eerie shadows in a macabre dance of swaying shapes as the fire grew behind him. Other refugees were few, but those on the streets picking through the ruins looked about them fearfully. No matter how quickly he moved, the light and heat behind him still seemed to grow and grow. Then there was a sound, a sighing rush of air as night became day, the bombs exploding behind him joining in a cacophony of horrific noise, rumbling like thunder, sighing like an oncoming train. Dust and ash filled the air as there was a sudden wind, knocking him down, pulling him back the way he had come. Desperately, he clawed at the street as he was pulled, rolling down the brickwork until he grabbed a crack in a concrete curb. His body swung and slammed into the curb with terrific force as he held on, fingers bleeding from the effort, mind screaming with pain, lungs wheezing.

Then he looked down at his feet, where the world had turned into fire.

A swirling cylindrical mountain of flame ascended from the waterfront five kilometers away, the inrushing air screeching across the wrecked landscape, the mountain twisting slowly like yellow, black and red stripes on a spring maypole, unburned gas rising to the top, burning, falling inside, and then rising again. The cyclonic wind pulled in everything—people, rubble, uprooted trees, bricks, wood, steel, bits of automobiles—consumed it all in its furnace maw, and then pitched the waste up in the air. An impossibly bright light lit up the British bombers three thousand meters above. The great sighing firestorm shrieked and whistled, rose and swirled, burned and burned and burned.

His boots were pulled off and flew down the street into the mountain of fire, the buttons on his uniform melted, his uniform charred, his fingers digging ever deeper into the few centimeters of shattered concrete curbing that separated him from the firestorm's voracious maw, clinging to it like a sea moss against the riptide. His arms and shoulders felt as if they would tear out of their sockets, his hair singed. He smelled the great heat and rotten stench of burning flesh and steel. Indistinctly he heard minor explosions. Bombs, probably, he thought with astonishing detachment, or exploding masonry. For an eternity that probably lasted all of two minutes, Thielmann held onto the gutter crack while the 150 kilometer-an-hour draft pulled everything into the inferno that would move or not resist. For an absent few moments, he thought he was gone, that it would be far easier to merely let go of that lifesaving crack in the gutter.

But then he decided he'd come this far, found his Elsa, and would not be denied. And with a brief image of their future together, the fiery light dimmed, faded, and went out as the storm collapsed, its two kilometer-high edifice of hell only a bad memory of dust and flickering flame, billowing across the burning rubble as it fell with the final roar of a dying predator.

He lay in the gutter for a few moments, gasping for breath in the dust-choked air, hands bleeding from the rough concrete. He rolled onto his back, finally letting go of the life-saving curbstone. Shuddering for breath, he suddenly felt quite cold, even though his sweat hissed and boiled on the pavement. After a lifetime of perhaps another five minutes of gasping, he struggled to his feet, his uniform in charred rags hanging on his frame. Though the pavement burned his feet, he staggered on, finding his way to the flak tower, hammering on the massive double doors with his bleeding fists. As the doors opened the smallest crack, he shouldered his way in, ignoring all others, sipping some water from a canteen, some brandy from a tin cup, and finally found Elsa, asleep on a stair landing between basement levels, a small child under each arm, her rose still clutched in her tiny hand. He collapsed at her feet, the remnant of his uniform crumbling off him like dried leaves.

Gunther sat at his feet, a watchful eye on all who drew near, growling at interlopers.

August 1943
Schweinfurt, Germany

From my mother's sleep, I fell into the State,
And I hunched in its belly till my wet fur froze
Six miles from earth, loosed from its dream of life,
I woke to black flak and the nightmare fighters
When I died, they washed me out of the turret with a hose

Randall Jarrell

C *rop Duster* got two new waist gunners for the Schweinfurt strike. One was a big, jovial Virginian named Tony Collova, and the other was a fairly small dead-shot from Columbus, Missouri, named Alvin Murphy. They joined the ship just in time. The bandits were out in full force that afternoon of the biggest strike of the war. Half the Eighth Air Force was hitting the ball bearing works at Schweinfurt, and the other half was hitting the Messerschmitt assembly works at Regensburg. The 299th was being hit once every fifteen seconds by a fighter pass. They fought each off with cannon shells whizzing by cockpits with cottony-white puffs of 20mm bursting all around.

Sweat rolled over Miller's oxygen mask in the 60 below chill, soaking him through his long underwear. The gunners swiveled and turned, bandits arching through the formation. One by one, the Fortresses staggered, exploded, flamed and fell. After a half hour of air combat, only a handful of the 299th's B-17s continued to the target, still forty minutes away. It was then they saw a sight that burned into their minds; awesome, hideous, beautiful, and terrifying all at once. A hundred... two hundred... three hundred...more than they could count...bandits, directly ahead of them, in a staggered checkerboard formation, headed straight for them.

"Mother of God," someone said over the radio. "What now?" As punctuation, five hundred rockets streaked for the bombers—each a forty- pound lance of high explosive and white-hot steel. The sky was suddenly lit by a million hornets as all the rockets exploded within split-seconds of each other. Miller thought vaguely that this was what it must be like to fly through a fireworks finale.

Angry fragments tore into *Crop Duster's* nose. Miller felt a peculiar hot needlelike stab in his right foot, then a strange numbness reaching halfway to his knee. "Pilot to crew," he called on the intercom while looking at the rents in the ship; his windscreen starred and cracked. "Report nose to tail."

"Bombardier to pilot: got a frag in the shoulder, but I'm OK. Navigator's had it." Miller flashed briefly on Harry Royce's face. Sorry Harry.

"Top gun to pilot: Running low on ammo." "Radio to pilot; I'll get some to you, Jack." "Belly gun to pilot: Still here." "Left waist to pilot: Running low on ammo." "Right waist to pilot: Two more bandits heading for the front." "Tail gun to pilot: another dozen bandits coming up."

"Co-pilot to pilot: OK here. All engines online." The huge formation ahead of them had disappeared, vanished as if it had never been there. Three more Fortresses were staggering out. Still forty minutes from the target...

A pair of Focke-Wulfs in a rare back-to-front stern attack caught everyone off-guard, twisting through the shattered combat box like a corkscrew through rotten pine. A 20mm round exploded in the tail section, nearly blowing Egan out of the ship and ripping off his left leg at the knee. "Right waist to pilot," Murphy called as the attackers looped away, "Tail gun's in a lot of trouble."

"Pilot to radio: Roy, get back and see what you can do."

Roy strapped on a walk-around oxygen bottle and worked his way back to the tail gun, deftly dodging the waist gunners who were ankle-deep in expended brass as they kept up their fire on the attacking fighters, diving through the rear of the still-reforming box. He pulled Egan back inside the airplane, rubbing his frozen face vigorously and putting his oxygen mask back on. He bound a tourniquet on what was left of Egan's leg, but the blood was still gushing. The morphine syrettes were frozen. Roy tried to thaw them out in his mouth but couldn't work up enough spit. Despairing of all else, Roy held the mangled remnant of Egan's leg in the frigid blast of air left by the cannon shell, freezing it solid. The bleeding finally stopped, leaving a bright red, icy lump. Roy tied the tourniquet tighter and went back to the radio hut, hauling the unconscious Egan with him. Still half an hour out...

The flak rose a few minutes later, butchering the leading group as the 299th pulled apart to spread the flak pattern. As they did, the bandits chose just that moment to dive through them again, paying particular attention to those airplanes already damaged. The gunners were awake, and the bandits were either short on fuel or ammo or both, because they only made one pass and did no serious damage to any more airplanes. Twenty minutes out...

The big billowing blooms of flak were so dense Miller could barely see through it.   One shell—probably a 150mm, Miller thought impassively—passed completely through *Midnight Lace's* right wing, leaving a sudden feathery wake of freezing fuel rising behind it. It exploded well outside the formation, but its victim was already spiraling to the earth. Ten minutes out...

Just before bombs away, a close flak burst rocked *Crop Duster*. With fragments still bouncing off the ship like hail, Miller called up for a report. "Bombardier to pilot: ten seconds to bombs away." Thomas was still at the bombsight, bomb release in hand, bleeding only slightly, waiting for the lead ship to release, mind fogged and tongue thickened by morphine, shivering violently in the frigid blast through the shattered glass in the nose, Royce's blood pooled frozen at his feet.

"Top gun to pilot: still here."

"Radio to pilot: belly gun doesn't look good," Roy said as he looked at rather incongruous pieces blown through his rear bulkhead. "Egan's still alive."

"Left waist to pilot: I'm still here, belly gun's had it," Collova called, watching red-black pools crystalize on the ball-turret hoist.

"Right waist to pilot: still here."

"Co-pilot to pilot: still here, all engines on line, fuel adequate for return."

Yeah, Miller thought bitterly, remembering Otto's craggy face and slender hands. We should live so long.

***

The engines were still warm, magnetos still clicking when Miller and his crew swung out of their aluminum coffin. Miller's foot hurt some, but wasn't too troubling. He glimpsed the remnant bits and pieces of the belly turret dragging on the ground, gazed impassively at the blood-spattered Perspex and aluminum framing, a gloved thumb still caught in a niche in the debris, the remains of what had once been a human being. The lucky medic assigned to clean up the mess started with tongs and ended with a sponge. The chaplains, eventually, took over.

The medics hauled Royce out of the nose, covered by a sheet above his chest, but still Miller could see that it had blown his head from his shoulders. Thomas, shivering, paste-white, drugged, was carried away behind him, followed by Egan, miraculously still alive.

Miller sat on the grass next to his ship, his crew beside him, not speaking, shivering not with cold but weariness, trying to warm in the remnants of the sun, trying to forget the nightmare vision of half a thousand rockets exploding in front of them, of the twinkling wings and icy grace of the bandits tearing through the formations, the screaming metal of flak and cannon shells all around them, and the red-black pools of frozen blood all over the ship. Doc Hamman later removed a small fragment of Harry Royce's skull from Miller's foot, painted it with iodine and marked him fit for duty.

***

Hit ball-bearing plant primary at 21,000 ... group got clobbered; lost ten ships....need new belly turret...

Miller put down his pen at a knock on his door. His roommate had just rotated to another group, so he did not know who this would have been. At the door he saw a tall, urbane-looking Captain, older than Miller by several years, wearing flight wings. "Miller," the captain asked, "I'm Ned Gillette. Billeting office said I was with you." Miller let him in, introducing himself with a handshake and a hoist of Gillette's trailing duffel bag.

"Well, it ain't much," Miller said resignedly, "but it's home for me."

"Better than a tent," Gillette agreed, gazing around at the bare walls. "Where's the latrine?"

"End of the hall, to the left. Don't talk about tents. I was in one for my first two weeks here."

"Oh," Gillette replied, genuinely impressed, "You're one of the originals here, then?"

"Yeah," Miller sighed, sitting in one of the two chairs in the room.

"Got here in November, flew missions in December." He studied the newcomer's uniform briefly. There were three rows of ribbons, flight wings, and some unfamiliar insignia on the lapels. "I don't recognize the branch. Something new?"

"Oh," Gillette said, stripping off his jacket, "Yeah. I gotta get some Air Corps brass, I guess. This is Intelligence; new outfit."

"Uh huh," Miller grunted. "You bring a new 'Fort, or are you a replacement?"

"Neither, really. I flew in the past tense—too old now. No, got my wings in '31, left the service for the footlights of Broadway. Got promoted in the New York Guard and then got called up last February. It was either intelligence or quartermaster, so I took intelligence. I'm the new squadron intelligence officer."

"I didn't know squadrons had real intelligence officers."

"New idea," Gillette said, rustling through his duffel bag. "Iron-Ass Lemay has had good luck parceling out the target profiling work, so they decided to try it in other groups."

"Oh. What'd you do before they called you up?"

"Oh, lots of things. I've been a theatrical agent, part-time actor, playwright, stage manager, and co-producer in my time."

"OK. How's that work in intelligence?"

"Well, it kinda fits. Working the stage, you get to know how to fit people to situations, how to find just the right guy—or gal—for the job, how it might look to somebody else. What'd you do?"

"I was in college in Wisconsin. Worked summers in my dad's flying service. Joined up and here I am."

"Yes. Here we are, all right. How many missions have you had?"

"Today was twenty-one." Miller said it with finality, as if the subject were closed. Gillette picked up on it instantly and was quiet. There's a point beyond which the stagehands should not question the actors, he thought, and a point beyond which the ground echelon should not question the flyers. This was that point.

"Um, I'm supposed to tell you that Colonel King wants you in his office at the earliest possible interval," Gillette said.

Miller dusted off his spare hat, put a quick buff on his shoes, and sauntered off to squadron headquarters. The clerks barely looked up from their work, each with a basket full of 'In' and precious little 'Out.' Miller had few illusions about where all the paperwork came from because as the senior captain in the squadron he wore a score of other hats including check pilot, elections officer, gas precautions officer, and, ironically, health and morale officer. Each additional duty required at least an hour a week of his time; some needed more than that.

"Captain Miller, sir," the sergeant muttered when he let Miller into King's office. Miller marched ceremoniously up to King's desk, snapped to attention, and threw off a salute. King returned the gesture.

"Have a seat, Miller," King droned in his tombstone voice. "Not going to stand around on ceremony much here, but," he handed Miller a typed copy of orders, "Teller got assigned a new job stateside, which leaves me without an air exec. As senior captain, you get the job, along with this," he handed him another typed sheet. "Stand up once and I'll pin 'em on." Miller read the second order in stunned silence. 'John Miller, having demonstrated great courage and leadership, is hereby promoted to the rank of MAJOR in the United States Army Reserve and the United States Army Air Forces.'

Slowly, still reading the orders, Miller stood. King, removing Miller's captain's bars, was still talking. "These are my originals, which tradition says I have to pass on to the first subordinate I promote to my old rank. Here's what came with the orders." Handing Miller a shiny pair of oak leaves, King offered his hand. "Your permanent rank is still first lieutenant, but you knew that. Now, as air exec, there's not a lot of difference between what you do now and what you've been doing, but as a Major there's a bit more money to do it and another fistful of reports. Clay Cole can help you with what you're supposed to know from the Command and General Staff School, which you haven't got yet, but I've requested orders for you. C'mon and I'll buy you a drink."

At Club # 4, it seemed as if the news of Miller's promotion had traveled fast. After they had slammed the first round home, Geoghegan stood up. "Pilot Miller; it is my incumbent duty as the founder of the Fraternal Brotherhood of Majors…"

"Hey!" Major Margaret Thorne shouted. "What about the Sisterhood?"

"You can induct him into that if you've a mind, Maggie my dear; now shaddap while I make the rest of this up. Where was I? Oh, yes: to induct you as our newest member," he shouted, laying his brogue on particularly thick. "Just remember our motto: 'we've enough rank to be noticed…'"

"But not enough to matter," the other patrons shouted. After the general gaiety had died down, Clay Cole sidled up to Miller's stool. "There's a short course—I think it's a week now—for executive officers down in Devon; I've sent your name in for a slot, which you should get in a week or so. They're pushing more and more units over here, and very few of the staff officers have any staff training; no matter: it's not that hard." Cole turned away from Miller briefly to order another drink, and Miller could see his glass eye dull in his head.

"You've been to staff school?"

"Used to teach there," Cole assented. "Not a lot to it, but a method of paperwork, and much of that you won't be doing, anyway. For us now, squadron check pilot's your most important job—that and leading the squadron in the air when the commander isn't there. Just remember: the unit belongs to the commander, but the officers belong to you now." The revelry got louder for a few minutes—someone just came in with another announcement that Sicily had been declared secured.

"Pretty quick work," Cole muttered.

"Yeah," Miller agreed. "Just wish we could get done with this job over here as fast."

August 1943

Oschersleben, Germany

You can always tell an old soldier
By the inside of his holsters and cartridge boxes;
The young men carry pistols;
The older ones, grub

George Bernard Shaw

I t had taken nearly a week, and Elsa's reluctant invocation of her father's name, before she and Thielmann finally reached Oschersleben in a police van. With his feet badly burned and his hands in bloody ruins, it would be some time before Thielmann could fly again.

They threw JG191 into something of a panic when Thielmann and his new bride arrived very early on a Sunday morning. Though Elsa was not news, the marriage was, and made for something of a problem since Thielmann had not sought permission from the Personnel Office to marry: were they legal or not? Kaltz, ever the effective commander, simply pointed out that there was a valid certificate of marriage, duly signed and witnessed, and he could only presume that both parties were sober and fully clothed when the ceremony took place. As for the reasons for the emergency...Hamburg was reason enough for him. He would straighten the matter out with the bureaucrats.

But wives were not common on *Luftwaffe* bases, and so the flyers and support staff of JG191 addressed this unique challenge in their own way. For lodgings, Taube gave up a little cottage he had been using for when his wife came up to visit. It was only two rooms with just a few crude sticks of furniture, but the roof didn't leak, so it was enough.

Pritzler's mother and aunt were working a farm some thirty kilometers east, and came over to get Elsa some clothes and other necessities, since she had lost everything she had in Hamburg, and the cabin in Austria that held the rest of her belongings was too far away. For food, the ration clerk was paid handsomely to look the other way when Elsa was added to the ration lists as a maid (and paid half a ration a day which somehow doubled under the heading of "wastage") under her first husband's name. She got permission to transfer her Red Cross job to Oschersleben, and the small pittance they paid her helped her to buy other things. After two weeks in the hospital, Thielmann was recovered enough to be given evening passes.

The ward he was in was typical of military hospitals—long rows of uncomfortable cots, patients in various stages of consciousness and pain, the pervasive smell of carbolic, stark lights and cold shadows. Elsa walked towards the back of the ward, where Thielmann shared a room with another Captain from a different group. As she approached, she noticed an older man in an ill-fitting *Kriegsmarine* uniform seated next to her husband, murmuring. He was a big man with large, raw hands and an orderly helmet of pale gray hair. They both looked up as she drew near.

"*Liebchen*," Thielmann said as she kissed his cheek, "my father. Papa, this is Elsa." The big man hugged her cordially, the way a father-in-law should.

"My, yes," Lothar said. "Otto has spoken of you, but didn't say you were quite this lovely. My belated congratulations, and welcome to the family."

"Thank you, er, Papa," she stumbled over the phrase. She had never met her first husband's family, so had no practice at all with in-laws.

"Papa has brought good news," Thielmann beamed, propping himself up on the bed. "Ulrich is a prisoner in America."

"Oh, good!" She was genuinely relieved. Otto had been brooding about his brother for months, and she did not want to have another "missing sickness" to deal with other than her own. "Do we know what happened?"

"We know a little," the elder Thielmann said. "The English shot his machine up over the Kanal and the pilot found an American airfield in a fog. He managed to land, and the Americans had to dismantle the machine to get Ulrich out. Apparently, he was injured."

"How severely; where?" the son asked.

"That is unclear. The Americans sent some specialist to extract him.

Something apparently went through the back of his neck and came out under his chin. It took a bit of doing, they said, to get him out without killing him."

"How do we know all of this?" Elsa was no stranger to secretive information, but often wondered about where it came from and what the information said about the sources. Her father, who she detested as a fervent Nazi, often spoke of secrets when he was a more ordinary policeman before the war.

"Several sources," he said evasively. "We have pieced together what happened. And of course we have a Red Cross confirmation of Ulrich's arrival in the prison camp in a place called Camp McCoy in America."

"Do we know anything else?"

"Only that the American *Festungen* where the machine landed were marked with a diamond M insignia. Our sources make this the 299th Bombardment squadron of the 610th Bombing Group. Both are near the English town of Bartlesby."

"Bartlesby," Otto tried the name on his tongue, "Bartlesby."

"Otto tells me your mother is in Salzburg, Elsa," Lothar said.

"Yes, but Papa...." Her voice trailed off. Her father was at his headquarters in Lubeck on the Baltic coast. He had not seen his family in over a year, and had no contact with his wife or daughter.

"Well, I shall have to arrange to meet with them." This was so difficult, old Lothar thought, but probably no worse than it was for my parents in the last war, when I married Elisabeth on leave.

"Oh, Mama would like that," Elsa said. "You should really meet with Uncle Peter, too."

"Yes, your famous uncle. How is he?"

"He is still angry that the Nazis are in power, and have seen fit to carry on with the war. He is just the same," she sighed. "Papa Lothar?"

"Yes, Elsa," he replied, slightly startled at the new form of address.

"Do you fly, too?"

"Oh, no. I'm strictly an administrator," he lied slightly. In truth, he didn't have to wear a uniform at all because he was a civilian "technician" who sifted information. Just then, a loud voice was heard at the end of the ward. *"Achtung; stillgestanden!"* and as one, the military idlers and visitors locked into a ramrod-straight posture, eyes front and unfocused.

"Gentlemen, please, carry on, be at your ease," another familiar voice said. Lutzow-Verein, in his pre-1932 uniform, walked casually down the ward, glancing and waving to the patients as he passed, the worried hospital Director following behind, whispering and motioning to staff as he, the head nurse, and several other doctors hurried behind the old soldier.

"We were not expecting you, General, or we would have prepared..."

"Doctor, please," the general said kindly, "this is not an inspection or anything official. I am only here to visit my nephew. And here he is," he said, stopping at Thielmann's door. "Elsa, my dear, I was so relieved to hear of you," he murmured, bussing her on the cheek. "Your mother called me yesterday." The irreverence, Elsa thought, a German kissing in public. But Uncle finds great amusement in it.

"You didn't even tell me you were leaving the mountains, uncle," Elsa said.

"I hadn't planned on it, but I wanted to see an old friend in Bremen."

"Hello, Uncle," Thielmann said, doing his best to rise.

"Stay there, Otto," Lutzow-Verein chided. "You are a sick man, they tell me. And, may I offer you and Elsa my heartiest congratulations and sincerest best wishes? I welcome you to the family of Lutzow-Verein."

"Thank you, uncle," Thielmann began, "but may I introduce my father, Lothar; Papa, this is Elsa's uncle, *Generalmajor* Peter von Lutzow-Verein." Lutzow-Verein shook hands with Lothar.

"You've a fine son, Thielmann, a fine man. Welcome to the family of Lutzow-Verein." Lutzow-Verein boomed.

"Thank you, sir," Lothar said, genuinely flattered, "and welcome to our family. Your niece has much to thank you for."

"Oh, she was my sister's doing, not mine. She told me about the marriage. Have you heard from Salzburg yet?"

"No. I was just telling Elsa that I have to write to her."

"You should hear from her soon. Her father already knows." They exchanged pleasantries for a time, the general sitting nonchalantly in the proffered chair, not touching the chair-back. The hospital staff clustered nervously in the background, barely out of earshot. Thielmann wondered if any of the staff would notice that his uniform was obsolete, or recognize who he was. Somehow, he thought to himself, I do not think they would notice, and if they did, it probably would not matter. The name Lutzow-Verein commanded so much awe after the last war they would fall all over him, even if he was not in uniform.

"I am released every evening, uncle. Would you join us in our mess?"

"I would be honored if you don't go to any trouble. It would be a privilege to be among common soldiers again."

It was not every *Luftwaffe* fighter group that could boast of having entertained a general officer, but JG191 prepared a sumptuous meal despite Lettow-Vorbeck's insistence that they go through no special trouble. He acted respectfully interested while touring the flying machines and the workshops, but his insistence on meeting the pilots and blackbirds, on seeing the barracks and even the enlisted men's latrines, caused some concern. Though they were clean, they weren't clean enough for a *Generalmajor*.

Thielmann introduced his father to his fellow officers, leaving Elsa to introduce her uncle. Lutzow-Verein, Kaltz wondered, the Lutzow-Verein? Lutzow-Verein was pleasant, even genial, to everyone in the unit, passing idle conversation, asking them if they were well-fed, if they'd heard from home or relatives. "Bär; Swabian, are you not?" Lutzow-Verein looked as if he were testing his memory. "Are you any relation to Wolfram Bär, of the Fourth Regiment of Artillery?"

"My grandfather, sir," Bär answered.

"How is the old boy? I served with him for a time."

"He is as well as a ninety-year-old man can be expected, sir. And he is long since deaf from the guns."

"Ah, yes. Good soldier."

"*Jawohl, Herr General.* He has spoken highly of you in the past."

"Remember me to him if you can, please?"

"*Natürlich, Herr General.*"

Though the bright-work wasn't especially bright and the dirty was quite filthy, he observed it all, having nothing but questions for the men about them. He passed no judgments on the obviously substandard, haphazard and makeshift; this was no inspection, just a visit. In the mess, after the veal and parsley potatoes, the conversation swirled around the endless shortages, on the General's experience in the last war in Africa, or on nothing at all.

"Do they want to call you up, *Herr General?*"

"Only as a courtesy," he chuckled. "Occasionally an old comrade will visit and ask politely what I think of such-and-so, but I know they are really being kind to an old soldier who knows nothing of this war. This unit is a perfect example. Except for the men and their accommodations, I know practically nothing about the *Luftwaffe* or how it works. Besides, the Nazis would as soon forget all about me."

"How can they forget the great Lutzow-Verein, sir? They still whisper about you in the training camps."

"They whisper about a legend, not me. Lutzow-Verein is an embarrassment, a throwback to an age when war was a nobler calling, not an efficient machine of death. With my 'von' they would as soon dispense, as they have dispensed with everything else that was noble about Germany, even though Elsa's father changed his name when he married my sister to gain a noble 'von.' We are fighting this war now to stay alive, and the Nazis to keep their plunder, or save their wretched necks." A few officers wearing Party chevrons on their sleeves were quietly indignant.

Smiling mildly at their agitation, the general turned to face them directly. "Do you know what war is, gentlemen? It is far more than just killing and destroying. There is no other human endeavor where the rewards of success are so great and the costs of failure are so dire. In this way, it is a sieve. War is the ultimate means by which both God and man decide what is evil, what is good; what is noble, what is craven. War decides truth, falsehood, memorable, and forgettable. War is the sum of all foibles of man and of nature. Men reach the height of their nobility and the depths of their depravity there. It destroys cultures and societies, and it creates them. It is the ultimate in human experience. War is where death and life have no meaning at all and where death and life are the only meaningful things. Human society is made and unmade by war. It is both the ultimate creator and destroyer of man. War sorts out all things through its meshes, and each thing is kept in its appropriate place.

"When this war is over, all will know the depths to which the Nazis have sunk to create their perfect version of society. But there will be a few who will misinterpret their depravity, and because of them, we shall have to sieve again. And there will be even fewer who will see that it is only another sieve, one of many defining moments in our history, and for them it will be a torment when we once again have to suffer war. I only hope that when my time comes, and I stand before my Creator, that where I was stopped in the sieve of war will allow me some peace."

September 1943

Northern Europe

The girls be'ind the bar they laughed an' giggled fit to die,
I outs into the streets again, an' to myself says I:
O it's Tommy this and Tommy that, an' Tommy go away;
But it's 'Thank you, Mister Atkins,' when the band begins to play

Rudyard Kipling

A week after the Schweinfurt raid, *Crop Duster* got two replacement gunners. A Nebraska farm kid named Bill Aitcheson, barely above height and weight requirements, squeezed easily into the new belly gun. For the tail, they got a new replacement up out of North Africa. "I know you, don't I," Miller said when he met him.

"We've met, sir," Don Milliken said, still growling as he'd done on their first encounter in Milwaukee. "I'm pleased you're still around."

"Not near as much as I am," Miller said. "Where'd you come from, anyway?"

"My last home was driving a gypsy cab in Chicago," he said. "And if one of your kids calls me 'Pop' or 'Pappy' so help me, I'll break him in two and dance a jig on his gizzard."

"Where have I heard that before? *Oh* yeah. Still, you gotta admit you're a little long in the tooth for this business."

"How old I am don't matter. Sir."

The group lead ship, *The Throne Room*, had some new gear installed, along with crew replacements trained to use it. That change got *Throne Room's* Jackson and Reynolds re-assigned to *Crop Duster* to replace Thomas and Royce.

Nate Jackson and Jack Reynolds were an improbable pair, a classic "Mutt and Jeff," but not because the two were fast friends and deathly

259

efficient in their work. No, these two were almost complete opposites. Jackson was the blue-blooded scion of a hopelessly rich and powerful New England clan with roots predating *Mayflower*, and Reynolds was a member of a tribe of sharecroppers and truck farmers in Texas. More than that, Jackson was the 299th's poker champion, while Reynolds couldn't make a pair with ten cards.

One weather-miserable day, the 1st Wing got so badly scattered no one knew where all the parts were. The castles of Fortresses stumbled around Germany through a heavy cloud deck over the briefed target (Bremen), then to the secondary, then to anything they could find to hit. With *Throne Room* still in Bartlesby getting fitted with the new gear, *Crop Duster* was the lead ship, and Jackson and Reynolds ran the flight deck—and the mission—flawlessly, leading the 299th wherever the Wing decided it wanted to go. Finally, a target of opportunity presented itself (some nameless ammo depot in Luxembourg that was probably never hit again) before the Fortresses had to turn back for lack of fuel. The 'Forts lined up on an I/P run and got bombs away only a few minutes later. Flak was sporadic but fairly accurate.

Miller was flying on fumes when he went into the first English meadow he could find in the darkening Kentish countryside. He pulled *Crop Duster* to a halt in the hardened loam about ten feet in front of a hedgerow. Aside from the fact that it wasn't an airfield, it wasn't that bad a landing. The crew piled out of the ship, Miller and Farr making a cursory check for damage. Collova, Murphy and Roy made a quick reconnaissance to find out where they were, coming back in a few minutes to report no signs of civilization.

"You sure we're in England?" Miller asked Reynolds.

"Yup," the navigator replied somewhat testily, "Somewhere in Kent. We should see some lights off to the northwest."

"In the blackout," Witt mocked. "We'll see lights in the blackout." Reynolds stared at him.

"What did Charles De Gaulle say when he saw the elephants coming over the hill?" Collova quipped. As one, the crew groaned at another of Collova's seemingly endless stream of jokes.

"I'll bite," Murphy said. "What did he say?"

"Nothing: he knows elephants don't speak French."

"Well, nothing more we can do here," Miller declared. "Guess we'll just have to find a phone someplace. Farr, stay with the ship and keep the crew together. Witt, you're in charge. Reynolds, come on with me.

I think I saw a road a few miles west. We'll be back as soon as we can." Miller and Reynolds trudged off in search of some sign of human habitation.

"Why do elephants paint their toenails red?"

"If I bite one more time, will you shut the hell up?"

"So they can hide in cherry trees. Ever see an elephant in a cherry tree?"

"Of course not, you fat turd."

"See how well they hide?"

"Collova, I swear by the Eternal I'll throw your lard ass outta this airplane one day..."

Darkness descended in the English countryside like turning off a switch in a windowless room. Soon, a blanket of stars appeared across the indigo blue sky overhead. Every hundred paces or so, Miller and Reynolds ran into another hedgerow and had to spend several minutes looking for a path through it. It had rained the night before, and the pair was getting quite soaked and cold.

Keeping a rough bearing with a hand compass, they finally found a road after a couple hours' march, and briefly discussed which direction they should go. After a scientific coin-toss they proceeded north. It was another hour before they found a small cottage on the edge of a sulking mass of trees. Miller knocked on the rough-hewn door, not seeing any signs of light within, but some sparks from the stone chimney. The door slowly swung open, revealing the dancing light of a fire on the far wall. Back-lit from the fire stood a little man, crudely dressed in the woolens of the gamekeeper's trade, hastily dragged over a nightshirt, bearing a rather large-bore fouling piece which he naturally aimed at the intruders. An unnaturally large dog stood at his side, showing unnaturally large teeth and an ungodly loud growl.

"What say ye?" the little man snarled over the dog's growl. The Americans turned quite pale and were already shivering in the cold damp. Oh, this is just what I need, Miller thought. If the Germans don't kill me, the English might.

"W-w-we-we're Americans," Miller managed. "We ran out of gas and landed a few miles east. We wondered if you had a telephone."

"Americans, is it?" the gamekeeper snapped. "There's no Americans out east, then, is there? Say now what's your business or I'll blow your Hun heads off! *Say* it, then!"

"We're flyer's sir," Reynolds replied, "and like he says, we ran out of gas. We just bombed Berlin, in fact. But we took too long getting there and..."

"Shamus," a woman's voice called inside the cottage, "who is't, then?" "They says they be Americans from out east a bit," the little man called back, "but I knowed there be no Americans to the east. I knowed these two be..."

"Aviators, Shamus," the voice called, ever closer to the door. "Of course they're Americans." The woman appeared in the doorway in a nightdress and cap, pulling a shawl tightly around her shoulders. "They said they *landed*, ye deaf old fool, not *came*. Put that silly gun away; thee haven't any powder for it in any case, does thee now? Come in, come in, lads, before thee catches your death. Shamus, don't just stand there, fetch the whiskey. Why they're soaked through, the poor dears." The tiny woman hustled the two flyers in the cottage while the gamekeeper and dog stood aside, still eying the strangers suspiciously. As much as they protested, Miller and Reynolds still welcomed the chance to stand near the fire, and did not turn down the offer of a very coarse but welcome whiskey.

"Do you have a telephone, ma'am," Miller asked his hostess as the cold faded from him.

"Now what would we be doin' with a telephone, then?" the little man said, genuinely astonished.

"Nay, I'm sorry, sir. We have no telephone. But his lordship has one, now doesn't he, Shamus?"

"Quiet ye, woman," the little man insisted. "They be Hun spies, I tell thee!"

"They be not Hun spies, ye old fool." This dickering when on for some minutes between his back-country Kentish lilt and her Irish brogue, with both Americans straining to understand what was being said. Finally, the arguing apparently stopped, though neither American could tell if anyone actually won.

"Go on, then, old man, and hitch up the cart," she chided, hustling the protesting gamekeeper out the door. "He's been this way since the Blitz, see," the little woman explained. "Convinced Germans are behind every stone and stick. Shell-shock," she added *sotto voce*.

"Yes, ma'am," Miller assented, as if he understood. "But if you could just show us the way to his lordship's..."

"Ach, I need do nothing of the sort. Shamus shall take thee there."

"Well, we can walk, ma'am, if you'll just..."

"Walk, sir, nay. 'Tis three leagues off." As the little woman was slicing bread,

"How far's three leagues?" Miller whispered to Reynolds.

"Nine miles, I think. Mighty long walk."

The woman returned with bits of cheese and bread, and some cold shreds of lamb. "We haven't much, but thee're welcome to what we have. Eat, then. Put some fire back in ye." The bread was salty, typically English, and coarse, but they hadn't eaten since mid-morning. "Do ye know Texas, America, then gentlemen?" the woman asked.

"Yes, ma'am," Reynolds drawled with pride. "I'm from Texas."

"Are ye then?" she brightened. "Our Adrian is in Texas with the RN. Some hush-hush with shipping, he writes. What's Texas like, then?"

"Ah, it's beautiful down by the coast. And it's right nice up in the north, too. In the middle and out west, well..." Reynolds had lost his drawl years since and Miller had never heard him put it on so broadly, but he resisted grinning.

"Trouble with red Indians, I hear," she whispered. "The cinema..."

"Oh, they ain't been much trouble for a long time, ma'am, 'cept on Saturday night when they get liquored up..."

***

The ride to the manor house in the small cart was bumpy, but quiet, the only sounds being the old horse's hooves clip-clopping on the hard road and the periodic muttering from the gamekeeper. The huge dog sat quietly next to the gamekeeper on the small bench seat, occasionally glancing back at its passengers.

The rising moon was brightening the sky as the wagon pulled up to the manor, a huge, rambling affair with immaculately trimmed hedges. Quite a few cars were parked in the courtyard by the front door, and on down the drive all the way through the gate that had opened by a sleepy gatekeeper without challenge. As he brought the cart to a halt, Shamus instructed his passengers to, "Wait here," motioning the dog to stand guard.

Soon, a man in evening clothes appeared from the front door, followed by the gamekeeper. "Hello there," the man said, "Shamus says you're German spies pretending to be Americans. Is there any truth to that?"

"Well, sir, to the Americans' part, I'll have to say yes," Miller replied, "but we're in an awful fix if we're spies."

"Come on, then. We're just breaking up our party. Thank you, Shamus. We'll take charge of these, er, spies. Go get something to eat." The little fellow shuffled off, muttering under his breath, dog alongside.

263

"Quite a character," Miller said to his host, "he works for you?"

"In a manner of speaking, I suppose he does. Richard Marlowe's my name, Major," he said, offering his hand. Miller and Reynolds both shook it. "His family owns that cottage and the land, deeded to them in perpetuity by my great grandfather, the first Earl. Shamus' grandfather took a musket ball meant for the first earl on the Peninsula in 1811. Great- grandfather gave him the land and an annuity. We keep them on as grounds men and gamekeepers."

"Little nuts, I think," Reynolds said.

"Oh, quite mad, yes indeed," Marlowe agreed, running his slim fingers through his black hair. "Shamus was first over the top at the Somme in '16, Father said, and the last on his feet in his battalion. All went down in the first few hours: all but him. Drive anyone mad, I'd say. Quite harmless, though." A commotion momentarily disrupted their conversation in the front courtyard, caused by the arrival of a truck-mounted hayrick containing most of the rest of Miller's crew.

"What're you guys doing here?" Miller yelled, "I told you to stay with the ship!"

"I'm responsible for that, I'm afraid, Major," a Bobby in the truck's cab replied. "They were starting a fire out on the field because they were cold. I took it on myself to bring them here. Can't have any lights, you know." And flight suits soaked with stink and sweat from a mission ain't warm either, Miller thought.

"Farr's back with the ship, skipper," Jackson said. "We only had two blankets, and we were getting mighty cold and ...."

"Hungry," Collova said. "We ain't eaten in damn near eighteen hours, boss, 'cept them damn K-rations."

"Go on inside, then, gentlemen," Marlowe said. "We've plenty of food. Major, I think you'll want use of a telephone." An impossibly British butler stood like a statue by the door, evening guests gathered curiously around the archways and windows of the manor house. "Simons," Marlowe called out, "see to it that our new arrivals have what they want, eh?"

"Very good, sir," the butler answered. "Ellsworth or Ralph, sir?"

"Oh, Ellsworth, naturally."

"Very good, sir; this way, gentlemen." The Central Casting butler led the crew into the dining room, where a large buffet was being restocked. Raising Bartlesby took only a few minutes, and relating their position took only a few more, an RAF Group Captain/guest providing coordinates.

"What's 'Ellsworth or Ralph,' skipper?" Murphy asked, mouth bulging with cold beef.

"Beats me," Miller answered, taking in the swirling multinational crowd of swells, diplomatic and military types that were the guests of the party. "Ask the butler."

"That won't be necessary, Major," Marlowe joined in. "It's a private code between us. My son Ellsworth and his son Ralph came home on leave before they shipped to Singapore. That first night, Ralph sat and ate in the kitchen just as he always had, and Ellsworth sat in the dining room just as before. Well, things weren't the same as before, now were they, especially since they were both sub-lieutenants with the same date of rank? Indeed, not. So Ralph joined Ellsworth in the dining room by their own arrangement. So 'Ellsworth' has become the dining room, and 'Ralph' the kitchen.

"We know the nobility is dying, gentlemen. A death started when those yellow devils we thought were so inferior sank those two British ships, and I am the last of my line. Both of them are dead, you see: Ellsworth and Ralph. They were born within three weeks of each other, they grew up together, and they died together on *Repulse*. I've left my estate to the Crown, but I've codiciled that Simons and his family can live here for as long as his family lives, rent-free. That which is noble in us survives, gentlemen, even if the nobles do not."

The all-night party (common in Kent just then, to avoid driving in the blackout) was revived by the appearance of the new "guests," even though there was little exchange between the dirty, weary, hungry, boorish Americans and the predominantly British society members. The English regarded Miller's crew as they may have regarded stray dogs suddenly appearing. The crew ignored them.

A small orchestra took up their instruments again, playing the lovely but somber chamber music typical of these occasions. The partygoers wandered seemingly aimlessly from room to room, passing small conversation about nothing. The handful of American guests (officers and diplomats, of course) were at least civil to their recently arrived countrymen while the leather and wool-clad airmen stuffed their faces.

"Ladies and gentlemen," an American called out, suddenly appearing from a side door. "I've just spoken with my State Department. The Supreme Fascist Council has thrown Mussolini out and asked the King to return. The Italians have surrendered! It's official. The Italians are out of the war!"

"Here, here," the English shouted.

"Bravo," the French applauded.

"Urrah," the Russians cried.

"Hooray," the Americans yelled.

"No shit," the crew of *Crop Duster* exclaimed, and suddenly Miller's men became heroes, gawked at and talked to, pumped by the hand and slapped on the back, even though only Milliken had flown against Italian targets. The small band started "God Save the King," which the Americans knew as "My Country 'Tis of Thee." The English, naturally, sang:

God save our glorious King;

And the Americans, perhaps a little too loudly for guests, also took up the tune:

Sweet land of Liberty;

While the non-English-speaking remained respectfully silent, except for a Russian who'd just discovered the wonders of Irish whiskey and belted out something to the same melody that no one else understood... except the other two Russians. But by the last verse, no one had thrown a punch, and the song ended to the familiar strains:

God save the King — Let freedom ring!

"Gotta hoe-down," Collova exclaimed, seizing a violin from one of the band. He crooked the instrument into his elbow and began to saw on the strings fervently, brilliantly, much to the visible amazement of the orchestra, as some reel echoed in the ancient hall. The ever-irreverent Milliken grabbed a woman—a septuagenarian marchioness—by the elbows and swung her around to the tune. At first clumsy, but with growing skill, the party transformed into a full-blown reel as the orchestra followed Collova's lead, Miller's crew leading even the stuffiest of partygoers into the uniquely American rhythms. The Scots in attendance, recognizing the sounds as based on a Fling, easily adapted their traditional dance to the American music. I'll be damned, Miller thought, watching this spectacle unfold. There may be hope for us yet.

"One down and two to go, sir," Witt yelled to Miller.

"Yeah," Miller managed. Of course, the two left were the worst of the bunch. Italy was out of the war; Germany would be next. All Miller and his friends would have to do was survive long enough to see it.

September 1943

Maastricht, Holland

And God still sits aloft in the array
That we have wrought him,
Stone-deaf and stone-blind

Edward Thomas

S till, they won't turn back, Thielmann thought bitterly as he watched his swarm form behind him, and Taube's swarm behind them, still climbing above the oncoming Marauders. We hit the *Amis* on the way to Schweinfurt and Regensburg with everything we could put in the air and still they did not turn back. Perhaps we can turn these Marauders back just once...

For the *Luftwaffe,* the twin-engine Marauders were becoming extremely dangerous. It wasn't that they carried more guns than the Fortresses or the Liberators (in fact they carried fewer), but because they attacked swiftly, closer to the ground, hitting smaller targets with the same size of bomb load as their larger cousins. If a Fortress herd attacked a factory, the Marauders would pounce on a single workshop; if the *dicke autos* hit a power plant, the Marauders would blast the railway siding next to it. Beyond that, Marauders seldom flew beyond the range of escorting fighters. Finally, and most ominously, Marauders spent much of their effort attacking the *Luftwaffe*—airfields, workshops, flak batteries, radar stations. But because of their altitude, size and speed, they could not attack the Marauders with the same tactics as the bigger bombers, and JG191 was to find a way.

Five kilometers ahead and five hundred meters below JG191, a spray of Messerschmitts flew in small knots of four, probing fingers, searching for the escorting fighters that protected the Marauders, if there were any today. The *Amis,* being practical, didn't always send an escort with the speedy, low- flying Marauders, but the *Luftwaffe* units that opposed them learned early on that it was very, very common.

Craning his neck, swiveling, changing speed and altitude with nearly reflexive detachment, Thielmann watched, listened to the ground controllers (today they were under ground control—somewhat unusual for JG191), waited for the contact. His stomach ached with a dull throbbing he had felt since Mosalsk: many pilots complained of stomach pains. Worse, his burns hadn't fully healed over yet, and the skin on his hands was still touchy.

Ground control had a plot on what looked to be a Marauder formation just ahead. The naval spotters had seen them crossing the Dutch coast, but escorting Spitfires had chased off the tracker planes. "Bitburg leader to Altmarck leader," the leader of the Messerschmitts called. "Contact on the right: Spitfires; may have Marauders behind them. Am engaging. Bitburg leader to all Bitburg units: engage, engage. *Pauke!*" The Messerschmitts wheeled in a wingover turn to the right, sailing for their ancient enemies, the British-built, American-flown Spitfires.

"Altmarck leader to Altmarck," Pritzler called. "Form for Indian action, right." With machine-like precision, JG191 quickly shifted from a search formation to a diamond fighting formation.

"Altmarck two to Altmarck leader," Thielmann called as he slid into Pritzler's left rear, "position action right."

"Altmarck three to Altmarck leader," Bär called, pulling in from behind to close the diamond to Pritzler's high rear, "position action right."

"Altmarck four to Altmarck," Taube called, rolling into the left side of the formation, "position action right. Unidentified targets approaching right up one five."

Thielmann looked to the right corner and saw the dots quickly descending on them. "Affirmative," he called, "Altmarck two to Altmarck leader: I have them."

"Altmarck leader to Altmarck two and four: lead attack two abreast. Altmarck one and three follow attacks. All Altmarcks attack. *Pauke!*" Thielmann led his swarm over the diamond, diving into position to Taube's right, the unknown targets growing. He replaced the initial rush of exaltation and fear with consternation and a growing pain in his stomach. What are they? These are not Spitfires, nor Thunderbolts.

Hawks, perhaps, or Tomahawks with new engines? What in...?

The strange Indians sped past and through them, guns blazing head on. Thielmann recovered enough to fire his machine guns, saving his heavier cannon ammunition for the bombers. He whipped his machine around for another go at the strangers, watching with amazement as they climbed, turned and still sped away. Am I dreaming, Thielmann wondered, or did I just see a climbing three-gravity banked turn by six airplanes in less than three kilometers? I could not have seen it. Such things cannot happen. "What are they?"

"*Amis* shooting at us, you idiot! Let's get after them!" JG191 swung around into a more customary attack diamond, just as the strangers attacked them from the high right. As Thielmann pulled his machine about, his stomach suddenly stabbed, tight and painful, as he imagined being shot, but knowing they had not hit his machine. The sudden agony was nearly blinding, tearing into his abdomen as he watched the silhouette of a stranger pass in front of him; squared wings, bulge under the cockpit, astonishing speed and maneuverability ...what in hell is it?

Still in agony, he pawed the cannon arming switch, pulling his kite around to get on the attacker's rear. The strangers swerved away swiftly, whipping about to charge again. But this time it was different, for JG191 had prepared, through long, grueling hours of precision flying, to meet their foes, identified or not. The strangers came around in their finger-fours, the Germans in their loose swarms, clashing in the frozen space again and again, climbing ever higher, now the Americans, now the Germans with the height advantage, the sun advantage, the deflection angle, range, energy, trading every secret and skill in their minds and machines for a clear shot. Twice cannon shells passed through Thielmann's machine. Three times he was sure he hit one of the mysterious Americans, once to see smoke from the engine. His stomach gnawing away at his strength, he finally decided that he could do no more. "Altmarck two to Altmarck leader: I must disengage. Altmarck two to group: follow Altmarck two three." With Reicher loosely following, Thielmann broke off the battle, as did the strangers, as mysteriously and wondrously as they had appeared.

***

The surgeon had recommended rest, for Thielmann had developed a peptic ulcer, probably from the rotten food in Russia. "Not an uncommon case," he had said. "The Army is forming entire battalions of them. You will be all right in a few weeks if you rest." This meant, of course, that he was not to fly. But since losing a leg had not kept Hans-Ulrich Rudel out of his Stuka, Thielmann saw no reason to stop if he felt well enough. In the mess that evening, the Jägern still tried to identify the strange *Ami* fighters they had encountered. The identification book they had was the most advanced, but what it was telling them made no sense. The strangers, according to the unmistakable silhouettes and tapered, rectangular wing shapes, were an underpowered British type carrying only four rifle-caliber guns they had encountered in the Channel battle. The fighters they had fought today were vastly superior in speed and maneuverability to those puny Tommy machines, and carried at least six heavy cannons.

According to the intelligence book, which all pilots agreed had to be wrong, the strangers were called Mustangs.

***

A week later, Kaltz entered the officer's mess where his pilots were relaxing after a harrowing day. Thielmann was quite weary, as was the rest of JG191. Another attack on those annoying Marauders had cost them three machines. "Gentlemen," Kaltz announced, "I have good news for you. JG191 is being transferred to the south, out of range of the American Thunderbolts. We're going to have a brief rest period at Bad Kissingen, near Schweinfurt. Intelligence thinks that after their severe beating last month that the Americans won't be back there for a while..."

Two days later, JG191's ground echelon arrived at their new base in twenty trucks and two trains about an hour after the FWs landed on a sloped piece of concrete that was supposed to be an *Autobahn*. The rolling hills around the ancient city of mineral mud baths reminded Thielmann of his home. Everyone knew the Americans would not fly this deep into Germany again soon.

Thielmann wondered how convinced he was of that, recalling what Belzer had said so long ago in Poland: "*I fear the Americans, for they do not fear us...*"

13 October 1943

Hail, ye indomitable heroes, hail!
In spite of all your generals, ye prevail!

Walter Savage Landor

T he officers in the stuffy operations room were still worried about a weather front over the North Sea, but they had their orders: Hit Germany hard, soon, before the weather closed in for the winter. They pored over the target profiles, looked at the endless succession of charts and tables and reports, stared at the maps, and finally reached the inescapable conclusion—Thursday would be the best day. The bombers would have to be ready.

Maximum Effort was their term for it. Every bomber and fighter in England would fly the mission. The target was deep in Germany, one of the deepest and the most important—ball-bearing factories—the German war machine moved on ball bearings. Those factories would have to be hit now, again...and again if need be. The Italian campaign was stalled. The news from the Pacific was mixed.

Only the Air Force in England carried the war to the enemy.

There was no one else.

"Cut the orders," General Eaker told them. "We'll have to sort this out the best we can. Issue a Warning Order for tomorrow. Let's see if we can do it right this time." After the disaster over Munster just three days before, Eaker felt as if he'd just signed his own death warrant.

The clerks began the tedious, furious business of typing out the scribbled notes that would become the Field Order sometime around midnight. For now, the teletype operators rang up the loops and started the Warning Order to the Commands, Divisions, Wings and, finally, the Groups.

WARNING ORDER—HQ8AF PINETREE TO ALL PINETREE UNITS—WARNING ORDER—ALL OPERATIONAL UNITS ALERT NEXT 24HRS NLT 2100 ZEBRA...

***

"The news from Russia is, well, discouraging," the briefing officer said, revealing another chart on his easel. "Fighter strength taken from Russia for the defense of the *Reich* has cost us air superiority over most of the central front. The Russians are no longer the country peasants in the air that they were in '41. Now they can easily sweep our bombers from the skies, and our fighter strength isn't enough of a deterrent for the *Sturmoviks.* They can strike us from the air with relative impunity."

The officers absorbed this grimly, without comment. Now the tables had turned on them. Just a year before, *they* commanded the air over the battlefield, using the Stukas as guided artillery. Now the supply of pilots and planes was thinning over the fighting fronts, and it was all they could do to defend Germany.

***

Miller was just emerging from the maintenance building as King approached him. There would be no mission that day (only three days after a Maximum Effort there usually wasn't), but there were repairs and endless modifications to be done. "Major Miller," the squadron commander called, "This is Lieutenant Penn. He just brought a new Fortress up from the depot. He'll be joining the squadron." Miller shook hands with the young lieutenant (probably no younger than his advanced years of 23), imitating the friendly manner he remembered from long ago, but no longer felt. "Miller's the air exec and the check pilot for the squadron. He'll show you around."

"You had chow yet," Miller asked the earnest-looking young man, looking him up and down without moving his head or eyes (a technique one learns when looking for German fighters).

"Not since breakfast, sir," Penn replied eagerly. If this puppy had a tail, I'd catch cold from the breeze, Miller thought.

"OK, come on." Miller led the way to Mess Hall #1 near the front gate. Of the four on the base, it probably had the best chow. On the way, Miller returned the salutes of several (but not all) enlisted men, but Penn noted that very few lieutenants would extend the courtesy. "Most of the time we don't salute anything under a full bull," Miller explained, "but some of the new guys haven't got used to it yet. Old sergeants are the toughest nuts to crack—accepting the 'unlearned reflex' idea. New guys show up with a lot of stuff we have to un-teach. Saluting's part of it."

After chow, Miller found Penn's billet (across the hall from Jackson) and left him for the night. Plenty of time to fix what he got at the intake and training center at Bovingdon and everywhere else, Miller thought...

If he lives that long.

***

Thielmann set his Focke-Wulf down on the smooth concrete gently, up the gradual slope. The wide open fields surrounding the strip were wide enough to launch and recover on good, dry days. The prefabricated huts and acquired farms on both sides were at least adequate for their purpose.

Steger and the ground crew were walking towards Thielmann's plane before the propeller stopped turning. Thielmann methodically turned off all the switches and valves, mentally pacing the ticking-down of the magnetos. His guns were empty and smelled of burned oil. His machine was still fairly new and still handled well, but the engine needed work. Gasoline impurities were fouling the plugs and injectors, probably pitting the pistons. He wished again that they too had the 100 octane aviation fuel the Americans and British had.

Richter landed just after Thielmann, handling his machine with admirable skill. In the past six months, he had become quite the aviator, with sixteen victories himself. Gunther bounded up to Thielmann's machine just as he was climbing out. Thielmann, as always, stooped to scratch his ears and give him a lump of dried horsemeat. "Do what you can for the engine, Steger," Thielmann called out. "It loses power in climbing turns. There's some damage to the tail surface, I think. I got too close to a Spitfire today."

The blackbirds began swarming over the machine, working their nightly miracles. "*Jawohl* Captain," Steger answered. "It's good to see you, sir." Steger always said that when Thielmann returned from a day's flying, and for a time Thielmann didn't believe it. But as the months wore on, Thielmann came to realize that his crew chief was genuinely what he appeared to be—a loyal comrade; and a friend who often did little personal errands for Elsa.

Inside the ready building, other pilots were recounting their experiences of the day. There was not much to recount. Spitfires and Thunderbolts over France and the Low Countries, Lightnings hit a rail depot at Amiens and an E-Boat dock at Maastricht. The group lost no pilots but two machines, claiming three Lightnings and a Thunderbolt for their trouble. Two to four, Thielmann thought wearily, and they outnumber us by four to one.

"Gentlemen," Kaltz called out, and everyone fell silent. "They alert us for this evening and for tomorrow. We do not know what is in the making, but we do know that the Americans have not sortied their heavy bombers in three days. We are told to expect the worst. Get some rest, gentlemen. It may be a long night."

As the pilots quickly finished their brandies (there would be no more until the alert was over) JG191 steeled itself for another rapid deployment to wherever the crumbling dike of the Third Reich was the thinnest, where they would stick their fingers in until they were told another place was worse. Every active day it was the same, but not every day was a night-and-day alert. That was unusual. In fact, it was unprecedented.

***

The late-night assembly bugle roused the aircrews from a light slumber. In a few minutes, the briefing room was filling up with men half-asleep, expecting to fly in eight hours.

Mitchell Canby tried to reassure his men as best he could. A late-night briefing for the mediums meant an early-morning low-level attack on well-defended airfields, radar stations, and flak concentrations on the penetration and diversion routes to Germany. Though most of the men would survive, they would have little chance of evading the flak or low-level fighters, and if they were badly damaged, they probably wouldn't have enough altitude to withdraw to England. Getting hit meant death or capture, and that was all there was to it.

***

In the darkness under the thick concrete canopies, the fuel trucks began their runs to the *Luftwaffe* fields. They said the British were bombing near Hamm, so the Hamm convoys would hold for the moment. But the fuel had to move now to the North and Central German fields.

***

The driver slid his truck away from the ordnance dock, watching in his mirror until the dull gray concrete slab slid away. The scene at the ordnance depot was eerie at first, but in the past year he'd become accustomed to it. The subdued lights of the trucks, the red lights of the forklifts, the reflective yellow-white strips on the arms of the traffic directors made them look a bit like ghosts. The movements every night of hundreds of tons of ordnance in relative darkness all over England made him wince when he thought about it too much, so he didn't think about it. The run to the B-26 base at Nichols in the dark with the bombs on board would take him about two hours. In the day it would take not quite a half hour. But at night, without lights, carrying some 80,000 pounds of high explosive bombs, he didn't move any faster than fifteen miles an hour.

***

Somewhere out in the darkness, Lothar Thielmann thought, the pathfinders were coming. The early reports of the intruders were already coming in, and the signs pointed to Hamm tonight. He watched the specialists tune their receivers for the invisible beams the British used for navigation. If they guessed correctly, they would pass the information to another unit, which would try to provide what looked to be another beam. Someday, he thought, this might work.

***

"Looks like nineteen aircraft by 0600 Hours, suh," Philukuzki drawled. "We maht have twenty if we kin get *Cobb's Crib* another magneto." Miller nodded absently, taking the report. Nineteen aircraft out of forty-eight assigned. Six laid up, two hangar queens, and two new ships with crews still passing stateside water. Even on a maximum effort, no one would take green ships up without a few weeks of training. A green crew on a maximum effort is worse than useless, Miller thought: its maximum murder.

"OK, Casey," Miller said, "let's just call it nineteen and to hell with Cobb's ship. He doesn't have a full crew, anyway." Miller duly reported

275

the 299th's ship count to King, who passed it to Throck, who passed it to the Division. Eventually, by about midnight, it would arrive at Eighth Air Force HQ, and they would have a complete accounting of all the airplanes they were going to send the next day. There had been a time when this was impressive, but now, after little more than a year of only mediocre results, it was just more paper to shuffle.

***

The train, laden with flak ammunition, rolled slowly through the darkened city. The engineer and conductor watched the signals ahead of them, listening to the radios. At every major railhead, the train waited for news of the situation ahead—was there bombing, unrepaired damage, a stalled train? In France and the Low Countries it was worse—were there terrorists ahead, had they destroyed another bridge, loosened the outside rails in the next curve, a stalled a lorry across the tracks? Before the war, a train might cross Europe in twenty-four hours. By October 1943, it took at least three days.

***

The huge doors on the bomb bunkers swung open with surprising ease, rolling out the first racks of bombs into the chill fall darkness. Thousand pounders, this lot, went for the lead squadron, the 610th. The ordnance men inside the bunkers were still assembling the tail fins for the 500-pound bombs that made up half of the 299th's bomb load for the next day. Across the ordnance site, a handful of men with chain hoists carefully moved the small, evil black incendiary bombs from their wooden racks in the bunkers to the carts, loading the boxes of small burster fuses in a separate truck, and moving the lot out to the ready site. They were destined for the 191st. The ordnance handlers working the incendiaries were far more careful than their counterparts across the way, their equipment far sturdier and more stable. You could shoot at an HE and it wouldn't detonate, but incendiaries had been known to go off when a handler sneezed while screwing in a fuse.

***

Thielmann stretched and grunted on the sofa, the watery dinner wine warming him. Elsa looked up from her book, smiled, inwardly reassured, and then went back to her reading. They did not discuss what would go on after midnight, when Thielmann would return to the field. Elsa already knew what could happen and wanted no reminders. Gunther scratched an ear. Thielmann listened in the distance for the lazy rumbling of British bombers. Occasionally, he heard the sharper rumbles of night fighters flying on vectors, some real and others false, all across Germany.

Sometimes, though he knew it to be his imagination, he thought he could hear the interceptor's guns and the bomber's guns high overhead, firing at shadows, flickering engine exhausts, silhouettes, flashes of the imagination. How much worse, Thielmann wondered, would it be if the Americans and we could not see each other, as we cannot see the Tommies at night? What value would your clouds of escorts and your herds filled with frightening guns be, eh, Americans?

***

Sally reviewed her list again, looking for boys she might know. Her four-week night shift was half over, but it already wore her out. There were over three thousand patients moving in and out of this facility. She had dressings to change for three more boys this evening (she'd already changed seven) before her shift ended at midnight. She had to find doctors for one patient whose wound had turned gangrenous, one who had slipped into a coma, and one who was burning up with fever.

Tomorrow, at noon, she'd start all over again.

***

There was symmetry, Anton Zimmer thought, to the curve of the small female breast when it was perfect. A symmetry that was often upset when the creature was awake and sitting up, as opposed to sleeping. This was why he insisted that the prostitutes that he hired every third night ("nothing in excess," the Party exhorted) either be drugged or act as if they were, though he preferred they were asleep when he approached them. When he was done, he didn't care what they did as long as they left soon, and he never saw them again. He had to move frequently because the number of women who fit his specifications was generally small.

Which was why he was so intrigued by the small photo of Thielmann's wife: she was a small woman in all the perfect ways. He tried to remember if Anna Thielmann's breasts were large or small:

small, he decided, or I would not have been interested in her. As he slipped out of his robe and lay on his latest "instrument" as he called her, he thought perhaps it was time the Thielmann question be resolved once and for all.

***

Miller lay on his bunk, watching the dust motes above his head swirl in the artificial light from the shops across the field. In the past 24 hours, he had slept probably twelve, and in another three hours or so, he'd be up for at least eighteen. Like most airmen, he rested the afternoon before a maximum effort, slept little the night before.

Miller tried hard not to think, not to feel, not to yearn for the long-lost innocence he had when he came to England with such high expectations. No one expected to be in England for a year, bombing Germany, expending bombs and bullets and perfectly good human lives for between-the-war theories disproved before Pearl Harbor. So many years ago, he thought, even though it was not quite ten months.

Just before he dropped off to sleep, Alex's face flashed in his mind. Then he thought about her hauling Tommies out of the English Channel, with an image of Grace getting drenched in a London air raid shelter, and tried to give some perspective to a place and time of peace, who had smelled death and tasted despair, who lived in terror most of their waking hours. But it was Alex on his mind as he drifted off.

***

Thielmann entered the dimly lit barracks hallway quietly, so as not to disturb the men there. Inside his tiny room, he undressed in the dark, smoking a last cigarette before retiring. His legs were vaguely stiff and the scars on his back itched and stung. He thought about the next day vaguely, with the same sense of dread and foreboding he usually felt about the next active day, but it was carefully compartmented in his mind, allowed to languish in an unnourished, untended part of his mental garden.

The active part, the part he tended to, worried about his brother, his father, his friends in the group, his wingman, and, above all else, Elsa. Will I make you a widow again tomorrow, dear one, he wondered bitterly, or should I have left you to the firestorm and saved you from this anguish again? But how can I have saved only you and not all of Germany? I still have to try to save Germany, even if only from itself.

14 October 1943

Schweinfurt, Germany

Go tell the Spartans, thou that passes by,
That here, obedient to their laws, we lie

Simonides of Ceos

I'm in my plane...got to stay in formation...crew's dead...bandits swarming after us...wind blasting through the windshield...got to keep up the box...I'm nosing in...flak tearing me apart...bombs don't do any good...falling down...on fire...coming apart...dying...

Miller shot up in bed, awake again. He couldn't remember sleeping, but he knew he must have because he had the dream again, the one he couldn't get out of, the one he died in. Sitting on his bunk, he hoped vaguely he was waking from a long bad dream. But the familiar shadows of his small room showed he was still in England. He always thought England felt cold in the morning. A glance at the alarm clock told him it was nearly two o'clock in the morning. Mission day; it's probably nearly time to get up. Wearily, he decided he was already up.

Stumbling in the darkness to the sink, he ran the hot water for his shave. He preferred hot water when shaving, but he wasn't getting any from this sink. He didn't even think about not shaving. The first time he tried that, his oxygen mask didn't seal right, and it chafed against the coarse stubble of his face for the entire mission. Swearing quietly to himself, he stumbled to the coal stove in the corner. Since cold water in the morning was a common occurrence, the stove was already coaled and oiled, waiting to be lit. Opening the stove door, he lit a piece of paper and threw it inside. The oil in the stove lit slowly, catching the coal, and the stove warmed up. Hot water in a jiffy, he thought. I wonder if their cold water has a relationship to their warm beer. Waiting in the gloomy chill for the water to heat up, he tried to remember the faces of his first crew, but couldn't...except for Farr.

The water was steaming on the stove, and he sat down to shave in the dark. The duty sergeant came around the billets, knocking on doors. "Breakfast at 0300, briefing at 0400," he intoned. Gradually, the billets came to life with sounds of tired men waking up to a daily grind.

Dressing quietly in the dark, Miller mechanically pulled on long woolen underwear over the silk he preferred. He hated wearing the cumbersome leather/sheepskin suits and coarse wool. Nice part is, he thought, this is the magic number. After this, I can go home.

After this 25th mission, he could rotate home to be an instructor. Then, all he'd have to do is show newly minted pilots everything he knew about staying alive in a B-17 shot full of holes in hostile skies with half their crew dead or dying. He couldn't teach them how to cope with crewmen who get lost in seas of despair so severe they take their own lives. He wondered vaguely if he wanted to leave his fellows with the job still undone when he could still fly.

Gillette groaned heavily in his bunk. At length, he sat up and switched on a light. "'Time is it?"

"Oh two fifteen."

"Damn."

"Not much sleep?"

"An hour. Last strike, John; don't screw this one up."

"I'll sure try not to. Listen, you guys know everything. Where are we goin' today?" Gillette typically worked late the night before each mission, working up the target profiles, identifying dummy targets on the ground, available fighter cover, antiaircraft defenses, and all the other details of the enemy's capacity to defend himself.

"Not a chance," he said, "but I can tell ya it ain't gonna be a lot of fun. And I will tell ya you've been there before." Wonderful, Miller thought. He didn't press for information Gillette couldn't give him for security reasons, but that Miller probably didn't want to know, anyway.

***

I'm in my machine, and I'm attacking the American *Festungen* again. I fly right at one, then another. They don't fall down. My wingman explodes, goes down in flames. I shoot at all of them. They don't go down. They drop their bombs as if I wasn't there. I attack again and again....they don't go down....they fill the air...Suddenly I am on fire, and my canopy won't open. A hundred...a thousand American bombers are shooting at me, and I can't get out. I go down...

Thielmann shot up in his bunk, reliving again his horrible dream. He looked about in the darkness of his room, heart pounding, sweat pouring. Why don't they go down...why don't they stop...why don't they turn back?

Thielmann looked closely at the luminous dials of his watch. It was four in the morning; time to get up. Gunther picked his head up sleepily, watching his master in the dark, ears perked. Wearily, he swung his feet down to the floor and stood on the cold concrete. Gunther grunted up from his warm bit of old carpet, prodding Thielmann's hand with his nose. Rubbing the little sleep from his eyes, he let the dog outside and staggered to the latrine, its glaring light hitting him like a physical force. Another day, he thought blankly.

Waiting for hot water from the tap, he examined his face. His gray-blue eyes were bloodshot and surrounded by dark shadows. As he shaved, other pilots stumbled into the latrine, sleep still in their eyes. Gradually they awakened, talked..."Klaus, how's your mother been?" one called to another.

"I can't say. I haven't heard since the last big Tommy raid on Berlin. I just wish Axel were still home..."

"Yes, why did your brother ever get it in his head he should join up?"

"I don't know. I suppose he feels he should serve the Fatherland..."

"The Fatherland," came an incredulous reply. "Of what possible use could a sixteen-year-old boy be to the Fatherland?"

"Dieter," another sternly rebuked. "The Russians killed his father, you remember? Perhaps he just wants revenge..."

"Oh yes," another voice chimed in, "we should all seek revenge against the Russian *Untermenchen*. As if that does any good!"

"Silence," another voice said. "Yours is not to question the desires or the motives of a good German boy who answers the call of the *Führer*..."

"HAH," another said. "Russian *Untermenchen!* You should fly against those *Untermenchen*, with fighters that turn   inside] our antiquated Messerschmitts; out-gun us, out-run us, and so many..."

"I SAID SILENCE," a voice barked, and the room was still, with only the sound of running water, the clinking of toothbrushes, the flushing of toilets. Thielmann finished his ablutions quietly. You idiots should have seen that muck-up of it we made at Crete, he thought.

Back in his room, Thielmann prepared for another day, pulling on his *langen Beinen*, the third pair he'd had since Russia. Gunther carefully licked his paws on his scrap of carpet.

***

Miller pushed the mess hall door open, leaving the dark, damp, foggy outside for the muggy warmth inside. Already the delays had begun; they had pushed everything back three hours for weather. Miller squinted slightly at the sudden glare of the bare bulbs hanging from the ceiling, contrasting with the predawn gloom outside.

Breakfast noise was comforting. The quiet roar of 500-odd voices in morning conversation, slinging steel trays, rattling flatware and sizzling food on grills, was a little dose of reality. The smells of hot coffee and frying ham were vaguely reminiscent of another time, another place. Miller got a tray of food, trying hard not to think about what it was. Walking back to the senior officer's section, he sat down across from Throck.

"'Morning, Miller," the big Russian sighed. "Last time you'll have to do this if we don't get scrubbed."

"That's right, sir," Miller said wearily. "I'll never get up before four in the morning again. Any chance of scrub?" In less than a year Miller had been briefed forty times and had bombed twenty-four targets, having been scrubbed the rest.

"Oh, yeah, always is. Bad fog up north; some here in East Anglia, too," Throck replied, not looking at Miller. "The eggs are sour again," he continued. "I wish they'd stop making powdered eggs with old milk. And this bacon — they only call it that because it's salted. God-awful coffee, and..." Throck stopped, recovering himself. "You know," he started again, "somebody ought to figure out some day exactly what the odds are that anybody survives twenty five strikes. I know how they came up with that magic number—I helped create it—but it seems arbitrary to me." Throck knew the odds were exactly zero, statistically speaking, with an average of four percent casualties for every mission.

Miller didn't say anything. "Somehow," Throck went on, "I know crews and planes in other groups have managed the trick—we haven't had any yet. I tried to get you the diversion for this one, but no soap."

"We appreciate it, sir," Miller said with some conviction. "I can't imagine a strike over Germany without at least one crewman getting hit, though I know it happens because I've done it. I think most of the ships that make it in one piece do mostly milk runs like Brest and Le Havre, where we've got fighter cover all the way. Without fighter escorts them Nazis just chew us up. And now they want us to go even deeper."

"That's what they say," Throck agreed, "but until we get enough Thunderbolts and Mustangs to escort us to the target, they don't dare send 'em with us too often, even if they've been going the distance since September. But we have to keep hittin' 'em where ...."

Suddenly, the mess hall fell silent as the sound of heavily laden engines gently rattled the building. The airmen looked up at the ceiling, counting as the planes flew overhead. Marauders, Miller thought, out of Nichols, going out early to hit the forward German fighter fields and flak batteries. They only did that when there was a big mission on for the heavy bombers. The last plane was rumbling in the distance when the noise resumed in the mess, but it was different now, quieter, more subdued, each man with his private thoughts. "Maximum effort," Miller finally said.

"Yeah," Throck said. "Every crate in England's going out today." The mess hall filled with breakfast noises again.

***

In the briefing room, Thielmann stretched out in his customary chair. After 123 aerial victories, he and Bär were entitled to the best furniture in the briefing room. Reicher shuffled in wearily. "*Gute Morgen* Otto," Reicher offered as he sat next to Thielmann, "I got a letter from Heinz yesterday."

"*Morgen* Felix. How is he?" Thielmann asked, genuinely concerned. Reicher's brother, Heinz, was an infantry platoon commander in Italy.

"He says he is well, but he says that all the time. He is worried that Mama and Papa are in danger in Stuttgart, and he is worried about me, but he says for us not to worry about him."

"Is that all he says?" Thielmann said dubiously.

"No. He says American tanks are worthless, but that there are many of them, and that Americans fight like demons. The British are tired, he says."

"When did he send the letter?" Thielmann asked.

"Last month," Reicher replied. Reicher went on for a time, but Thielmann tuned him out. If the Tommies are tired, he wondered, why do they keep bombing us?

As the briefing room filled up, Thielmann greeted the other pilots in the group, passing a word or a grin to each. Of the 48 pilots, he had flown with six of them since he'd joined it. Most of the rest had passed the "Giant Killer's" methods on to other groups and were now flying in Italy, France, and Holland. A few were dead; some were wounded so badly they could no longer fly. Some had simply walked away, gone to Florida or, just...left. Kaltz entered the room, and the pilots stood as one man. "Seats, gentlemen, if you please; active again, eh?" he said, just like every other active day.

"Alert order is group Thielmann first, Bär second, Taube third, and Pritzler fourth. Air time should be no more than three hours. I am to read this from *Reichsmarshall* Goering: 'If it becomes apparent that the target today is the ball bearing plant at Schweinfurt, the cowardly fighter groups are to redeem their shameful behavior and show their National Socialist fervor by attacking the bombers regardless of antiaircraft artillery.'"

Kaltz went on, droning about new bomber tactics, vulnerabilities, zone coverage in case all the planes are attacking at once, the use of the new rear attacks on trailing Fortresses, and so on. Thielmann listened, writing the call signs and frequencies on his hand mechanically.

Attack through the flak...

***

"Take your seats, gentlemen," Throck began, his voice easily carrying to the back of the briefing room. "Our target for today is the Krupp-Thyssen AG ball-bearing works at Schweinfurt," he said, unveiling the briefing map on the dais. There was a painful moan as they saw the innocuous little strings of yarn that marked their flight vectors. Innocuous little strings of yarn—a cats-cradle of death—stretched across the map from England across the North Sea to the Dutch coast, then plunging south into Germany, jagging left and right to avoid the flak centers and to confuse the fighter controllers as to the real target, ending in central Hesse on the Main River, then turning back to England, detouring only to avoid the Bonn flak center and the immediate vicinity of Abbeville, home of the "Abbeville Boys" of JG26. Just four days after a big mission to Munster, this was a fine thing. "Expect flak over the target to be heavy," Throck went on, "and bandits on the way in and on the way out. Everybody and his brother's hitting this one today, so it'll be crowded."

Oh God...Germany, Miller thought. Yeah, heavy resistance over the target, all right. Throck went on with station times, engine start, squadron positions. "Any questions?" he concluded. This was rhetorical, a mere formality, because everything was already laid out. There would be no questions about the next round of high-altitude horror.

"Navigators and bombardiers stand by. Squadron briefings are to begin in twenty minutes." That ended the group briefing for the pilots and co-pilots, who filed out like condemned men and headed for their individual squadron briefings where the target assignments were laid out in more detail. 190th was to bomb the steel storage facility. They targeted other squadrons for the fuel depot, the plant itself, and the machine shops. Everybody had their place, and the aircraft would be loaded appropriately. Since the steel was invulnerable to everything, including direct hits, more than half the squadron would carry the dreaded incendiaries. The rest would carry high explosive bombs to make dust, craters and noise, hampering the firefighters on the ground.

"Make enough dust and you get more fire," Witt muttered.

***

Thielmann and the other pilots listened intently to the intelligence officer recounting the morning. Early morning attacks by medium bombers had caught weary night fighters on the hardstands, and tired radar operators nearly napping at their coastal posts. They had hit several radars and fighter fields in Holland, Belgium and northern France, making the *Luftwaffe* fighter command suspect an attack from that direction. Radio intercepts indicated a very large attack in the making.

***

Miller and Witt rode the truck with a dozen other pilots and copilots, each man deep in his own thoughts. If they had been scheduled to bomb rail yards in Holland or a truck factory in France, there would have been a lot of chatter and maybe even some horseplay. But this mission meant that at least two of each hundred men in the 299th—at least two ships—wouldn't be coming back...and the crews knew it. The truck barely slowed down as the fliers jumped off near their planes. Lugging their parachutes and flying suits in their kitbags, they trudged wearily to their planes, only raising their eyes off the ground when they reached it. Pair by pair the trucks emptied, each pair heading for their four- engine war machines squatting silently on the hardstands, ground crews scurrying around them like drone ants tending to a queen, getting them ready. Carefully, Miller and Witt began their preflight checks. Some pilots let their crew chiefs and flight engineers preflight their planes. But few pilots survive twenty-four missions, so Miller did it himself.

Farr was already at the plane. One by one Roy, radioman; Aitcheson, belly gunner; Collova, right waist; Murphy, left waist; Milliken, tail gunner; Reynolds the navigator; Jackson, the bombardier, trudged, walked, or otherwise arrived at the ship.

One by one, the crew struggled to 'turn the props through,' manually hauling the four engines through a full revolution. This exercise, sometimes seen as wasteful torture, ensured that the lubricating oil was present in all the engine cavities, and that the cylinders were freely moving before attempting to start the engines.

Wiggling the control surfaces, running a hand along the leading edges of the tail, Miller reassured himself of the plane's airworthiness before each launch, as he had for every plane he ever flew. For him, his pre-flight drill wasn't just a routine. It was more of a silent communication—almost a prayer—a communion of sorts between the metal and fabric of the plane and the bone, muscle and skill of the pilot.

He liked to think he could tell that the ship would fly well one day, poorly the next. He felt they understood each other and knew how to keep each other safe. As long as he flew the plane well, she would always bring him home.

Soon the armament truck arrived ("this late," Farr grumbled) delivering the heavy machine guns. The gunners lugged the ponderous guns to their stations, mounting them with the greatest of care.

"We're a high ship today, skipper, tail of the formation," Jackson said to Miller. "Fourteen 500 pound General Purpose AN-M-64s; altitude at drop 25,000 feet; 0.1 seconds delay on the nose fuse and 0.025 seconds on the tail should dig a deep enough hole so's we can kick up some dust. Tail fuse..."

"In theory," Miller said sardonically. "Thanks, but I really don't need to know." Jackson, unperturbed by the rebuff, simply turned away. Miller admired his bombardier's dedication to his job and the details of the ordnance they delivered, but hearing about it simply made him uneasy.

While the guns were being mounted, the bomb truck arrived, and the 500-pound general-purpose high explosive bombs were unceremoniously hoisted onto the trolleys, fitted with their tail sections, hoisted into the bomb bays and carefully positioned. Each bomb was lifted into the racks, fused, wired to the arming mechanism in the plane, and the safety-fuse links checked with great care and speed. As the guns and bombs were mounted, the ammunition arrived. Belts of 0.50 caliber ammunition were lifted to each gun on the plane, linked in the gun's feed trays, and one end loaded into the guns, 250 rounds per gun. Every third round had a red nose of phosphorous—incendiary tracer ammunition so the gunners could track their shooting.

Miller and Witt finished their outside checks and Witt followed the navigator and bombardier into the nose of the ship. Reynolds was securing his charts and checking his instruments; Jackson was carefully checking the bombsight. The gunners were checking their guns, their suit's heater connections, the oxygen outlets and masks, their body armor and the myriad other details under Farr's watchful eye. Philukuzki was outside, making sure nothing was left undone.

Farr stood up in his turret after making his preflight checks of the guns and the plane. He had checked each gun, each mount, each sight, and each feed tray carefully, ensuring himself and the rest of the crew that the guns would hit what they pointed at, and that the ammunition would feed flawlessly. Trying to clear a jammed gun or feed ramp wearing heavy mitts in flight, with angry fighters shooting at you, was nearly impossible, so he made sure on the ground that the guns would fire reliably in the air.

After the checks and lock-downs were done, there was nothing to do but wait. Depending on the weather, they could wait for half the day or more. One by one, the crew piled out again and lay around in an air of nervous tension, waiting for the first flare of the day. Murphy and Collova tossed a baseball back and forth in an easy rhythm.

"So these two barflies climb up to the top of the Empire State Building..."

Roy, Aitcheson and Milliken played gin without keeping score.

"And the first one jumps off, goes down about twenty stories, an' floats back up..."

Reynolds read another of his western novels.

"'See? Wha'd I tell ya,' he says..."

Jackson played poker with three other men from next door.

"So the second one jumps off and hits the pavement. Splat...!"

Witt dozed fitfully.

"And the first one goes back to the bar..."

Philukuzki and Williams played mumblety-peg with a screwdriver.

"And the bartender says, 'Ya know, Superman, you sure can be an asshole sometimes.'"

Farr tossed a football back and forth with the flight engineer of another ship.

"Shaddap, Collova!" Miller watched the control shack and the weather, off and on, watching his crew and throwing a stick for Tripod, the 299th's three-legged mascot, waiting...

***

Stretching his aching legs, Thielmann gazed off into the diminishing darkness to the west. Over the Spessart Mountains, over the Westerwald, over the sea, he wondered if the Americans were looking back to him, into the rising sun. Is today the day I gain another victory, or is today the day my dream falls true, and I fall for the last time? Or, perhaps, today nothing happens? He thought of his brother Ulrich briefly, glad his daily terror was over. Come ahead, then, American, come ahead, he thought, watching Gunther charge after a partridge.

***

"That's it," Farr called, watching the red flare rising in the gray sky. "Suit up. Mount up." The crew broke into their bags and stared donning their heavy suits; heaving their body armor into the ship just before crawling in themselves. Miller, as usual, was the last to get in. Once more, he scanned the plane for any defects, any flaws. One last glimpse at the plane.

One more time, old girl, just once more...

Taking a long, deep breath, he grabbed the nose door combing, swung his feet up into the hatch, and crawled inside. The armorer left, the bomb safety link flags trailing in his hip pocket. That left only Philukuzki with his fire extinguisher outside for the wait to start engines. As Farr finished checking his guns again, he called to his pilot, "Top gun to pilot: everything's OK, skipper." "Navigator OK, bow gun loaded and ready...Radio ready; codes entered and locked, radio compasses checked and on-line, gun loaded and ready...Ready in the belly...Left waist; manned and ready...Right waist; manned and ready...Tail gun; ready...Bomb sight checks completed. Bombs mounted and doors closed." With everything done, they settled down to wait for the next flare. Soon, all too soon, the bombers clambered into the air separated by only a few seconds, each thousand horsepower engine straining under the weight of their burdens.

The Mad Russian...The Throne Room... Finnegan's Alley...New Orleans Special...Mary...Hell on Wings...Flak City Fugitive... Hammerin' Hanna... Warsaw Willie...Detroit Demolition...Alamo Mike...

Miller guided *Crop Duster* to the end of the runway, waiting for the plane ahead of him to get off the ground. Gradually he built up engine power as Witt watched the gauges. At just the right moment, the brakes were released and the ponderous plane began the long roll down the runway, gradually building up speed...tail up...controls getting lighter. At just the right moment, Miller eased the control yoke back and *Crop Duster* was airborne once again.

Philukuzki and the other crew chiefs watched them roll off the hardstand and launch, sharing their private terrors with no one, absently passing around their ritual canteen of watery gin silently, stoically.

It's up to them now. Thirty-four straight hours of work to get 'em up and nothing we can do now...but...wait...

***

City of Denver...Wrath of the Lamb...Phoenix...Kansas Cyclone... Boozer... Killer O'Caney...Sugar Tit...Fall River Flush...

Banking to the left, Miller began his spiraling climb to the assembly area above the field, the engines throbbing roar a concert for Miller's ears, the once per minute beeping of the Bartlesby buncher beacon ringing in Witt's headset.

As he was climbing behind the other planes, it struck Miller as he always was by the exhilaration of takeoff, the apparent weightlessness of the plane, the blazing sun just as he broke through the cloud deck that always seemed to cover the field on mission days. He still loved flying, but somehow the purpose of flying had become corrupted. Breaking away from this reverie, he went back to looking for the gaily colored assembly ship for his squadron.

"Up there," Witt said, pointing out the right window. "About another 5,000 feet." He was pointing to the rest of the squadron's formation, falling into echelon formation for the climbing run-in to the enemy coast. Miller eased the power up and brought the yoke back slightly, turning the lumbering plane to join her sisters. Just as they began a formation turn while waiting for the rest of the planes, two bombers collided in mid-air. One either hadn't seen, or couldn't avoid, the other. Now the two were inextricably joined as they vaporized together in a cloud of exploding fuel and ordnance, the mass falling into the cloud deck, never to be seen again. Though he'd seen it before, Miller watched the tragedy while trying not to think about it. They'd find out who it was when they got back…if it was someone they knew. It was bad enough that flak or enemy fighters shot bombers down, but to die like that was just not something anyone wanted to think about. He just wanted to think about something that wasn't related to where he was, that didn't smell of wet wool and khaki, stale coffee, cigarettes, oil and sweat, that didn't sound so terrifying. But the horror was so much a part of what he had become, it was almost impossible to avoid.

About ten minutes after Miller joined the formation, the squadron moved up to join the group, and then turned east into the sun and toward the target. There would be no talk between planes for a while. Each ten-man crew sealed off into a private world of noise, cold, and fear.

***

After checking their planes, Thielmann and the other pilots headed for the mess. The smells of fresh bread and coffee filled their nostrils as they entered. For the present, there was no war, no bombers. For a few moments, there were only men eating breakfast. Bär sat quietly in a corner. He'd just come off night duty, vectoring the night fighters to the British bomber streams. "How are you this morning, Bär," Thielmann asked, sitting at a nearby bench. "You had the duty last night?"

"We lost three last night in the air, and the night intruders got a dozen on the ground in France. I actually spotted three bombers through the jamming and the *Düppel,* and scored a probable on one," Bär sighed. One bomber, Thielmann thought. We lose three *Jägern* in the air, another dozen on the ground, and we score—perhaps—on one. How can we win with such mathematics?

Taube sat next to Thielmann. "*Morgen,* Taube," Thielmann began. "Another day, isn't it?"

"*Morgen,* Thielmann. I was in Bonn last night. I think I've seen the way we can win."

Thielmann regarded his friend carefully, skeptically. "How," he said.

"I was at an experimental aerodrome last night, one the Messerschmitt plant runs at Reichlin," Taube began. "I think they've finally gotten *der Schwalbe* right."

Thielmann gulped hard, his mind racing at the word "swallow." "What do you mean?" he said, incredulous, afraid to hope.

"Those idiots in Berlin have finally let them fly it as a fighter. I SAW it, Thielmann," Taube said, his voice racing, blue eyes gleaming, excited. "I saw it sitting on the ground. Six cannons in the nose, swept-back wings, and two engines without propellers. It looks like it just LEAPS into the air. And they are having the best pilots test it. Nowotny has decided it could win the war!"

Coming from any other source, such a statement would have carried no weight whatsoever. But from Walter Nowotny, one of the best pilots in the *Luftwaffe*, it meant something. It meant everything. "Imagine, Thielmann! We can fly faster than the latest Spitfires, perhaps even faster than those Mustangs," Taube continued, "and we can attack bombers at higher speeds than their guns can track."

"What does Galland say?" Thielmann asked, still finding it hard to believe such good news himself.

"He isn't sure, but he thinks we can test it in combat," Taube said. "He has reservations about fuel consumption, that at high altitude there's only enough for one pass on a bomber formation, and he's right, and they say the engines are unreliable. But in one pass, a group can down ten, fifteen bombers. We HAVE to have these planes!"

"Well, Taube," Pritzler said as he joined them, "I hear you've seen it." Taube looked about quickly, seeing no one paying much attention. "Yes, and it's a dream. It looks as if it could shoot down the whole American Air Force at once!"

"I'm certain of that, Taube," Pritzler grinned, slightly amused. "Tell me, what makes this one so much better, eh? Did *Dicke Hermann* promise he would change his name again?"

Thielmann and Taube grinned at the small joke. "No," Taube said, "you have to see it. I saw films of it. It outruns even our Focke-Wulfs, Pritzler. It flies as a dream might." Pritzler stared hard at his fellow group commander, incredulous. It was hard for him to conceive of anything that could fly faster than 700 kilometers an hour.

"Has anyone heard about the raid on Hamm last night?" Richter sat down with the others. "I heard the Tommies lost fifty bombers."

"Nonsense," Pritzler snorted. "If the Tommies lost fifty bombers in one raid, we could all go home. Perhaps ten..."

"Hamm," Taube said, incredulously. "But they hit Berlin just the night before last..."

"And Hamm last night," Thielmann said. The conversation suddenly swirled around the British bombers, ignoring the amazing new jet fighter that no one believed they would ever see. All knew that it would become a bomber because the *Führer* said so. No one tried to believe in the wonder weapons any longer. In a few moments, though, the conversation shifted again, now ignoring the war, now in the thick of it. For hours they talked about anything except today, except now, except the next few hours.

***

"Navigator to pilot: crossing the coast on time and on course." Miller hunched his shoulders reflexively, as he always did when he entered enemy territory. Already airborne for over an hour, he always got cramped in his leather-and-wool cocoon at about this time. He reached up for his throat microphone.

"Pilot to crew: OK gunners, fire 'em up. Deploy belly gun." As Aitcheson climbed into his Plexiglas ball and lowered it into position, the plane shook gently as ten fifty-caliber machine guns roared and bucked, initially alone but shortly joined by all the planes in the formation. Hundreds of tracers laced across the void ripped the clear blue sky. If I didn't know better, Miller thought, I'd say that anybody who wanted to attack a formation like this was plain nuts. But Miller did know better, and he was consistently amazed by how many enemy fighters could get through the apparent wall of bullets. But, already, without firing a shot, the Germans had killed twenty guys in the assembly area, and the bombers hadn't even seen a German yet, hadn't even gotten into enemy-held territory.

"Belly gun to pilot: one's falling on the right, skipper." Miller looked, but not for long. *Mary* was falling out of the sky for no apparent reason. No fire, no structural damage, no nothing; another clear-air crash. Miller tried not to think about it happening to him. Now, he thought, with any ... no, better not think about luck.

***

"Gentlemen," Kaltz said, entering the mess. "The Americans are in the air. There are as many as thirty-two herds, probably over three hundred bombers. The first of them made landfall thirty minutes ago." Suddenly, the free exchange of ideas and stories ended as the pilots stared, openmouthed, at him.

"THREE HUNDRED," Bär gasped, "have you gone mad!?!"

"I wish I had," Kaltz said, fatalistically. "We are alerting fighters all over Europe and Scandinavia. There are so many we cannot calculate where they are going. We have to put up every available plane, including bombers. Even night fighters are coming on-line, and we are pulling in reserves from Russia. No one scrubs today. Be ready at a moment's notice. JG26 is attacking them even now. We go on fifteen minute standby in thirty minutes. All pilots to your planes."

The pilots fell silent after the group commander left. Now it was time to think of the next few hours, the next exchange of human lives for a few other lives, for a few more months of the Thousand Year Reich.

Three hundred machines...thirty-two herds...each three hundred meters high and 350 wide, two and a half kilometers apart. They would attack the leaders head-on and be in gun range for just under three seconds each pass, and would be in enemy gun range for over ten seconds—twenty-four kilometers—as they passed each herd in succession. The longest seconds any of them could imagine, while they could not shoot back as a thousand heavy machine guns fired at them. Not even JG26 could overcome that.

***

Far ahead of the 299th, as it plowed majestically through the frigid sky, the air battle had begun. As far as the rest of the crew was concerned, it was on another planet, but Miller heard it over the command net, deafening with bad news.

"Up ahead up ahead—bandits closing ahead...Here they come again...Close up close up...still gotta get there...Ridgeline nine to group: falling out...tell Mama...Bandits six o'clock low...Twenty minutes to next turn...Stockade three to group: I'm on fire...going down...bailing out... Close up close up...Ridgeline two to group: pilot dead, losing height... Somebody call this off..."

***

"Pilots to your planes," the tinny loudspeaker blared through the mess.

The size of the cloud of Fortresses staggered Thielmann's imagination. Three hundred or so, they said. Three hundred! Over England, the best the *Luftwaffe* could muster was two hundred. Now these *Amis* and Tommies put up that many at least once a month, and twice just this week. Thielmann rubbed Gunther's ears perfunctorily just before jumping up on the wing of his machine, the little dog watching him as Steger strapped his pilot into the seat. "Start engines and launch aircraft. Accept ground control in three minutes," the loudspeaker blared.

Thielmann pumped his throttle once, shouted "CLEAR" over the nose, and pressed down on the starter handle. The engine whined satisfactorily as the starter wound up, and at just the right pitch, he pulled up on the starter handle. The propeller spun lazily at first, then with growing speed as the engine caught and Thielmann adjusted the mixture and throttle controls, pulling the canopy down and locking it shut once again. And once again...

Four at once, JG191 scrambled into the air, quickly forming their four-machine swarms before they locked their landing gear up, arming their guns on the rise. "Intercept leading bomber herd vicinity Kassel," the controller said, the Focke-Wulfs climbing as quickly as fuel and prudence would allow.

"She sounds pretty," someone said over the radio.

"She's probably as old as your mother," another said.

"Quiet, I can't hear," Thielmann rejoined. "Altmarck leader to Altmarck: form diamond."

Ahead, he could hear the other *Luftwaffe* units on the attack.

"Coburg leader to group: come around again; come around again... Where are the Indians...Who cares, as long as they are not here... Coburg four three to Coburg leader: I am badly hit. I have to go down... *Horrido*...Riemer leader to Coburg: clear out, we are headed in...Stettin three three to anyone: I am in trouble...on fire..."

***

For nearly an hour, the top turret had been hammering a foot over Miller's aching head, the concussion driving an invisible spike between his eyes. Through the static and jamming of the radio, he listened with bare detachment. "Bandits coming up...On the left on the left... Three inbound ahead..." Shell casings fell like rain as the Fortresses drove relentlessly onward while a continuous stream of bandits dove and roared and swung into the castles in the air. "Ewald's hit..." *Detroit Demolition*..."I got one...Fencepost six: bail out, you're on fire..." Boozer...The ground in their wake was dotted with the wreckage of downed bombers, burning brightly, smoldering. Occasionally, there was a German fighter in a heap. "Jesus they're still coming...Got one... Close up, close up..." There goes another, Miller thought, watching *Spirit of Jersey* explode, four shimmering fireballs that were the fuel tanks left to tell the tale, falling in the autumn sky. "There goes Ewald....Where the hell's the escorts...Jesus God, another forty of 'em, two o'clock high..."

Murphy and Collova in the waists were stumbling and falling on spent casings and links, dodging the odd cannon shell they saw coming their way. A fragment bounced off Murphy's steel helmet and he sprawled to the floor. The gunners were getting tired, and the ammunition was running low. Miller was drenched in sweat despite the cold. Witt struggled mightily not to taste the gorse rising in his throat, not to think about his own waste he had expelled. The intercom shouted and shrilled as the German fighters kept pouring in and Miller wildly avoided this head-on attack and then another, as this diving pass fell short and that rising lateral attack broke off too soon. The interceptors were showing no sign of letup; ME-109s, ME-110s, FW 190s, ME 410s, JU-88s, everything that could fly and shoot. And the Fortresses lumbered on, the formations oblivious to the huge rents torn into their very fabric...

Miller clutched the yoke with renewed determination as an ME-109 bored in from ahead, ducking his head down slightly, steadying himself for another joust, praying again that this wouldn't be his last act on earth, frozen sweat in a ridge just below where his oxygen mask met his face. Here he comes here he comes steady right NOW...Nose down... cheek uncovered...top turret hammers away...cheek gun sputters... bandit guns sparkle...tracers fly by, changing color...bandit jinks up... missed this time...where's the next one...back into line...

Over and over and over and over...

***

"*Pauke,*" Thielmann shouted into the radio, leading JG191 in a 48-machine head-on charge, twelve swarms on-line abreast, sallying into the leading herd. Rapidly, Thielmann's target grew in his Revi sight, the top turret flaming in defiance, the cheek gun chattering. The Festung swerved hard and Thielmann's aim was thrown off, barely avoiding the Fortress as he skimmed over the wing.

Richter called back: "Altmarck one two to Altmarck leader: three good hits. No change... wait, I think he's falling out...Altmarck leader to Altmarck: Report positions...Altmarck two to Altmarck leader: all here, coming around behind you...Altmarck three one to Altmarck leader: coming around...Altmarck three down." Taube, Thielmann thought; Taube is down... "Altmarck four to Altmarck leader: down two, coming around...Altmarck leader to Altmarck: come around again, attack the rear...."

***

"Flak ahead," Reynolds said as the red-gray-black cottony billows burst ahead of them. The flak burst under them, next to them, above them. It was indiscriminate. It didn't care, but worst of all, there was nothing the bombers could do about it.

"Beginning evasion," Miller said, as he started the irregular, clumsy dance the formation performed when the antiaircraft guns got their course, height and speed. Up, left, down, left, up again, right, right, down — a random pattern intended to keep the enemy ground gunners guessing, staying as tight as they could, so there were no holes in the box. Miller never thought evasion did any good. As if to punctuate this thought, *Kansas Cyclone*, to the left and below *Crop Duster*, was hit, staggered, and began her long, too-rapid descent to earth. Resisting to the last, Miller counted crewmen escaping: two, three, four, explosion.

Oh Christ, what's this for....

***

JG191 found fuel and rearming at Bad Kissingen to be fast, as other interceptors found fuel. But JG191 was closer to home, and down three aircraft, including a swarm commander.

***

"Navigator to pilot: Initial point in two minutes. Turn left to a course of 70 degrees in two minutes."

"Roger," Miller called back. "Turn left to zero seven zero in two minutes." The crew held on when flak came too close, hoping this wasn't their last. Jackson had once compared flak to going down a flight of stairs in a garbage can: a deafening thud, an awful vibration, a sickening drop, and starting all over again. Miller compared it to being in a sewer pipe with someone dumping crushed stone and gravel on it: roaring noise, bone-rattling vibration, gravel pinging on the sides. From each near miss, the plane recovered, droning on, bumping in the turbulence, sometimes violently shaking and tossing the crew around inside the tiny spaces. Occasionally, a quick crewman could see daylight between the skins.

"Initial point," Reynolds said.

"Roger," Miller replied, banking the big plane to the left. "Course zero seven zero." As Miller turned *Crop Duster*, the rest of the formation also turned, as if guiding around an invisible corner.

"Navigator to bombardier: release point coming up." Jackson bent over his bombsight, throwing the switch to activate the gyroscope that would stabilize the optics. He made his calculations, dialed in the altitude and airspeed, checked the optics, and watched *The Throne Room* for the drop.

"Bombardier to pilot: I'm set. Lead is on final approach," he said over the intercom, preparing himself.

Miller reached for the switch, batting it with his heavy mitt. "Pilot to bombardier: Autopilot on. Hit it hard and get us home." Suddenly, billowing ribbons of smoke streamed into the formation. The rockets burst into gray-black balls of smoke and lethal steel. But they fired those before a fighter attack, not over the target when the flak...

***

Thielmann wondered as they launched again how many of the new green pilots would be killed before they even saw an American, and how many good aces they would take down with them. The fighter schools were turning out pilots with barely a hundred hours of flying time, and there weren't enough Focke-Wulfs to intercept the bombers effectively. Attacking a Fortress with a Messerschmitt was nearly useless unless the pilot was an extremely good shot or extraordinarily lucky. These new pilots were barely good enough to fly in the correct formation long enough to become good shots. The radio crackled in Thielmann's ear. "Altmarck to all Altmarck units; bombers over Schweinfurt. All Altmarck units select targets and attack." Far below him, the Fortresses were making their bomb run. Now, he thought, the flak will break them up and we will kill them.

"Pauke," he shouted in his microphone when he spotted the dim dots, we accept the challenge....

***

"Heads up." Farr said on the intercom. "Bandits at 11 o'clock!" Roaring towards the castle of the Fortress formation, dozens of FW-190s charged towards the bombers as they flew perfectly straight-and-level on their bomb runs, scattered by the flak and the rockets, billows of flak still renting the air. As the deadly attackers closed on the Fortresses the air was alive with cannon shells, hurtling and wheeling fighters, lumbering majestic bombers, deadly bombs jettisoned by cripples, bullets, tracers and debris. The intercom buzzed with the gunner's shouting and cursing each other, calling out to each other in the desperate scramble to kill the swarming fighters before they certainly killed them.

"Right waist get 'im get 'im. Belly gun, what're you, asleep...I got plenty more coming up from the stern low. Jesus, they look mad."

The bandits were diving and climbing through the combat box with relative impunity, all the Fortress guns blazing away. *LuAnn,* in the middle of the formation, caught fire, quickly spreading along the wings and fuselage. The bomb bay doors opened and bodies tumbled out, the pilot still at the controls, holding it up so his crew could get out. Miller watched the scene in front of him, trying hard to be detached.

"Tail: hey Milliken, wake the hell up! You let two by you...I had two above me I was shooting at, asshole...Top turret, I think you nicked that one...Nicked, hell, he's dead: look, he's bailing out! Score one for the home team...Here they come again...FWs 11 o'clock!"

The gracefully lethal fighters swarmed down, rolling slowly for better gun angles, silently shrieking past the bombers. As one fighter passed by, the roof of *Crop Duster* shook and roared as heavy cannon shells ripped into the Flying Fort's fuselage and left wing. "Where'd that one come from, top gun?" Miller called. The enemy fighter dove just ahead of *Crop Duster.*

"Right on top of me—dead space," Farr answered...

***

Straining against the G-force, Thielmann whipped his machine around for another attack, this time from below. Who is that going down? I'll try the same Fortress; it'll be weakened now...

***

Witt said to Miller, off the intercom, "We're losing oil pressure on number one."

Miller tapped the gauges to ensure they weren't just sticking. "OK," he said, "If we have to, we fall off to the left."

"Bombardier to pilot: bombs away!" As the mortal ballet raged, the bombs tumbled out of the bomb bays like rain, whistling death and destruction to the target on the ground, and the fighters were coming back for another pass.

Miller felt the plane get lighter, more controllable as the bombs fell into space, and felt the slight surge in speed as the doors closed on the bomb bay. "Pilot to bombardier: are the bombs gone?"

"Bombardier to pilot: roger. Fourteen 500 pound GP delivered at fifteen twelve on target, I hope."

"Roger."

The intercom crackled with warnings, expletives, and exaltations. "Andrews's falling out...on fire..." *Finnegan's Alley...* "Got a bunch of bogeys coming up from seven o'clock...Hey, Piesec just blew up." *Berlin or Bust...* "Aw, shit. His old lady just had their kid, too...Adams's in a nosedive. They won't get out." *Sugar Tits...* "We got those Nazi bastards good this time...They're gettin' us pretty good too, ya know."

***

Oh, to hell with these damned Fortresses, Thielmann thought. Good strikes from above and below and still they don't fall down. Again, JG191 turned around to charge the lumbering bombers as they turned towards home. The fighters knew they were having some effect; two cripples had already left the formation, and another bomber had blown up. "Altmarck leader this is Altmarck four one: Altmarck four is down..." Pritzler, Thielmann thought, *Pritzler...*

***

"Close it up, keep it tight," Throck droned in his unmistakable voice.

"Ignore the cripples. We gotta get home. OK, everybody turn on the lead." Shakily, the formation turned to the northwest. Then, from within a blast of ferocious flak, yet another fighter attack.

"FWs at five o'clock...shit, I'm hit!" the intercom crackled.

"Who's hit?" Miller shouted.

***

More bombers were staggering in the air, threatening to fall out. Though they were not without losses themselves, the German interceptors turned around and attacked again like hungry sharks devouring a school of fish. "Altmarck two to Altmarck one; Otto, I'm making a kill pass. Watch me..." Bär had picked the cripple Thielmann had hit twice, staggering now in the formation for the *coup de grâce.*

"No, wait..." The German climbed from the right side stern to the left front, concentrating his fire on the bomber's vulnerable wing root. Suddenly, Bär's machine blossomed into a ball of flame as a burst of flak blew his machine apart.

The wreck kept rising toward the lumbering Fortress...

***

Atchison saw the fighter blow up and yelled over the intercom, "SHIT! HOLD ON FELLAHS!!!" As if in slow-motion, the blazing mass of metal and fuel kept climbing, arching toward the left wing. Miller glimpsed a flicker of the fiery wreck before it hit *Crop Duster's* engine. As he reached for the engine controls, the wreck exploded not more than ten feet away. As if struck by a tremendous sledgehammer, *Crop Duster* rolled up on her right wing, then nosed down into a steep dive. The explosion blasted him to the right, jamming the throttles fully forward.

"Christ," a voice on the radio said, "Miller just bought it."

Crop Duster...

"Twenty four strikes and he goes down on 25. Damn," another voice said.

For most bombers, this is the beginning of the end, and all those who flew the B-17s knew it. But Miller was too busy to think about that.

***

Thielmann watched Bär as he died; colliding with the Fortress he was so intent on killing. *I hope your family will be proud. I am not. Your death was a hideous, stupid waste.* He watched the Fortress in its long, dying dive, and decided he would watch it until it crashed. Circling lazily, he banked slowly downward, watching as the Fortress died, spiraling down as the air battle raged above him...

***

"PULL BACK JERRY!!!" Miller screamed at Witt, "ALL YOU'VE GOT PULL FOR GOD'S SAKE OR WE'RE ALL DEAD PULLLLLLLLLLL BAAAAAAAAAAAAAAAAAACK!"

Miller strained every muscle in his body to the effort to recover from the impossibly steep dive. He hauled the yoke back towards him, thrusting his left leg to straighten under the unbelievable strain of controlling thirty-five thousand pounds of metal rushing to earth at over three hundred forty feet per second, and speeding up. His shoulders and upper back dug into the hard seat, the parachute dangling uselessly under him. Every muscle and tendon in his body howled at the unexpected exertion after sitting quietly for hours in the numbing cold; he screeched, stretching the oxygen mask strapped across his face with his jaw as it fell suddenly loose, squeezing his eyes tightly shut against the rising red tide of acceleration, straightening his back in his seat, wrenching the control column and jamming the rudder pedal in a desperate act of simultaneous fear and rage. In more rational instants he glimpsed the airspeed indicator as it spun wildly out of control and the altimeter spun down even faster, felt the icy blast of freezing air from what was once his side window, wondered vaguely how he could still be alive.

***

Thielmann was still watching as the Fortress sped up ever faster. *For you, life is over...*

***

Oh come on, baby, come on pull out pull out pull out we've been on 24 strikes so far and by God you'll bring me home for the last time if it kills us both pull up pull up if the control cables hold and the wings and tail don't tear off I'll bring her up pull up pull up oh shit I can't oh baby I have to straighten out straighten out why am I still alive pull out pull out I can't feel my face pull up pull up...

***

Are you fighting hard to stay alive, American? Can you fight the laws of nature, of gravity, of physics, of averages long enough and well enough and hard enough to stay alive and get home...?

***

Witt wrapped his wrists under the yoke; holding on to the control shaft itself, pulling back all the while the crazy patchwork of ground came ever closer... Pull up pull up I don't wanna see the Fatherland or my maker or anything or anybody except my bunk in England come on pull out pull out pull out oh God oh God pull up pull up pull up straighten out straighten out oh Jesus how long do I have to do this I can't hardly feel these controls oh God don't let them be gone he can't do it himself come on pull out pull out...

***

How well can you pray, American? How worthy are you to survive when my friend died such a stupid death? How kind are the Fates and Gods to you today...?

***

In the nose Reynolds was trying to come out of his daze from the explosion behind him that slammed his forehead into the cheek gun. *Crop Duster* was practically standing on her nose, with Germany rushing towards the shattered glass as she shook and roared, the wind screaming through the rents in her skin and the blown-out windows. Pull out pull it out pull it out oh come on I may have washed out of pilot's school but oh God now I wish I'd flunked the flight physical and got some desk job someplace oh shit skipper pull her up pull her up oh shit come on pull up pull up pull up pull up my head's busted I can't see oh God I don't wanna die like this come on skipper pull her up...

***

What possible difference would your death or your life make, American?

***

The explosion threw Farr onto his left side in the long agonizing dive, the hard rim of his turret digging deep into his ribs. Come on skipper this is twenty-five and I get to go home and teach some other poor bastards to do this for God and country so I don' have to anymore come on pull out pull out...

***

One American more or less cannot make a difference to the cosmos...

***

Hail Mary, full of grace, blessed art thou among women...the tail surfaces shook and roared, the wings vibrated like the too-tight skin of a drum; the engines roared uncontrollably at full throttle...hear, O Israel: the Lord is our God, the Lord is One...

***

Did you bomb Hamburg last July? Did you save my brother? Wait: is that a diamond M on your tail, American...? You can't pull out; too low now. No, you can't....

***

The blast threw Roy against the roof of the ship, still holding tight to the grips of his gun as the antenna handle dug deeply into his back ... oh good jumpin' Jesus what the hell is going on oh Christ oh Mama will I ever get outta here oh my back is broke I know it is oh good Christ get me outta here... The waist gunners were thrown against the radio room bulkhead, one of them dislocating his shoulder as he was yanked forward by the drop, the other slowly bleeding to death in the freezing, spinning hell ... oh god I can't feel anything oh shit oh god oh I gotta get back home again oh oh oh oh Rosie I'm sorry it had to end like this oh oh oh ... Jackson had been thrown first against the right side of the plane, then forward into the nose, twisting his leg around the bombsight pedestal, breaking it in two places... Goddamnit I wish I'd taken that damn exemption like Dad told me to oh Christ skipper pull her out pull her out pull her out oh God my leg hurts oh pull up skipper pull up is that my leg bone poking through my pants oh Christ pull up pull up blood that's blood coming out of me pull up pull out pull up...Milliken, now falling backwards, watched the air battle shrink above him and vanish, watched the tail section vibrating, listened to the straining control cables stretched well beyond their intended limits, and watched a lone Focke-Wulf slowly circling, following...Jesus Christ I had nothin' like this in the last war in Cuba or nothing oh God why didn't I just stay home with the rest of the old men oh God I swear by the blood of my children if I get outta this I'll never drink again so help me please...Atchison was staring directly at the horizon in an upside-down view of a world gone mad through his reflex sight, too terrified to turn or to think... Mother I didn't want to go but all the rest of the guys were going and I didn't want to be left behind again oh mamma oh mamma... The whole war machine appeared to be bent on its own destruction... Bless us sinners now and in the hour of our death amen up up up up oh sweet Jesus Mary and Joseph pull up pull up my help cometh from the Lord who made heaven and earth oh God pull up pull up pull out pull out pull up yea though I walk through the valley of the shadow of Death oh Jesus Christ I'll never drink again so help me I swear for Thine is the Kingdom and the power and the glory for ever and ever Amen...

***

You're too late; too late...I can see more of your wing now. Is it possible you may survive...? You have done it, American. You have done it. The Gods and Fates have smiled....

***

After long, agonizing moments, Miller and Witt loosened their grip on the controls, Miller finally backing the throttles to a more rational level. The airspeed dropped steadily; 240...180...160...130...120 miles an hour. Gradually they leveled the plane as best they could, but they were descending faster than was comfortable. The altimeter read

1,250 feet and was still winding down, albeit at a less frightening rate. But they had done what no one had never done before: recovering a B-17 from a 20,000 foot power dive.

Miller checked the damage to his plane he could see, numbed by the cold, the physical and mental struggle. The left engines were still attached, but the inboard was practically falling out of the wing, its propeller completely gone. The outboard was still running, intermittently, uncontrollably changing its pitch and speed, parts of the left side of the fuselage flapping in the wind. Miller's side window had been blown out, and several windows in the nose were gone, and paint blistered and scraped off the nose and left wing. He also took stock of himself. Even without a mirror, he could feel he had several splinters in his face. He couldn't hear out of his left ear, and he had difficulty focusing. His left shoulder was bloody and throbbed terribly.

"Jesus," Witt said, rasping through a dry throat, "Did we really do this?" Miller was too weak to speak just then, as the reality of what had just happened sunk in. After a moment, he numbly bobbed his head up and down, reaching for his throat mike while recovering his composure. "Pilot to crew: we've been hit pretty bad," he rasped. "They'll think we're dead. Report nose to tail."

For long moments the intercom was silent, wind whistling through the many holes in the plane's skin and the lumbering throb of the remaining engines the only sounds heard, the guns finally, mercifully, silent.

***

Thielmann was now concerned about the rest of his unit. Pulling into a steep climb, he searched for familiar markings in the maze of interceptors around the American herds. "Altmarck: Recover immediately. Altmarck: Recover immediately," the radio crackled, the possibly pretty fighter controller growing hoarse from the long effort.

***

"Bombardier to pilot: I busted my leg. Ugh, bad. I can still move around. Bombsight's gone. I'm gonna have a look at the bomb bay as soon as I can."

"NATE I CAN'T SEE," Reynolds shouted over the din, shaking Jackson's shoulder, blinking and rubbing his eyes, blood running down both sides of his nose and a large round patch where the cheek gun hit him in the middle of his forehead. Jackson, dosing himself with two syrettes of morphine, extricated his left leg from around the bombsight pedestal. Screaming from the agony of the splintered bones grinding against muscle and nerve endings, he bound his shattered leg in rags, pausing only to wipe his hands on his flight jacket. He held Reynolds's face in his hands, peering at his forehead and eyes. Equal and reactive, Jackson decided, having heard his physician-uncle say that once.

"Jack," Jackson shouted through the din. "You hit your head. It's only temporary." Somewhat reassured (at least outwardly) Reynolds felt around his station quickly, and then called in.

"Navigator to pilot: my panel's shot up, gun's OK, and about half the glass got blown out from the nose. I hit my head and I can't see good, but I'm OK. This is a real windy ride up here."

The bombardier made his way past the flight deck, pausing only to ensure that both pilot and co-pilot were still alive. When he saw Miller, he masked his horror with the generous help of his agony, and the morphine that was finally taking effect.

The left side of Miller's head was mangled, with metal fragments sticking out of his face, but he seemed to fly the plane as if he were only slightly wounded. A ghastly, huge stick of metal was poking out from the left side of his flying helmet, but Miller seemed unaware of it. Don't dare get him off the flight deck, Jackson thought, but we'd better think about getting out of this tub...

"John, I got some splinters in my legs," Witt said off the intercom. "Hurts some but not bad," the copilot finished, feeling the blood soak up his underwear. He could feel nothing below mid-calf.

"Top turret to pilot: The right wing is in good shape, and the left looks structurally OK. The number two engine looks like it'll fall off any minute. I see no damage to the tail or control surfaces from here. My guns work and the turret moves. Number three and four are operating as expected. We'd better think about shutting off number one."

"Negative. We'll need to get all the power we can get, and even if the prop twists off, it'll burn up fuel we may not be able to transfer."

Jackson called in again, his voice weak. "Bombardier to pilot: we got fuel leaks in the bomb bay."

Aw hell, Miller thought. "Are the doors open?"

"Negative."

"Can we stop the fuel leaks?"

"Don't know. I think the main transfer line is OK." Christ, Miller thought. We may be able to fly home if we don't run out of gas. The bombardier was glad nobody asked how he was now.

Not too bad, Miller thought, but the added drag from the blown-out glass would cost precious fuel, fuel that was now leaking out through the bomb bay and probably from the number two engine.

"Radio to pilot: I've got the command transmitter but nothing else. Lots of holes back here, and my gun's jammed up—ruptured case, I think. My IFF's gone, but the radio compass checks OK. I hurt my back, but I'm OK."

"Can you get air-sea rescue?"

"I'll try, skipper. Go out with tone then I'll try voice." Good, Roy, good, Miller thought.

"Belly gun to pilot: I can move the turret, but one gun is out. The bomb bay doors look OK but I see some liquid coming out. The left wing is real bad underneath and the left tire is gone. Other than that, everything looks good from here." Other than being a flying junk pile and losing gas, we're in pretty good shape, Miller thought.

"Left waist to pilot: Collova's lost both legs below the knee. The tourniquets seem to stop the bleeding, but his suit's bad off—soaked with blood all the way up to the neck. We got some holes through the floor and bulkheads, but I don't see any damage to the control cables from here. I think the oxygen back to the tail's cut, though. I dislocated my left shoulder, I think. I can't feel my hand and my arm hurts like hell." Getting better all the time, Miller thought bitterly.

"Tail gun to pilot: I got nothin' coming in my line. I can't breathe, but my guns still work."

"You won't need oxygen because we'll never get that high again. How do the tail surfaces look to you, Milliken?"

"Other than some little holes, not too bad. Both elevators and the rudder are still on, but after I saw them shake during that dive, I don't know how."

Miller considered his options quickly. "OK, the Krauts'll think we're dead, so it'll be a while before they come looking for us." I hope, he thought wearily. "Aitcheson, get outta that ball—nobody's gonna hit us from below, anyway. Go have a look at Collova and Murphy. Then come back up here and tell me what you think." If he had to abandon the ship, he wanted everybody to have at least an even chance to survive. Collova may not survive an inbound trip, but riding a cripple back to England alone wasn't the way to a long life, either. "Farr, get into the bomb bay and help the bombardier." Instinctive, not rational, he thought. Can't think straight, can't concentrate...

In a few minutes, Aitcheson appeared on the flight deck and shouted into Miller's good ear, masking his fear and shock at the sight of his pilot. "No good, skipper. He's barely awake and still losing blood. He'll be dead in an hour at most." Miller nodded understanding, and reached for his throat mike.

"All right everybody, listen up." Miller said, "We're hit pretty bad. We've still got two good engines on the right wing and one on the left for the moment. As long as the controls last, we can keep her in the air. We won't need oxygen, but we gotta decide to get out or try to get back. We're closer to Switzerland than England, but on two reliable engines we may not get high enough to make the frontier and Spain's too far away, so if we want we can try to get home if we've got the gas. If we can't get the wheels down, we may have to bail out, but I'd rather do it over England than occupied territory. What do you guys say?" This kind of decision wasn't one every pilot gave his crew a choice about. But Miller had no thought of forcing anyone to ride out a cripple, knowing what a risk he was taking as a lone bomber in hostile skies.

"Bombardier to pilot; I'll play the hand out...Navigator to pilot: I don't like parachutes...Co-pilot to pilot: they'd kill me down there... Top turret to pilot: I go where you go, skipper...Left waist to pilot: I stay with Collova...Tail to pilot: what the hell, why not...Belly gun to pilot: I don't like sauerkraut...Radio to pilot: aw hell, guys, I guess I'll make it unanimous."

Miller allowed himself the luxury of a small smile. They were going to try to pull the old girl back home.

"OK," he said over the intercom, "we'll have to lighten the ship. Throw the oxygen bottles out and anything else we don't need to stay flying and protect ourselves, or what don't work. Navigator, I need course and speed to the English coast. I make our current heading at 300 magnetic, airspeed 120, altitude 1,200. What's the sanctuary ceiling today? 800?" Sanctuary was the altitude that wounded planes stayed at, or tried to, when they didn't have a radio or an IFF transponder to identify them.

"Navigator to pilot: Affirmative; 500 to 1,800, but I can't see, skipper. I really can't."

"OK. Jackson, can you get me a plot?"

"Yeah, if I can get back up there; my leg's real bad."

"Aitcheson, get the bombardier back forward; Farr, get into the bomb bay and see about those fuel lines. Jackson, I'm gonna try to hold her at 120 and 1,000."

"I'll have a plot as soon as I get a fix."

"Tail gun to bombardier: Lieutenant Jackson with all due respect, you sonofabitch, sir, you'd better live long enough so's I can win my markers back."

Miller, enormously tired and preoccupied with something he couldn't quite put his finger on, cracked into a grin.

***

Jockeying his fuel-hungry plane back to the field, Thielmann's gaze wandered around him. Other FW-190s were coming in, some intact, many damaged, all running out of fuel, ammunition and boost nitrous. In hours of air battle, dodging and weaving, they had pushed the FWs to their upper performance limits. The headphones still crackled with chatter.

"All Altmarck units recover immediately. Repeat; all Altmarck units recover immediately...Group Taube arriving in 10 minutes. Need medical assistance...I have no landing gear, no controls left, my wingman is down. Request assistance...We have 15 Messerschmitts needing fuel and ammunition now. You are nearest. Request instructions..."

Far above, the battle was still being fought by other fighters, some far removed from the Spessart Mountains. Although it was not quite four in the afternoon, Thielmann felt he had been up for days. Landing gently on his home field, he taxied to the fuel truck, hoping he wouldn't get too much trouble from them. He didn't want to have to explain what he had to do. Jumping out of the cockpit while the propeller had barely stopped turning, he yelled at the Gefreiter to fill his tanks quickly.

"But, sir, other planes are here ahead of you, and I can't..."

Drawing his pistol, Thielmann pointed it at the corporal. "Fuel NOW," he repeated. The corporal carried the hose to the plane. Commandeering a car in like manner, Thielmann raced to the munitions hut where Goetz, an overage major from the last war, was arguing with Kaltz.

"But I simply don't have enough 0.77 centimeter ammunition. I only have 2 and 3 centimeter ammunition stocks. I have some of the smaller caliber, but not enough for fifteen Messerschmitts..."

"'Forward ammunition depots shall maintain adequate current stocks to provide for foreseeable needs.' That is what the regulation says. Why do you not follow regulations?"

"Sir," Goetz replied, trying to be as patient as he could, "this is not only not a forward station, it is not a depot. It is only an ammunition dump. If I could get anything else I would, but as it is, I have trouble enough getting what I HAVE to have. Now if you want…"

"Sir," Thielmann interrupted breathlessly, "Excuse me, but I need to get reloaded; now." Kaltz and Goetz both regarded Thielmann curiously. He looked quite disheveled and out-of-breath.

"Yes, Thielmann," Kaltz said, "yes. But what happened to you? Your unit is only now recovering. The Americans are quite thick today, so you'll have another chance at them in an hour or so. Take a moment to compose yourself."

"I cannot, sir. I have to get back airborne quickly." He quickly related a version of what had happened. "I have to get back up there. I have to find him."

"Quite admirable, Thielmann," Kaltz muttered, "but quite impractical. The Destroyers or the coastal flak batteries will bring him down, don't worry. If it is as you say, he may not even get that far. I'll ensure we credit Bär with the victory. Just you go and…"

"*Nein*," Thielmann spat. The older flier regarded his young colleague for a long moment, then drew him out of earshot of Goetz.

Kaltz watched him and then looked out into the sky. "Long, long ago I watched something like this. I had badly damaged an SE-5, an Englishman. He somehow brought his plane under control just high enough off the ground, and he started back for his own lines. I watched him and I thought 'you brave, skillful man! Today is not your day to die.' So I followed him for some time until the antiaircraft guns shot at me and he landed in a meadow near those guns." He shook his head wistfully. "I often wondered if he flew again." He glared back at Thielmann, and then softened. "Yes, go then, and if anyone gives you any trouble, have them contact me." Kaltz had to shout the last to Thielmann, already dashing for his plane.

***

They set a course for England and estimated a flight time of three hours. It was to be three long, grueling hours for a crippled bomber alone over hostile territory with angry fighters and antiaircraft guns studding every mile. Miller held *Crop Duster* at 1000 feet and about 130 miles an hour when the number one engine wanted to cooperate. Its performance was so erratic that they couldn't depend on it, revving up then down on its own. The oil pressure was near zero; Farr expected it to seize any moment.

The crew jettisoned anything that wasn't nailed down. Flak jackets, flight suits, steel helmets, oxygen bottles, ruins of radios, rations, coffee bottles, extra maps, code books, aircraft manuals, damaged machine guns, and the belly gun turret were sacrificed to save weight. Former necessities of war were now liabilities. "Aitcheson to pilot: I gotta set Murphy's shoulder. Anybody know how it's done?"

"Reynolds to Aitcheson: pay attention. Murphy: grab hold of something with your good arm. Now, Aitcheson, feel Murphy's shoulder and compare it to your own. Murphy, tell him where it hurts the most." There was a brief silence, followed by a loud "OW." "OK. Aitcheson, push or pull or twist that shoulder so it feels like yours, but try not to go in the direction where it hurts."

"It won't move."

"Give it a good sock, then."

"AOOW, SHIT," Murphy yelled. "Damn, that's better."

"Aitcheson, tie his upper arm to his side. Murphy, try not to use it." Silence again.

"Tail gun to pilot: I got two shots of morphine into Collova and the bleeding's stopped. He's out of it, but I don't know if he'll last three hours."

"Can we throw him out?"

"Yeah, I guess so." Miller considered that for a moment. Crippled bombers expect to have to defend themselves, and needed every gunner they could get. Still, Aitcheson and Jackson were essentially without work and they could man the waist guns.

Miller's head and shoulder ached terribly and his face was quite numb, but he dared not investigate too closely. Don't dislodge anything, he thought...can't concentrate...sleepy...

"Right waist to pilot," the intercom crackled again, shaking Miller out of a daze. "Boss, I wanna go out." It was Collova, his voice thick from morphine. "I've got a better chance after a few minutes in the air than I do waiting for somebody to maybe get me home. I wanna go. I'll just get in your way, anyway." Unfortunately, he was right. In his current condition, Collova was of no use to anyone aboard.

"You sure that's what you want?" Miller called back.

"Yeah, sure, boss."

Miller pondered for a long moment. "OK, go on then. Good luck. I'll buy you a beer when you get back."

There was silence aboard the plane for the next few moments as Aitcheson and Murphy jostled Collova to the rear door. "I told you I'd throw your ass out," Murphy whispered, pulling the D-ring as Collova tumbled into space. "Left waist to pilot: He's clear. His 'chute opened."

Only the rushing air and the engines were heard on the bomber again. Everyone knew that Collova's chances were at best even, and at worst, nil, even if he survived the jump. Miller felt sleepy again, remembering the roly-poly Virginian with his dumb jokes and rolling laugh only dimly, as through a haze in his brain.

"Radio to pilot: I need some help back here." Miller was jerked back into wakefulness again, feeling he had drifted off to sleep.

"OK." Miller said, "Aitcheson, get into the radio room, then onto the right waist. Gunners, stay awake: Farr, get those repairs done. They'll be after us like flies on shit."

Roy was lying on the floor, wracked with pain. "I broke my back," he yelled. "Strap something to my spine and I'll be able to move." The only straight object to be found was a piece of plywood decking, which Aitcheson clumsily tied to Roy with wire. Somewhat relieved, Roy sent Aitcheson back out. The belly gunner promptly reported to the waist.

Witt watched the pilot with growing horror and respect. If he only knew...but Witt wouldn't dream of telling him. Miller had been passing out off and on, and after a brief conference with the other officers, they decided to leave him alone, to see if he could do it on his own. No one even thought about removing him from the cockpit, Witt thought grimly, not after he pulled us out of that dive. Jackson can't sit straight, my legs are gone, Reynolds can't see, can't spare Farr from... somebody's gotta be in charge while he flies it.

"Copilot to crew: what's our ammo situation?"

"Navigator to copilot: I had about fifty rounds...Top gun's about twenty...Tail gun's about thirty...Left waist about a hundred...Right waist about a hundred...Radio about a hundred fifty."

"OK," Witt called. "Aitcheson and Milliken; redistribute the ammo. Get everything out of the cheek gun and the radio and get it to the top turret. Cut the waists in half and get it to the tail gun. Roy, can you stand?"

"Better than I can sit."

"OK. Get forward into the top gun. You won't have to sit there. Reynolds, can you move?"

"Yeah. Can't see, but I can move."

"All right. Aitcheson, get Reynolds aft into the radio room. Reynolds, crank the Gibson." The Gibson Girl was an hourglass-shaped emergency radio, hand-cranked to emit a steady, fixed transmission that the rescue stations monitored.

"Copilot to bombardier: Jackson, can you work the radio?"

"Sure. Nothing up here works anyway. I can do plots from back there." "OK. Aitcheson, help the bombardier to the radio room when you're done with the navigator and the ammo, then get back on the waist. Farr; how long before repairs are done?"

"Few more minutes."

"Get into the waist when you're done." Miller looked over at his copilot. Good decisions...had to be made...can't think straight.

For long, tense moments, the intercom was silent, each crewman alone with his private terrors. Roy scribbled down the message for Jackson. "How good's your Morse?"

"Good enough for a merit badge in Boy Scouts."

"OK. Send this in tone three times, then voice twice. Rest for a while and repeat until you get an answer. Don't send if you don't think you sound right. A garbled message could be as bad as none at all."

They finished the movement of crewmen and ammunition in a few more minutes. Jackson gave himself another morphine injection and swallowed a pep pill from his survival pouch. "Copilot to crew: Everybody take a goofball," Witt called; "we'll need 'em..."

**

Where are you, American? There are only a few logical routes for you to follow. I hope the Indians don't sortie out to find me all alone...was that a diamond M on your tail?

**

The top turret turned ceaselessly. The gunners searched the skies for the enemy fighters they knew would be coming. All had the overwhelming feeling of impending doom, like the silence over the prairie when twisters were near. "Right waist to pilot: there's another cripple below us to the right." The pilot and co-pilot looked in the indicated direction and there was another B-17 on two engines with one sputtering and several pieces shot out of the wings and tail.

"She's pretty bad, skipper," Witt said, "worse than us. Looks like there's another off to her right."

"Yeah, and another behind her; God, four cripples in one formation. Still, four's safer than one," Miller replied, banking slightly to a position some hundreds of feet above the other cripples. He labored to keep *Crop Duster* in a steady position, but the other planes were almost too slow. The leading bomber was having no apparent trouble, even though most of her nose was gone. The fourth seemed to fly on one only occasionally running engine. Miller scanned the trailing B-17, named *Lights Out,* sporting a scantily clad young lady on her nose, pulling a light chain while exposing her bare bottom. There were no gunners in the waist positions, the top turret had sizeable chunks torn away, and the flak had practically shot the nose off. Can't even defend herself, Miller thought; oh God. Miller felt the sick sensation that he was going to get caught, as though he could smell the impending thunder and hail even though he could not feel his face.

"Flight engineer to pilot: I'm just about done here..."

"Hurry up! We're gonna have company any minute." As if the fates were reading his mind, the tail gunner came over the intercom.

"Two bandits coming up on our tail fast." Milliken touched his trigger to fire at the approaching fighters. As if they sensed *Lights Out* plight, the ME- 109s ignored *Crop Duster* and the other planes and bored in on her, firing as they passed. Her tail gun had not fired. Miller's gunners and the other Fortresses fired furiously at the attackers, knowing that they would be next as soon as they dispatched this poor cripple.

It was over quickly. The right wing of *Lights Out* smoked, and two bodies hurtled out of the bomb bay, opening the parachutes almost as soon as they were clear. The nose of the bomber pointed downwards and, like an enormous bird, rolled onto her right side. It was over when the right wing sheared off. The blazing debris of the once- proud war machine floated to rest on the ground below like autumn leaves, blown by a passing breeze.

The fighters arched around in the air, now seeing their other quarry still had some teeth. The two split out to attack *Crop Duster* from the nose, the most vulnerable places even on a healthy plane, but in *Crop Duster's* condition almost certainly fatal. As it closed, the first grew in size. Miller and Witt braced themselves as 20mm shells slammed through the nose of the plane, destroying the instrument panel and filling the cockpit with glass and debris. Roy fired his guns as the fighter approached, looming large in his sights as he put a continuous stream of heavy machine-gun bullets into the air. Peeling off, the fighter turned around again for another head-on attack. Roy called back that he was nearly out of ammunition. The second German rolled gently into position and headed inward.

Fate and the number one engine decided that at that moment that the propeller would seize up. As it wobbled, *Crop Duster* shook from the imbalance. Miller, in frustration and rage, reached into his shoulder holster and retrieved his .45 pistol. Furiously he thrust the weapon through the shattered windscreen and commenced firing, all the while yelling at the top of his lungs, "GET THE HELL AWAY FROM ME! GET THE HELL AWAY!!"

Suddenly the fighter veered off, streaming back over the top of the bomber , faltering in a slight climb with black smoke belching from its engine. Gradually it turned, dove, and headed downward. The pilot opened his canopy and rolled out.

"Got him," Atchison called, "no chute."

Score one for us, Miller thought. Now we're even.

Witt stared at his pilot, not sure of what he'd just seen. Roy yelled back to the crew to bring him more ammo, as he'd just fired off his last round. The second fighter closed on *Crop Duster* from below and ahead, skillfully avoiding the top gun's firing arc. Just as it was in range, the intercom sprang to life. "Engine away!" as the number two engine sheared off and fell away. Inexplicably, the number one engine smoothed out and resumed normal operation. The Messerschmitt fired only a quick burst before swerving violently, but misjudged *Crop Duster's* speed. As it swerved, the attacker turned on its left wing to pass the bomber on its left side, hardly more than fifty feet from the left waist just as Aitcheson clamped down the gun's spade triggers, sending a stream of heavy slugs into the belly of the Messerschmitt. As the fighter reached the end of a long bank, tracers from the tail guns streamed into it, and it exploded in a silent ball of flame. Dropped an engine and two fighters at the same time, Miller thought. "Good work, you guys," he said over the intercom. Now, if he could just hold this crate together for another hour and a half or so, he might just be able to get home. For some reason, he felt quite drowsy, and though he knew he was cold, felt warm.

***

Wearily, Thielmann searched all around him in the most likely escape route for a crippled Fortress. Twice he had swooped down on cripples, only to find it was the wrong kite or the Fortress put up more resistance than Thielmann thought he could. He knew what the American should have looked like and kept heading northwest, north and west towards the sea.

***

Miller swiveled his head to the left, squinting in the glare of the sun over the western horizon as if he had just woke up. For an hour he'd been flying by dead reckoning, gauging engine performance by sound and feel, keeping the sun in the same relative position because he no longer had a reliable compass. Never felt so tired on a return trip, he thought, studying the shattered window to his left, and the shards of windshield in front of him, concentrating on their condition rather than his own. Gotta stay awake...

The instrument panel was a wreck. Witt held control of the crippled *Crop Duster* when Miller nodded off. The controls were stable enough that Miller could afford to release them for short periods, but not long enough to see how bad his head was. He knew it had been a while since they started back, but for some reason, it didn't feel that long. Everything hurt. His head and shoulder throbbed, and his uniform felt sticky... probably blood...but otherwise he felt OK. If only he could stay awake...

***

The radio operator at Great Yarmouth Air-Sea Rescue station, executing an idle sweep across several frequencies, picked up the crackly, weak call: "...Fencepost three; low on fuel and ammunition. Route sugar how, height sugar minus. Please reply. Any station: this is *Crop Duster*; Fencepost three. Any station..."

The operator rang his phone while whipping off his headset. "Sir," he said into the instrument, "I have an American in trouble. Aircraft name is *Crop Duster* from Fencepost: Bartlesby, with a Gibson signal we've been tracking for some time at the same plot..."

That set the machinery into motion. ASR called USAAF, who called down to the air station, and Bartlesby identified the caller as one of their own.

"Good *God*," Throck exclaimed, "we wrote *him* off *hours* ago. Where the *hell* is he? Smitty, get me Pinetree Main. And get *my* airplane ready," he yelled into his orderly room.

Fuming because none of the fighter escorts had even launched while they butchered his group for better than three hours over Germany, Throck struggled mightily not to break into his native tongue. "Ira; Throck. Listen, Larry Miller's boy's a cripple inbound. I want every available airplane in the air...*Goddammit* Ira, you'll do it or by the Eternal *God* when this war's over I'll have your *nuts* for a watch fob... Ira, we hung Larry Miller out to dry twenty years ago and today we've proved he was right. I'm not gonna have his boy pay for our twenty years of feeding 'em bullshit if I can help it...I don't give a fat rat fart what Fighter Command's weather is! Tell those yellow bastards to get to hell up in the air! They can call it blind intercept training or they can call it suicide drill but get 'em up...get 'em up Ira or by *God* I'll shoot you myself... and don't make me mad Ira you sonofabitch..."

***

By the time the North Sea coast was a hazy smudge on the near horizon, the other two survivors of the cripple formation had fallen out, one crew bailing out before the bomber fell down, the other lowering his landing gear in the unwritten but well understood gesture of aircraft surrender, heading down for an open space to land.

As the haze cleared and the coast drew nearer, *Crop Duster* might hope for a friendly fighter escort, but the inbound twin-engine bogie coming up fast from behind wasn't friendly, and everyone aboard knew it.

The Brits had answered Jackson's call for help, and said someone was on the way, but Miller had no illusions about the range of the Spitfire, and even fewer about the willingness of the Air Force to send out fighters for a lone Flying Fort cripple after a day like today....

***

Is that you, American? It cannot be you. There is too much of you left.

***

The Messerschmitt ME-110 banked around to the front of *Crop Duster*, by then barely a thousand feet off the ground. These lone aircraft that lingered along the coast were called "destroyers" by the

Germans, but the American bomber crews called them "jackals" and "vampires" because they hunted for cripples to blow apart with heavy cannon and rockets. This one, with an even two dozen victory marks, rolled slowly around, just out of machine gun range, sizing up the most likely avenue of attack.

The twin-engine fighter slipped in behind *Crop Duster*, just beyond the arc of the tail machine gun, and began firing three 30mm cannons as both planes crossed the coast over the open sea. The heavy shells slammed into the struggling bomber as Milliken fired the last ammunition on the ship in useless frustration. Pieces of *Crop Duster*'s tail section and left wing tore off and tumbled down into the sea.

NEIN...!

From high above both airplanes, a stream of tracers lanced across the German fighter's path, forcing it to divert. Just as suddenly, a lone FW-190 descended between the German twin and *Crop Duster*, taking up a position between them. The Focke-Wulf flew in almost perfect synchronization on the big ME's nose, blocking the heavy guns.

For once I am glad these big destroyers are so clumsy, Thielmann thought, or this would be far more dangerous than it is...

As Miller and his crew watched the silent ballet of fighters, too awe-struck to speak, too confused to even try to make any sense of the apparition, the FW/ME pair expertly executed two perfect head-on attacks without firing a shot. The ME, try as it might, could not get around the FW. Changing position for different angles of attack, the FW easily intercepted each attempt. Finally, the big Messerschmitt broke off and headed back towards land.

What am I doing, Thielmann wondered, as the Messerschmitt gently banked away. He sidled his FW-190 up to *Crop Dusters* left wingtip, and for a few moments he stared at the ship.

"Why are you still in the air, circle M," Thielmann muttered to himself; "I have seen better-looking wrecks. That name on your nose... *Crop Duster II...* what does that mean? You are lucky, *Crop Duster II*, and I may be in a great deal of trouble. Well, I think you will appreciate it. I salute you..." Aiming his flashlight at the *Festungen's* cockpit, he flashed out a message.

"What in hell was that all about?" Witt wondered aloud. A light flashed in the German's hand, seemingly in Morse. Witt scribbled the dots and dashes down on his hand. Didn't make much sense, he muttered to himself, and I know German. Farr, watching the scene out of the left waist position, used a pencil to scribble the tail markings on the sleeve of his shearling jacket.

***

Indians...they will go after the destroyer...I had better head them off...

***

"Gents, today is not our day to die," Miller said, watching the Focke-Wulf execute a fast climbing bank over the top of *Crop Duster* and dive away.

"Or today's not his," Witt said, pointing to a half-dozen British fighters plunging out of the west toward the little vignette.

"Spitfires, by God," Roy called out; "never thought I'd be so glad to see a goddamn Englishman."

The six sleek fighters circled around *Crop Duster* as she lumbered across the sea, two taking off in pursuit of the Focke-Wulf. "That's it, guys." Miller said, more than a little relieved. "Thirty minutes to England, and we even got an escort. Roy, flash the Spits and tell 'em thanks for the rescue. I think I can hold this crate in the air until I see Dover."

Roy tapped out the message with a flashlight to one Spitfire off the right wing. The Spitfire replied with a flashlight. "He says Coastal Command'll pick us up in a few minutes to take us in. Air-sea rescue is already shadowing us." The crew let out a cheer that shook the ship. Miller allowed himself to smile again, but was still anxious about landing and, with his cold-benumbed face, the best he could manage was a sad grimace.

Minutes later, a Coastal Command flying boat flew majestically under the crippled *Crop Duster*. "He wants to know if we want to ditch," Roy called on the intercom.

Miller thought about it for a moment. With extensive nose damage and casualties aboard, it didn't seem like a real good idea. But why can't I decide, Miller thought. Tired...gotta land...come on old girl, get us home... "Ah, negative on the ditch," Witt answered on the intercom.

Miller stared at his co-pilot dumbly. "You guys wanna bail out?"

"Too low," Witt answered. "Besides, I gotta see how you're gonna land this crate."

Roy flashed over to the flying boat the reply, then read the other plane's signal. "He says he'll follow us to the coast just in case," he called back on the intercom. Soon the air around Crop Duster was alive with airplanes, American fighters, bombers, British fighters, bombers, and aircraft of every description. Miller watched the coterie dumbly, still unable to concentrate, dazed by this outrageous show of force.

Just a little longer, Miller thought, just a little while longer...

***

Eight hundred feet below the crippled Fortress. two Air-Sea Rescue boats motored after the flying junk pile above them. One veteran American Coast Guardsman whistled in amazement that it was still in the air.

There must be a God, he muttered, and He has one *hell* of a sense of humor.

***

"English coast dead ahead," Roy said over the intercom. "Looks like we can do it, skipper."

Miller tried but lacked the energy to work up much relief. "Yeah, if I can set this bus down. Is Coastal Command still out there, or air-sea rescue?"

"Left waist to pilot: I see some boats in the Channel just off the coast. They might be fishing boats..."

"I don't care. At least they can pick us up," Miller replied urgently, clearing the cobwebs from his head. "Listen, you guys. I don't know if I can get the gear down. Whadda' ya say you guys bail out...Aw hell, you can't. I can't climb above 600 feet."

"Wouldn't go anyway, John," Witt said.

"OK. Jackson, give me a course to the nearest field. I can't take this crate all the way back to Bartlesby. Probably don't have much fuel left..."

"Jackson to pilot: steer 210 degrees magnetic as soon as you cross the coast. There's a Coastal Command base about three miles inland."

"Roger: 210 magnetic after landfall. But..." There was something wrong with Jackson's instructions that Miller couldn't quite put a finger on. "Co-pilot to Jackson: what's 210 magnetic if we don't have a compass?"

"Roger wait...Jackson to Witt: put the right side of the nose about two points to the left of the sun."

There was a light mist over the coast as *Crop Duster* headed towards the misty hills, and the intercom was filled with chatter again. "Gettin' myself proper drunk when I get back; yessir, proper drunk...Not me, brother; I'm for the rack and a nice hot stove…Creature comforts, all of you. Why, what you should do is find yourself a good woman and …"

"OK, shaddap," Miller rebuked mildly. "We ain't back yet. I don't think we'll need the guns anymore, so pitch them over the side." Furiously the crew tossed out the guns, the last crashing on the beach. "OK, everybody assume crash positions. I'm not even gonna think about landing gear."

"There's a field," Witt said, pointing out through the shattered windscreen to a barren strip. Miller thought it looked abandoned, but right then, he wasn't about to go looking for another.

"We're gonna make one circuit—give 'em a chance to recognize us and get ready." Miller started a slow bank to the left, recovering immediately to the right for a long turn around the field.

***

Men on the ground, not expecting a crippled B-17, dropped their mundane tasks and began scurrying all over the field, some to push other planes aside to clear the runway, the rest dashing to ambulances and fire trucks to prepare for *Crop Duster's* touchdown.

***

A nearby veterinarian—the first the area had seen since the war started—had just injected another of his wooly patients with an experimental sheep-pox vaccine. This flock of his four-legged patients was part of the large grazing herd that kept the Coastal Command fields on the Channel coast tidy.

He noticed the commotion on the field as his assistant, a second-year veterinary school student, dragged up another patient. He heard the laboring engines of a heavy airplane and looked up to see a badly damaged B-17 banking over the field. Thinking he may be of some help to his fellow Americans, he shed his overalls as he strode to his jeep.

***

Circling around to the end of the runway, Miller carefully lined his plane up with the end, feeling his head and shoulder throbbing again. "Farr to pilot," the intercom crackled, "We're ready. Set her down." In the radio room, the crew huddled under the wreckage of Roy's radios, pulling the ditching strap tight around them.

Miller made to reach his mike, but Witt beat him to it. "Copilot to crew: hold on," he said simply.

Miller called back on the intercom. "Roy: fire two flares." Miller shouted to Witt off the intercom; "Figure we'll probably be heavy on the right, so I'll keep the left wingtip just a hair down and maybe we'll keep from spinning on the right wing. As soon as I say, cut the engines. It'll be just before we set down, but I don't want to belly-in with power up; all we need is prop blades shearing off." Miller glanced over to Witt, seeing the fear glinting behind his otherwise passive eyes. "You ready?"

"Ready as I'll ever get," he replied, left hand on the switches, eyes intent on the end of the runway. One thing that I've got to do sometime, Miller thought dimly, is figure some way to simulate a belly landing. He knew the theory they taught in school wasn't worth the match it'd take to burn it.

Crop Duster descended toward the runway. "Steady now...steady," Miller droned, sweat breaking out on his frozen face. "Hold it... hold it steady. When we hit the ground, cover your face with your arms." Ever so lightly, *Crop Duster* flared down to the end of the runway. "Cut engines," Miller said, and Witt dutifully chopped the switches. As the engines stopped, the sudden silence was deafening. The roaring blast through the holes and blown- out window frames was the only sound anyone could hear. *Just hope it's not the last.*

"Hang on," Miller hollered. The tail settled on the runway, squealing and smoking before the rest of the plane slammed down and both pilot and copilot covered their faces. They skidded for another thousand feet as the well-ordered emergency landing became chaos.

Crop Duster spun around while rising on the left wing, dragging down the field, rocking up onto the right wing, and then slamming back down on the left wing. Along with the roaring noise and vibration, the debris that had lain harmlessly quiet during the ride home had suddenly come alive, angrily flying everywhere, threatening the crew one last time.

As suddenly as it had started, the swirling and roaring stopped as the plane lurched, finally, to rest. At first, Miller and Witt were stunned by the silence, but the screaming sirens of the rapidly approaching ambulances and fire trucks roused them.

Oh Christ, Miller thought, *we made it.*

"Everybody out," Witt yelled, "this tub may go up any minute." Turning to Miller, he said, "Come on, John. It's over." Unbuckling the pilot's safety belt, Witt hoisted Miller by the arm. "Out over the nose," he grunted, pushing the pilot through the shattered windshield. Numbed by the exertion, cold and dizzy from what he didn't know, Miller scrambled out of the cockpit over the nose of the plane, now a hopeless wreck. Firefighters were dousing a small fire on the crumpled wreck of the left wing, but the right wing was still intact, as if in defiance.

"Come on outta there, mate," a voice said to Miller. The face attached to the voice was of a ruddy, mustachioed corporal. "Come on, then," the voice said, "We don't mind you Yanks using our aerodromes, but you should try not to make such a bloody mess, eh?" Miller smiled broadly, despite a sudden, blinding agony in his head and shoulder.

Oh God, he thought, I'm back.

Then everything went black.

***

"ICE," Cooper yelled at his assistant, who was standing dumbfounded near the nose of the airplane. "GET ME ICE!" Startled into attention, the young man dashed to the jeep, poured the serum out of the ice chest, and ran back to the doctor with it. Cooper kneeled next to where Miller lay, the base medics and doctors clucking their tongues in disbelief.

"Fancy meeting you here, doctor," Witt grunted as he crawled on his hands and knees, leaving a faint trail of blood behind him.

"Yeah, real fancy," Cooper muttered, packing a blanket with ice and laying it around Miller's head. "Ashton, bring that jeep around here," he yelled at his assistant again, "DO IT!!"

Another litter carried Jackson out of the radio compartment, pieces of his lower leg bone protruding from his pants. Reynolds was being hauled out of the radio room by three rescuers, dried blood running out of his ears and down his face. Roy lay on the ground, writhing in agony. Milliken, Aitcheson and Murphy helped each other out of the wreck.

Farr clutched his ribs and held a dressing over a bleeding hole in his behind, watching the doctor labor over his pilot, holding a Godawful stick of metal poking out of his skull. Oh, this one'll be a great one for the grandkids, he thought: shot in the ass on my last mission.

"Jeep's not big enough," Cooper said urgently. "Need something wider. Gotta hold his head steady. Group Commander," he called to an officer staring agape at the wreck and the bleeding lump of flesh that

323

had once been a pilot, "the farm has a truck—uhn—lorry. Think we can borrow it?" As the officer turned to find someone to 'requisition' the vehicle, he saw Milliken and the ruddy corporal already at a dead run across the field.

***

A tale for the grand-kids: local Bobbies in pursuit of a hayrick lorry traveling way too fast for a narrow road, only to be warned off by pistol-brandishing speeders in American military uniforms who absolutely refuse to stop, then joined by American MPs called to assist the pursuit, which—with the belated recognition of a medical armband flying from one of the truck staves—ultimately becomes a high-speed escort to the hospital.

***

It wasn't an ambulance that screeched up to the emergency room door. It wasn't even a military vehicle; it was a farmer's stake truck that backed up to the hatch, driven by a Chicago cabdriver, and escorted by the screaming sirens of MP jeeps. When the gate opened, there was a litter surrounded by sandbags, and a black man kneeling over a patient on the litter—a patient covered with blood, whose face was barely recognizable as human. "Boy," the emergency room medic shouted up, "just what in hell do you think you're doing?"

"The *doctor* is holding his patient's head still, Corporal," Farr growled, pushing his .45 into the corporal's face, "and if you don't want me to blow your ignorant head off, you'll get one of them carts out here and take Major Miller inside *RIGHT GODDAMN NOW.*" The cart was quickly produced, and the litter carefully lifted onto it, Cooper still holding Miller's head and the dangerous splinter absolutely still, packing ice around it. Farr, even while helping Witt out of the truck, still brandished his .45 at anyone showing the slightest hesitation in helping his pilot.

"He's *alive,*" doctor after doctor clucked, incredulous that this lump of blood and flesh still had life in it. Plus, no one was about to argue with Cooper's shouted assurances...or Farr's pistol. They began IVs, took blood pressure, pulse, cleaned up the mess, applied bandages, sutured, and shaved, all while Cooper stood at the head, packing ice, and keeping the deadly splinter completely immobile.

***

Grace was fast asleep when the phone rang. She answered it distractedly, but instantly it gained all her attention. "When?" she said into the phone, pulling herself together. "Is it serious...Yes, Sally, I know. I'll see what I can do." She hurriedly pulled on her robe while searching for her address book. She found the number and dialed hurriedly.

"Hotel Corinthian, please." There was a silence. "Yes, may I please speak with the Duchess? This is Duchess Mayfield....It's an emergency... yes, I'll wait...Olivia? Grace. That American that Jean and Alex were so fond of...yes, John Miller...He's been injured...No, not dead, but severely injured...Yes, at the American Hospital....His sister's there, she just called me...Yes, I'll do what's needed...Yes, ...Yes, ...oh, *thank* you..."

***

The conversation was brief and to the point. "Winston, you know I would not ask if it were not vital, but we need action now. He's badly hurt. If you could get Lord Favington permission to have a look, the Montefalcon government would be quite grateful. And as for the rest..."

"Olivia," the Prime Minister replied patiently, "you do not know what you're asking for. Why, it would take a *miracle*..."

"Winston, I made you look good as Armaments Minister in the last war, so you will, by *God*, make *me* look good as a *mother* in this one. Besides," she purred, "what would Clemmie say if you made Alex unhappy, when with a few telephone calls...?"

"Olivia, you leave my wife and my goddaughter out of this." He stared at her at first with malice, then with a touch of admiration, then with desperation. "Oh, *bloody* hell." He picked up the telephone impatiently. "Get me Brooke; yes, *immediately!*"

***

Field Marshal Alan Brooke, Chief of the Imperial Staff, was not accustomed to official callers so late in the day, and certainly none who were unannounced and anonymous, regardless of the PM's assurances. Nonetheless, he prepared to receive his visitor with his usual fastidiousness.

Aroused by a great commotion outside his office he rose from behind his desk in alarm as two Special Branch officers swept into the room, followed immediately—to his surprise and dismay—by Her Serene Highness Princess Margaret Alexandra Victoria Charlwood-Mountbatten of Montefalcon, General Andre Vauchand of the Montefalcon Air Force (who had been a Group Captain until the afternoon before), and Captain Steve Groves of the Coldstream Guards (also known as the 9th Duke of Blandon); in all, probably the last people he had expected to see.

"Field Marshal," the princess began, "this is a request of a somewhat personal nature, but with ramifications that strike at the highest levels of the alliance. The King, my step-father, has requested that he be flown out of Switzerland to Britain immediately, and that a Doctor Foer, his personal neurologist, accompanies him. His Highness Prince Jean will fly to Geneva tonight. Can you help us?"

"Ah, your Highness, I would be happy to..." Brooke stammered.

"Most urgent, we're told," Vauchand explained, "my government has directed us to create a diversion on the North Sea coast. We hope that a diversion of yours, with one of ours, may be more effective..."

"Yes, absolutely," the Field Marshal managed. "I shall contact Pound and Portal at once. Is there anything..."

"Oh yes indeed," the Duke of Blandon added. We have arranged for Lord Favington for a consultation on an American patient who is a friend of the Crown. There's an American doctor who should arrive at London Airport in a few hours. Can you see that he's escorted to the American Hospital with dispatch?"

"Naturally, milord; naturally."

***

And thus began the Great Raid of 1943, marking the first combat mission of the Montefalcon Air Force since the spring of 1940. Two Type XXI submarines and twenty other vessels were sunk or damaged by cannon-firing Lightnings and accompanying Mosquitos at Zeebrugge. Naval gunfire accounted for another score of damaged vessels all along the Dutch coast. Further north, the surprise air attack at Ostend sank a German destroyer at its moorings. The spectacular attack, sometimes called the German Pearl Harbor, was without a single Allied loss.

Leading the Zeebrugge attack was a small group of B-17s that dropped thousands of incendiaries on the docks and quays, led by a Fortress that more than one German survivor swore had a Cossack painted on the nose.

***

After such catastrophic losses, Kaltz wondered, how could we ever be whole again? He watched as Thielmann wrote his brief report as the senior surviving officer. His dark eyes were filled with tears, but his hand was as steady as stones. Then, Kaltz realized Thielmann was talking to him. "What time was our first launch, sir?"

Kaltz looked down at the unit diary. "At 1203; first reported contact was twenty minutes later, at 1225. Can you recall who else was attacking them?"

Thielmann looked puzzled, then determined. "Other than the flak, Bromberg was just withdrawing. *Whose* mad idea was it we attack through the flak over Schweinfurt? There's no better protected place in western Germany!"

"You heard the edict. 'To compensate for your cowardice,' *Dicke Herman* exclaimed, 'you will attack through the flak over all German cities.' You heard it when I did."

Thielmann flashed an angry face. "Our 'cowardice' has wiped us out. What will he say now?"

"What he needs to say to stay alive."

***

Cecil Thornton, Lord Favington, Chief of Neurology of the Royal Medical College, Most Distinguished Fellow of the Royal Society of Physicians, and Royal Neurosurgeon by Appointment of His Britannic Majesty King George VI peered carefully into Miller's left eye, shaking his great, shaggy mane ever so slightly. Good Lord, he mused to himself, no apparent damage. Pulse weak but steady, EEG inconclusive, but vitals are strong. Carefully, he formed his questions to the doctor standing beside him. "Ice, you say?"

"Yessir," Cooper replied, while thinking please, please, please don't ask how I got the idea. I'll have to make up something grand and dramatic instead of the truth, which is...a cat fell in an icebox.

"Where would you have gotten that notion?"

Oh Christ, here it comes. "I had a patient with a nail stuck in his head. On a hunch, I used ice to reduce the cranial swelling, which also seemed to reduce any secondary damage, especially to forebrain function. The major's face was already cold from the wind blast through his windshield, and I came to believe it was what kept him going. I just sought to preserve what a happy accident had already saved..."

"Why didn't we think of it before? Serendipity itself!" Favington exclaimed. "Why, my good fellow, you've not only saved this young man's life, but you've initiated an entirely new course of treatment for brain trauma! We must publish immediately! Tell me, where did you get your training?"

"Howard University and East Tennessee State, sir," Cooper replied carefully.

"You must be the Doctor Cooper who completely reorganized our parasitology studies."

Huh? "Yessir," Cooper replied, "but all I did was..."

"Bring veterinary training into human medicine," Favington finished with a flourish. "And long past time, frankly. I knew a Doctor Havens from Howard University, worked in India. Do you know him?"

"He was one of my instructors, sir."

"Of course; he had some insight into the prevention of malaria. Do you have any interest in malaria?"

"Some, yessir...but as for our current patient, should we plan on removing the splinter?"

Late October 1943

Now the war has become invisible to me;
A visiting spectre...
All that is left now is for the soul to endure it,
Agony and catastrophe are perhaps no more common than before,
Only more real, more active, more visible

Rainer Maria Rilke

The telephone was an unwelcome interruption of Zimmer's train of thought; it was late at night and he was thinking of another prostitute.

"Hallo; Zimmer here. What is it?" He listened intently to the voice. "Where is this pilot...Put him on...be careful what you say....yes... yes... are you certain...the markings must be exact...yes...very well; put the inspector back on...get that statement in writing and get that pilot to a safe place."

He hung up, thought for a moment, and then picked up the receiver again, switching it impatiently. "Get my car ready, and my best...let's see...*Gestapo* uniform. Yes, I am serious. Pack food for three days. We leave within the hour for Bad Kissingen."

***

Eaker sat quietly at the end of the table as the officer droned on. "... And given current pipeline loss rates of under 1% we should be able to make these casualties good in just under three months."

The other senior Eighth Air Force officers—Group, Wing and Division commanders, senior staff, and Spaatz from Fighter Command—had been listening to the dimensions of the Schweinfurt disaster all night. Over three hours of air battle, sixty ships lost, over a hundred returned that would never fly again, three groups with over fifty percent casualties of aircraft launched. And the fighters and one entire Bomb Division never even took off. Altogether, more than six hundred men killed, wounded or missing on the last mission to Schweinfurt—nearly fifteen percent of VIII Bomber Command in a single mission. Coupled with the losses over Munster the previous Sunday, Eighth Air Force had lost thirty percent of its bomber strength in less than a week. Pickett's Charge was only slightly less catastrophic. All for less than five hundred tons of bombs dropped, of which less than a quarter would have had any real effect.

Now if everybody here isn't shipped to Alaska on the next leaky boat, he thought bitterly, Hap Arnold and George Marshall ought to be cashiered. I'll be lucky if I'm not shot.

***

"These are serious charges, Thielmann. You answer them by giving me lies and superstitions. Surrendering his airplane, you say. Well, the destroyer pilot tells a different tale. And where were you when your comrades were fighting the Americans over Schweinfurt? Out hunting a ghost?"

"As I said, I arrived at the scene far from Schweinfurt, where I wanted to shoot down the American. But he was lowering his landing gear, and the *Luftwaffe* has recognized that signal since we started using it over England during the Channel battle. The destroyer pilot was simply too preoccupied to see it, that's all. And I had permission from Colonel Kaltz to pursue this American because he shot down my wingman. It's really that simple."

"That SIMPLE!" Zimmer raged. "These murderous gangsters, these American thug-Jews are killing innocent children and you accept their surrender!?!? That's not simple, Thielmann. That's TREASON!"

Zimmer drew nearer, his small doll's eyes shining dully in triumph, stinking sweat breaking out on his forehead. "I've got you now, Thielmann; you and your whole rotten family. I've got you all now. You'll hang for this, Thielmann, you'll hang!" Roughly Zimmer jerked Thielmann out of his chair, pushing him towards two NCOs by the door. "You, Kaltz," Zimmer shot the older man a glance. "You will be next. Your unit has only hours to live. Make preparations to end your career honorably, Colonel, if you have the courage," Zimmer sneered as he left, following his men.

***

The reporters and senior officers huddled around the beds as the crew of *Crop Duster* spun an amazing tale: "... I seen this FW come up and I figured he was gonna hit us sure. He did, too...Yeah, that's right; twenty thousand feet of power dive, pulled out like it was nothin', on just two engines and the controls shot away...I'm tellin' ya, that's what happened. He fishtailed this two engine 'Fort in the face of a dozen Kraut fighters.... no, I ain't gonna ever drink again; took the pledge right then and there I did...Yeah, right through the windscreen. Fired that old 'forty five at them Nazis as they was comin' at us, and him losing all that blood and all, yelling for them to get away. Damn if that Hun didn't go down in flames...Naw, I was outta ammo, I'm tellin' ya. Now didn't I tell you guys to pass me up some...And then this FW jumps in front of this jackal and flies right in front of him for maybe five minutes. Damnedest thing I ever did see...Came down on that runway just as easy as you please, flared and dropped and that's all there was to it..."

By God, the generals thought, we may just be able to pull a legend out of this cock-up yet.

Great copy, the press flaks thought, I can see the movies now, with Bogart firing a forty-five as Hun fighters swarm around, or maybe Cagney...

Now don't you be shooting your mouths off about that FW, the public relations officers admonished; not until we figure out what went on. Can't have everybody out there thinking there's some guardian angel out there...

***

It was evening when Gillette and King found Witt alone in his room. The lieutenant was just having his legs redressed when the two officers came in. "Sir, Ned" he groggily nodded to his squadron commander and intelligence officer, "I take it this is not a social call."

"Well," King said, moving a chair next to Witt's bunk, "I didn't bring any charge sheets, but we really gotta know what went on up there." Witt shook his head wearily, as if to shake off a dream.

"Didn't buy the crew's story, huh?" King shook his head slowly, regretfully.

"It's not a question of me buying it. It's a matter of someone being able to sell it."

"Well, I tell ya, with a few exceptions—we never had less than three engines—what we told the reporters was God's truth." He paused to let it sink in for a moment. "God's truth." he repeated.

"Start at the beginning, Gerry," Gillette said. "We really gotta know. There's some big-assed brass wants to hand out a bunch of medals and we need the *truth*, or at least something we can make look good."

Witt reached into a drawer and fished out a piece of wadded notepaper, handing it to Gillette. After flattening it out, he peered at it carefully. "Where'd you come across this?"

"The FW pilot flashed it at us just after we crossed the coast. I've tried to break it, but it's just gibberish. Make any sense to you?"

"Nope, I know what it is, though; tap code the *Luftwaffe* uses when they can't use radios. Uses old *Fraktur* characters that were never translated into American Morse. That's why you can't read it." Gillette pocketed the note. "I'll run it past some friends of mine in cryptanalysis— they'll break it in no time. It may take some interpretation, though; doesn't translate that well." He motioned to King to go out of the room, handing him the note as they left. "If this is what I think it is, it is proof positive that at least some of the crew's story is true because the only people that see tap code are *Luftwaffe* pilots."

"Yeah, but then what," King muttered. "There's some goody two-shoes flying top cover for crippled Fortresses? Do we want to make that case?"

"No," Gillette said with finality. "But we can make a case that not every German is a butcher all the time, that 'clemency of the enemy' isn't just propaganda. We can say that if Collova and all the others like him hit the ground alive, they may be OK." He thought briefly about the markings that Farr wrote, adding up in his head what his score would have been, and more important what the whole thing meant.

Some German ace saves an American bomber from destruction? Why?

***

Kaltz contemplated his future, the future of his country and his unit as he reached into the bottom drawer of his desk. Removing the contents, he pushed on the front edge of the bottom. The spring popped the false bottom out, revealing a small notebook. Paging through the numbers, he reached for the telephone receiver, dialing carefully. "Karinhall, please....Frau Karin, please, Heinrich Kaltz here...Bunny; this is Hoso. My last leader was just arrested. A Gestapo thug named Zimmer.... yes... yes, thank you..." and the line went dead. He hung up the receiver and nodded to Steger, who was waiting by the door. "It is your turn, Steger." The old farmer nodded and left.

**

Steger's journey to the little cottage took all of five minutes, but Elsa was ready for him, near tears. This woman is younger than my oldest daughter, Steger thought, but already she's a widow...perhaps twice. He bundled her into the car and drove to the base communications center. The *Unteroffizier* on duty, who had already been told what he was about to do, hustled the operators out of the room. Sitting down again, he rang the connection, already made.

"Mama, do you know where he is?"

"No, dear, I don't, but your father can find out. I don't know that he will, but I can try to ask. I haven't seen him in for some time, but..."

"Thank you, Mother," Elsa said severely. "I knew this would be a waste of time." Both hung up at the same time; Elsa collapsed into Steger's arms...

**

Magda stared severely at her husband just a meter away. "Adam..." she whispered, "If you *don't*..."

He nodded, threw down the dregs of his whiskey and left.

**

Somewhere near midnight, the two officers were walking to their jeep, exhausted from hearing the same unbelievable story at least three times. As the copilot said, it was essentially as the crew had said it: Miller had flown the plane nearly all the way back with at least a quarter of his brain gone, vision in one eye at least impaired if not lost completely, and having lost more blood than anyone thought was possible. "Could it be, sir, that it really happened that way?" Gillette asked his commander.

"Ned," Throck groaned, dragging heavily on his cigarette, "I have no idea if it's possible or not. I've seen some pretty amazing things with sheer determination and airplane strength. You saw what they left of his ship; you know he couldn't have flown on manual control. You know what the medics said—a quarter of his brain gone, and was probably at least half blind—he could not have flown that ship. I don't know what's possible, but I know that what that young lieutenant just told us is what's going in my report and I'll be *damned* if anyone will dispute it. They may kick my ass out, but I'll see to it that that young man gets the highest medal his country can award, or my name ain't Boris Vissaryonovitch Throck."

***

Thielmann felt nothing but pain. He was still in his flying suit, stinking of old sweat, blood, and filth. The small cell was of cement block and poured sand, not quite two meters high or a meter in any direction. A bare bulb dangled over his head, and leaking pipes above it dripped cold water down his cell wall. In his waking moments, he considered his future, but Elsa was the most consistent image that came to his mind. *What have I gotten you into, my darling one? What lies ahead for us?*

The hours—or days...he didn't know which—since his arrest were a painful blur. They had methodically beaten him in a long room with pipes on the walls and benches down the middle while tied or chained or handcuffed to stools, chairs, pipes or a post. No questions were asked, and no tools were used. Only rarely was he hit in the face. The blows to his chest, kidneys, and abdomen had been bad enough. He had soiled himself and was subjected to alternate cold and hot water sprays, then dumped into this cell, a routine repeated over and over again until he had completely lost track of time. He'd been given a crust or two of bread from time to time between beatings. He had eaten nothing substantial since his cheese, coffee and bread just before he launched after...*Crop Duster*, was it...?

***

"Sorry Ira, but the brass just doesn't have any confidence in daylight precision bombing anymore." Doolittle let the idea soak in. "We just don't have the know-how, the gear or the numbers yet to make it work. I know you and Hap and Possum barked about it for years, but this Schweinfurt mess..."

"Yeah, I know, Jimmy. So what's Hap want me to do? Just go home?"

"No, no, nothing like that. We have something else planned for you in the Mediterranean. For *now,* for *here* anyway, we're saying that the self- protecting bomber is a failed concept," Doolittle said with finality. "Should have been twenty years ago when Larry Miller said it was nuts. We all knew the truth two years ago—when the Brits proved it— we just didn't want to admit it. We knew that pursuit aviation and bombardment aviation were just two sides of the same coin, but we let Congress think that the less expensive option—bombers—would be all we needed. But then we kept developing fighters, and so did everybody else. Now the fighters have the advantage. Maybe someday the bombers will, but right now they don't."

"So now what?" Eaker grunted.

"Well, there's a new plan. We think that strategic bombing still may have its merits, but with our current know-how and numbers, we're going to treat it as a means to an end. Under 'Pointblank,' we're to get air superiority over Europe for the cross-Channel invasion. To do that, we have to knock out the *Luftwaffe.* That means meeting their fighter force in the air and on the ground and killing their best pilots while draining their resources. Simply put, we detach the fighters from direct escort. Then the bombers..."

"Are bait," Eaker said, thinking of the sacrifices of his friends, the random, hopeless struggle over Germany. "They have to *try* to intercept the bombers—for *political* reasons—but we jump them before they get that far."

"That's right. Their propaganda machine and their whole justification for a war-based economy and consumer shortages depends on their intercepting, on their fighting back, on the only fighting front that the public can really see without Goebbels' interpretation—the one right over their heads. The bombers draw the fighters up and we pick them off. No other way to get them to come up that we can figure."

"Didn't the *Luftwaffe* try that on the RAF in '40?"

"Yes, but they got sidetracked into letting the RAF off the hook and blitzing London. Besides, the Brit's resources were pretty limited then, and ours aren't. Hell, the way our intelligence is reading it, the *Luftwaffe* loses more pilots in accidents than our bombers shoot down. Doesn't mean we'll take the guns out of the bombers. Just means we'll rely more on the fighters for now, using strategic bombing as bait for air superiority."

Doolittle was quiet again, staring out the window. All those men, all that sweat, all that emotional and physical capital, spent for bait.

God damn it, Larry, why didn't we listen...

***

The crude slab door to the cell swung open once again, and two burly NCOs pulled him up by the shoulders. "Up," one of them grunted into his ear, "play the good traitor." Too weak and bruised to walk, he allowed himself to be carried while his feet dragging behind. Once again, he was delivered to the long room with pipes on the walls and benches down the center. They plopped him onto a chair and shackled him to a pipe while a pair of officers watched from his right. Zimmer, resplendent in a dress uniform, observed with relish.

"So, Thielmann, we come to the end of our time together," Zimmer started, strutting slowly in front of him. "I am pleased to report that your entire family has been arrested, as I promised." He stopped, allowing his statement to sink in. Thielmann barely moaned, grunted. "They are being most cooperative, of course, and your wife," he paused, raising Thielmann's chin with a gloved thumb, "has dutifully reported to my suite in the SS officer's barracks." He drew close to Thielmann's face, grinning. Thielmann looked back dully. "She is not yet...compliant, but that is merely a matter of time. And training, of course; a great deal of training." He let Thielmann go and strutted away. "When we catch up to your sister—the Japanese authorities are being most helpful—she, too, will comply after much, much training."

He turned in the dank glare, clicking his heels together. "These... gentlemen...are going to take you away to be disposed of like the sack of filth that you are. My only regret is that I cannot put the noose around your foul neck as I am called to higher things, thanks to your family's treason and my ruthless pursuit of that treason."

He quickly strode back to Thielmann, who barely understood what was going on and had little recognition of what was being said. Zimmer grabbed Thielmann's hair and yanked until the back of his head nearly reached his back. "When I killed that old man, Thielmann, it was because he was an enemy of the Party and I serve the Party," Zimmer spat. "When I destroy your family, it will be because they are enemies of the state, and I serve the state. You were unwise to dismiss me all these years. Take that into the next life." Zimmer tossed Thielmann's head away, and it lolled around like a rag doll's. "Take this piece of shit away to the punishment he deserves." They unshackled Thielmann from the chair, picked up roughly and carried down the long room. The two officers followed.

The haunting image of the torchlight parade in Nurnberg came back to Thielmann, intermixed with Zimmer's gloating face and the reek of his sweat under the cologne. And there are far more Americans than there are Germans, he thought, remembering the words of long ago, an age almost forgotten...

I fear these Americans and Russians, for they do not fear us...

***

"General Eaker for General Arnold....Hap? Ira. I think we should send Boris Throck on that job with Possum Hansell... I don't *care* if he's a Russian, and I know *damn well* you don't either...because he's the bravest sonofabitch in the Air Force and one *helluva* operator, that's why, and we need Boris the Bastard out there..."

***

Alois Zimmer's life was transformed from apparent obscurity to the highest exaltation in the Nazi party. They promoted him to Colonel in the Waffen SS, presented him with a personally autographed photograph of Heinrich Himmler, congratulated him by telephone for smashing the "Thielmann ring," and put on a special train bound for his new unit.

That evening, as he was being pleasured by a cinema actress in his stateroom aboard a train plunging through the night, Zimmer felt he was finally getting the much deserved and long-overdue recognition of his talents.

***

Ernie King and Clay Cole stared at the manning board, wishing it yielded some more palatable answers. No complete crews with more than five missions; no complete crews that had been together for more than six; only eight operational ships and all would be in the shop for at least a week. With the air exec in a coma, the next senior officer on flying status was a first lieutenant. "What in the hell are we supposed to do?" King asked.

"Whatever it is we can do," Cole answered. "Ten new ships to the group. We get three. Seven new crews available: we get them all." He threw the paper down on his desk. "We started from scratch two years ago; we'll do it again now." He glanced at the status board. "First flight, lead ship: *Adam's Apple*; Pilot Lieutenant John Hudson; backup Lieutenant Michael Hall. Second flight, lead ship..."

***

Kaltz threw back another brandy, hardly feeling it burn any more. Another week like this one and the Allies would be completely unopposed over most of western Germany. Another week like that third week in October and the *Luftwaffe* would be finished. The alerting network had been completely overwhelmed, there were no spare parts or aircraft left, pilots were being put on intercepts with less than fifty hours of training, fuel was used only for intercepts and other mission-essential purposes (none for training), and still the Americans and British came on as if the hundreds of planes they lost were as nothing, merely a beginning. He had a vision of a continuous cloud of American and British planes covering Germany, blocking out the sun and the stars. He thought if that American Thielmann saved would train just two more like himself, and those could train another four...it was near torture to dwell on it.

The Giant Killers were no more. Taube and Bär were dead; Pritzler had a shattered pelvis and may never sit up again, let alone fly. Germany lost a hundred planes in a week to combat and non-combat causes, and at least as many pilots. The Americans could make such losses up in a month, Kaltz thought, but we can never replace those pilots.

But the Americans had not turned back, not in the face of the *Luftwaffe*. The Americans fought their way through to the target, fought their way back, and through it all, not once did they retreat in the face of German opposition. That their bombing was inaccurate did not matter, Kaltz knew, because every time the Americans and the British approached an important target, the *Luftwaffe* had to rise to fight. In the early days, the RAF had turned away from strong opposition, but the Americans never did. The *Luftwaffe* high command gloated that the Americans were beaten, that Germany had achieved air supremacy over Europe once again, that they will never lose it, and that Germany will rise from the minor setbacks of recent months to its ultimate destiny.

***

Throck set the flimsy aside, contemplating his future. His transfer to the Twentieth Air Force was a promotion of sorts. Why were they giving him command of a bomb wing in India, of all places? He thought Hansell, who would be his immediate superior, was a fine flyer, but in command...? Throck had orders for that Zeebrugge stunt...well, he had orders for a low-level strike, which perhaps did not *mean* "strafe with B-17 machine guns," and that big 'X' he painted on the target may have been taking his hand-drawn orders too far. Had he been so angered...he thought again about his last conversation with Eaker. Eaker was a good man and a brave flyer, but he was also a practical man. He didn't want someone as insubordinate as Boris the Bold under his command. Was this a demotion, then?

***

Thielmann could remember snatches, bare images, and impressions of the next few moments—or hours—he couldn't decide which. He found himself in a bathhouse, seated in a hard yet comfortable chair. A uniformed physician was examining him, peering into his eyes and ears, holding his mouth open. His flying suit had been removed, yet the bathhouse was warm and damp.

"He has at least three broken ribs, and I don't like those bruises on his abdomen," the doctor was saying. "He needs to be seen by an internist and he needs x-rays. I fear for his spleen."

"How serious is it?" someone behind Thielmann asked. "Would it be too dangerous to wait another day?"

The doctor palpitated under his ribcage, and Thielmann grimaced. "He needs a hospital tonight; now. How does that feel, Captain?" the doctor asked as he pushed hard into Thielmann's lower gut.

"It hurts. I had an ulcer repaired..."

"I know." Thielmann stared at the doctor for a long moment, not understanding. "Now, Captain, I understand this fellow here is to help you get cleaned up." Thielmann was too ill to struggle with the well-groomed and impeccably dressed older man who bathed him, shaved him, and combed his hair with remarkable speed and efficiency. As they stuffed Thielmann into a coverall, he felt as if he were meat for the sausage press. Someone offered a small glass of brandy, which he choked down, followed by a glass of distilled water, surprisingly chilled in the warm bathhouse. They gave him bread and sausage on an elegant porcelain plate, which he nibbled at. He didn't feel at all well, but he was too hungry to ignore the food. Suddenly, he was alone on a well-upholstered divan—his time sense completely gone—as he drifted in and out of a light sleep.

Finally he was awakened when a *Sicherheitsdienst* Colonel with close-cropped hair, a lantern jaw, and peculiarly china-blue eyes gently jostled him. "Captain Thielmann," the senior man whispered, "come with us, please." An *Unteroffizier* helped Thielmann up and out of the bathhouse to a limousine idling on a hard-packed gravel drive in the late day sun.

Thielmann was sick, hurt in many places, hungry and confused, but he could add up a few things. If he were in real trouble, the Security Service would not be calling him by his rank. His last clear memory was his being hauled off by Zimmer, with clear threats to his family and his unit. "Come with us, please" did not fit into that equation.

It had apparently rained during the day, and the damp mixed with the clear mountain air was like a tonic to Thielmann's tired brain. By the time he had staggered, then walked ten meters, he felt as if he'd slept for a week. He entered the front car door held open by a *Feldwebel*. Inside, sitting behind the steering wheel, was an SD Colonel. Thielmann could have sworn he had seen those eyes before. "First, Captain," the Colonel began, "I want to congratulate you on your success. One hundred twenty victories, is it?

"One hundred and twenty-two," Thielmann responded dully, suddenly exhausted in the dry heat of the limousine. The rain started again, rhythmically drumming on the roof and leaving cat's paws of rain on the windshield. "Thank you."

"Here," the Colonel pushed a heavy portfolio across the seat at Thielmann. "There are the police, SD and *Gestapo* files on you, your family and some of your unit. Your father's record has been replaced by one that tidies up some of his associations so he can continue to work with the *Abwehr*. Your uncle's record is nearly spotless, but with the *Gestapo*, one can never tell. If they have no record, they can't come for him. I have included your wife's files...short, but there nonetheless. Her uncle's files have been destroyed...all of them. It was safer that way. Besides, there were so many." Thielmann glanced at the contents, not believing what he held. "I am to tell you that the Luftwaffe may be young, but it has a long memory." Thumbing numbly through the papers

Thielmann marveled tiredly at the number of stamps and agencies that had reported on the activities of a handful of patriotic Germans. Something called a "resettlement office," a "sanitary commission," and even a "labor bureau," had something to say about everyone. Germany survived on stamps and files, suspicion and inquiries.

"Zimmer said that Elsa..."

"Yes, I know. She is quite safe." Thielmann tried to push the heavy folder back, but it was pushed away again. The Colonel turned briefly to face Thielmann, and Thielmann thought he recognized something in his face, something long forgotten. "No, you dispose of it as you see fit. Those flimsies, you know, make terrific toilet paper."

He returned his gaze to the front, nodding towards another limousine rolling up the road. "In a few hours, you will be in a *Luftwaffe* hospital. Your wife will meet you there." The car stopped and Steger jumped out of the passenger's seat. Standing in the rain by the back door with an umbrella, he stood at a rigid attention like a statue, holding the umbrella as if it were a rifle on his shoulder. "You should go, Thielmann. Good luck to you." The Colonel held out his hand. "I should hope that the next time we meet, it might be under better circumstances."

Thielmann shook the hand briefly. "Perhaps..." he began.

"Just go." The Colonel had turned cold, commanding. "And don't forget this." Thielmann took the folder, opened the door, and Steger rushed across the gravel, opening the umbrella as he approached. Thielmann hesitated, staring back at the Colonel. What was it, he wondered, that made him so familiar?

***

As the limousine turned around and sped away, the Colonel stared after it for a long moment. "*Herr General*," he said at last, "I have obeyed you, followed your guidance, and done your errands since you pulled me out of that gutter years ago. I never asked questions. I have had to do things that are distasteful, both to get ahead and at your behest. But this time," he pushed open the curtain behind the seat and twisted around to face the rear seat's occupant: a broadly built, meticulously groomed man in his late fifties, dressed in a dapper suit of the finest gabardine. "I am completely at a loss for explanations. What just happened, and why? I have watched that swine for some months for you, not understanding what he was up to...or why you wanted to know until...I found the marriage certificate in Hamburg." A tear formed in the corner of the Colonel's eye.

Adam Greitz steyer von Lutzow-Verein gazed out the window, as if to interpret the rain. "My daughter must never know my role in all of this. Our little ruse might work for now."

"'The Luftwaffe has a long memory?' What of it? You are his father-in-law..."

"That is precisely why, my dear Baumer. While it was Goering who called me, it was because Kaltz called his wife. Imagine how Dicke Hermann must have felt being goaded by his wife's cousin into intervening in Himmler's realm! Ha! The very thought of it!"

"But the records..."

"Destroying the official existence of Thielmann's family and friends will prevent any of Zimmer's friends—and even little turds like him have friends—from taking matters into their own hands. But not even Goering can destroy an official existence the way we can."

Lutzow-Verein sipped wine out of a crystal goblet. "Eventually, my daughter or her husband will put what we've done together, but that is for later." He paused, shifting his gaze out the window. "I can see that Otto Thielmann is a good man, a smart man. Elsa has chosen well." He spoke with some pride, the pride of a father. "But for now, the further my daughter is from me, the more I can protect her from the wrath of the future. You, Adelmar Baumer, know as well as I do that this loathsome Nazi edifice cannot endure for our lifetime. When it crumbles, he and she must be far from me."

"When Zimmer destroyed my uncle," Baumer began, "I wanted to..."

"Yes, and you were sensible enough not to take on such a thug. As you rose in the Party, you realized that there were better ways to destroy people like him with grudges and Party cards in the New Germany. Now come, we must be off."

Spring 1945

So, stand to your glasses, steady;
This world is a world of lies
Then here's a toast to the dead already
Hurrah for the next man who dies

Bartholomew Dowling

The comparative cool of the office was welcoming to Witt as he walked in from the fiery glare of the Pacific sun. It wasn't even summer yet, he mused, and already we're cooking. He was ushered down the short corridor, created by communications cubicles and filing cabinets. Above the door, the sign read FIRST STRATEGIC SERVICES WING (PATHFINDER/WEATHER), and below it read: "Boris V. Throck, BG; Commanding."

Throck was at his desk writing on a flimsy. "Major Witt, sir," the orderly muttered, ushering the young officer through the door and closing it behind him. The air conditioner hummed behind Throck's head, next to a scrawled sign that read, "Speak Up: I Bombed Schweinfurt Twice so I Should Be Dead."

"So you drew short straw," Throck growled, not looking up. He finished his note, placed it in the OUT IMMEDIATE tray, and tossed his pen down. "Before you start the bellyaching, I have news of old friends. Have a seat."

"Thank you, sir." Witt was grateful even for the wooden folding chair. The drive from one end of the Tinian base to the other was three miles in the equatorial sun. Witt had already heard about Farr, who had died of peritonitis just a few weeks before, and about Ernie King who had been wounded in the spring of '44 and invalided home.

"So, first off, your pal Miller, based on three citations, was awarded the Distinguished Service Cross and is now up for a Medal of Honor."

"Jeez," Witt whistled, "how is he?"

343

"Home, finally. He started walking on his own just before Christmas, '43. Spent six months in a hospital in England, shipped back to the 'States last June. He wrangled himself a job up in Wisconsin, something about emergency landings. With all his press, it was hard to say no. That head wound, though, is not very photogenic. The war bonds people don't want any part of him."

"Wow. So, he's flying again?"

Throck paused, blinked briefly, pulled out a cigar, and pointed it at Witt.

"You know better. That kind of head injury...he'll never fly again for the Air Forces. Same goes for Reynolds. We don't know what might happen with oxygen deprivation or low temperature." He lit the cigar. "Some investigators are coming from Washington to see you in a few days. Make yourself available. But Milliken, remember him? Died in his sleep last November...I just got the twix here...found his birth certificate among his effects. He was born on 23 January 1880, which made him sixty-four." Throck made an incredulous face. "*Helluva* gunner though, eh? Nineteen kills on his sheet. He used his son's birth certificate to join the Army. Apparently, the boy got killed on Guam. The Marines were trying to clear up the records for some medal or other, found the discrepancy in Social Security numbers."

"Wow," Witt agreed, remembering his feisty neighbor. "Some story there. But, about tomorrow's strike: the bomb wings are concerned about a few things. No formations to save fuel; incendiary-heavy because of the paper buildings; even night bombing to cut down on the fighter threat, but they need the gunners on board. Can't see the whole airplane, you see."

Throck appeared to be deep in thought for an instant. "OK, I get it: I'll get Lemay to take out all but the tail guns, and leave all the gunners aboard. How's that?"

"OK," Witt agreed, "but the flight level: ten thousand? They'll be sitting ducks..."

"Well, we haven't seen any night-fighters yet," Throck began, "and Jap flak gunners are a modest threat at worst. At night, maybe not at all: tech intel is saying their radar is very primitive. The reason for the low level—and the lack of formations—is that the Boeing reps think the engines are blowing up so much because of inadequate warm-up. Lower the flight level, the temperature difference disappears...."

***

It was the symmetry of the Comet that Thielmann particularly admired. As he walked around the last three rocket fighters left on the field, he wondered at the terrors his pilots must have felt as they rocketed into the *Viermot* formations. He knew that nothing either the Americans or the Russians flew could shoot them down, but he also knew that his pilots could barely land their...kites... safely. The only reason he got the job of instructor to this unit was his experience with gliders, and these things spent most of their time as heavy, clumsy gliders.

But his affections were not with the rockets, but with the Arrows that sat, elegant and eager, at the end of his long runways near the launching ramps and over the hydrazine tanks. The odd-looking Dornier push-pull interceptors were far more dangerous to allied pilots than the rockets, and the German pilot casualties were far fewer. The Arrows flew with regular aviation fuel that would irritate a flyer if it leaked; the Comet's fuel dissolved pilots.

Gunther seemed to hear something off in the distance, but could respond only with shifting eyes and a slight whimper. The veterinarian did not know how old he was, but he seemed to simply be wearing out. He'd been slowing down for a year, and now as they waited for the Americans to come, Thielmann would do what he needed to do for his old friend. A small syringe of morphine was all it would take.

His men had left; Thielmann had received orders to move them to Spangdahlem, but couldn't bring himself to send his boys to another unit to stave off the inevitable. Instead, he abolished his tiny command (as a newly minted Lieutenant Colonel he could do that, or so his clerk said, based on a century-old Prussian law), discharged the men and sent them all home. Steger had wanted to stay, but Thielmann had ordered him demobilized and sent him home under an escort. Thielmann hoped he could get there before the Russians, so he could evacuate his family.

As the sun rose and another pod of Mustangs flew overhead, Thielmann pressed the trigger on the explosive charge that touched off the rocket fuel and destroyed the Arrows under their camouflage nets, and blew the launching ramps apart. Now, the Comets were just so much metal.

Going back to his car, Gunther did not stir; his eyes languorous. Goodbye, old friend, Thielmann thought, a tear welling in his eye as he pushed the hypodermic into his flank. He was happy that poor Gunther, a veteran of many campaigns, passed—like Kaltz had last Christmas—of more-or-less natural causes.

There was, however, some small measure of solace, in that another dog had found Thielmann, a smaller one than Gunther, but perhaps just as eager and attentive as Gunther had been so long ago. Thielmann called him Heinrich.

It was Heinrich that first barked at the American vehicles that roared onto the airfield that afternoon. An American Major with pilot's wings speaking fluent German questioned him just after dark. "You disbanded your unit based on an Imperial regulation from...1876?" Ned Gillette seemed incredulous.

"Yes. The old regulations were never truly repealed, you see. They were...suspended...between Versailles and 1936." That's what his clerk had said, and that's what he was saying to all comers.

Gillette chuckled lightly. "Well, you know, there will probably be a new German Air Force some day. Hope you can sell that one to them."

"Well, what of it? The *Gestapo* can't arrest me now." Gillette nodded in agreement.

"No, but your men won't get their mustering-out pay..."

"They already got it..."

"In *Reichmarcks*, yes? They'll be worthless..."

"No: in old *Geldmarcks*. I don't know where they came from, but we had just enough to pay off the men."

Gillette looked impressed, but surprised. "How would you know...?"

"Believe me, Major," Thielmann said, recalling the snippet of conversation from decades before, "I know."

***

The formation was neat, tidy even. *Unteroffizier* Georg-Hans Thielmann marched carefully down the ranks of old men, children, invalids and government officials that made up the parade of the Marburg Defense Battalion. In the group's front, braving the chilly wind from the east in his outdated uniform, was Generalmajor Peter von Lutzow-Verein. Separate, yet part of this assembly was another formation of some three hundred *Polizei*, firemen, and other civil warriors in uniform, fronted by over a hundred refugees from as many army and *Flakartillerie* units that had reached Marburg ahead of the onslaught, the lot commanded by a tired and frightened Captain from an engineer unit. Satisfied that he could do little else, Georg-Hans marched forward to report to his commander.

"*Herr General*: Four hundred and nine *Soldaten* are in formation and awaiting instructions."

"Thank you, Thielmann," the old general growled, barely able to be heard over the battering wind. "I believe instructions are coming from just up the road."

A light tank, armored car and jeep that rattled over the hill just a few moments later stopped just below the crest. A figure stood up in the jeep, appeared to be scanning the horizon around the formations, and began moving again, slowly rolling towards the town. The armored car and tank rolled off the road on either side, turrets twisting, searching warily.

Two halftracks topped the crest and pulled off the road, their infantrymen spilling onto the wide and nascent fields. The Germans watched passively. Two more tanks crested the hill and spread behind the infantry. The jeep stopped some ten meters from where the officers stood. A figure in the back of the jeep brandished a submachine gun, standing on the seat, while the driver and front seat passenger got out. The driver unslung a carbine; the passenger drew on a cigar.

"*Guten morgen*," the passenger drawled in a passable *Hochdeutch*. "*Hier ist Marburg?*"

"*Ja*," the old general replied, and then continued in English. "This is the Marburg garrison. We do not wish to fight."

"So we understand," the passenger, a stubby major of infantry, answered. "My German is not that good, *Herr General*. An interpreter will be here momentarily." He looked around the formation, still searching for potential traps. "We are to disarm you and begin processing your people. First, we need the *Gestapo...*"

A staff car speeded down the hill from behind them, honking a horn furiously. As the staff car skidded to a halt, a half-dozen men clambered to the road, led by an American brigadier general.

"Halt," a German in a badge-less army uniform shouted from the general's side. "Don't move unless instructed." The American general walked slowly up to the German. "Major General von Lutzow-Verein, I believe. Brigadier General Robert Lee Lesard," the American drawled, "West Point Class of '30," as he threw off a snappy and crisp salute. The interpreter, with a broad Bavarian accent, rattled off the greeting.

The old General drew himself up to his full height, a full head taller than any of the surrounding Americans. "Lutzow-Verein," he said, "*Bavarische Kriegsakademie* class of 1890. We are your prisoners," he finished, returning the salute. "My officers are at your disposal." Turning slightly, he called over his shoulder. "*Unteroffizier* Thielmann!"

Georg-Hans marched stiffly to the front of the formation. Briefly, his elbow hurt where there had once been an arm, but he dismissed it. Not daring to salute with his left hand, he stopped at the prescribed five paces, clicked his heels, and loudly said, "*Herr General!*"

"These gentlemen wish to disarm our men. Will you please assist them?"

"*Jawohl, Herr General.*" Turning stiffly, Georg-Hans bowed first to his general, then to the American. "Forgive, but *mine* arm *nach* Stalingrad, I leave. *Mine name ist* Thielmann, und *Mine* English *ist* bad *nicht...ich denke*," he struggled mightily, but broke into German at last, "but I have a lad to help..."

"*Ja, ja*," the interpreter interrupted, "they will understand. I would not speak of Stalingrad, however. There are Russians nearby, observers of a sort. Some may not understand. First, we need to speak with the Police President, the fire chief and the head of sanitation. Next, we need to enquire about any combat units in the area."

"Yes, very well. The civic leaders are at the end of the formation there. I must ask, however, if you have a medical staff nearby because our hospital is quite full and our doctors are overworked. We need medical supplies and whatever rations we can get. My niece, you see, is here but is not well..."

***

In a small and crowded barn that passed for a hospital, the SS *Standartenführer* lay on a soiled and crude cot. Alois Zimmer tried with all his remaining strength to determine what had gone wrong with his life. He remembered arriving at his first command, Detachment Zimmer. Of the six hundred men in his command, nearly half of them were Balts and Ukrainian auxiliaries. The Germans roughly described their mission as "rear-area security" but from the day he arrived to take command in November 1943 to the day his last officer died in the air attack on the road between Budapest and Vienna, they never actually engaged any armed partisans. They had, however, hung, shot and burned a great number of civilians for "aiding" the partisans simply by speaking Russian.

He had suffered from malaria since the summer of 1944 and from dysentery since the fall. A few days before he arrived in this hospital, he had contracted diphtheria. Struggling for breath through cracked lips and crackling lungs, he dreamed of parades, burning villages, honor ceremonies, gang rapes, and meeting the *Führer* (which never happened the way he dreamed of it).

The last German he heard said: *Leave them; they won't last long, anyway.*

His last dreams were of a pretty blonde girl from his youth who was far beyond his reach even then.

The last words he heard were guttural Russian: *these are not worth a bullet. Torch the place.*

Fall 1945

Once I moved about like the wind.
Now I surrender to you, and that is all

Geronimo

T he prisoners gathered in small groups—bomber crews and fighter pilots, reconnaissance and dive bomber, German, Italian, Hungarian, Rumanian, and Japanese—as bored men and women in isolation often do. General Galland mounted a platform near the fence, his staff handing him the lists for the day's announcements.

"*Deutcher,*" he called, so that the translators would not try the unfamiliar names. "Aluss!" he shouted, waiting for the response.

"*Jawohl, Mein Herr!*"

"Your brother..."

"Johann..."

"A prisoner in France; Balzer!"

"*Jawohl...*" And so on he went, calling out the names and the dispositions of relatives: camps, homes, graveyards. They announced only those known. The unknown remained silent.

"Thielmann!"

"*Jawohl, Mein Herr!*"

"Congratulations, Thielmann; you have a daughter, born in August. Mother and child are well." A warm glow spread over him while fellow pilots, strangers all, shook his hand. Other detainees in the Technical Intelligence Pool looked on, grinning at the news.

***

The Lieutenant Colonel between the MPs looked somehow smaller than Gillette had remembered, and was followed by a small but clean and well-fed mongrel dog. His uniform, clean and neat but bereft of all badges and insignia like all his fellow detainee uniforms, seemed almost to hang on his massive shoulders. Mud slightly spattered his boots from the tent-city camp where he now lived.

Like his fellows, he spent much of his free time maintaining his appearance since his interrogations/debriefings took up only a few hours each day, and the difficult transition from flying combat to doing essentially nothing was, as yet, wholly incomplete.

"*Herr Colonel*," Gillette greeted him when he drew near.

"Colonel," Colonel Thielmann replied in heavily accented English. Thielmann had been working with several interrogators since they captured him. Most of them he liked or at least respected, except the one who insisted that he answer for the concentration camps, and who kept asking questions about the *Gestapo* and the SS and other organizations that few of the prisoners had direct knowledge of. The others wanted to know about airplanes, engines, tactics, ground control vectoring, military organization, and other pilots. Thielmann and his comrades answered the questions put to them. They only did their duty to their country as they saw it, just like the Americans and the English and the Russians. The Germans just had the bad fortune to lose. But everyone in the camp knew of the trials of leading Nazis at Nuremberg, and they dreaded the day when they were going to be put on trial. Perhaps, Thielmann thought, that's what this Colonel was going to ask him about.

Inside a musty tent, the two colonels sat facing each other with a table between them and a bare electric bulb dangling overhead. A third Colonel sat silently at the end of the table, watching the German. Thielmann idly scratched the dog's ears.

Gillette offered him a cigarette, usually a good sign. "Colonel Thielmann," Gillette began, "are you being well treated? Is there anything you need?"

"Well, yes, in fact. The Japanese in the camp here are not accustomed to our food, and the latrines have become intolerable. Perhaps you could arrange for a change of diet for the Japanese, and more cleaning supplies, bleach especially. The Japanese are far too—no, proud is not correct—stubborn, yes stubborn—to ask themselves." The handful of Japanese flyers from the Pacific was a recent addition to the aviators and technicians at Spangdahlem, and had been a source of some trouble since they arrived, sick and weak, ill- nourished and sullen. I know this man, Thielmann thought, then said, "We have met before, I think." Those days seemed far away.

"Why, yes," Gillette answered, slightly surprised as he scratched down some notes. Thielmann watched the other American out of the corner of one eye. He was a flyer, a very senior flyer, judging by his wings. The other hasn't flown for some time, he thought.

"I'm here to ask about your activities on 14 October 1943, the day of the last big raid on Schweinfurt in '43. Do you remember?" Gillette asked.

"Yes, I remember Schweinfurt. My group was at Bad Kissingen at the time, in FW-190s."

"Are you certain," Gillette said. "I have information that you were still in the ME-109s."

"No," Thielmann replied, familiar with the interrogator's ruse of making the source confirm his own information, "JG191 was always in FW-190s."

"All right; tell me, do you remember one particular Fortress that survived a collision with a Focke-Wulf that day?"

"How could I forget? My best friend flew that Focke-Wulf; killed by our own flak and then collided with the *Viermot*. A stupid waste, really."

"I see," Gillette murmured, writing. "Then, do you remember seeing that same *Festung* over the North Sea a few hours later?" The other American shifted in his chair, cocking his head towards Thielmann.

"Yes, I do," Thielmann answered. "A destroyer was trying to shoot it down, but I intervened, believing it was trying to surrender. Well, I was wrong about that, but I paid for that mistake. The *Gestapo* had me for a time."

"*Ach, so?* Do you remember sending this message to that *Viermot?*" Gillette handed him a copy of the note in the original tap code as Witt had scribbled down. Thielmann read it once, then again, placing it back on the table, a small smile on his face.

"Yes, I recall. It had seemed such a waste, such a fine pilot. Two stupid wastes in one day were just too much for me."

"What does the message say?"

Thielmann turned his head to stare at the other American, who leaned towards him. "It says: 'Live long and fly well, my brother; Thielmann.' That is all."

Gillette shifted his eyes between Miller and Thielmann for a few moments, both intently staring at the other. "*Liebt lange, fliegt schone, bruder,*" Thielmann whispered, extending his hand to the stranger.

They shook hands and Thielmann left, a little man with cliff-like shoulders and over one hundred and fifty aerial victories, in a sagging uniform between two burly American MPs, going back to his fellow aces in the tent camp where he worried about the nutrition of Japanese allies he had never known, a mongrel dog trotting along at his heels.

Summer 1965

London, England

Now sit down ye warriors bold,
Eat, drink and sing as in days of old.
'Tis said that man and beast and bird someday has its inning.
The turn comes now for men who fight;
Give thanks above "La Guerre Est Finiş"

Unknown

W hy is it, Miller wondered, that the sunrise always looks so glorious in London, the golden orb rising majestic, triumphant over the dark, warming the land, chasing away the demons of the night. Standing on the hotel roof, coffee in hand, watching the day begin with the freshening breeze and scudding clouds overhead, he felt strangely at peace, without the stabbing headaches and dizziness that had plagued him for twenty years. "Good morning, my friend," a familiar voice behind him said.

"Hello, Otto," Miller replied without looking. "Is it me, or does the sunrise in London look different?"

"I'm sure it is because the sunrise is so rare in London, the event must be celebrated. Quite lovely, yes?"

"Yessir, right pretty. How's your brother?" They had corresponded briefly, setting up a trust fund for the maintenance of German PW graves in the US, reciprocating with a German organization looking after American PW graves in Germany.

"Ulrich is well. He sends his regards. He was *Kriegsmarine*, so he wasn't invited..."

"I know. You barely were. I had to fight tooth-and-nail just to get you *Luftwaffe* veterans invited."

"Yes, and thank you for that struggle."

"We fought the same war, Otto, fought the same enemies. Stupidity, arrogance, greed, and fear..." Miller broke off as they both turned to watch a B-52 taking off, the plumes of ten engines thundering in the quiet dawn.

"And now we are on the same side," Thielmann said. "There can never be another war like that one; never again."

"Not with those monsters in the inventory," Miller answered, still watching the Stratofortress, Boeing's latest, largest, heaviest bomber leaving for a station high above the earth, to wait for orders no one ever wanted to send. "That one ship can carry more conventional ordnance than my entire group. Somebody said if we fight the third world war with nuclear weapons..."

"...We would fight the fourth with stones. Einstein. And he was right." "Not much comfort in being right, is there?"

Thielmann smiled, tired and sad. "Dead and right and dead and wrong are still dead. We should leave as many as we can to live, yes?"

"I didn't understand that," Miller thought aloud, "until you taught me. I've never forgotten."

"You saved my brother. I saved you. We taught each other, *Mein Bruder.*"

Not Long Ago

Arlington, Virginia

We meet 'neath the sounding rafter,
And the walls around are bare;
They echo our peals of laughter
It seems that the dead are there

Bartholomew Dowling

The last echoes of the trumpets and roll of drums still resonated, the honor guards stiff in the cold, the flags ruffling. A young staff sergeant presented the meticulously folded flag to Collova's widow and their daughter "with the thanks of a grateful nation."

After all the rest had left, only the flyers were left: Lieutenant General Jackson; Senator Reynolds; multi-millionaire industrialist Aitcheson; aircraft engineer Miller; math teacher Murphy; and prize winning authors Witt and Thielmann. They stood silent as the last bugle faded.

After a few moments, Miller cleared his throat, the piece of metal in his hand. "She's carried us all home, and her mission done at last. I say we let her rest."

"A piece of her, anyway, skipper," Murphy complained. "We gave Milliken a slab in England, and I gave up my piece for Roy 'cause I couldn't find his. Farr, I couldn't find another for him. I was kinda hopin' I'd get one last ride with the old girl..."

"OK by me. You guys...?"

"Fine for me, skipper...OK...all right, John...sounds fair...I'm game..."

"I promised them a beer," Miller told Thielmann as they walked from the cemetery. "We would be honored if you'd join us."

357

"As would I, my friends, as would I. Let me tell you about old friend Bär. You know, he only ever made one mistake, but that one killed him..."

Thielmann spoke with the boyish exuberance that only flyers know as they walked away, hunter and quarry together, talking and gesturing like the old comrades they both were...and were not.

Historical Note

I will fight no more forever

Chief Joseph

The US Air Corps Tactical School (ACTS) at Maxwell Field, Alabama, devised the doctrine of daytime horizontal precision bombardment using optical bombsights and integrated flight control equipment (autopilots) between the world wars, in part because of the horrors of the trenches in the 1914-18 war. While the doctrine's proponents, including HH "Hap" Arnold, Heywood "Possum" Hansell and Ira Eaker, sincerely believed in its validity, parts of the theory behind its effectiveness (especially the "people will rise up" parts) had been disproved by the Germans and British before the Army Air Force (AAF) even *tried* to follow the doctrine beginning in 1942.

Nonetheless, the Americans convinced themselves that they could make it work. The RAF was *never* convinced and tried to get the Allied leaders at the Casablanca conference in January 1943 to direct the AAF to join them in their night area bombing campaign. Eaker, as senior American airman in Europe, sold the leaders—specifically Winston Churchill—on "round the clock" bombing just so he could keep *trying* daylight precision.

In the worst year of the war for the Eighth Air Force, 1943, one in three aircrewmen were killed or injured badly enough to be sent home for a theory that the leaders were becoming increasingly aware was invalid *with the equipment they had then*. In late 1943, the Eighth switched to area bombing completely, based on the "drop on lead bombardier" practice. This was more successful than precision *ever* was because of the far greater number of bombers available. Yet, the AAD insisted that these were still *precision* attacks because all the bombers still carried optical bombsights...even if all the bombers didn't *use* them on *all* the missions. Precision bombardment, that was never as precise as it *needed* to be and certainly *not* as precise as prewar theory held it *could* be, was *de facto* discarded as a failed doctrine. The specific reasons for this subterfuge are beyond the scope of this essay, but had to do with *war crimes*, and the possibilities of future prosecutions.

By late 1944, the American bombers were doing considerable damage to Germany's infrastructure because they had far greater numbers and better targeting radars.. By March 1945, it was a *dying* issue in the Pacific theater, though "precision" attacks with huge numbers of aircraft were conducted by the Twentieth Air Force's B-29s right up the end of the war, but the Superforts had far superior equipment than was used in Europe.

The POINTBLANK offensive in early 1944 gutted the *Luftwaffe* of many of its aces; the plague of accidents caused by pilot inexperience and equipment failures—that started in 1941—made the German fighter force weaker by the month. The appearance of a few advanced German fighter aircraft late in the war was not enough to reverse the tide of overwhelming Allied numbers in the air, fewer and fewer aces, and the success of the ground offensives both east and west.

The most surprising thing about the air war over Germany was that both American and German pilots and aircrewmen could take themselves off flying status at any time, for any reason, or for no reason at all. That so many stayed at it, risking their lives and health in an apparently hopeless fight for questionable outcomes is remarkable, but, as Miller was told more than once, it was all the Allies could do in the dark days of 1942-43. Similarly, Thielmann's persistence in staying in the fight can best be explained by his love for his country and his comrades still fighting.

The introduction of second-generation American fighters in *Crop Duster* is admittedly early. I moved the *Luftwaffe's* first encounters with the P-47 Thunderbolt up by two months and the P-51 Mustang up by six months, to give Thielmann and his comrades a glimpse of what they would be up against in 1944 and beyond. Of the over 26,000 German fighter pilots who flew in the *Luftwaffe* from 1939 to 1945, fewer than 2,500 survived, though an unknown number of that total stopped flying missions before the end of the war for several reasons, mostly health, both physical and mental. Given the technological and numerical advantages their adversaries enjoyed, the perseverance of even that 10% was remarkable.

The 1939-45 air campaigns over Europe were unique, and we will never see any like them again. The advent of surface-to-air missiles alone precludes the need for intercepting fighters, and that has reduced the typical strategic bomber's crew count by half and more. That and the emphasis on standoff weapons such as ICBMs, cruise missiles, and precision-guided ordnance means that we will only know tactical disasters like the two 1943 Schweinfurt raids from the history books.

This conflict and *this way of war* made global war between world-power belligerents practically unthinkable. For *that*, perhaps, we should all thank those brave fighters for peace.

Milton Keynes UK
Ingram Content Group UK Ltd.
UKHW010640021023
429777UK00001B/105